I0702774

INTO INFERNAL PARADISE

THE LAST ALLOY
BOOK ONE

MICHELLE TORO

DELUSION
ENTERTAINMENT

This is a work of fiction. Names, characters, places, and incidents either are the product of the author's imagination or are used fictitiously.
Any resemblance to actual persons, living or dead, events, or locales is entirely coincidental.

Copyright © 2023 by Michelle Toro

All rights reserved. Published in the United States by Delusion Entertainment.

www.michelletoro.com

Cover design and illustration by Rena Violet.
Edited by Mandi Andrejka.

ISBN 979-8-9880666-0-6 (hardback)
ISBN 979-8-9880666-1-3 (paperback)
ISBN 979-8-9880666-2-0 (ebook)

CONTENT WARNING

This book includes mentions of past self-harm, thoughts of suicide, physical and emotional child abuse, graphic violence and murder, mild gore, and profanity.

To Erin, because sisters are everything.

CHAPTER 1
DAPHNE

Six Years Earlier

After weeks of brutal brilliance, the angry Texas sun was finally shrouded in gray. Still, the asphalt radiated a blistering heat, but the air now radiated something more...electric.

Daphne rolled up the sleeves of her drenched shirt and wiped ceaseless sweat into her black hair. As she widened her stance over the once-white arc beneath her feet, her foster sister bounced the basketball once. Twice. A breeze tousled the trees bordering the park and the leaves that piled underneath. A single stray leaf drifted into the space between them.

Do it again.

Ember drove.

Daphne beat her to the left, but Ember stopped short, dribbling the ball between her legs and out of Daphne's reach. Though Daphne stayed with her, shuffling on the balls of her feet, never losing sight of her foster sister's green gaze. It'd taken time to grow accustomed to their near-neon brightness, but after two years, Daphne had learned that they also gave Ember's every move away.

The ball continued to bounce. Bounce. Bounce.

Her sister's eyes darted to the right, and Daphne was there before she could even cross the arc. But Ember didn't hesitate, spinning on heel, charging to the left and—

Daphne was there again, smiling, chest heaving. She might have been much shorter, with much less muscle than her older sister, but she was faster. She could jump just as high. At this range, Ember wouldn't be able to get off a clean shot.

Ember spat in the grass and wiped her face, lying flat the few stray strands of blonde curls that had come free from her ponytail. Then she drove again.

Again, Daphne was there. Ember cut right; she was there. Ember cut left; she was there. Ember tested her again and again and again, but Daphne stopped her again and again and *again*.

Finally, Ember pulled all the way back to the top of the three-point line, her expression souring into a glower, and Daphne dutifully followed her all the way back, hands wide, ready to stop the next drive.

Except, Ember shot the ball.

And it was nothing but net—well, if there had been a net. This wasn't exactly the best-kept court in Dallas. Graffiti paint alone doubled the thickness of the backboard.

The ball hit the asphalt before rolling into the yellow grass. Daphne dropped her hands to her knees and sighed—panted really—before catching sight of her sister's foot.

"Two," she said.

"What?" Ember said between labored breaths. "Three. I was behind the line when I jumped."

"No fucking way, you stepped on it. Besides, you're up by

like twenty points. You want me to compete with the next star of the WNBA *and* a rigged score?"

"I'm not rigging the score. I was behind the line!"

"Whatever."

Daphne jogged over to retrieve the ball, grass crunching with each step she took. The trees were hardly healthier, their crowns packed with orange and yellow and brown. The scorching heat of the metal slide had scared away any parent or child months ago, and the carousel hadn't been touched in half a year—though today, the wind blew strong enough that the carousel whined on its own.

She looked up at the leaden sky, desperate for the rain to come faster, to wash away this fall and bring on the winter. Things had become way too hot.

She threw the ball back to Ember. "Fine, three. But when you go pro, I get ten percent of whatever you make."

"*If* I go pro, you get five," Ember said as she dribbled the ball between her legs. "But I gotta make it out of high school first."

"Maybe if you didn't spend so much time fighting, you'd have more time to study."

"Maybe I'll stop fighting when people stop fucking bothering me."

Daphne folded her arms and said nothing, letting the judgmental brow she raised speak for her.

Ember sighed, and the tension in her forehead loosened. She caught the ball with two hands, eyes turned to the ground. "It happened again."

Daphne nodded. "I saw the locker room. Coach says the power is completely fried."

What a fun surprise that was, rushing to get to practice this morning only to find the entire locker room dark, the other girls shining their phones' lights and speculating as to why.

But when Daphne had seen the black streaks that scorched the walls, as if every wire behind them had surged all at once, she'd immediately known *exactly* why.

"What did the police say this time?" she asked.

"That I'm on their shit list. Not like I wasn't before." Her sister released a mournful chuckle. "I guess I'm lucky that they still haven't found a way to prove it was me."

"And yet you keep giving them every opportunity to."

The tension in her forehead returned. "I'm not giving them anything. It's not like I did it on purpose. I don't even remember what happened."

"You never do. But you know you woke up angry."

"Yeah, and? What if I did? We don't know for sure that that's why—"

She cut herself off suddenly, her eyes darting around the empty playground as if someone might still be listening in on their conversation. "We don't know that that's what led to the outage," she whispered.

Daphne rolled her eyes. "You're not the only one who gets mad, you know. You have to learn to control it."

"But it wasn't my fault! The power just went out." But when she saw Daphne's lowered brow, she sighed. "I'm working on it."

"Are you? Didn't you just pick a fight with a senior yesterday?"

"I'm *working on it*. Can we stop talking about this?" Ember dropped the ball, crossing it between her legs, behind her back. Then she pulled up, jumped, and shot it. Two points. She didn't even hit the rim.

"Sure," Daphne said as a small green fire lit within her. "I wanna talk about last Friday's game anyway. How the hell did you make every single shot you took?"

Her sister landed another basket. "I didn't."

"Forty points, Ember. As a sophomore."

"And I got blocked twice. So no, I didn't make every shot. Only the ones I could get open for." She cocked her head, eye on the hoop. "But it was cool wasn't it?" Then she smirked before shooting the ball. Perfectly. Again.

Daphne scowled. "Okay, second question. How am I supposed to compete with that?"

"What? You're worried about making the team? Seriously?" Another shot. Another swish.

"I'm like half your height and have half your skills."

"And, you're already better than most of the other point guards. Even better, you still have another year to practice before you become a freshman. They should be the ones worried, not you." Still dribbling the ball, Ember shrugged. "Plus, who knows? Maybe I'll get expelled before then."

"How is that a plus?"

"Another opportunity for a spot on the team."

"And Richard would kill you."

Lightning flashed across the sky. Her sister straightened and lined up for another basket, her eyes narrowing in on the rim. She shot the ball again, though this time, the odd light, like electricity, tailed it; it landed in the basket, of course, but so much *faster* than it had before. Daphne never did get used to seeing it—whatever *it* exactly was.

"Dick wouldn't dare try," Ember said.

Daphne touched her rib—the one for which she had sat in a tub of ice for an hour several months ago—the one she told the doctor at physicals yesterday was a result of playing a guy at school. That bone was healed now. The bone in her cheek still hurt. *Richard tries, alright.*

"The doctor really didn't tell you anything?" she asked, avoiding thinking anymore about their foster father.

Ember rebounded and laid the ball back up into the basket. "Nothing."

"Literally nothing?"

"Yep. He did all his fancy tests and poked me with a million needles and came to the conclusion that I need anger management classes. So—" she passed the ball to Daphne "—nothing."

"That can't be right. People don't just pass out." Daphne set the ball on the asphalt. "Whatever is going on with you isn't normal."

"Tell the doctor that." Ember's hand moved to the locket hanging around her neck. "Honestly, I don't even care about a cure or anything. Like, most of the time, I feel fine. I just wish I knew what happens *while* I'm blacked out; I'm tired of being blamed for hurting people I don't remember even talking to."

"I'm more worried about it getting worse," Daphne said, curiously watching her sister twirl her metal heart. "You're lucky no one was in the locker room with you."

Ember shot her a glare. "I didn't do that. The power was already blown when I woke up."

"You mean like the mall bathroom was? Or Lincoln's gym? Or your last foster home?"

Ember drew both the chain of her necklace and her lips tight.

"You know they're afraid of you, right?" Daphne continued. "Your team is afraid of you. Your coach is afraid of you. Richard and Martha only keep us because they're terrified of what you would do to them if you were separated from me."

Thunder rolled through the galvanic air. Ember twisted her necklace so tight that the skin of her neck purpled. "Are you afraid of me?" she asked.

Daphne met her sister's too-green, hurt-filled eyes. "No. I'm here for you. We're getting out of this together."

Lightning cracked the sky open, finally releasing a torrent of rain upon the neighborhood. Water rushed the pavement, filling the cracks in the sidewalk and potholes in the street. Caked-up oil and chalk drawings were flushed down the gutters. Wire and wooden fences alike bent under the unrelenting cloudburst. And yet, the girls stood on the blacktop a moment longer, in silence, in thought.

At last, Ember looked up. "I guess basketball is done for today."

Daphne rubbed her eyes and face, brushing what water she could away. "You were crushing me anyway. I'd rather end it before I'm completely humiliated." She bent down to pick up the ball, and when she rose, she found Ember staring at her.

No, not staring. Fuming.

"What?" Daphne asked.

"He hit you."

Her hand snapped to her face, her cheek sensitive to the pressure of her touch. The concealer was gone. *Shit.*

"It was from basketball," she said. "Some girl spun around and elbowed me in the face. It was an accident."

"You're lying. You're protecting him again."

"I'm not," Daphne insisted. "It's from basketball," But she couldn't even look at her sister when she said it.

And Ember didn't believe her for a second. "Is it Martha, then?"

"No," she said forcefully. "I'm not protecting them."

That, at least, was the truth. Daphne could never stomach intentionally protecting their foster parents; she had only ever meant to protect Ember. But that unfortunately required shielding Richard and Martha *from* Ember—they kept the roof over the girls' heads. They kept them fed. And they kept quiet. If Ember hurt them, even accidentally, there was no telling how they would respond.

Daphne marched back to the house.

Her sister followed. It should've been difficult to hear her in this rain, with this thunder, but her voice pierced through as if it were a perfectly clear day and they stood only inches apart. "Why are you lying to me?"

Daphne sped up without a word. Richard and Martha were truly the least of her worries. But the cops and social workers —they only needed one good reason to take away her protector, her confidant, her sister of two years. And though Ember might have deluded herself into believing that there was no connection between her blackouts and the accidents that accompanied them, that the power surges and outages were all happenstance—that all the people she'd hurt were lying— Daphne hadn't. How could she? She'd seen the glow in her sister's eyes one too many times.

"Daphne, please!" Ember shouted from behind. "He's hurting you. Why are you lying for him?"

Daphne shook her head as they both turned the corner, her sister inches behind her. She knew there was something different about Ember. She wasn't blind. But she also wasn't new to foster care. One whisper about something going on with her, that she was a problem, and the two would be separated faster than they could blink. As long as they were still in the system, they had to keep whatever this was hidden.

Anyway, this wasn't forever. The plan was to run away. Somewhere in Dallas, so that Ember could finish out high school and get a scholarship to play in college. Then, Daphne would move with her so that when she got drafted to the pros, they could all make this hellhole a distant memory. She didn't exactly know how they'd do it, but they would. Until then, she would endure whatever she had to endure in silence.

When Ember caught up to her on the porch, she yanked

her hand. "Would you fucking answer me? Why are you lying to me?"

Daphne shoved the ball into her chest. "For us. I'm trying to keep you from doing something that puts you in jail. Happy?" She turned to open the front door.

Ember shut it. "No, I'm not happy that my little sister is being *beaten by our foster dad.* I thought this stopped months ago. Why didn't you tell me? I can talk to him!"

"Are you kidding? After the locker room?"

"I didn't do that!"

And there it was, the familiar glow. As if her eyes were radioactive. As if to warn Daphne to stay far, far away. And though Ember's hair was drawn straight by the weight of the water that doused it, the corner of her lip still managed to curl. "But the thought of seeing Dick fry..."

"Stop it. You shouldn't want to hurt him."

"Why not?" Ember spat back, and it was like her voice was laced with venom. "He's abusing you. I don't think a little pain is out of the question."

Daphne shuddered from the cold and fear. She hadn't been lying earlier: she wasn't afraid of her sister. But she refused to believe this being *was* her sister. It held too much rage. Its remarks were too vile. Too evil.

"You shouldn't want to hurt people," she said again.

"Dick isn't people. He's abusing you. How many times do I have to say it?"

Daphne pulled on the doorknob, but Ember was leaning all of her weight on the door.

"You're not actually trying to get in there, are you? It's 7 p.m. He's been drinking for hours already."

"Ember, please. I'm tired. Can I just get out of this rain?"

"I can't understand why you won't let me fight them for

you. Do you actually like living here? Do you enjoy being raised by those two dipshits?"

"Of course, I don't. I *hate* it here," Daphne hissed. "I hate being poor. I hate these people who pretend to be our parents. I hate knowing I have an actual family somewhere in China, and yet I was dumped here before I could learn to read the freaking takeout menu. But this isn't about just me, or did you forget?"

And like the light from the sky, the glow faded from her sister's eyes. Ember set the ball on her hip and grabbed her locket again, pulling on it like a leash. "Can't we at least tell someone? The cops?"

"You think that if we rat on Richard and Martha, they won't rat on you?"

"But I didn't *do* anything."

Daphne grabbed the bridge of her nose. "No, we don't know *what* happened—what*ever* happens. But how often can you wake up where the lights went out, where it smells like something's burning, and not think that you have anything to do with it? The school might be old, and the wiring might be crappy. But the mall's wiring wasn't. Lincoln's gym was new. You won't always have some lucky excuse to give the cops. And I'm certain our doting foster parents can give them at least one clue that connects you to any of it. To *all* of it."

Ember's jaw shifted. "Then what about the social worker? Isn't it her job to make sure we're safe?"

"No. They'll separate us, and I refuse to be separated from you." Daphne met her sister's eyes. "Just, please, listen to me. I don't need you to hurt anyone, and I don't need you to call anyone. The best plan is the one we've had since day one: get our shit together and get out of here. And I can't do that on my own." Water dripped from the hair glued to her face. "I *need* you to help me escape."

Her sister was quiet then. And though the glow was gone, her eyes shone so green and vibrant, even through the rain.

Daphne swallowed. *I need you to help us escape. I need to get you help.* But Ember would never listen if she thought someone was taking care of her—especially if that someone was the little sister she tried so desperately to protect—and so Daphne kept those thoughts to herself.

The door opened. That was the worst part of their house: there was no such thing as privacy here. It was so small that from the front window on the door, you could see all the way through the kitchen and out the back, and it took little effort more to hear everything in between. Their foster parents had to have been watching them for a while now.

"You're wet," Martha said, and the air around them warmed.

Daphne shot Ember a warning look, and she released her clenched fists. When the temperature returned to normal, Daphne turned back to their foster mother.

"We got stuck in the rain."

"You should dry off, then. Dinner is on the stove."

With a curt nod from Daphne, the two sisters stepped onto the cracked beige tile and crossed the patchy carpeted floors. The room smelled of boxed pasta and meat sauce, and then smoke, as Martha's cigarette added to the already yellow walls. Some news channel blared on the TV in the living room, though no one was there to watch it, and Richard sat at the decaying kitchen table, whiskey in hand—just as Ember had predicted. *Home, sweet home.*

After patting herself dry with the bathroom towel, Daphne grabbed a paper plate and plastic fork. But as she served herself, the handle of the spoon slipped from her hand. With a furrowed brow, she wiped the sweat from her palm onto her pant, only to feel a new bead form on her hairline. She swiped that one too, then realized someone had clicked off the TV. In its place rumbled thunder and whistled wind, and when she looked up, she knew exactly why it was so damn hot inside.

Ember hadn't moved from the doorframe of the kitchen. She stood there like a starved predator, staring daggers at her prey. And, like an arrogant idiot, Richard stared right back. He set his glass down.

"What?" he barked.

Her eyes flicked to Daphne, though Daphne was already furiously shaking her head. *Don't you dare. He's not worth it.*

And so Ember drew her lips to a pout and wordlessly grabbed a plate. As she fashioned her dinner, she still kept her eyes on Richard, but Daphne breathed a bit easier.

Richard retook his drink. "That's what I thought."

Fuck.

"I know you didn't just say that."

"Calm down, Ember," Daphne said.

But her sister charged Richard anyway. He stood suddenly, drunkenly, and though he might have meant to intimidate her, he gained only an inch over his eldest foster kid and had nowhere near her athleticism.

"You hit her," Ember hissed with a new glow in her eyes.

His own eyes widened, like a toddler scared and about to cry. He had the balance of a toddler, too, swaying and holding onto his chair for dear life. "I didn't mean to."

"Why don't you ever hit me, Dick? Pick on someone your own size for once?"

"He told you already," Martha said from the entryway, voice shaking. "He didn't mean to." She dropped her cigarette in an ashtray and moved toward the table to stand by him. She was much shorter than him, but at the moment, she seemed twice his size. "Stop it, now. Before you hurt someone."

"You never ask him to stop before he hurts someone,"

Ember spat. "I just want the father-daughter dance I've been waiting two years for."

Richard paled as if he might throw up, and Martha grabbed his shoulders to brace him, or to hold him—Daphne wasn't sure. But she was more than sure of the look her foster mother gave her. It was a look of desperation, filled with too-late apologies.

She exhaled.

"Ember, please," she said. "You don't want to do this."

"I think I do, actually." Ember spoke with a hint of relish, and as she delicately held Richard's chin, an insidious smile formed on her lips. "I really, really do."

"No, you don't. This is the anger talking. That thing that makes you pass out. This isn't you."

"This is me."

"It isn't," Daphne begged, water trickling down her forehead. "Basketball is you. Competition is you. But not this."

"I'm protecting you."

"You don't need to hurt them to protect me."

Thunder rattled every shingle on the roof. Wind rattled every pane out of place. Ember let go of Richard's chin, and their foster parents didn't hesitate to skirt toward the stove, where Daphne stood, defiant and sweating. *It's way too hot in here.*

"I wasn't going to hurt them," Ember said calmly, the glow still flaring in her irises.

Daphne nodded slowly as the rest of her body trembled. But she made sure to meet her sister's luminescent gaze. "Yes, you were."

"No, I wasn't. I was only protecting you."

"That's not true," Daphne whispered, her face flushed and tears nearing her lashes. A crack of thunder again rattled the windows and walls. She didn't let it rattle her. "You were going to kill them. I know it. You know it."

Ember's frown morphed into a grimace and a growl. "And so what if I was? Who cares if I kill them? Maybe some people *should* die!"

She snatched the whiskey from the table and chucked it at the cabinets behind their foster parents, shattering the glass and causing Martha to scream.

"I care!" Daphne seized Ember's wrist, forcing her to look back at her. "I need you."

Ember glanced at Richard and Martha, then back at Daphne, and the four of them stood there like that for a minute. Maybe two. With every blink Ember took, the glow receded slightly, until her eyes nearly returned to their original unnatural hue.

"Damn it," Richard said. "Sit down already, before your dumb ass kills us all."

Ember's eyes sharpened, glowed brighter, and the air grew stifling.

"No!" Daphne shouted. "They don't deserve it. You are meant to become the best basketball player of all time and let me be your agent and live in your penthouse. Do not let this, this hatred take that from you." She shook Ember's shoulders, but her sister wouldn't look at her. "Please. For me. Let it go."

The silence returned, as did the thunder, the lightning, and the winds. Ember rolled her neck, then grabbed at it. And abruptly, she walked away.

"Don't follow me," she said, swiping a sweatshirt from a living room chair and rewrapping her dark blonde curls into a loose bun.

Daphne trailed her sister toward the front door anyway. Now, the sky was completely black except for the occasional lightning strike that illuminated it, and the rain poured sideways.

"Where are you going?" she asked.

"I need some time to think."

"In the storm?"

"I think best during storms."

"Sure, during them. Not in them." Daphne watched Ember retie her shoes. "C'mon, don't be stupid. It's not safe out there."

Ember straightened at that, her eyes still glowing, the air still warm and...electric. "It's not safe in here."

"I know, but there's not—"

"Daphne!" Richard yelled from the kitchen. "Apologize to your mother for scaring the fuck out of her!"

Daphne winced but glanced down the hall. Martha was sobbing into her napkin. Richard had one hand on his wife's back while the other poured a new glass.

And Ember's attention remained on her, begging for her permission to do something.

"Daphne! Get in here, *now!*"

She winced again, instinctively raising her hands to shield her face. He must've been too drunk to realize that Ember hadn't left yet, and Martha was too distraught to keep him in check. Daphne didn't look at her sister this time, though she knew those glowing eyes hadn't wavered. She could feel them. Their protection, their care. Their ire.

"He's going to hit you again." It wasn't a question.

"I'll be okay as long you don't do anything. Remember that we're supposed to be in this together. We're supposed to get out of this together. We won't escape without each other."

Ember slammed the door behind her, rain pouring in her absence.

"I swear to god, Daphne, if you don't get your fucking ass in here this minute, I will—!"

And once again, Daphne covered her face.

And then, a crack of thunder deafened her. It was so loud, she barely heard the window shatter. So loud, she hardly heard the kitchen stove explode. She caught only a hint of Martha's scream. Richard's scream.

But when the ringing in her ears finally did quiet, she heard coughing. Then silence. Then her own screams.

Because it was hot. *Way too hot.*

CHAPTER 2
EMBER

Present Day

Ember shot the ball at the same old graffitied hoop that hadn't had a net for as long as she could remember, and she made it—because she hadn't missed a shot in just as long. A prickle of electricity lingered on her fingertips as she wiped her face with the small, dry part of her t-shirt.

The alarm on her phone went off. 6 a.m.

She stuffed the ball into her bag and headed toward her apartment for a shower, a breakfast bar, and a change into her uniform. She accomplished all three within half an hour, and before long, found herself sitting in the middle of her white-walled living room on her hand-me-down sofa, one hand scrolling through her social media on her phone, the other toying with the locket around her neck.

She typed in the name she checked daily—*Daphne Rui Liang*—and hovered her thumb over the request button.

Daphne had changed her profile picture again. Over the years, Ember had watched her jawline slim, her figure mature.

She'd smiled at waist-length hair and pixie cuts. Chuckled at braces and too much eyeliner. She would never forget the day *Georgetown University* was added below the name; she'd never been prouder of her little sister.

This new image had been taken from the shoulders up, on the background of the American flag. Daphne sported a black blazer and turtleneck, her black hair cropped below the chin. And her smile was just as big and cheesy as it had been six years ago.

This was all Ember knew about her now. All that her sister would let her know.

The screen went dark. She stared at her blackened reflection, her finger still shaking over the glass.

She would reject me again anyway.

Twirling the metal heart of her locket, she tucked the phone into her jeans pocket, grabbed her lunchbox and backpack, and went out the door.

The aisle of toddler-tempting colors and animals assaulted her sight. Clouds of processed sugar assaulted her nose. And static-laden pop radio assaulted her ears. But despite her aching back, she continued on, restocking the cereal shelves in perpetuity.

She pulled the collar of her red polo higher, hoping it would dull the sensation on her neck.

"Ember, you okay?"

She looked up. Her co-worker Rachel looked back at her with wide, bright brown eyes. "You don't look so hot."

"I'm fine," Ember said as she pulled out another cereal box. She tucked her locket beneath her shirt, feeling the icy metal against her chest. "Just thinking."

"Not about Ethan, right? He's not worth the mental energy."

She smirked. The guy who she'd let cheat on her while he'd bought her groceries for a month? "Definitely not."

"Well, good. I need you back in action tonight. This time, we *will* find some guys worth the effort. But no more fights, okay?"

"Weren't you the one who said that douchebag deserved it?"

"Yeah, but somehow I was also the one who got in trouble, dragging your passed-out ass out of the bar in heels and a mini-skirt. Thank god, you woke up before we had to go far." Rachel grabbed the newest box from her hand. "Speaking of, I don't think you had that much to drink. Watch your glass tonight, alright?"

Ember handed her another box.

"What even happened last week?" Rachel continued as she placed it on the shelf. "When I came out of the bathroom, he was on the ground, you were collapsed in a chair, and all these people were throwing around these wild stories about you punching him and pulling out a Taser? I didn't even know you owned a Taser!"

Ember shrugged. "I don't remember."

"I can't believe you got him to apologize to me either. Normally, they're too pissed that slapping my ass didn't suddenly make me swoon." Rachel leaned one arm against the shelves. "You know that's what I admire about you? You don't ever let anyone push you around."

Thunder cracked outside; its remnants echoed throughout the store. Ember threw her hand to her neck, trapping an unfortunately familiar prickle beneath her heated palm.

"I think it's time for a break," she said.

"Break? It's not even ten."

"Feel free to keep working." She closed the box of cereals, leaving it in the middle of the aisle floor. "I'll be in the back."

Despite her protests, Rachel followed Ember around shopping carts and produce displays, down an aisle of canned goods, and through the back doors into the tiny orange break room. Ember rummaged through the fridge before dropping into one of the two plastic chairs, feet propped up and phone in hand.

"If Heather finds us back here, we'll both be fired," Rachel said.

"Eh, this is my third job this year." The wooden table creaked underneath the weight of Ember's shoes. "There's always something else."

Laughing, Rachel took the seat across from her. "I seem to recall you saying the same thing about Ethan. He didn't treat you right, you know."

Ember took a long sip of soda. "I know."

"You shouldn't let anything he did affect how you see yourself."

"I don't."

"Because he was a scumbag. I mean who cheats on someone with not one but two other girls—"

"Ahem, Rachel?"

Her co-worker popped up straight in her chair. "Yeah?"

"Though I do appreciate it, you really don't have to fake concern for me."

Rachel looked as if her breath had been stolen. "Wait, what? I'm not faking anything."

"Uh...huh." Ember swung her feet to the floor and set her phone on the table. "We've known each other for what, three months? And we only ever see each other at work, where we're miserable and sober, or at the bar, where we're miserable and drunk."

"And that means I'm faking concern?"

She shrugged. "All I'm saying is you don't have to. You don't need to care about my love life or my career plans or anything like that. You and I are co-workers with a shared interest in drinking our worries away. This," she gestured between the two of them, "is a transaction to facilitate that. Nothing more, nothing less. No emotions necessary."

Rachel narrowed her eyes—not out of anger but curiosity. "Why not?"

Ember blinked. "What do you mean, why not?"

"Why can't I care about you more than that? Why can't you care about me?"

"Because all transactions eventually end anyway," she said, frowning, "and I don't overinvest in dead ends."

And then, Rachel laughed so loud, it startled her. Her howls echoed off the brick walls.

"That's dumb as fuck," her co-worker said, fighting hiccups. "I am neither a transaction nor a dead end. I'm a person. And I'm your friend."

Grimacing, Ember grabbed her phone and threw her feet back onto the table. "Yeah, well. I'm not yours."

"If you say so. I don't think people often go out of their way to fight the harassers of their so-called dead ends. But whatever helps you sleep at night."

Ember stared at Rachel over the edge of her screen, wondering where she'd gone wrong. She'd had this conversation a number of times before, and it usually ended in yelling or tears or well-deserved cold shoulders. But this was the first time anyone had ever simply ignored her. She was tempted to reconsider her position.

Then her eyes drifted to the three scars on her wrist. One year, eleven months, and three days without reopening them. Their red hue had faded to the point where she no longer needed concealer. And she remembered why she couldn't.

"I'm not going out tonight," she said without looking up.

"Okay, that's where I draw the line. Say we're not friends all you want, but you cannot back out of our partygoer contract. I won't let you."

"It's going to storm the entire time. No one will even be out."

"We'll be out. I think we count as someone."

"I need to save some cash anyway. You know I desperately need a car."

Rachel shifted back in her chair and folded her arms. "Hm. You do need a car. I can't believe you ride the DART so late." She tapped her chin. "Fine, but you owe me. Mark's Halloween party is next week. I expect your presence plus interest."

"What's interest?"

"A drink." She held out her hand. "Deal?"

"Fine." Ember shook it. Though after this little incident, she had no intention of seeing the deal through.

Her hand then went to her locket. It was heart-shaped with the name *Ember* inscribed on the front, *Slade* on the back. Below *Slade*, her supposed birthdate: *January 10*. That was all anyone had known about her when she'd been found on the doorstep of Parkland Hospital, swaddled in fleece in a woven basket...on January 11.

"Hey," she said, "we don't have pliers laying around somewhere, do we? One of the links in my chain is bent out of place."

"Try the stockroom," Rachel said. "Where the box cutters are."

Nodding, Ember said, "Thanks." And as quickly as she could, she left.

When she entered the stockroom, she was greeted with

more offensive color combinations and reacquainted with the overwhelming smell of sweets. But to her right was a wall of hammers, screwdrivers, and the like, and suddenly the room was bearable.

She skipped the pliers, ripped open the drawer of new box cutters, and pointed a blade straight at her chest. Then she pulled her necklace taut.

It didn't cut.

She sawed faster, pulled the necklace tighter, hoping that this time something would finally give. But in twenty-two years it never had, and today was no different. No matter what tool or technique she'd tried, nothing came close to breaking the chain. Nor had she ever been able to squeeze her head through its loop, even when she was little. And the clasp itself was apparently fused shut—a strange thing to do to a necklace on a newborn infant, in her opinion.

She let go. The once-sharp edge of the blade was now ragged and dull. The blade itself had warped at a slight angle. The back of her neck bled from the way the chain had cut into her skin.

Her necklace was still pristine. Every link shined silver and bright as if it had never been touched by anything—even air. Even blood.

Thank you, Mom and Dad, for leaving me this stupid broken necklace and absolutely nothing else. Number two on my ever-growing list of abnormalities you failed to warn me about.

Number one was, of course, the spark.

Ember waited on a metal bench underneath a metal awning in the middle of the concrete jungle and stared at the oasis of green across the rails. The historic Dallas High School hadn't been a school for decades, but it always reminded her of her own—well, what she remembered of her own.

She rubbed the spark on the back of her neck so hard her skin became raw. *Fuck, it's dark tonight.*

When the train finally pulled into the station, she boarded it, dropping her bags in the front—as far from the other three passengers as possible—and finally let loose the tension of a twelve-hour shift. As her body succumbed to the train's sporadic jolts, she laid her forehead against the cool window. One after another, droplets hit the glass, and she traced each one, dragging her finger along their paths as they fought their way to the bottom, pooling, separating, until at last, they slicked out of sight.

The three other passengers exited the car.

Thank god.

With the drop in temperature, the hairs on her skin raised and a shudder ran up her spine. Her palms, though, remained heated, as they always were of late. *Abnormality number three.* As a precaution, she refocused her attention on the water sliding down the pane—a technique she'd picked up years ago, during her stint on the streets. In those three months, the rain had been the only thing that kept her mind off her aching stomach, off her exhaustion and guilt. Off the spark on the back of her neck.

But it was a delicate balance, relying on rain. Because although the rain calmed her best, it usually came during storms—and storms were when she lost control.

Raindrops. The drops merged into streams. Then rivers. *Raindrops. Raindrops.* She rubbed her forearms, and thankfully, that was enough to keep the heat from spreading, even if it wasn't enough to make her hands cool.

The train pulled to another stop. Two new passengers stepped aboard.

They were twins; they had to be. And yet, they contrasted one another so starkly. The furthest one had snow-white hair, matching her sharp white eyeliner, and she brandished a toothy grin. But her sister's hair was blacker than charcoal—a similar shade to what also lined her eyes—and her expression was stone-cold. They both had deep tawny skin, and they both wore gaudy white, full-body jumpsuits that fit closely to their figures, with tacky white capes trailing behind them.

Ember turned back to the window, hoping they would choose a seat at the back.

"Excuse me." The twin with white hair hovered over her, eyes green as grass. She pointed toward the empty seats across the aisle. "Mind if we sit here?"

Ember glanced around the car, ensuring it was as empty as she thought it was, and sighed.

"Sure," she said, then pulled out her phone for a riveting game of crushing candies. She doubted she would be able to race the droplets in peace any longer, and this was the next best option.

A hand blocked her screen.

"I'm Nieve," the same woman said, holding out her arm. She spoke with a slight accent, like she was Puerto Rican or Dominican. "Pleased to meet you."

Ember feigned a smile and grasped Nieve's hand. "Ember."

"Pretty name. This is my sister Sombra."

The stone-faced, black-haired sister extended her own arm. "Pleasure," she said, though her tone suggested it was no pleasure at all.

"Likewise." Ember shook her hand, too…and caught Sombra's ever-so-subtle flinch.

She ripped back her arm and poured herself into her phone. Surely, the twins would take the hint.

"Do you live in the area?" Nieve said.

Or not.

Ember nodded once before returning her phone to the back pocket of her jeans. The candies were glitching from over-heating anyway.

"Sombra and I recently moved here," Nieve continued. "We're ecstatic to live in a large city."

Ember gave another toothless smile before putting her elbow on the window and resting her head on her fist, ignoring the scalding sensation underneath her chin. *Why on earth, if you've entered this world with your own built-in companion, would you go out of your way to bother me?*

Raindrops.

"So, what is there to do around here?" Nieve asked.

Lightning struck. An earsplitting crack followed. Raging winds howled outside the cabin, and Ember let them speak in her place.

Sombra gazed out the glass. "The weather is growing hostile."

I'm growing hostile, Ember thought, finger on the pane. *Rain—*

The train lurched sideways, and the women went with it. Like they were in a pinball machine, she and the twins tumbled between the seats, forward, sideways, backward. A knee there, a wrist here. The floor became the roof, then the floor once more. The excruciating sound of metal-on-metal pierced her ears. A sharp pain stabbed her mouth, then warm liquid filled it. The train tipped onto its side once more. But at last, thank god, it all came to a stop.

She flew into the seat in front of her with a grunt, straining her shoulder in an attempt to brace herself. Only when she was sure the train wouldn't move did she force herself to stand up.

The sides of the cabin were dented. Several windows—

now below their feet and above their heads—were completely smashed. The PA system blared static.

Ember tasted metal. When she touched her lip, a deep red colored the tip of her finger, and in her left arm and upper back pulled a vicious soreness. "Is—?" she started before a throbbing pain bolted across her shoulder. She inhaled deeply, waiting for it to pass before trying again. "Is everyone okay?"

"I'm alright," Sombra groaned as she sat up. But her sister remained on the ground, silent. Sombra must have noticed Ember staring because she nodded at Nieve and calmly said, "She's alright as well."

Ember wasn't so convinced. "What the hell was that?"

"I'm not certain," Sombra said, slowly lifting her sister's head onto her lap and shielding her from the rain.

"I'm going to take a look."

The twin shook her head. "Don't bother."

"What? Why?"

But then she was still as a statue, staring into nothingness.

Okay, weird, Ember thought, taking the moment to evaluate the scene, noting every possible way out of the crushed tin can. Unfortunately, there was only one: up.

Finally, Sombra blinked. "It's completely off the tracks." Were her eyes...glowing? "Someone pushed us. I assume they used the wind."

Some*one?*

"The straight winds can be brutal here," Ember said dismissively, her eyes turned back to the window-roof. "And tornadoes. Pretty common during a storm like this."

Sombra blinked again, and the glow receded. "It was the wind, but there was nothing common about it."

Before Ember could ask for clarification, Nieve gasped, and she no longer cared about the weather. The woman's eyes flickered, and red trickled from her head, staining her white hair, but she was alive, thank goodness.

Ember spotted her bags sitting just a few feet away from her, having tumbled during the crash. They looked even more rumpled and dirty than usual but seemed otherwise fine. She rummaged through her lunch bag for her ice pack.

"Here," she said. When Sombra eyed her, she gestured at Nieve. "She needs it more than I do."

Sombra grabbed the box and moved it to her sister's neck. "Thank you."

"Don't mention it."

Then, though her left shoulder ached terribly and broken glass threatened to slice her every inch of the way up, Ember grabbed the makeshift ladder of sideways seats and climbed, pushing herself through the smashed window ceiling. At the top, the rain and winds limited her vision, but from what she could see—

Oh my god. They'd made it as far as the suburbs, but they were off the tracks. Entirely. Incredibly. Torn away. The last few train cars piled in the now rubble of a church. Mangled rails littered the parking lot. Glass and cracked pavement scattered the front yards of six neighboring houses.

How did Sombra know?

Some of the passengers from the other cars climbed out as well, joining nearby homeowners as they gathered where the few vehicles in the street had been flattened.

But Ember couldn't yet pull her gaze from the church. At this time, it was unlikely anyone was in it, and it didn't appear as though any of the passengers were severely hurt, but still... Still, her stomach turned at what she couldn't see—bones and bodies and blood. Screaming.

I should call for help.

She pulled her phone out of her back pocket—or at least,

what was left of it. The screen had been smashed into thousands of bits of glass. The back was falling off, exposing the components to the weather. She pressed the power button over and over again, but the shattered black screen only taunted her.

Her luck. *Raindrops.*

She climbed back down.

Nieve was sitting up now, her vibrant green eyes opened wide, mouth shut—but she stared at nothing too, just as her sister had. Several seconds later, she blinked.

"Sombra," she said. "We've got to go."

"You were knocked out," Ember said. "We should get you to a doctor. Where's your phone?"

But Nieve ignored her and reached for her sister's collar, yanking her down. "You see them too, Sombra. We have to go *now*."

Sombra nodded, understanding something that Ember had clearly missed, and helped her off the floor.

"Nieve, really," Ember said, "you need to get checked out. You could have a concussion. If you don't have a phone, I'm sure we can use someone else's to call for a ride."

But neither twin was listening. Sombra climbed toward the windows at the top, and when Nieve started to do the same, Ember put a hand on her shoulder.

"You shouldn't be moving right now," she said more sternly. "Not until you get medical attention."

Oddly, Nieve laughed. "We ought to first get you out of here." She kept one hand on the ladder of seats but held out the other, her white-lined eyes asking for Ember to follow her up.

Ember stayed on the ground. "You hit your head. What we need to do is find a phone."

Nieve sighed. "Come on, Alloy."

Then, she grabbed her by the wrist and forced her completely *off* the ground.

"Ouch, goddammit!" Ember's legs dangled in the air. Her shoulder seared. "What the fuck do you think you're doing? Let go of me!"

"Not a chance. Not after coming all this way."

She continued to kick and jerk, her mind too focused on keeping her shoulder intact to contemplate what the woman meant by "all this way."

"Stop this, Alloy. You'll need your strength."

But eventually, she was able to push off the seats, and she turned. Nieve yelped as her own arm twisted, and Ember landed on the ground with a thud.

Nieve shortly followed, landing without a sound, her white bangs plastered to her forehead with a mixture of rain and blood.

"You have two options, Alloy. I can either levitate you, or you can climb."

She can't be serious, Ember thought, rising to her feet.

"I'll stay here," she said, "where I get to keep the name Ember."

"Pick again, Alloy," Nieve said, eyes unwavering. "Levitation or climbing?"

Ember massaged where the woman had grabbed her and looked up at Sombra who stood on top of the train, gazing into the rain with her charcoal hair flipping in the wind. There were two of them with that strength. Whatever Nieve had meant by "levitation", or whatever these extraordinarily strange people thought that she resembled, she didn't want to find out.

"I'll climb," she said finally, the heat in her forearms intensifying. *Raindrops.*

Nieve smiled. "Wonderful."

Once Ember returned atop the car, the twins' attention

diverted elsewhere, scanning the scene below as their capes fluttered behind them. They could've been superheroes.

Maybe that's what they think they are. I really should call 9-1-1.

The rain fell harder and lightning sheared across the sky. Ember started toward the side of the train.

An arm jutted out in front of her.

"Don't," Sombra said.

Ember folded her arms. "Why not? I'm not trying to become a lightning rod tonight."

When they didn't reply, she balled her scorching fists. *Raindrops.* "Is anyone going to tell me what's going on?"

Again, no response. What were they so mesmerized by?

She tracked their stares. It was far away and, given the rain splashing against her face, difficult to see, but if she squinted, she could make out a shadow. No, two shadows, out by the houses on the other side of the rail and who happened to be running toward them. As they grew closer, she could just make out their black sweatshirts with the hoods up, black sweatpants, and masks.

"Do we fight?" Nieve asked.

"Not with her," Sombra said. "She's a liability."

"Who are they?" Ember asked.

Silence.

Raindrops.

"Let's get going," Sombra said.

Suddenly, the twins leaped. Ember, overly cautious of her footing about the slick metal of the train, leaned over the side to watch the twins casually land the ten-foot drop to the ground. She remained frozen where she stood.

"Come on," Sombra said. "We need to go. Jump."

"Um, no thank you. Y'all sort out whatever issues y'all have with them, and I'll wait for the ambulance." Ember lowered herself onto the train, legs dangling over the broken window, preparing to climb down into the cabin once more.

"We don't have time for this," Sombra said. "*Erigo.*"

Ember's calf burned, and her stomach pitched. She moved into the air, her mind racing to understand how. Had she somehow slipped? Did she fall off the train?

And then she landed. Hard.

She rolled to her back, coating her polo in mud. Her curls were matted with rain and grass, and her foot throbbed.

But she didn't have time to complain. Nearly the moment she landed, the twins had her—one at each hand—dragging her as they walked away from the shadows. They followed the train tracks north, passing the crowd at the church.

"What are you doing?" she shouted, shaking out the pain in her ankle. Only then did she see the red streaming down her calf, her jeans torn beneath the knee. Shards of glass stuck to her with blood and denim. "I swear to god, y'all need to let go of me. Now."

"No," Nieve said. At the sound of police sirens, they turned again, left this time, away from the tracks and into the town. "We have to protect you."

"Protect me from what?"

But at the intersection of a body shop and convenience store, they stalled. The shadows stood a few dozen feet to the left, in the middle of the street.

"Them. We need to move."

They ran with Ember in tow. And Ember did what she could to focus on those peaceful, calming, sliding raindrops... rather than the increasingly loud thunder, her incredibly close proximity to these women, and that damn spark blazing on the nape of her neck.

"You don't know who you're dealing with here," she pleaded. "You'd be better off letting me protect myself."

Nieve squeezed her hand tighter, pulled her harder. "We know you're an alloy," she said. "We know your magic is strong. But have you ever fought with it? Have you trained?"

The pouring rain made it difficult to hear, but did she just say "magic"? *And what the hell is an alloy?*

"Have I *what?*"

"That's why you need us. These aren't average Agarthan soldiers. They're high-level operatives who have spent their entire lives working magic into combat, and they're here for you. You'll be made an Agarthan slave unless you let us help."

What are these girls high on?

"We need to get out of sight," Sombra said. "The rain isn't providing nearly enough coverage."

But the moment they hopped the wooden fence to find some trees in some unlucky family's backyard, they stopped. A foot in front of them stood the shadow figures, as if they had appeared out of nowhere, as if they had been waiting for them for eternity. *But how? Weren't they...behind us?*

Ember reminded herself that she didn't know any of the people in her company—that they were all equally as untrustworthy—but the hooded ones did bring on a particular dread. Especially now that she could see their eyes—their *scarlet* eyes.

"Fuck," Sombra said.

The left shadow muttered something inaudible and the raindrops *sharpened*. Like needles—or, wait, actually needles? And like a million tiny darts, they flew. Ember threw up her arms.

A noise surged above the roar of thunder. A voice. *A song?* Even stranger, she recognized it, though she couldn't quite identify it.

And the million pinpricks never came.

Hesitantly, she lowered her arms, finding the needles frozen an inch from her face. She touched one, and it stuck, like a dart in a wall. The shadowy figure that had created them moved like he was set to slow motion. The shadow to his right had disappeared. And Nieve was...singing?

Ember glanced around, past the singing twin and the slow-moving figure in black. Past the mirror—that she was certain hadn't been there before—lying flat on the ground at the other end of the yard. Through the missing plank in the fence, and to the street. The park. *My escape.*

"Where is it?" Sombra said. "Where's the other mirror?" She walked in front of Ember, head on a swivel.

With Sombra, Nieve, and the slow-motion shadow man distracted, Ember took the opening, hopping the fence as silently as possible.

Something in her periphery caught her eye, and she threw herself to the ground. A hunk of metal—*from the train?*—hurtled over her.

The thud echoed the thunder. The sheet of metal smashed the fence and the twins flat against the side of the house. And like his counterpart, the shadow figure disappeared.

Sombra stumbled as she picked herself up from the ground. "Godsdammit!" she shouted, holding her head. "Show yourself, you coward!"

Ember shot back to her feet, looking from one house to the next to the park, one yard after another, unsure of which direction to go. Unsure *if* she should go.

Before she decided, a black-gloved hand wrapped around her arm. Her legs went rigid, and her spine stiffened. The faceless man, returned to normal pace, dragged her away.

"Who the hell are you?" she cried, twisting in his grasp, hoping the rain would make her skin slick. But instead of weakening, he gripped tighter, cutting blood off from her forearm entirely. "Let me go!"

The shadow mumbled, and in front of them, the paved

road lightened from black to gray to silver, and then became reflective like a large mirror. Yet, when the shadow tapped it with his shoe, it rippled like water.

I need to wake up.

"All you have to do is walk with me," the shadow said. "Step into—"

The sound of shattering glass reverberated above the winds, and Ember was shoved to the side. When she looked back, the shadow figure still stood over the mirror, but an arrow pierced its center, fracturing it into thousands of shards as if it was never liquid at all.

She bolted. There was no hesitation this time. Her legs moved on their own, and panic guided her. Rain pelted her face, wind roared in her ears. She found the first best hiding spot she could see—a large oak tree in the nearby park—and ran for it. And she made it.

She collapsed against the trunk, inhaling what she could, water and air, but her pulse didn't slow. Her thoughts didn't slow. *Raindrops. Raindrops,* she thought and her hands still heated. Her neck still sparked. *I have to get out.*

Something covered her mouth. She screamed again.

"Shush, Alloy," the voice said behind her. He wasn't the same shadow who'd grabbed her before. "We don't want to harm you."

Then, he mumbled something she didn't understand, and another mirror appeared in the grass.

No, wait. Did he *create* that mirror?

"It's time to go," the shadow said. "Take a step forward and you'll be safe."

Step? Into whatever reflective hell that *is?*

Hilarious.

She ripped to one side and thrust her knee up toward her assailant's groin. But he caught her knee, leaving her unstable on one leg as she tried to throw a punch. Then a kick. Anything that would land and set her free. He blocked all of them.

"Who *are* you people?" she said, thrashing in his grasp. "Get the hell off of me!"

He let go, and she fell on the grass inches from the mirror. Then a dagger shot over her head so quickly, she didn't notice it until the shadow snatched it from the air.

"I don't want to fight you," he said, holding his hands up. The blade glinted as he spun it between his fingers. "But if you want to fight, I promise I'll win."

If I survive this, I'm calling in sick for a week.

Nieve's song filled the air.

"Shit," the shadow figure said. "Stay there, Alloy. Hopefully, this won't take long." He hopped over the mirror and sprinted across the playground, across the pavement of the basketball court, and to where the fight had moved to on the other side of the park.

Ember wanted to run again, but fear paralyzed her. She didn't know where she could go, where another mirror-man wouldn't appear to take her away. And her palms were *hot*; her arms were *hot*; the dizziness was already setting in. At this point, escaping was useless. She needed to focus only on the—

"Raindrops." Her voice shook as she said it, but another, "Raindrops," and her vision started to clear.

Not fifty yards away, the twins fought the black figures—at least, she thought it was fighting. Waves of water and gusts of wind and singing and mirrors...so many mirrors. Daggers thrown. Spears thrusted. *Is that a sword?*

She shook her head as if that would clear whatever it was she was seeing, but the fight raged on in front of her. *What is going on?*

A streak of light tore through the clouds, joined by a vociferous thunderclap, tearing away her attention in turn. The lightning was getting closer. They needed to get out of this storm.

She pushed herself to sit against the oak tree and pulled her knees to her chest. Her head pounded. Her breaths came faster and faster.

She grabbed at the spark on her neck. *She* needed out of this storm.

The wind then blew hard, and she latched onto the tree. The gusts pried at her hair and clothes, but fortunately, won none of them.

The twins were less fortunate, blown off their feet like a leaf in the breeze. But as Sombra flew back, she dragged her hand on the ground, and wherever she touched, the grass liquified, creating a river in the middle of the park. Where she landed, she regained her stance and dipped in her hand. Then water rose from the stream, and, as if from a hose, it surged toward the shadows.

One figure dodged. The river hit the other squarely in the chest. The twins stepped in unison like they had rehearsed this dance a thousand times, moving their hands from the sky to the ground, to the newly formed creek. The stream grew to a swell, then a tidal wave. And then it crashed over the fallen shadow and tossed him in the currents. The shadow squirmed inside, unable to breathe, let alone escape.

But near the twins surfaced a mirror, and the second shadow stepped through.

"Behind you!" Ember shouted, though the women spun as if they already knew. In one swift motion, they dropped the river, flooding the park, and disarmed the figure, his daggers falling next to the mirror. Nieve forced his arms behind his back and him to his knees.

Ember exhaled. *It's over.*

Then the wave hit the twins.

She stiffened. *What?*

She searched the area, but she still didn't understand. The water had come from behind the kneeling shadow—from the ground. From thin air.

Sombra and Nieve fell, sputtering. Before they could catch their breath, another deluge of water assaulted them. The kneeling shadow figure reclaimed his knives and stepped away from the geyser unharmed. The once-drowning shadow was nowhere to be seen.

Another wave hit out of nowhere. Then another, and another.

Lightning flashed against the sky...and against the ground. *The mirror.*

When the twins dropped the river, they'd dropped the drowning shadow, too. And when they'd disarmed the dagger wielder, his mirror had never shattered.

Now, the drowning shadow was gone. He had to have been the one siphoning water. And he had to have used that mirror to do it—he was still using that mirror to do it.

And now the twins were drowning. They were trapped. They needed an escape.

She had to do something.

No. I can't do anything.

But that thought didn't stop the heat from filling in her chest and her abdomen. It didn't stop the trees and grass from splitting into two. No, now her stomach turned as she watched four assailants fight a set of quadruplets, her vision shifting in and out of clarity.

Sombra extended an arm, coughing, reaching for her sister. Nieve didn't reach back.

Something. Anything.

No, I can't. I wouldn't be saving anyone.

The waves stopped. The missing shadow reappeared, and

together, the figures sharpened the rain. A million needles, once again, glinted with the flashing light of the sky.

Ember snapped her eyes shut, only to see an image of a young girl with short black hair, dark brown eyes, a bruised face. The girl stared at her, waiting for her sister to protect her, to save her, to help her escape.

The girl screamed.

Her eyes sprung open. The back of her neck burned, and her body was ablaze. Her vision cleared, hearing sharpened, electricity surged.

I have to.

She took one step forward—

The spark at her neck burst like a firework, the locket at her neck seared like a stovetop, and she doubled over in tears and sweat.

One of the shadows stretched his arms above him, holding the thousands of raindrop needles over the nearly lifeless twins that lay at his feet. As he drove his hands down, it took all of her strength to point at him.

But she did.

And she slipped out of consciousness.

CHAPTER 3
ADEMURE

"Te envidio." *I envy you.*

As she said it, the queen waved to the thousands lining the sand-made streets below. The Nysan people wore green linens and green shoes and looked up at their royals with bright green eyes. The queen adjusted her diadem about her crisp, hairspray-saturated locks and smiled.

Ademure was too weary to respond. Her mother had been saying the same thing to her for months now: about her youth, her beauty, her health. She could only imagine what the queen meant by the statement this time. So, she kept her lips tight and hoped the bit of sunlight she was allotted today would return the color to her once brown skin.

"How have you so solidly won their affection?" the queen continued in Spanish. "They cling to every word you say."

So, it's about my station today. Not sure what there is to be jealous about. Perhaps how glamorous my life is, hours upon hours spent at the library?

"They don't love me anymore than they love you," Ademure said casually.

"Now, that's not true."

The queen was right about that. As Nysan tradition dictated that each member of the royal family participate in el Día de la Reina parade, both Ademure and her mother had given their speeches from the upper deck of the ship-shaped royal float. Princess Ademure received a roaring round of applause—Queen Esmerelda, reluctant clapping.

"What do you do, then?" the queen continued. "Sneak into town and hand out diamonds? Smuggle hordes of healing water to the hospital? Or maybe you gift the people your feminine wiles?"

"I haven't left the castle, Amá, just as you've asked. If I've done anything to gain their affection, it's wave and smile in public for the first time in months."

Their stalled float jerked to a start—the servants who manipulated the float weren't adept at sailing a carriage so large. The vehicle might have been controlled like a landsailer —with skis at the bottom that required a manipulation of sand and wind to push—but it didn't move like one. It was nowhere near as streamlined. The royal veterans, however, handled the stutter with grace.

"They'll be gone by this afternoon," Esmerelda said, still smiling and waving.

"If you think it's necessary."

"Of course, it's necessary. If they can't do the job correctly, they have no right to serve me."

We've already let go of forty servants this month, Ademure thought. *What's five more?*

The two-tiered float continued its path down the main boulevard of the island's central town. In front of them marched dozens of Nysan navy sailors dressed in their gray and green uniforms, followed by another dozen royal guards. Two of the white-clad estrellas patrolled on landsailers, and all of them were there to protect the float from whatever wild intruder her mother thought might attack them this week. *There's no harm in a little extra protection*, she reminded herself. *Just let her imagination run its course. It will pass, eventually.*

When they reached the plaza, they cruised to a stop. Thousands of Nysan civilians stood shoulder to shoulder in whatever space they could find, squishing up against the nearby storefronts or else covering every grain of sand the square had to offer. Several children sat on the shoulders of their parents. Several more stood precariously on the edges of the plaza's stone fountain.

From the railing of the upper deck, just in front of the helm, her mother blew a melodramatic kiss to the masses; the gesture received moderate enthusiasm. Ademure hardly pecked her hand and soon covered her ears from the resulting ovation.

"Your father, too, had them in the palm of his hands," Esmerelda said over the noise. She still smiled for the crowd, but her tone had gone icy. "The cruelest man I've ever known, beloved."

"I wouldn't know," Ademure said. "I hardly remember him."

"The horrid man has everything he could ever want, has taken everything from me, and now, you're doing the same."

These allegations are growing tired, Amá. Surely you can sing a new song?

"Apá didn't take everything from you," she said. "He took the sunless lands, yes, but left you paradise." She gestured toward the town beneath them.

"He took my son."

"But left me. If we're apportioning by children and not skill, you must believe that's a fair divide."

"Not if his intention was to have you take my place."

The air stilled.

Has your delusion strayed so far? You now believe the twins' lies?

"You truly think Apá contrived a plan that relies *entirely* on his estranged, young, and impressionable daughter to somehow influence the people of Nysa to usurp her only parent's—her *mother's* throne? Wouldn't an invasion be simpler?"

"You are meant to inherit *his* throne, too," the queen said. "And you did get our alloys killed."

"You know as well as I that that was an accident. And it is not as if I knotted their nooses."

"The estrellas have also confirmed your father is already building an army. I assume because you didn't overthrow me quickly enough. Thank goodness you're more diplomat than dictator. And you've always been a bit slow."

Ademure left the railing. She loved her mother, but *damn it* if she had to take any more of this garbage. She had grown so weak, she couldn't conjure even a dagger anymore. What made her mother think that she was strong enough to overthrow her, or rule a nation in the aftermath? Perhaps, if she acted quickly, she could have a guard escort her on a landsailer and be back at the castle before anyone noticed her absence.

But as she reached the top of the stairs at the backside of the "ship", hidden from the crowd with a curtain, she was met with a man and woman in white uniforms, both of whom were twice her age and both of whom towered over her.

"Estrella Capote, Estrella Bailón," Ademure said, "I didn't realize you were in the parade. I thought you two would be welcoming the alloy at the castle."

"Alteza," Bailón said before bowing with the grace of a ballerina, not a hair out of place; Capote refrained from a deep bow, probably for fear of ripping his suit.

Ademure meanwhile recoiled at the honorific—the

estrellas had always used "Alteza" when speaking to her, but the word lately seemed more a curse than a reference to her royal status.

"The Delfinos are watching her," Bailón continued. "We're on strict orders to guard the queen and you."

Of course, you are. These days, Ademure never went anywhere without an estrella breathing down her neck. Bailón told her it was for her safety, but she had her doubts.

"Well, I'd like to head back now," she said, attempting to push past the pair.

"I'm afraid we can't allow you to leave without orders," Bailón said as she grabbed her by the wrist. Capote held her by her shoulder.

Ademure met Bailón's eyes. "I'm giving you orders."

"Orders come from higher up, Alteza."

"My mother knew I would try to leave?"

"Actually, the orders are mine."

Ademure threw off their grip and flitted her eyes between them, but the estrellas stood stern.

"When was this decided?"

"At the last meeting, Alteza."

"You mean the meetings I'm never invited to?"

Bailón merely lifted her chin.

Ademure stormed off, back to her mother's side along the railing. The queen hadn't stopped waving, despite how the people below had thinned.

"Amá, the estrellas tell me I no longer have authority over them. Is this true?"

"Yes," the queen said tersely, still maintaining her all-important smile.

"And this was decided without my knowledge?"

"It was."

Ademure gripped the railing so tightly that her arms began

to shake. This psychosis of her mother's was much worse than she had feared. Limiting her activities was one thing—she had always assumed that was protective in nature. But to limit her command? What in the world was her mother thinking?

"For what reason might I ask?"

"In the case you decided to stage a coup. I can't have you turning my own council against me."

Too slow to overthrow you, yet clever enough to incite mutiny. "Amá, I'm the princess of Nysa. Your *daughter*."

"And," Esmerelda said, casting her a sharp look, "you are turning the public on me as we speak." She shifted her gaze to the people below. They'd quieted and now stared curiously at their royals. "Your popularity is a blessing, but your fickle emotions will lead the public to revolt."

"I understand your frustrations, Amá, but this is absurd."

"No, this is precautionary. I can't let your father win."

The queen left the railing, and Ademure trailed her. The cheering returned behind them.

"Win what? We're not at war."

"Not yet." Her mother ducked behind the curtain. Estrellas Bailón and Capote bowed their heads as she walked toward her seat. "But it'll only be a matter of time before they strike, and when that happens, I'll need more than the estrellas to defeat him. I'll need resources and recruits, love and patriotism. Our people will have to support us more than his people support him."

Ademure reeled. This sort of nonsensical banter was exactly why she avoided speaking to her mother—a mistake in hindsight, because the banter was no longer simply nonsensical. No, her avoidance had allowed it to evolve into something conspiratorial, something deadlier—something her mother had the elite force to act on.

"You sound like you *want* war."

The queen struck quickly. Ademure held her face tentatively, heat emanating from it, and her mother shook her own wrist.

"How dare you," Esmerelda said. "I want peace for Nysa. But what do you expect me to do? In less than six months, two top officials have been assassinated. I can't ignore that. We're the last nation. I'm the last world leader. We won't have peace until the Agarthan threat is eliminated."

No one knows who sent those assassins, Ademure thought, still holding her cheek. *Agartha is the last nation that would attack unprovoked. Our estrellas on the other hand...* But she knew better than to speak her thoughts aloud.

"How do you win, then?" she asked instead. "How do you plan to gain support?"

"You have their support. They'll listen to you."

If I'm with Apá, why would I help you? Trying to understand her mother's logic was futile, it seemed. "I'm not going to convince the people we need a war without reason."

"I've just given you the reason."

"If he attacks, then I'll do it. I'll persuade them. But I won't do it beforehand. Not without proof that there will be war. That there needs to be a war."

"And what if when he attacks, you're in the crossfire?"

Her breath caught. The crowd's muffled clapping and cheering and music burned in her ears.

"You mean if the father I'm in league with were to kill me?"

"He's done far worse before. If he attacks and you're killed, what do you suggest should happen then? Who will persuade the people to fight then?"

Her mother wasn't wrong to ponder the possibility, but the question—it didn't feel like a hypothetical.

"If I were to be killed in such a manner, I...," Ademure tugged her skirt, "I would hope that the people would recognize the wrong and fight back without need for persuasion. On their own and out of love. For their nation. For justice. But Apá wouldn't—"

"So, you're saying," Esmerelda interrupted, "in the event you can't give the people reason, your death alone would be reason enough?" She tilted her head as if she were actually considering the idea. "Interesting."

Ademure frowned. Surely her mother wasn't insinuating... No. She was the queen's one and only heir. Her *daughter*. Esmerelda would never—no, *could* never—hurt Ademure.

Except for the occasional strike of the cheek.

"I don't know that," Ademure said. "And I hate talking about this, Amá. I don't plan on dying anytime soon. Besides, when the time comes, I sincerely doubt Apá will be the reason for the occasion."

Her mother laughed. "Perhaps not. But you can't know when you'll meet your end, Ademure. Though you can suppose the aftermath. The clues lie in the present."

Queen Esmerelda then pulled back the curtain and was welcomed with soft applause. When Ademure followed, the crowd's reaction elevated to boisterous praise. It was so loud, she barely heard her mother, and still, the words, on a warm October day, made her shiver.

"Just like your father. So beloved."

CHAPTER 4
EMBER

Ember jerked upright and gasped for air. Beads of sweat dripped down her temples as she blinked away the flashing lights, echoing screams, and stench of burned flesh.

Just a nightmare. Though, she couldn't remember any of it.

She lay back down. Her fingers rested on the sheets, and her back sunk into the mattress. In the soothing darkness, her eyes felt heavy, and she drifted away, lost in thought of how grateful she was to be at home in her bed—

Her eyes sprung open.

With horribly aching muscles, she pushed herself up and limped over to the curtains to draw them open. When she did, light flooded the room, exposing every foreign corner and alien decoration.

Whoa.

To her right sat a set of forest green drawers that expanded from wall to wall. To her left, a gilded closet stretched from the floor to the high ceiling. An enormous crystal chandelier meant to hold dozens of candles hung above the canopy bed. And at the front of the room stood a large vanity with tiny intricate roses carved along the ridge of the mirror frame. Strangely, however, no mirror sat inside it.

This was clearly not any of the hospitals in which she'd awoken before.

She fell back onto the bed as she rubbed her forearms, sliding the soft fabric against her skin...a delicate, unfamiliar fabric. She looked down. She was wearing chartreuse silk pajamas.

Not just a nightmare.

The door swung open.

"Oh good, you're awake," said a woman dressed in white, hair charcoal black, arms full of blankets.

Ember pulled the sheets tight over her body and wondered if her aching muscles would still let her throw a punch.

"The closet has a number of gowns and other outfits you can wear," the woman continued as she gestured toward one of the half-dozen doors in the room. "Change and I'll take you to the dining room for breakfast."

Ember didn't move.

The woman frowned. "Alloy? Something wrong?"

"Um, yeah," she said, hand moving to her head. "Who...who are you?"

"Sombra." The woman raised a brow. "We met on the train the night before last."

"...Uh-huh. And where are we?"

Sombra's frown deepened. "Nysa."

Ember chewed the inside of her lip. This was always the worst part of her blackouts—piecing together what had happened. She recalled the ride from work, at least. There were two women, some men in black, maybe a wreck? But then, a blur.

"You have a sister...with white hair. Her name is..."

Sombra set down the blankets in a chair. "Nieve."

"Right. And you were...struggling with some people? Wasn't one of you hurt?"

"My sister. But you saved her. Do you not remember?"

I saved her? Ember glanced at the scar on her wrist. *Doubtful.* "My memory is usually a little fuzzy after an episode."

"An episode?"

"Where is Nysa?" she asked, toying with the chain of her locket. "Is this a hotel?" She looked around the room once more. *Dear god, I hope not. No way can I foot this bill.*

"No. We're in the Magick Realm. Alloy, are you certain you're okay? Is it normal to not remember basic geography after an 'episode'?"

"Um, sorry. There's been a lot of construction downtown lately. I'm not super familiar with all the new bars or restaurants."

Sombra shook her head slowly. "I don't think you under-stand. You're not in Dallas anymore. You're not even in the Soulless Realm. You're in the Magick Realm, on the island of Nysa, hundreds of miles from anywhere in the States."

Ember snorted, but the woman's worried gaze told her she wasn't joking.

"Wait," she said quietly. "You kidnapped me?"

Sombra's gaze sharpened. "We rescued you. We've returned you home."

"Home?" Ember sat up straighter, burying her hot palms into the sheets. "What are you talking about? Who even are you people?"

"Apparently, we have more to review than I thought. We'll talk over breakfast. Get dressed, and I'll be back in a moment." Sombra slammed the door behind her and yelled "Nieve!" down the hall.

Staring blankly at the jade duvet, Ember raked her hands through her hair. "What the hell happened?"

Her stomach grumbled. *Ugh.*

If she had had her wits about her, she would've taken the opportunity to climb out the window and hightail it to the nearest airport. But she hadn't yet been murdered, and, without cash on hand, she couldn't pass on the opportunity for free food.

But why did they say this was my home?

She dragged herself to the closet, holding her hand to her head, in desperate need of some ibuprofen and an energy drink. She didn't know why the recovery always resembled a hangover, but this one felt like she'd had a night of tequila shots.

And of course, when all she wanted was a t-shirt and a pair of sweats, she found none. Rather, the closet was filled with floor-length gowns she thought fitting for bridesmaid dresses or a red-carpet event. The footwear consisted of jeweled heels and strappy flats. There was even a pair of glass slippers.

I thought I was abducted, not asked to prom.

Eventually, deep behind the dresses, she found an assortment of simple pastel linen shirts and shorts and a single pair of lace-up boots. Not ideal, but at least they'd be easier to run in when she made her eventual escape. She settled on a blue skirt and white tee.

There was a knock on the door.

"Alloy, are you ready yet?" Sombra called. "Breakfast will be cold."

"Coming," Ember said, pulling on the shoes and choosing to ignore whatever the hell "alloy" meant for the time being. With the trusted hair tie she wore on her wrist, she drew her curls back into a ponytail and met Sombra in the hallway.

"You look...common," the woman said.

"Thanks. This was the most common look I could create."

"Incredible," Sombra muttered, then started down the corridor.

Ember walked beside her in stride. *Well, you don't get to kidnap me* and *tell me what to wear.*

"Su Majestad y su Alteza would've joined us for breakfast this morning," Sombra said, "however they are in town for el Día de la Reina. Instead, they will meet you tomorrow evening at dinner with the rest of the estrellas."

"I'm sorry, what? I'm meeting with royalty?"

"Right. We've a lot to cover so I'm going to need you to keep up."

She did not just roll her eyes at me. "Can we start from the beginning? Like why you kidnapped me?"

"We did not kidnap you. The royal family asked us to save you from the Agarthans and return you to your home."

"I literally don't understand half of what you just said. Why should some royal family care about my safety?"

They arrived at a large arched doorway. The doors were shades of green which, apparently, was the color of choice in this...castle? Green stained-glass windows. Glassy green floors. Tan and green geometric patterns on the ceilings and walls. Though when she looked closer at the walls, Ember saw tiny granules in what she expected to be concrete. *Sand?*

"I promise, we will explain all of this, Alloy. But surely, you must be famished. Can't we first have a meal?"

Sombra pushed the doors open, and a wave of smoke and sugar wafted through the air. The spread comprised of sausage, fresh fruit, pancakes, yogurt, eggs, bacon. Even several boxes of cereal. And Ember's mouth watered as her mind, body, and soul prepared to fill her gut.

"Please, sit," requested what looked to be a butler.

Another woman, identical to Sombra save for the white

hair, was already seated at the mahogany table. She grinned as Ember took a seat across from her.

"We hope it's to your liking," the woman—Nieve, she vaguely remembered—said. "We wanted you to feel as comfortable as possible, so we had the kitchen make all the foods common to the United States. Please, eat as much as you desire."

Hesitantly, Ember took one cube of pineapple, intending to eat no more until she could be certain it was safe to do so. But the moment the citrus hit her tongue, her hangry and hungover sides possessed her, and like a machine, she guzzled food down faster than she could process its taste, inhaling butter and grease galore. It wasn't until she dropped her fork that she realized the twins hadn't been eating.

She played with her locket, surmising what poisons she'd ingested. But a moment later, when her hunger subsided, her rationale returned: if they wanted to kill her, it would've been easier to accomplish when she'd been unconscious for over twenty-four straight hours.

Of course, that didn't mean they weren't ever going to kill her, so she kept her knife within reach.

"Finished?" Nieve asked, grinning.

Ember nodded once and mumbled, "Thanks."

"Oh, I hope you enjoyed it. I do believe el Alcázar de Maldojo has some of the best chefs in the Magick Realm. If you're ever hungry for anything in particular, don't be afraid to ask them."

"I'll be sure to." She fidgeted with the knife at her fingertips. "So. Magick Realm. Stupid big sand castle. Royal family. What does all that have to do with me?"

"Don't be modest, Alloy. You belong here. But I am curious as to how you found a tutor in the Soulless Realm. Who taught you?"

Tutor? "You mean my basketball coach?"

Nieve laughed. "No, your *tutor*. I know you're rough. And you may not have yet properly refined your skills, which is entirely fine—we will help you with that. But we saw your strength the other night. You surely didn't learn that on your own? Who taught you to use that magic?"

Ember's hand and the utensil it toyed with stilled.

She should've asked why Nieve thought someone had taught her anything. Why she'd ever been in the *Soulless Realm*-thing in the first place. Or how the twins had known just where to find her.

She should've asked about her biological parents.

But she was too distracted by the thought of her foster ones. The same ones she'd...

Magic. Not what I would call it.

She kept her gaze on her silverware. "Magic doesn't exist."

The twins exchanged glances, Sombra's seemingly less surprised than Nieve's. Nieve then tried to speak, but her mouth only opened, and any words she might have wanted to say died in the back of her throat.

So Sombra spoke instead, with none of her sister's geniality. "You don't believe that."

Ember stared at the knife's reflection of her odd, green eyes. As odd of a green as the twins'. *I don't.*

"You can train me?"

As if she had just regained the ability to breathe, Nieve nodded vigorously. "We would love to train you. Profe Ozamiz is waiting to begin lessons as we speak."

"What's the catch?"

"You have us wrong, Alloy. It only benefits us to train you. Other than your attention and discipline, there is nothing else from you that we need."

Ember eyed them both. Though Nieve was much kinder

than her counterpart, neither was exactly kind. *Why did they really bring me here?* she thought, and she remembered the men dressed in black.

"Who were you fighting yesterday?"

"Agarthans," Nieve said. At seeing her confusion, she added, "Agartha, like Nysa, is a magical hub, but instead of an island paradise, it resides beneath the Earth's crust. They are not allies."

Ember pursed her lips. "What was yesterday's fight about?"

"You."

"Why?"

The sisters again exchanged looks.

"You are the last alloy in existence," Nieve said. "And they wanted to use you against us in the war to come."

Ember leaned back in her chair. "So there is a catch."

"Alloy, believe us when we say, we would train you regardless. You are a Nysan, a magick, and you deserve to develop your powers on those qualities alone."

"But make no mistake," Sombra interjected. "War is imminent. And we need your help in defending our home."

"But it's not my home." Ember twirled her knife between two fingers. "Dallas is my home. And I think I'd like to go back."

"Alloy, please," Nieve said. "I'm sure it seems quite a bit to ask—I know it is—but the Agarthans won't see reason anymore. They've grown their army considerably and will stop at nothing to get their way. They will decimate us and every innocent man, woman, and child on this island."

Ember flinched at the word "decimate."

"And you think I can stop them?"

"With the right training, we know you can. You're an alloy after all. The strongest of all the magicks."

"And how do you know that? What exactly is an alloy?"

"Alloys are exceptional magicks, and no normal magick can do what you did. Two extremely powerful Agarthans in one single spell? That's nothing short of remarkable. Think for a moment. You're a novice who produced *lightning*."

The knife fell.

The lights, the screams, the stench... It all returned to her. She was sprawled on the sidewalk again in the heat, in the shadows of the flames engulfing her house.

Then she was at the hospital. Daphne's heart beat as if her chest was made of glass. The ventilator pumped like her lungs had been poked with holes.

After all these years. Ember rubbed her fingers together, phantom sparks dancing about them. Another played at her neck. *That's what this is.*

She picked up her knife, gulping down the memories. "What do you mean, 'lightning'?"

"You really don't remember," Sombra said.

Nieve gave her sister a warning look and a subtle shake of the head.

Then, she looked back at Ember, saying, "I mean, exactly that. Lightning. You managed to control and direct it at the Agarthans. You distracted them long enough for Sombra to levitate both of us out of the chaos. And I drove to Houston and sailed us here last night."

She leaned forward. "I've never seen a magick conjure lightning before—not even other alloys. I honestly thought it was impossible. Even among alloys, you're strong. You will be nothing short of vital to our success against—"

"No."

Nieve cocked her head. "I'm afraid I don't understand, Alloy. Could you—"

"No." Ember met their eyes, her knife pressed so hard into the plate, a small crack formed. "I'm not fighting."

Sombra's jaw looked tenser than before, but Nieve laid a calming hand on her sister's thigh and nodded.

"Okay," she said smoothly. "You don't have to fight. Or train. You are a guest after all."

Ember's eyes darted between the sisters, the black and white, the pissed and friendly.

"When is the next flight out of here?"

"We can take you back in two days' time," Nieve said.

"I've already lost two days of pay as it is. I can't afford to lose two more."

"We will compensate you—for the time and the stress." Though she seemed disappointed, she gave a soft smile. "I'm sorry this didn't work out as we had hoped."

Well, that didn't sound too bad.

"And what am I supposed to do until then?"

Nieve shrugged. "There is the dinner tomorrow night with Su Majestad. And before that, we could give you a tour of the castle. If you're interested, of course. We don't want to be more of a bother than we've already been."

Ember eyed them again, cautious, but curious. They claimed to know what she was—what she could do. That she belonged here. *My ever-growing list of abnormalities... Maybe they can explain them.*

"I wouldn't mind a tour."

CHAPTER 5
EMBER

"This is the royal family's personal theater." Nieve walked to the front of the stage, arms outstretched.

Dark green velvet curtains draped over the raised flooring. They shimmered in the dim light of the candlelit chandelier that hung past the orchestra pit. And past that, in the audience, stood four plush green chairs, bordered in gold and vines. It was difficult to tell from the stage, but it appeared only one of the chairs held the imprint of a person.

"It's gorgeous," Ember said, meeting her side. Sombra stayed at the back of the stage, arms folded.

"Stunning," Nieve agreed. "Some of the best players in the world perform here. It took ages to perfect the acoustics, but we happen to have some of the finest engineers in the world too."

"And where exactly are we in this world?" Ember asked. "Like, where in relation to somewhere I know?"

Nieve set a hand on her chin. "It's hard to define where Nysa is at any given moment. The nymphs cloaked the island long ago to ensure the soulless didn't stumble upon it. Anyone entering must be guided by someone already shoreside. Of course, that means we don't know exactly where we are either."

She hopped off the front of the stage. Sombra climbed down the steps and met her sister near the chairs. The two then walked toward the back of the theater in unison, and Ember realized she was expected to follow.

"I know for certain that currently, we're in the Caribbean," Nieve continued when she caught up. "And I believe the soulless have referred to the area as the Bermuda Triangle, if that means anything to you."

So we're not as far from the States as I thought.

"And how did you find me?" Ember asked.

"Relatively easily."

They exited the theater, turning down another green hallway entirely made of sand.

"And you're sure I'm from here?"

"You have eyes green as ours."

They walked in silence for a while. Apparently, Nieve wasn't going to say more.

"Then why did it take twenty-two years to bring me back?"

At the end of the corridor, at the top of a grand, jade staircase, the sisters halted. Nieve looked at her with sad eyes.

"We didn't know you were there," she said softly.

"Your parents didn't say anything to anyone," Sombra added.

My parents?

The charcoal-haired sister traipsed down the steps ahead, waving a hand about as she spoke. "Not unexpected, but you would think if they were going to send their only daughter to the Soulless Realm, they'd at least hire her a tutor."

Ember turned to Nieve. "You knew my parents? Were they alloys, too?"

"We didn't know them personally," she said. "They were not alloys."

"But they are infamous," Sombra called from the bottom stair.

"For what?"

Nieve shot her sister a look that could cut glass, and Sombra lifted her chin in response. But neither answered Ember.

So she tried again. "Where are they?"

"Gone," Nieve said simply. "Come. You must see the Sculpture Hall." With that, the twins descended the stairs into the depths of what seemed to be a ballroom, weirdly and unsurprisingly covered in sand.

But Ember couldn't yet make herself move.

Infamous.

It wasn't the first time she had thought poorly of her birth parents. Though she had spent most of her life wondering who they were and where they'd gone, she'd spent nearly as long wondering why. Why not leave her with information about herself? Why had they left her alone?

Still, she hadn't ever thought them quite ill-willed. She'd even once wished they were field medics or firefighters—that they'd died saving another. Of course, when she'd realized how peculiar it would be to leave a newborn at a hospital—*outside* a hospital—before presumably dying in the line of duty, she reconsidered the notion that they were good. But bad?

Yet as she considered Sombra's words, only "bad" made sense. And not just bad, but awful. *Infamous.* Because who else left a baby with no guardian, no note, in not only another city or country, but another realm?

Her fingers heated the metal of her locket. *Raindrops.*

"Alloy?" Nieve called from the bottom step. "Are you coming?"

Ember glanced at the indoor beach below and let go of her necklace. "Yeah. Sorry."

The twin nodded, and Ember hurried down the stairs. And though she was hardly impressed from the top step, when she became level with the floor, the true wonder of the room grew clearer.

The first sculpture was that of a tree twice her own height. Each ridge of the trunk looked as if it were crafted with a needle, each leaf as delicate as tissue paper—and the sculptor had constructed it entirely out of sand.

Another sculpture was a more traditional one: a castle. But the artist of this sand castle had carved out every window and turret, hollowed out each room. Every single speck of sand seemed to be glued on with intricate perfection, and yet Ember couldn't see the glue.

"A single artist manipulated each," Nieve said. She looked like an angel, drifting through the dozens and dozens of gravity-defying sculptures, while she herself was all clad in white. "The finest magic."

"Magic created this?"

"The very same magic you possess."

Ember's hand hovered over the twisting vines of a molded rose. Each thorn was so sharp, she was sure a prick would draw blood. "So, I could make this?"

"With training, of course." Nieve lowered her chin. "Perhaps you would like to try?"

Ember shook her head as she continued to admire the rose. "I won't fight for you."

"I'm talking only of a trial. One session, so you can get a feel for the craft. Then, when you go back, you'll have some foundation to work from."

She dropped her arm. "You would let me do that?"

"You are Nysan, whether you claim it or not. And you have

talent. I would hate for that to wither when you return to Dallas."

She looked back at the rose. Then the tree, the castle. Each one had such precision. Such finesse. Such control. *Control.*

"Yeah," she said, moving her hand to her locket. "I think I'd like that."

Nieve smiled. "Wonderful. I'll let our tutor know. Sombra will lead you back to your room. There's a change of clothes laid out on the bed. I'll meet you both in the courtyard."

When Ember returned to her room, she found the clothing Nieve had mentioned: a jumpsuit and cloak just like the twins wore. But instead of white, this set was an unfortunate shade of green.

Once she fastened the cloak to her shoulders, she looked down. The suit was clearly new, but the fit felt archaic, like it was a century or two behind. The shoulders were wide and the waist was tight, and the cape weighed heavy on her back. She could've been at war or on her way to an opera, or perhaps both. She felt ridiculous.

After tying her boots tight, she marched out to the hall to meet Sombra, who then led her through the dining hall before stepping outside.

The courtyard was both massive and perfectly manicured. Each blade of grass peeked through the sand at the same height as the next, and each was as deeply green as the forest that lined the area hundreds of yards to the north.

And with respect to that forest, she could see why the castle went without a northern border. Its densely packed trees spanned from one wall of the courtyard to the other, locking all its inhabitants in and likely locking others out. Not even light peeked through the canopy, and the forest seemed to expand forever north. Ember wondered if anyone had ever gotten lost in it.

Perhaps, after being blinded by the stupidly white building that stood at its edge, someone had. The edifice must've had fifty columns and a hundred stone steps, and it looked as if it had been plucked from Athens itself. A temple.

What if that's been my problem, not praying? Maybe I should start.

Much closer to the castle entrance, another white fixture gleamed, though it was a third of the temple's size, with far fewer stairs. Still, the gazebo was not small, and it had far more elaborate detailing about its threshold with green-painted engravings along the pearlescent railings and moldings. On the gazebo's steps waited two women: Nieve and another woman that Ember didn't recognize.

"Alloy Slade," Nieve said, "this is Profe Ozamiz. She'll be your tutor for today."

The woman didn't wear the cloak that the twins and Ember wore, but she wore a similar dark green jumpsuit that stretched thin over her bulging muscles. Her braided hair lay taut against her head, and she stood like a marine, stern and erect.

"Alloy Slade." Ozamiz bowed her head. "Encatada de conocerte."

Ember, unfamiliar with proper etiquette, but somewhat familiar with Spanish—*thank you, reggaeton*—returned the gesture. "Uh, likewise, Profe Ozamiz."

"Sombra and I will stay to observe, but Profe Ozamiz will take you through the basics of magic and combat." Nieve turned to the tutor. "Profe, if you will. In English, please." The twins took their seats on the bench inside the gazebo.

"The Delfinos tell me you know nothing of magic," Ozamiz said.

"Um. Yeah."

"Then, we must start with something else." The tutor reached into her waistband and pulled out a pistol.

"Whoa whoa whoa, what are you doing with that?"

Ozamiz loaded the weapon. "Testing your abilities."

"With a gun?"

"Have you never used a gun?"

Ember scoffed. "I'm from Texas." She then shook her head, trying her best to turn her thoughts into words. "Why do I need a gun? Aren't I supposed to be learning magic?"

"You will learn magic, eventually. But as of now, your connection is too weak. You need to build up your athleticism so that you don't faint each time you cast a spell. Until then, practice technique." The tutor presented her with the handle. "Technique defeats physique."

She grasped the pistol slowly and with both hands, keeping the barrel pointed down and away from everybody else. "I don't understand how shooting teaches me magic."

"If you can't aim a gun, you can't aim a spell," Ozamiz said simply. She moved a distance away, past the twins and the gazebo, and knelt on the ground. Ember couldn't hear what her tutor said, but the ground swelled around the woman until it broke into a column, growing tall, wide, and roughly shaped into something like a person. Two circles whitened at both the top and the center—the head and the chest.

Her mouth fell open. *Magic.*

Ozamiz returned to her side and pointed at the newly formed target. "Can you hit the head?"

Trembling, Ember glanced at the twins. Nieve seemed a bit more eager to be there, but both stared back, arms folded in wait.

She looked at her hands. *If you're ever going to control it...* Then she focused on the target and raised her arms.

Small breeze, still target, white circle.

Raindrops.

Click.

Boom!

She flinched at the deafening shot, dropping her aim and covering her ears. "Damn it! No earmuffs?"

"If you're in need of pulling a gun, you'll have time to decide whether to protect your hearing or your body. Not both." Ozamiz started toward the target. "Alloy, come here."

Ember returned the gun to both hands and walked with it pointed toward the forest. There would be no accidents on her watch.

"Yeah?" she said, and gasped.

Not only had she hit the target, but she had hit the proper circle, and almost squarely. A faint tingle faded from her fingers.

"Quite the beginner's luck," Ozamiz said. "Do you think you can do it again?"

Ember made her way back to the south side of the courtyard, near the castle wall. *Raindrops.*

This time, there was no flinching. The gun felt as natural as a basketball, the trigger an extension of her hand. She connected with the weapon, the magazine, the bullets, and fired the remaining shots—all sixteen of them.

Ozamiz looked at the target and laughed. "Delfinos," she called to the twins, "gather me some rocks. We're about to have fun."

Moments and another magazine later, Ember fired at levitating rocks, then orbiting rocks, then accelerating rocks, then not rocks at all but whatever material her tutor decided to turn the rocks into: metal, clay, paper, plastic. Each caught a different amount of wind, and each was struck the same.

Though her shoulders tired of the small recoils, she barely heard the shots now. But not because they deafened her. No, rather it was as if she was more in tune with her surroundings than she had ever been—even more so than when she played basketball. She could spot the centers of the rocks. She gauged the wind that pushed them. She knew which blade of grass each piece would land on.

So it was also easy to see, in her periphery, Nieve lean into her sister and whisper something—something that absolutely incensed her twin. Ember couldn't make out what they were saying exactly, but she wondered if it was at all about her.

When the gun clicked, and the final rock shattered, she finally lowered her aching arms.

"Very impressive, Alloy. Very impressive. *Erigo*." The fallen rocks rose into the air. Ozamiz plucked a singular rock and let the rest fall down. "You may consider making this your method."

"Method?"

"Of fighting. Generally, magicks have one or two weapons they fall back on—manipulation defaults."

Ember furrowed her brow. "What's manipulation?"

The tutor held out an open palm, asking for the gun. She obliged.

"*Reditio*."

In an instant, the gun became sand, sieving through Ozamiz's fingers and piling onto the grass below. She pointed at the miniature dune that sat on the otherwise perfect courtyard.

"That is manipulation," she explained. "It's the most common form of charm magic. As long as the mass before equates to the mass after, you can make most anything into anything. Or make most anything *do* anything. But depending on how different your original material is from your final, manipulation can become quite complicated and energy-consuming. For that reason, I normally wouldn't recommend guns as a method. They are much more complex to manipulate than blades or arrows, and the accuracy of most magicks isn't great. Plus, guns require bullets, an additional hassle."

There were so many questions.

"Then why recommend guns to me?"

"Well, your alloy connection may make all those disadvantages moot." The tutor held out her palm to reveal the rock she had turned into clay. "And your accuracy is terrifying."

No wonder they thought I was trained. The clay had no cracks or angles in entry—just a perfectly centered hole.

"So, what do you think?" Nieve said, smiling and clapping as she walked toward them alone.

Out of the corner of her eye, Ember noticed Sombra walking away. *Definitely about me.*

"How do you feel?" the white-haired twin added.

Ember looked down at the pile of sand that was once her gun and answered, "Shocked."

"It's exhilarating, isn't it?" Ozamiz said. "And you haven't even manipulated anything yet. That's where the real fun is."

She looked back up. "How long would it take for me to learn how to manipulate something?"

"From nothing? Perhaps a week or two."

"And then I could manipulate lightning?"

Ozamiz frowned. "I'm not certain."

"Ah," Nieve said. "Seeing as you are the only known magick with the ability, you would have to practice that on your own."

Ember's eyes snapped to the twin's. "I can't do that."

"I could teach you focus techniques," Ozamiz offered, her face lighting up with the possibilities that seemed to dance in her mind. "And we could always build up your strength. I'm not certain of the exact intricacies of your lightning, but neither option could hurt. And I can act as a safeguard: if you lose control, I can clock—"

"Of course," Nieve interjected, "that would all take more than a couple of days. And I know you're eager to return to Dallas."

The phantom electricity tingled Ember's fingers. She shook her head. "It's not that," she said. "I'm willing to make time to stay and learn, but you want me to kill for you in some impending war. I'm not willing to do that."

"We want you to learn and train, Alloy." Nieve held both hands out by her waist, gesturing to the courtyard around them. "We want you to return to your home."

Home.

But Dallas was home, wasn't it? It was where Ember had grown up and where she'd gone to school. She knew all the gyms and the parks and the schools and the malls. She had an apartment, a job, and was working toward a car. It was where she'd gained a sister.

It was where she'd lost a sister.

"Would I learn…to control it?"

"Control it and much more."

Ember toyed with her locket. Six years she'd waited for this moment, desperately and faithfully so, yet certain it didn't exist. Certain she would never be able to live without fear ever again.

Six years.

She'd be back before her next rent payment was due. And she'd said it herself, there were always other jobs. Plus, it wasn't like anyone would care that she was gone, right?

Rachel?

No. Rachel wouldn't care either. And if she did, surely

Ember had made it clear why she shouldn't. Rachel would move on, just like everyone else before her.

But if she could finally learn some way to get a handle on all this, maybe, just maybe...they'd come back.

Maybe, Daphne would come back.

She released her necklace.

"I'll do it," she said. "But I won't kill anyone. I'll stay, I'll train, but I don't kill people, Agarthan or otherwise. And I want access to a basketball court."

Something sparked in Nieve's eye, and she beamed. "I believe we can accommodate that."

Ember nodded, but inside she could hardly breathe. A chance—*her* chance—to finally, *finally*, take her life back.

And once she did, she would leave this place. Long before this war arrived.

CHAPTER 6
ADEMURE

The princess's balcony overlooked the courtyard below, where Profe Ozamiz trained the latest victim. Ademure leaned against her railing, watching as the tutor walked the alloy through a combative combination. The alloy attempted to repeat the steps—a punch, kick, duck, another kick. She was quick to pick up the choreography, though she replicated it clumsily.

How unfortunate it was that the previous alloys weren't actually the last. *Has it already been seven years?* she thought. *Seems like they died yesterday.*

But at least this woman was older than that batch of teenagers, even if—based on what little Ademure could hear—she was much greener to the craft.

How did she escape the nymphs? How did she elude the twins? Incredulous to think that an alloy could live for so long in the Soulless Realm without an incident, without anything to tip off the Magick Realm of her existence, especially considering how thorough the Delfinos had been in creating that database all those years ago.

Ademure pondered on that thought. If the alloy had truly grown up soulless, what would she know about the Magick Realm? What about the royal divorce? Nysa's relationship with the nymphs or with Agartha? Atlantis? Lemuria?

Likely nothing. Which meant everything the alloy learned would be filtered through her mother's conspiracies and the twins' lies.

How wonderful.

Ademure strolled back inside, somber at the thought of yet another joining in her persecution. Like she needed someone else to remind her of the faults she committed at fourteen.

She glanced at her vanity—a habit she still had, though it'd been over a decade since her mother had destroyed the mirror, or since Ademure had last seen an Agarthan...or since Ademure had last seen her reflection in anything but her silverware.

That was the day her parents had finalized their divorce. After fifteen years spent establishing new lives on the island, Agarthans had been banished from Nysa and Nysans from Agartha. Ademure had become the princess locked away in a tower. Even now, she could smell the stench of destruction magic—the stench of a rotting corpse—emanating from the leftover shards that stuck in the frame.

She ambled down the hallway, her loose gown sweeping behind her. Without allowance outside the castle grounds, and with few acquaintances within them, the library had become her sanctuary. When she needed comfort, books provided refuge. When she needed an ear, parchment listened. And, when she needed to cry, she found solitude within the depths of the shelves.

What she needed now was a distraction. From this morning's events and for tomorrow evening's torture. A story, real or not, that could whisk her away to another world. One without the threat of war.

The library arced around her, a cylindrical structure at the center of the castle, walled with hundreds of shelves of books. At the center of the cylinder floated a glass platform, and two grand staircases spiraled around the perimeter. From the railing that lined the top floor, she could see only two of the five stories down—the two that were above ground.

She stepped onto the platform and held out her hands, palms facing down. Though invisible, the magic of the glass whirred at her fingertips.

"*Demitto*," she said.

The platform descended. She pushed her hands down firmer against the magical connection, willing the platform to move faster, and she kept them there, passing one floor, and then another, before pulling them back. As the glass slowed, she brought her hands to her sides, and the platform stopped level with the third floor.

Modern History and Literature marked the ceiling of the rotunda. Ademure stepped off the platform where she was met with aisles upon aisles and shelves upon shelves of nothing but books, many of which she had already read through.

She beelined through the modern history and toward the literature where her fingers brushed the spines of assorted titles. Action, horror, mystery, drama...romance. *Love Between Leaves*.

Perfect, she thought and pulled the book from the shelf. A title she hadn't read.

The cover was forest green, the pages deckled. At the bottom, the name *Thea* embossed in gold—a nymph had written this.

Not unheard of, but unusual. The nymphs rarely came south of the northern forest at all, much less since the massacre. Though the courtyard shared a border with the nymphs' home, the library had few texts about the nymphs and even fewer from them.

She took the book to a desk, opened to the first page, and skimmed. The book itself was fine, but the real entertainment came from between the lines. She had always thought the nymphs were so different from humans—not in the manner the twins believed: she never thought them monstrous. But she never thought them quite human either, and here this book implied they maintained analogous relationships. They similarly valued loyalty and pride. They even seemed to fall in love the same way.

Apparently, they also wrote the same love tropes. This particular cliché featured a female nymph adored by two males. One mysterious and rugged, the other a lifelong acquaintance. The story begging the question: who will she choose?

After thirty pages or so, she lost interest, nearly returning the book to where she'd found it. But when she flipped the page one last time, she paused, a single word catching her eye:

"Rhythms."

She read on. How many people knew they were empaths? What were these rhythms? Her eyes flitted down the page, looking for answers, piecing together facts from fiction. In two hours, she burned through half the book but gained little more understanding.

"Surely you know more than anyone about the nymphs, Alteza. I'm surprised you find the need to read more."

She snapped the book shut. *Very bright decision*, she told herself, *reading about the nymphs in plain daylight.*

"Afternoon, Bailón," she said, pretending as if the estrella's comment didn't bother her. "Is there something I can help you with?"

The ballerina woman loomed over her. "As a matter of fact, you can. You know, the Agarthans are expected to attack soon."

Ademure scoffed. "Yes, of course. I hear it nearly every day now. 'The Agarthans are going to attack. The Agarthans are going to attack.' We've already destroyed all the mirrors, cut off most of our trade routes, and we reside on an undiscoverable island in the middle of the ocean. What exactly would you like me to do about it?"

"You could stop burdening our duties, Alteza."

"Excuse me?"

Bailón used one hand to lean on her desk. "It's difficult to guard the castle's boundaries and yourself if you continue running off."

"Running off?" Ademure suppressed another incredulous laugh. "I've remained within the castle walls for over seven years. I'm not running off."

"Yes, but the castle is large, and our estrellas are fewer than they once were. We'd prefer it if you limited the venues you ventured to."

She frowned. "You're cutting me off from the library? For how long?"

"For as long as it takes to keep you safe from harm."

"That's preposterous. The library is internal to the castle. I'm a story below ground. I'm as safe as I would be anywhere else within these walls. Probably more so."

The estrella then slammed the desk so hard it might've cracked. Ademure jumped.

"You don't seem to understand," Bailón said. "What if one of those assassins disguised themselves as a servant? What if they hid behind any one of these thousands of bookshelves waiting for you? Your throat would be cut before you could scream." She moved alongside the desk to meet Ademure eye-to-eye. "Or what if there was a nymph? We know castle walls are little deterrence for such horrible creatures."

"We haven't had an outsider on this island in over ten years. You're being ridiculous. I'll speak to my mother on this."

"Be my guest. These are her orders."

Ademure leaned back in her seat then, taking a moment to comprehend the news. But she struggled to. Banning her from the library in her own home? How did that protect her at all?

Unless that wasn't the point. Cutting her off from the island's most resourceful hub of information was not intended as a security move—well, at least not one for the princess's sake.

"My mother's jealousy has grown unyielding," she said, staring at the teardrop that newly stained the cover of her book. "She's paranoid of her own daughter."

"You dare speak that way about your queen?"

"It's true. She's sick. And I've only let it grow worse."

"Alteza," Bailón warned. "You should say nothing more and leave at once."

Ademure instead looked at her with a reddening gaze. "Let me replace this book first."

The estrella eyed her for a moment but nodded and gestured toward the aisle. Ademure then grabbed the nymph romance and slowly slid it back into place, holding on as long as possible. Finally, she followed Bailón to the glass platform.

As they rose, she looked down, admiring the rows of books that had once been her friends. Her gaze drifted to the last shelf she'd touched, where she replaced *Love Between Leaves*, and her heart sank further. Had she known that these were her final moments in the library, she would've reread a favorite.

CHAPTER 7

KIVA

Kiva dropped two triangular diamond chips onto the counter before grabbing the roti wraps and rum punches and returning to the stands. The anticipation of tonight had his heart racing, and it took every effort to not spill the drinks. As the bell rose above the tracks, he inhaled the salty air and smiled. The landsailer races were about to begin.

He handed his former tutor her cocktail.

"Gracías, mijo," she said.

"Anytime, Profe," he said in Spanish as he sat down. He was out of practice, but the language came back to him all the same. "And thank you for accompanying me. It's been some time since I've been to the tracks."

"Of course! I wish I could come more often. There's something about this environment. It's invigorating." Profe Valentina shimmied. "I feel alive!"

Kiva laughed. *She hasn't changed a bit.*

And she was right about the feeling. The landsailer races were one of the most exciting events Nysa had to offer. There weren't many places in the world that had an expanse of flat sand vast enough to host hundreds of professional and semi-professional racers completely out of soulless view. Add to that the jovial steel drums, maracas, buleador, and guitar that filled the evening air, and anyone could get swept away in the night. And, today was el Día de la Reina—not that the Nysan people needed any more excuses to party.

At the sound of the earsplitting bell, the contestants were off, and the cheers from the crowd drowned out the marimba-made melody. Sails pulled taut as the racers leaned into their handlebars, and a cloud of sand flurried about the landsailers as they cleared their first lap.

"I've missed these," Kiva said.

"I bet you've missed a lot of things."

"You're not wrong."

"I rarely am." Valentina grinned. "So, how is your father? Is he still that picture-perfect loving parent that I remember him to be?"

"Skipping the small talk tonight, then?" He grimaced as his favorite rider, the yellow sailer, narrowly escaped a wreck.

"Oh, Kiva, I do believe that family is generally regarded as small talk."

"Not my family, and you know that."

"I do." She stirred her drink with her straw. "So?"

"If we must talk about them, let's talk about my sister. We never discuss her. You know, she's come into quite the good fortune recently."

"And I see that you're not bitter about that at all. The apple does not fall far, does it? When can I expect your ego to over-inflate?"

He sighed. "Why do you insist on ruining my night?"

She glared at him with the same look she would've given him for speaking out of turn—when he was eight.

"If you want small talk, we can do small talk," she snapped. "Our queen is declining, our princess is a prisoner, the estrellas are inciting war, and my bookstore was rated the third best in town. So everything is going swimmingly."

He took in a deep, careful breath. "I'm sorry."

"Thank you."

"Your bookstore is definitely second best."

She smacked his shoulder as he chuckled. Her annoyance then softened to a smile, and she delicately rested the same palm on his arm.

"I only press because I worry about you, Kiva. You've been dealt an unwinnable hand, and yet you act as if the man still cares for you."

"And how do you know he doesn't?"

"Is that not self-evident?"

He clenched his jaw a bit tighter: it was.

The yellow rider rounded his tenth turn, edging out the blue rider ahead of him. Unfortunately, the resulting applause wasn't loud enough to drown out Valentina's lecture.

"What happened was tragic and unpredictable. And you were what, sixteen? As far as I'm concerned, that was your father's misstep. Not yours."

"Please, Profe, I really don't care to talk about this. My fault or not, I stopped trying to win back his affection a long time ago."

She straightened. "You surely had me fooled."

"Yes, well." He rapped his fingers on his glass. "I do still want to please him. But it's not because I personally care. I simply have to get back what's mine, and it's much easier to win him over with honey."

"Mhm. And what hive does he want you to destroy for it?"

The participants looped the desert track for the twentieth out of forty times. As they turned the corner, one contestant clipped the edge of another, sending them both toward the stands with an audible crunch of their vehicles. The crowd gasped, and Kiva grinned. If he could live any other life, he would be behind the handles of a landsailer on that very track tonight.

But he couldn't.

"He wants me to find a girl," he said. "That's it. No destruction necessary."

His tutor sucked her drink dry and raised an unsatisfied brow.

"He does think it'll be impossible," he admitted. "But you said it yourself, he's an irrational man. Perhaps, he's irrational to think me so incompetent with women."

She set down her glass. "An ego that rivals Icarus does not mean he's dim. How many women have you won over before?"

He felt his cheeks heat. "That doesn't matter, only that I can win one over now. Besides, charming *is* his specialty. Perhaps, we'll find that I've inherited more than one of his endearing personality traits." He leaned back on the bleachers and puffed out his chest, side-eyeing his tutor. "What do you think?"

"That you'd have an easier time saving the princess."

He slouched and pouted his lips. "Very funny. Are you done with your food?"

With a snicker, she handed him the empty containers.

Then, he climbed the sand steps of the sand stadium to head toward the sand stand. Everything was made of the stuff; time and magic and a meticulous architect had carefully crafted the dusty particulates into this epic arena. How many hundreds of hours were put into such manipulation, especially in so much detail? Even the trash cans were made of sand.

He had never appreciated the arena enough as a child—when he and his sister would race each other up and down the stairs, their father egging them on, their mother chiding the three of them. After a time they would eventually collapse on the top step and lay back to catch their breaths. But their mother would never let them collapse for long. She'd force them to sit upright, to appreciate the green flower-shaped track below, the town square not far from the arena, and the castle on the hill in the distance. She'd wanted them to take in the rhythmic waves and salty air and all-around perfect day. Honestly, he was glad she had. Lately, perfect days were hard to come by.

He stood at the top step. Below, the flower-shaped track was alight with racers and music and an exuberant crowd. Outside the arena, the town square glowed green, blue, and yellow—no red, queen's orders—beneath the starry night sky. And in the distance, el Alcázar was dark, cloaked in the shadow of its own government. And though he knew it had only been a joke, he considered his tutor's words.

I could save her, he thought as his eyes lingered on the dismal structure. *I could return this island to its former glory. I'd be a Nysan hero.*

One day. There were other things he had to do first.

He headed back to his seat. Three of the racers nearly collided while executing a particularly tight turn, and he stopped a moment to make sure he didn't miss a spectacular crash.

"You didn't bring me another drink?" Valentina yelled over the gasps and cheers. "What good are you?"

"You're less than five feet tall." He sat down, watching the sails billow below as the racers leaned in, chasing sand. "Another drink would have you on the floor."

"Don't underestimate me, Kiva. My alcohol tolerance is at an all-time high."

That, he understood. Even now, on the most revelrous of

holidays, during one of the most anticipated of races, there was an uneasiness in the quiet. He heard hushed but frantic mumblings; parents hugged their children a bit tighter.

"The people are worried," he said.

"Of course, they are. Tartarus, even I'm a little nervous. We're teetering on the edge of war as it is."

"I guess it's not the ideal time to be dealing with a couple of rogue assassins."

"Well," she bobbed her head from side to side, "it probably is for them."

He raised his brow. "What do you mean?"

"The more unstable a nation, the easier they are to target. That's all."

"Speaking from experience?"

In response, she took a large bite of roti and watched the yellow rider fall to third.

Kiva ignored the race altogether. "But if you're targeting Nysa, why kill the leaders of other nations? Why not go after Nysa herself?"

"That is admittedly curious. I don't know."

"You think they want to provoke Nysa to strike first? To expose the queen?"

"It would be easier to attack the island. No, I doubt they're trying to provoke a war that was already bound to happen. I think it's something greater than that. These assassins are far too skilled for a goal that easy."

Thirty-five laps in and distantly, he realized the yellow rider had regained the lead. "Any chance the assassins attack Agartha first?"

"I wouldn't do it."

"Why not?"

She considered him for a moment, then lowered her voice.

"Because it might be home turf. If it were me, I'd make a grand finale out of it."

Are the assassins Agarthan, then? He supposed it made the most sense, given the ability for Agarthans to mirror anywhere around the world—and Agartha's complicated past with Nysa.

But still, the Atlantean pharaoh and the Lemurian president? Those deaths didn't sit right with him. They were neutral. *Why them?*

The first landsailer—blue—crossed the finish line; yellow was a close second. The crowd roared, startling him out of his daze, and, at the sound of the energetic music, both he and his tutor jumped to their feet to join the clamorous applause.

Valentina leaned into him. "Not that I endorse either plan, but you should forget the assassins. Stick to finding your girl."

He shook his head. "I'm not certain I can do that, Profe. At the moment, I'll take any victories I can get."

CHAPTER 8
EMBER

Sitting on the emerald banquette in the oriel window of her room, Ember wondered if she would ever tire of this view. The sky was cloudless, an untouched canvas of blue that draped over the island. The crystal waters below reflected that brilliant color and added touches of white that appeared and vanished with the will of the tide. Ivory sands bounded the sea and blanketed the coastline as if it were a fresh layer of snow. She'd never seen anything like it before. She wanted to traverse it.

She brushed her hand over the simple jade linen pant she wore. *But not in this.*

Unfortunately, this was the best outfit here. The rest of the closet comprised of satins and velvets with padding and boning and anything else meant to make her miserable. Even the day dresses zipped tight. She missed very little in the two days she'd been gone, but the one thing she did long for was her clothes.

Well, perhaps not her work polo.

She tugged on her locket. She was supposed to be working

today, actually. And instead, she was here, on an all-expenses-paid island getaway, staying in a luxurious castle and learning about magic. It was almost too good to be true.

Has anyone noticed I'm gone? she wondered, rolling her chain between two fingers.

But then again, did it matter? She'd never cared for the job, and she didn't plan on going back. Honestly, her boss and coworkers were probably delighted by her absence.

Rachel probably isn't.

There was a knock, and her attention whipped to the door.

"Come in," she said.

A young woman in a pastel yellow dress entered and bowed her head.

"Good afternoon, Alloy Slade. I'm the princess's lady's maid. Pardon my intrusion, but the Estrellas Delfinos sent me to help you dress for the dinner tonight."

Ember glanced at the clock on the wall. "It's not even three."

The woman nodded. "Estrella Sombra said it may take some time."

Without any mirrors, she couldn't confirm she looked ridiculous, but Ember certainly felt that way. Within an hour of a shower, she had crusted curls, heavy lashes, and a corset digging into her back.

The twins stood on either side of her, Sombra in a black gown and Nieve in white. Sombra opened the sand doors.

Filled with so many people, the dining hall was unrecognizable. Three men in tuxedos sat in gunmetal chairs. At the other end of the white-clothed table, chattered two women clad in gold and silver. And were it not for the twinkling candlelight, Ember would have missed those people near the kitchen, napkins cloaked over their arms. Next to them, she spied a teenager with a kitchen towel around his head and an apron on his chest.

The teenager approached them.

Nieve stepped forward with a bright smile. "Buenas tardes, Damian, ¿cómo estás hoy?"

"Bien, Señorita," the boy said distantly. He peered around the twin and stared at Ember with his head inclined. "Usted es…lenta."

"Excuse me?" Ember said. She understood the Spanish but was offended nonetheless.

"You're slow," the boy repeated, this time in English. "Why are you slow?" He continued to watch her, clearly as confused as she, but clearly for another reason.

Just then did she realize how vibrant his eyes were. She had never seen such a green hue—it was even brighter than her own. That color might have been plucked off a neon sign and dripped into his irises, as if his eyes could pierce through hers and see every thought she had ever had. She wasn't entirely sure he couldn't.

Nieve cleared her throat. "Are you not needed in the kitchen tonight?"

"Mateo is fine without me, Seño," the boy replied without hesitation. He flicked his wrist as if to dismiss her. "He said I could meet the alloy."

It took everything in Ember not to laugh, though, Nieve didn't seem to find his gesture nearly as entertaining.

"You have free time, then?" she said. "That's wonderful to hear. I'm glad to see you're finally able to pick up training again. It's been a while hasn't it? At least several months."

Damian seemed to consider his words. "I've been busy."

"Yes, you've made that very clear. But tonight, you are free.

You have the entire dinner to practice. And in the nick of time, too. This war will be taxing. We'll need to exhaust every resource, employ every able body that we can."

"If I'm going to be an estrella, shouldn't I get to meet her?" He nodded in Ember's direction.

"You *are* going to be an estrella then?" Nieve mused.

His lips remained sealed.

"You're still welcome to, of course," she continued. "I wouldn't want to destroy your dreams. It seems like yesterday you were crying to me about how much becoming an estrella meant to you."

He eyed her. "That was years ago."

"Oh? Has your motivation waned? You were so staunch back then, so determined." She placed a hand on his shoulder. "I think Daddy would be disappointed."

"How dare—"

"I suggest," Nieve interrupted, her smile unwavering, "that you think a moment longer on what you want to say next." She squeezed his arm, and judging by his wince, she wasn't gentle.

He fell completely silent, then turned back to Ember, looking her over once more before saying, "Pleasure to meet you, Señorita."

Both twins narrowed their eyes, and Damian must have known he had over-extended his welcome because before she could respond, he dragged his feet toward the kitchen doors.

Ember frowned. *That seems like a lot to unpack.*

So she turned her attention back to the busy room and changed the subject. "Which ones are the princess and queen?"

"None of them," Sombra said with her usual stoicism. With Ember, she observed the crowd while her sister kept an eye on the teenager. "These are the estrellas. Nysa's elite special operations unit."

"Spies?"

"If we need to be, sure, but more like—I think you call them Navy Seals. Estrella Bailón was recently appointed captain of this force." Her lip curled with a hint of disgust. "We are her vice-captains."

"And we've earned our place," Nieve added, returning to the conversation with a hand on her sister's arm, smiling as if her interaction with the kitchen boy had never happened.

Sombra pulled away from them before the moment could grow long.

"Where are the queen and princess, then?" Ember asked Nieve while she watched the other twin's bout around the room. Sombra met with a bodybuilder-like man in a too-small suit, a plump woman with hair drawn into a long, chunky braid, and another man tall enough to post up in the NBA. The other three estrellas were talking and laughing, and still, Sombra was resigned.

"They'll be here soon," Nieve answered. "Actually, since we have time, let's introduce you to everyone." With that, she tapped her glass with a fork, and the room fell silent. All eyes were on them.

"Estrellas, good evening," she said. "We are so thankful to have you here, as tonight is cause for celebration. For years, we thought the alloys had been lost to magicks across the globe. I'm here to tell you that we have found one more, and a Nysan no less. Please welcome Ember Slade, guest to el Alcázar de Maldojo and future savior of Nysa."

Ember's eyes darted to the side. *Savior? That wasn't the deal.*

But Nieve applauded with the crowd, and the room's sudden collective attention paused anything she might have said to counter the notion. That, however, was probably for the best, as it gave her time to realize just how heavy the twin's gaze could be—heavy and...commanding.

You knew that, though, she thought to herself. *Didn't you?*

As if in response, Nieve's smile grew wider, waiting. Biting back her tongue, Ember surveyed the room. There were at least seven estrellas, not to mention kitchen staff and whatever guards surely waited outside the doors. She wouldn't win a fight now.

Do what they want you to do today, and it will keep their eyes off of you tomorrow. A lesson she'd learned after the incident, when she'd run away and was forced to resort to shoplifting. Thankfully, she hadn't needed to in years, but back then, it was the only way to stay out of jail and stay alive.

Against all instinct, she bowed her head.

The estrella raised an impressed brow. "Alloy Slade is a magick who, in yesterday's training, displayed incredible raw natural talent. Mark my words, she'll be a force to reckon with. Please acquaint yourselves with her, as she may be on your team in the future."

And when the twin left her side, Ember steamed. *Raindrops.*

But before she could do more, a woman stepped forward to greet her. Her lavish gold dress glowed against her umber skin, and she stood as tall as Ember, chin in the air, black hair taut on the top of her head.

"Ember Slade," she said before curtsying. "What an honor it is to meet you. My name is Marisa Bailón."

Ember peeled her attention from the snow-haired twin that wandered to the other side of the room and plastered on a smile for the estrella in front of her, reminding herself to play along. "Pleasure to meet you, Captain."

Bailón raised her brows, a twinkle catching her jade eyes. "Being in and around the castle, I expect we'll be seeing a lot of each other. You must reach out if you're ever in need of someone to talk to. We all have our talents, and the Delfinos are fantastic estrellas. But conversationalists they are not. I don't want you to feel as if you're alone here."

"Thank you," Ember said. "That's very generous of you."

"Of course, of course. Anything to make your experience more enjoyable. We're all expecting quite a bit from you. And truthfully, I hope you're better than the last alloys we had. They were strong, yes, but not very durable. They didn't last long."

Her fake smile fell. "I hope to last longer, then."

"Ahem."

Both Ember and Bailón looked down. At their hips stood a squat man in a tweed suit, adorned with a monocle attached by a gold chain. His eyebrows were large and bushy and his eyes unsurprisingly green. Bailón frowned.

"Yes?" she said.

"I believe it's my turn to meet the alloy."

"Why is it always when I'm in the middle of something, it suddenly becomes your turn? Fine. If you must." Bailón sighed and walked away.

The man stepped closer, holding his lens to his eye, looking Ember up and down and up again. At last, he let go of his monocle, said *"vincu,"* and the chain snapped back into his pocket. He then bowed, his bare head catching a gleam of light.

"My dear, at last! We thought it'd be at least another decade before we saw an alloy again." He took hold of her hand and shook it excitedly. "Oscar Cadeña. Pleased to meet you."

"Likewise," she forced herself to say. She reclaimed her arm.

"Oh, you're like a living relic. I have *so* many questions to ask you! If you're available sometime, I'd love to have a chat with you over lunch or perhaps a morning tea."

"I...um, I—"

The sand doors swung open, and the room silenced. The

two women at its entrance looked remarkably similar but were ages apart. A chartreuse dress hugged the middle-aged woman's curves, popping against her light brown skin and accentuating her emerald eyes. In her hair was fastened a diadem with a single green rose to replace the gem. Though petite, she puffed her chest like she was the tallest woman on the planet.

Conversely, the young woman next to her stood with her hands folded in front of her and her shoulders curved inward, her eyes turned to the floor. She was a bit taller than the older woman, yet she somehow found herself in her shadow. Her pale blue dress hung about her like a rag, washing out her brown skin, and her tiara barely clasped to her stringy brown hair.

One of the men in a black suit cleared his throat. "Su Majestad, Esmerelda Maldojo y su hija, Ademure, la Reina y la Princesa de Nysa." The estrellas bowed.

With a slight delay, Ember followed their lead, also bowing, but she did so slowly, keeping her head raised. As she straightened, she couldn't help but notice that the room had gone still, like all the air had been vacuumed out.

"Alloy Slade." Queen Esmerelda strolled toward her, inviting every eye in the dining hall her way. "It is good to see you awake. You gave us quite the scare there for a moment, being out for so long. I trust your lodgings are to your liking." She held out her hand expectingly.

Without hesitation, Ember took it in her fingertips and did a stuttered curtsy. "They're lovely."

And as if it were a mark of approval on her behavior, the queen grinned, sending a small simmering heat to Ember's hands. *Oh, I do not like that at all.*

Queen Esmerelda then continued her walk throughout the room, and the silent watching of Ember's own interaction vanished. As each estrella imparted their greetings to the queen, chatter and laughter renewed, and the princess took her mother's place.

"Alloy Slade."

"Princess Ademure," Ember said automatically, watching the queen waltz around like she was the next coming of Christ.

The princess dropped her voice. "I know it can't mean much, but I'm so sorry for what my mother has done."

That caught her attention. "No need for apologies, uh..." she took a moment to think of the proper title "...Your Highness. I'm happy to have returned home."

"Are you truly?"

Ember swiftly gauged the hall again. The estrellas were otherwise occupied, yes, but that didn't prevent any of them from passing furtive glances her way.

She looked the princess in the eye. "Of course."

"You're not," Ademure said, shaking her head. "It's written all over your face. But I acknowledge why you must put on a façade."

Ember touched her cheek, then chuckled, torn between incredulity and amusement. "Princess, I think there's been a misunderstanding. There is no façade. I *want* to learn how to use my magic. I *want* to learn more about where I came from. Yeah, I'm not thrilled with how all this happened, but I'm also not in any hurry to go back."

"Oh," the princess said. "Of course." But the sympathy with which she said it only sent more heat to Ember's palms.

"Look. I know I'm not some royal princess witch who owns some stupid huge castle or is in charge of an entire fleet of servants, let alone a country." She put a scalding hand on her chest. "But I can make my own decisions, and I *chose* to stay here."

The princess looked at Ember's hand, then, after some seeming realization, returned to Ember's frown.

"I apologize," she said with a bow of her head. "It was not my intention to upset you. I only wanted to...well, apologize. Best wishes on your training."

With that, she curtsied, then headed toward her chair at the end of the table, opposite her mother. And before Ember could consider the exchange, everyone else followed them in taking their seats.

Naturally, Ember had the luxury of sitting between Sombra and Nieve. Bailón sat across from the three of them.

"Welcome to this day of honor," Esmerelda said to the room. "Thanks be to Demeter, to Hermes, to Dionysus for their efforts in bringing us this feast—"

Oh, not Christ. The next coming of Zeus?

"—And thanks be to Pan for blessing us with the homeland to sustain such a meal. Please, eat to your heart's content."

On cue, a parade of fish, crab, rice, and beans floated in from the kitchen door and settled on the center of the table. And with each subsequent course, Ember became so aware of her corset, that by the time the mango sorbet was served, she was certain the buttons would pop.

After an hour or so, when the eating slowed and the conversation picked up, Esmerelda tapped a spoon to her glass.

"I hope you've enjoyed yourselves."

Everyone nodded in agreement. *Everyone except Princess Ademure,* Ember noted.

"A toast, then." The queen raised her cup higher. "To the estrellas that brought back the alloy. Cheers, Estrellas Delfino!"

The twins stood and bowed at the applause.

"We are so thankful for you two. Your hard work and

loyalty have not gone unnoticed." The queen sipped her wine. "Now, Alloy Slade."

Realizing the animal she must've looked like hunched over her plate, Ember straightened. "Yes, Your Majesty?"

"Welcome home," the queen greeted, though it sounded more like a curse. "I'm fascinated by you, Alloy."

Ember raised her brows and set down her spoon. "If I'm being honest, I'm fascinated by me, too." She chuckled as everyone laughed—everyone but the princess again who frowned, almost as if she were worried. Her own smile fell. *I've seen that look before.*

The queen's grin lingered behind her glass. "Tell me, Alloy, how is it that someone of your birth could go for so long undetected in the Soulless Realm?"

Ember shrugged. "Luck, I guess."

"Luck indeed," the queen said. "You know, it's really not so much that you eluded us that perturbs me. But how on earth did you elude *them*?"

At that, her brows knit together, but before she could even ask, Nieve resolved her confusion.

"She's referring to the nymphs in the north," the twin said before turning to the queen. "Majestad, as it turns out, our alloy has very little understanding of our culture and history. I believe you will have to be a bit more direct with your interview."

"Oh, you mean she's dim."

Heat erupted in Ember's palms. *Excuse me?*

"No, Majestad," Nieve said. Her eyes flitted to Ember as if to say, *I've got your back.* "You will find she's quite sharp. She's simply unacquainted with the Magick Realm."

"But she is an alloy, right? You said she could manipulate lightning."

"That I can guarantee. My sister witnessed it."

Sombra nodded with her customary indifference.

"Good. Nikita may have a greater military, but I know he doesn't have an alloy." The queen adjusted her crown as she eyed Ember. "And your lightning ability could make you worth three armies."

And though she appreciated Nieve's initial assistance, this time Ember looked at the twins with narrowed eyes.

Being a savior is one thing, she thought. *Being a weapon worth three armies is something else entirely.*

Yeah, no. I'm not doing this bullshit.

"Actually, Your Majesty, I'm not here to fight anyone. I'm just here to train."

Any drop of joy in Esmerelda's expression evaporated, as did the joys of Sombra and Nieve. In fact, now that Ember read the room, the only one with any humor left was the princess—and her humor was mixed with astonishment.

A grin grew on Nieve's lips but only her lips, falling very *very* short of her eyes. She spoke out of the side of her mouth. "Now, Alloy, that's not exactly what we agreed to before, is it?"

Ember whipped to her right. "I told you I wouldn't fight."

"No, you told us you wouldn't kill, Alloy," Sombra said to her left. "Fighting was always a part of the agreement."

She whipped the other way. "You said you would train me even if there wasn't a war."

"But there is a war," Sombra snarled. "And you're meant to take part."

"I am not a soldier, and I am definitely not your soldier. You said I was here to learn my potential. You said—"

"And how are you to know the extent of your potential if you don't fight with it?" the estrella hissed, coming within inches of Ember's breath. "The opportunities to learn in this war are infinite, Alloy. You'd be foolish not to take them."

"Have you all forgotten? There is no war yet."

The princess maintained an air of innocence when she said it, responding to her newfound attention by delivering a spoonful of sorbet to her mouth.

A bit stunned, Ember tilted her head.

"Princess Ademure is right," Estrella Bailón said from across the table, and the dinner party seemed to take a collective breath. "There is no war yet. And there is somewhat of a chance that there will never be one." Bailón grabbed a dinner knife and held it upright on the table. "But if the time comes, Alloy Slade, we will ask you to fight."

Ember shook her head vehemently. "I won't kill anyone. For any reason."

"I realize that, Alloy, but I do feel I need you to comprehend the broader implications. As I understand it, you have very little control over your powers. And with an ability as lethal as lightning, aren't you afraid...?"

Bailón didn't need to finish the sentence; the screams already drowned her out. The air reeked of smoke, and the temperature boiled hot.

Ember stared through her dinner plate, tracing the raised skin of her three scars with her thumb. It was almost other-worldly when she thought of how she'd earned the marks. Six years was often a long time.

And other times, not at all.

"Ah, I see that you arrived at this crossroads long ago," Bailón said. "Then, I guess you already know my position: when forced to kill, I'd much rather my dead be those I intend to make so." She stuck the knife into the tabletop, shooting adrenaline through Ember's veins.

Bailón then extracted the dinnerware and aimed the point across the table. "Of course, who knows? Perhaps you will never need to kill. Or perhaps you become so skilled you can incapacitate without casualty."

She flicked the knife.

Ember jumped to her left, and Nieve caught it above her. Panting, Ember took the moment in Sombra's apathetic lap to wait for additional flying utensils to pass. When she finally returned upright, Nieve stared down the estrella captain.

"Forgive me, Alloy," Bailón said. "I had only hoped to see this lightning trick for myself." She raised her brows at Nieve as if to express her apologies, though she didn't wait around for her vice-captain's acceptance. Instead, she returned her gaze to Ember, with all amusement having escaped it. "I should add that this is not a negotiation, but a perspective shift you should adopt. You will fight for us either way."

Still breathless, Ember's eyes flitted to the princess, hundreds of questions thrown into a quick glance.

And the quick glance of the princess answered: *Tread lightly.*

"Fine, whatever," Ember said, avoiding everyone's gaze as she held tight to her wrist. "I'll fight. I'll learn self-defense. Or, like you said: how to 'incapacitate without casualty.' But I *won't* kill anyone."

Bailón smiled. "I'm glad you see things our way, Alloy. And under Profe Ozamiz, you will become a master in no time."

Sombra drew her usual lip of disgust, and for a moment, Nieve wore the look as well. The moment was fleeting, however, and soon the snow-haired twin became chipper once again, leaning into her ear and saying, "I'm sorry for the confusion, Alloy, but I'm glad we've come to a solution."

Esmerelda waved off the exchange like it were an unwelcome insect. "Yes, yes, that's all dandy, but that doesn't answer how some soulless-raised dimwit uncovered the key to producing lightning! So tell us, did your traitorous parents teach you?"

Ember's arms instantly re-engulfed in invisible flames.

Raindrops, raindrops, raindrops, she told herself, and only when she could loosen the grip on her wrist did she answer.

"I don't know my birth parents."

"Of course, not," the queen derided. She shook her head and looked at Bailón. "Honestly, we could learn the charm and leave the girl."

"She's still an alloy," the captain said softly. "And learning the charm does not prevent Alloy Slade from using it. The entire point was to gain an advantage over Nikita, was it not? If you abandon her, you may as well give her to him."

Esmerelda narrowed her eyes, which, for a split second, Ember could have sworn glowed.

The queen turned to her. "Well?"

Suppressing every instinct that had plagued her youth— that still plagued her, now, she said, "You probably know more about my parents than I do, Your Majesty. They didn't teach me anything."

"Then how did you manipulate the one thing no magick can?"

She exhaled—"*raindrops*"—and the blaze lowered to a simmer. "I don't know. That's what I'm trying to figure out."

"Stop lying, Alloy. Someone had to have shown you. Who taught you?"

"My god, don't you get it?" The heat was in her face, on her neck, behind her eyes. "*No one* taught me."

A hand rested on her forearm.

"Perhaps," Nieve said calmly, "you stumbled upon the charm. Perhaps, it was simply fated."

Ember looked at her, then the rest of her audience. The queen was enraged, the estrellas were bewildered, but the princess...the princess was curious.

Her gaze stayed on the princess. "Yeah. Perhaps."

"So what is the charm, Alloy?" the queen seethed. "Or are you not grateful enough to teach us what you know?"

Ember closed her eyes to douse her anger with raindrops, but her false cordiality had run dry. "I don't know anything, Your Majesty. Much less what a fucking charm is."

The queen laughed. "You cannot be serious. A power the world desires, that you have, and you don't know the charm that controls it? Exactly how dense are you?"

"And what about you, huh?" Ember shot back. "You've known about magic and how to control it for what, like fifty years? And what lightning do you have to show for it?"

"How dare you! I give you food and shelter on an island that rivals Elysium itself and you repay me with insults?"

"You *kidnapped* me, lady. You're lucky I stopped at insults."

They both jumped to their feet. Ember hardly felt Nieve's second pleading touch.

"I've suffered quite enough from you," the queen continued. "Might I remind you that you are in the presence of royalty and half a dozen magicks who have decades more experience than you?"

"And might I remind you, that you want to fight a war that depends on *me* to win? It's *my* presence that matters, Your fucking Majesty."

Now, there was no question. The queen's eyes were luminous.

"You vile, insolent, miserable—"

"Amá, that is *enough*." All eyes turned as the princess stood too. "She doesn't know anything. She will learn. But only if you don't scare her away."

The queen slammed the table. "You do not tell me what to do!"

Ademure defensively raised her hands. "I was not trying to tell you what to do, Amá. I was only—"

"You were only trying to take my crown."

At that, the room stilled, and the princess dropped her head—in a way that was all too familiar to Ember. Despite the lack of storm, the spark returned to her neck.

Shit. Not here. Raindrops.

But fire rolled through her body anyway, and her vision blurred. And she rocked about her heels, vaguely aware of the eyes on her, of the silence that had formed about her.

"You stupid, stupid girl," the queen ranted, oblivious to the heat. "You think you know what's best for this queendom? You cannot possibly fathom what it takes to rule. It's so much more than what you can find in a few fancy books. It's so much more than selling out your enemy's top soldiers to the highest bidder."

"Amá, you know that's not what happened. And you know that I was fourteen. Can you not forgive the mistakes a child makes at fourteen?"

"Mistakes? Don't make me laugh. You're an insult to the Maldojo line. To this nation! To your people—and your people don't even know the truth."

"Amá, I am not working with—"

The queen slammed the table again, shaking all of the dinnerware and sending several glasses to the floor. "Silence! I will not suffer another lie that comes out of your mouth!"

Then, Esmerelda raised her hand and, though nothing came of the gesture, the princess winced.

Ember grasped at the nape of her neck in vain. *This can't happen now*, she thought. *This cannot happen.* She couldn't lose control. She had to keep the scars to three.

Raindrops raindrops raindrops raindrops, she told herself, but her vision wouldn't clear. The spark wouldn't cool.

And so, abruptly, she left.

CHAPTER 9

ADEMURE

The alloy's sudden departure ended the dinner party on quite an awkward note, and for that, Ademure was thankful. She still reeled from her mother's accusations—both from the parade yesterday morning and the dinner tonight—but more than anything, she grieved. The mother who had once taken her to play in the ocean waves, who had been by her often-feverish side, who had tucked her in and kissed her forehead every night, was gone. With nothing but a ghost in her place.

But the ghost was still a queen. She knew more about el Alcázar de Maldojo's curiosities than Ademure, and after that show for a dinner, the alloy was surely a curiosity worth knowing. So, Ademure remained within earshot of her mother as she and the Delfinos walked the corridors, though the princess made sure to keep her distance.

"I have half a mind to execute her," Esmerelda said from down the hall. "This is your fault, Nieve. You were the one who sought her out, and I cannot fathom why. She's not the quality magick I would expect someone vying for captain to recruit."

"She's simply on edge, Majestad," Nieve said. "She is quality; she's still adjusting. She'll come around soon enough."

"She disrespected me in front of my estrellas. That is an unforgivable offense."

"I don't disagree, but perhaps it is wiser this time to show a little mercy. We've worked so hard to acquire her. Why waste that effort so soon? If she proves useless, we can remove her then, but we can't yet be sure she is."

"Am I to trust your judgment? Perhaps the alloy would be better with Bailón."

"No," Nieve said quickly. "Leave her with me. She'll become the estrella you want, ten-fold."

"And the lightning?"

There was a pause.

"We will know the magic in a month's time," Sombra said.

"What if you don't?"

"She's still an alloy," Nieve said. "She'll be useful either way."

"Assuming she cooperates."

Another pause.

"She will cooperate, Majestad. It's fated."

"I hope so, Delfinos. I hope so."

Only when Ademure heard the doors shut did she finally turn the corner. The estrellas remained outside the queen's chambers, holding a discussion under their breath. She kept her head down and steps quiet, hoping she could sneak past the oracles' sight—the physical and metaphysical. Only fifteen feet more and this nightmare of a day would be finished.

"Alteza," Nieve called behind her. "Let's talk."

Damn. Ademure slowly turned around. "Yes?"

The women approached her, close, forcing her several steps back until her heel hit the wall. What little light there was glinted off their black and white hair and shadowed their menacing emerald eyes. Her breathing hastened, but she stood as tall as her petite frame would allow, using every inch of her heels for height. Still, the twins loomed over her.

"What are you doing?" she asked.

"We should ask you the same," Nieve said.

She grasped the wall behind her for support. "I don't know what you mean."

"So dinner was a slip of the tongue? Come now."

Sombra leaned against the wall on one shoulder. "The queen may believe you slow of mind, but we are not so convinced. What are you trying to do with the alloy?"

"The alloy?" Her eyes flitted between the sisters. "I said maybe three words to her tonight. And she wasn't fond of any of them. I'm not trying to do anything with her, except perhaps prepare for her funeral."

"So you plan on selling her name to the nymphs, too?" Nieve said.

Ademure pressed her lips shut as the blood rushed to her cheeks.

"You know the war with Agartha is inevitable," Sombra said. "Why did you lead her astray?"

"I didn't lead her astray," Ademure said curtly. "I was putting an end to *your* argument. She's not like the last ones, you know. She wasn't raised here. She has no sense of who you or I or anyone else is. You can't expect to win her over by throwing your authority at her."

"You told her there was no war."

"There is no war."

"And so you let her believe she will not become a part of it when it arrives?"

"No, I believe that fault lies with you. You're lucky Bailón has a way with words."

That familiar disgusted lip pulled on Sombra's face and even tugged at Nieve's.

"Pitching knives is not a way with words," the charcoal-haired sister grumbled. "But I don't have to tell you that. You're obviously no novice at eloquence. Su Majestad envies that about you."

"And fears that about you," Nieve added.

Ademure brushed her hands over the skirt of her dress. "She doesn't fear me."

"Alteza, please," Nieve said. "With your few words, you kept the alloy's attention all night. You're telling us that that didn't mean anything? That you're not trying to recruit help for your treasonous exploits?"

"Treasonous?" Ademure scoffed. "I'm anything but. I love this nation more than the gods themselves." She stomped her heel to make a point but instead felt like a child throwing a tantrum.

"Alteza, we all heard it tonight. You want your mother's crown."

"I denied those allegations. I'll deny them to my dying day."

Sombra gave her sister a knowing look. "Then why defy her tonight?"

"Because she's wrong! She's wrong for stealing the alloy from her home. She's wrong for berating the alloy as she did tonight. And she's wrong for wanting war with Agartha in the first place. Agartha is not our enemy!"

Ademure's sentiments echoed down the empty halls, drifting into oblivion. Nieve chuckled, and even the corner of Sombra's mouth upturned. Then, without a word, Nieve dragged the back of her icy, sharp nails down Ademure's cheek...and Ademure let her, frozen where she stood, too petrified to insist otherwise.

"Is she wrong?" A single nail scratched along her chin like a small blade. "Or do your loyalties lie elsewhere?"

Ademure winced. "My loyalties lie here, Nieve. I love my people and I love my mother."

"More than your brother and father?"

When the oracle's fingers finally left her face, she met her estrellas' eyes. "You can't ask me to choose."

"So that's a 'no' then? Princess, you must realize what this looks like. You insist on challenging the Nysan queen in public. You openly admit to your love for the Agarthan king in her presence and ours. You're his next-in-line for the throne. And, how can we forget your role in the death of our alloys? Hundreds of lives and the Nysan advantage, you threw away like it was a lunch gone rotten."

"I'm not a traitor," Ademure insisted. "I want to see our people thrive."

"It'll be difficult to thrive if the Agarthans decimate us."

"It'll be difficult to thrive if we kill each other in war! The Soulless Realm takes more of the Magick Realm's land and resources every day. We don't need to assist them with ending our existence."

"Alteza," Sombra demanded. "*You* are the only threat to our existence."

Suddenly, the air around them grew cold and heavy, pressing on Ademure's chest so that she could hardly breathe. The corridor felt as if it were shrinking. The candlelight as if it were dimming. The oracles' eyes as if they were…strangling.

My mother wants me dead. They all want me dead.

The realization paralyzed her. She couldn't even prevent the twins from touching her cheek. How was she to stop them from killing her?

At last, Sombra and Nieve backed away, but that only allowed for the air around her to grow colder.

"You will have a guard to escort you about the castle by tomorrow night," Nieve said as they turned down the hall. "Stay away from the alloy."

~

Ademure didn't sleep at all that night.

She skipped breakfast the next morning to write—the estrellas could take away her library but they couldn't take away her mind. She hunched over her dark green vanity as her pen soared across the page, brainstorming plans to win back her mother's favor, to fight off the estrellas, to leave the island. Maybe she could live with her father in Agartha or take refuge in Atlantis or Lemuria.

Or, maybe she could hide in the Soulless Realm. It would be the last place the twins would think to look for her. But without other magicks around to protect her, it would also be the most dangerous.

At that thought, she set her pen down. There were so many variables she had to consider. How would she set sail without the estrellas catching her? Could she even make it to the harbor without them knowing? Could she even sneak out of the castle?

No, she couldn't. Not alone. She was a princess, not an estrella—and a pathetic princess at that. She leaned her head back against her chair.

I need help.

Then, she remembered dinner: how the alloy had spoken to her when they'd met, how she'd stood up to both Sombra and her mother. The alloy wasn't afraid of authority. In fact, she didn't seem afraid of much at all.

And then Ademure remembered that *heat*. There was a

serious magic within Alloy Slade—perhaps the type of magic that could help her.

But *would* she help her?

Unfortunately, regardless if the alloy would or wouldn't, she had only until sundown to speak freely with her about it.

Or ten minutes, she thought, *depending on how fast the oracles see me and lock me away.*

A quick, quiet knock on the alloy's door.

"Princess?"

The alloy was red-faced and sweat-drenched and peeking through the threshold.

"Alloy Slade." Ademure curtsied. "I apologize. I would've thought you refreshed from training by now."

"Was there something you needed from me?"

To keep from twiddling her thumbs, Ademure folded her hands. "Um, yes, Alloy, I—"

"Ember," the alloy said, still hanging on the doorframe. "I've never been a big fan of titles."

"Okay, Ember. I have an urgent matter I was hoping you would help me with."

"And what's that?"

"Do you mind if I come in?"

Alloy Slade looked into her room, then back at the princess, and sighed. "Sure."

Thank the gods.

She opened the door wide. Drawers were thrown open, various shoes hanging out of them by their heel. Linens and nightgowns lay strewn over the bed. Near the closet, day dresses and evening gowns sat in piles of heaping fabric.

Ademure did her best not to wrinkle her nose. *Oh Pan, does she need a maid.*

When she stepped in, the alloy shut the door behind them before sitting at the end of the bed. Ademure grabbed a seat in the chair where the fewest number of garments resided.

"So, what's up?" Ember asked, pulling her hair out of its ponytail and shaking loose her sweaty blonde curls.

Ademure peeled a sock off her armrest. "How are you feeling this morning?"

"I'm fine, thanks." The blonde curls were now fixed back into an overflowing bun. "Is that what you urgently needed to talk to me about?"

"Um, no. Actually…," she adjusted herself in her chair, "I need help preparing for a trip."

"A trip," the alloy repeated. She pulled two curls free, letting them hang on either side of her face. "And you…want me to help you? You don't have servants for that?"

At the sound of footsteps and a thump, Ademure glanced at the door. It wasn't the twins, but if she didn't hurry, it would be.

"Well, no," she said. "This trip—I expect it will be danger-ous. Something beyond a servant's skill set."

"And you think I have the right skill set?"

"I think you're the only one with the proper skill set."

"Where are you going?"

She glanced at the door again, drawing her skirt tight. "I don't know yet."

"Okay." Ember stopped messing with her hair. "How are you getting there?"

"Not sure. Sailing, most likely."

"Do you at least know *when* you're going?"

At that, Ademure nodded. "As soon as possible."

There was a pause while the alloy made any number of faces, ultimately settling on what seemed to be utter confusion. "Not to be rude, but what princess leaves her castle both without a plan and in such a rush?"

Ademure averted her gaze to a spilled wastebasket. "A princess in name only, as I've recently been made aware. It seems the island has given me all it can give, and I don't foresee much more for me if I stay."

"So the trip—" Ember narrowed her eyes "—is one way."

Ademure didn't answer, because she wasn't entirely certain she could.

"Uh-huh. Okay, I'll be honest, Princess. I just want to learn how to control my powers, and unfortunately, I can't do that on my own. And after last night, I also can't afford to get on any more nerves. But really, if you want to leave, you should just go. You're a princess after all. You shouldn't need me."

"Ember, believe me, I would if it were that simple. But the estrellas have limited my freedom to barely more than that of a hardened criminal. In seven years, the farthest I've gone beyond these walls without an escort is the courtyard."

"Then go when they're not looking."

"I can't."

The alloy was quiet again, probably trying to discern what Ademure had meant by that. Ademure didn't blame her—she would have been suspicious too—but she also didn't really have time to explain how her own ineptitudes had gotten her here. She looked at the door a third time.

Gaze following her own, Ember said, "You're not supposed to be here, are you?"

She turned back to the alloy. "I'm sure it's only a matter of time before the oracles see me."

"Oracles?"

"They didn't tell you?"

The alloy shook her head.

"The twins are descendants of Pythia," Ademure said,

pulling at the ends of her hair. "Gifted with visions and sight. They receive prophecies whenever the gods decide to grant them. And they can see the present whenever they desire. As if they were birds from above or flies on a wall, they can see *everything* that happens within a mile radius, if they so choose to look."

She gripped her skirt again, her attention on the door. "Lately, their eyes haven't left me. It's why I want to leave. I don't have any freedom with them around."

"They can see us now?" Ember asked.

"They are probably watching us as we speak."

"Then they already know what you're trying to do. What's the point in coming to me about it?"

More chiffon balled into her hands. "They can see us; they can't hear us. Truthfully, they probably believe I'm only trying to befriend you." *Or trying to stage a coup.* "I've never attempted to leave before."

"Okay," Ember said, frowning. "But even if they can't hear us, they can still see the future, right? Won't it be kind of impossible to get by someone who literally knows our next move?"

"No, it doesn't work like that. They don't even really *see* the future if I'm not mistaken. It's more like something hits them, their eyes glow, and they start writing. At least, that's what they've told me. I've never seen it happen."

The alloy's brow furrowed, lines creasing on her forehead. She inspected Ademure's every tremble, every breath, every thought. Ademure let her. If she was going to survive, this had to work. Ember had to trust her.

"The twins go on missions all the time," the alloy said finally. "Why don't you make a break for it while they're away?"

"There are five other estrellas, and soon there will be

dozens more. I can't do this on my own." Ademure moved to sit on the bed next to her.

Oddly, Ember recoiled, shifting away from her without meeting her gaze. "You know I'm not trained right?" she said. "That that's like the entire point of me being here?"

"The twins sought you out because they believed your magic could singlehandedly win a war, and that was before they knew you could produce lightning." Ademure leaned into her line of sight. "Do you understand how powerful that is?"

"So I'm told," the alloy said, turning further so that she only looked at her from the side. "But I don't know how to use it."

"You could learn. Profe Ozamiz's training could trigger something. And when the time is right, we leave for the harbor."

"And then what?"

"We sail. Or rather, you sail. I'm quite out of practice."

Ember laughed. "Princess, I've never even been on a boat. You sure you don't want to fly?"

"Sailing is the only way off this island. Visit the harbor and ask for Admiral Guerrero. He's a dear friend of mine." *At least, he was.* There was no telling who else had turned against her. "He's very accommodating to the Crown. Tell him who you are, and I'm sure he'd let you sail anytime you desire. He always let the last alloys practice their sailing. And when you become a master as I know you will, come back for me."

"Princess, really, I'm sorry that you feel trapped here, but I can't—"

With reddening eyes, she took her hands. "Ember, please, I wouldn't have bothered you if it wasn't urgent or if I thought I could do it by myself. But I can't, and I'm not sure how much time I have left." She glanced at the door. "I need out straight-away. Desperately. And I need *you* to help me escape."

Ember ripped back her hands and jumped from the bed, stumbling over her vanity as she backed away. Her eyes shut. Her hands grasped onto anything and everything, knocking over makeup, styling tools, hangers. She looked as if she were trapped in a nightmare and was trying to do whatever she could to wake up.

Like at last night's dinner, the room heated.

"Raindrops," she whispered. "Raindrops. Raindrops."

Sweat formed at Ademure's brow. She squirmed further back onto the bed and closer to the door, becoming increasingly conscious of the alloy's ability to shoot lightning from her fingertips.

Meanwhile, the alloy clenched her teeth and cocked her head as if she were in pain. She gripped tight to the dresser behind her, still not opening her eyes. And, even when tears spilled down her cheeks, she stayed mostly silent. Instead, her legs quaked, her breathing shallowed, and her arms shook the furniture hard enough that Ademure felt the floor beneath her vibrate.

But then, she stopped.

"I'm sorry," she said, blinking away the water on her lashes. "I-I don't know... I'm sorry."

"It's okay," Ademure whispered, wiping her forehead. "It's okay." But when she slid back down to the end of the bed, she kept a foot angled toward the door, just in case.

Ember stayed at the edge of the room, arms folded tight to her chest. She was still for a while, staring out the window like she was deep in thought, until she said, "You hide it well."

Not knowing what had set the alloy off the first time, Ademure didn't respond. She didn't want to make the same mistake twice.

Thankfully, the alloy continued on her own. "Someone else I knew, she hid it well, too."

Furrowing her brow, Ademure spoke slowly. "I don't think I understand. What did she hide well?"

"Fear." Ember looked over her shoulder. "You don't want to leave just because you want more freedom. No, you're scared to stay, right?"

Heat rushed to Ademure's face while her mother's conspiracies and the oracles' words rushed to her mind. *Crossfire. Threat to our existence.* The coldness of Nieve's nails still lingering, she touched her cheek, and she nodded as the tears overwhelmed her.

"Fuck." Ember closed her eyes and shook her head. And though she hadn't moved from the window, she felt so much further away. "Why didn't you start with that?"

"And would you have believed me if I had? How many people do you know whose mothers want to kill them?"

It was the first time Ademure had said it aloud, and suddenly, it felt real. She could have vomited.

"Kill you?" Ember whirled around. "Why would she kill you? Aren't you her heir?"

"It's *because* I'm her heir...and have my father's blood. You saw her last night. My mother is blinded by her jealousy of him. So much so that she trusts no one he associates with—including me, though I haven't even seen him in eleven years. It's why I have to go. It's why I need you to help me go."

But rather than respond, the alloy stared at her—stared *through* her—as she toyed with her locket. And she stayed like that, completely silent, lost in some train of thought that Ademure didn't dare interrupt. With her free hand, the alloy rubbed her fingers together, like she was touching a memory... or perhaps, reliving one.

"I can't, Princess."

Then came the knock. Ademure's chest hollowed, and her eyes snapped to the door.

"Alloy Slade?" Nieve said from the hall. "Is everything all right? You're late to lunch."

No, no, no, Ademure thought, desperate. *I cannot give up on this now.*

"Everything's fine," Ember said as she turned back to the window. "I'll be out in a minute."

Ademure sprung from the bed, rushed to her side, and grabbed her arm. "No, Ember, please. I need you. I need your help."

"You don't want help from me." She pulled her arm away. "The people I help get hurt."

"What?" Ademure whispered, one eye on the door. "No, you'll train. You'll learn. You won't have to hurt anyone."

"Princess, I can't help you." There was another knock from Nieve. "And it seems as if I'm behind schedule."

"Is this because of something Bailón said last night? You have to ignore her. Ignore all of them. This is what the estrellas do. They get in your head."

"This isn't about the estrellas."

"Alteza," Nieve said, and her stomach plummeted. "I appreciate you welcoming the alloy, but she really must be getting on with her day." The knocks turned into pounds.

The alloy gestured her head toward the door. "You'd better get going."

"No, you have to help me!" Ademure pleaded. "Please! *Please!* I'm going to die!"

Ember kept her gaze fixed on the oriel window. "Not by my hands."

The door broke open, and Nieve's white-lined gaze sharpened on Ademure's puffy face. No amount of crying could get the alloy to turn away from the window. No thrashing nor screaming could garner even a glance.

Ademure was going to die alone.

CHAPTER 10
KIVA

Kiva hated wet socks. Unfortunately, the only way to make it to the cave was by walking through the shallow waters outside of it. Even more unfortunately, he still stood outside of it now, his head nearly reaching as tall as its mouth, waiting to access the shrine inside.

Well, truly, he meant to people-watch. Now that the castle's temple had closed, nearly all of Nysa was forced to make the trek to the cliffside of the island. Inconvenient for them, of course, but it was much easier to sort out faces here, where everyone stood in a line, than at other gatherings like the arena or plaza, where everyone got lost in a crowd. And he could not lose his girl.

Finally, it was his turn. Exactly as the others before him had, Kiva climbed the mound of loose rocks, laid down his mangoes and coconuts before the statue of Pan, and bowed his head. Unlike the others, however, he kept one eye open to survey the young blonde woman that had done the same next to him.

Adrenaline surged as he contemplated how to approach

her, what to say when he did. He brushed his hair back and cleared his throat, and then she fully lifted her head.

Lovely, he thought. *And not the one.*

He groaned as he pushed himself from the ground and exited the cave. Once back above sea level, he swung one leg over his landsailer and started the hour-long drive back into town.

As had become his daily routine, Kiva walked the town, exploring the shops along the colorful pastel main street. For being so isolated from the world, Nysa still managed to have an exuberance about it. In his travels, he had never seen a nation that blasted music in the streets at all hours of the day or held so many celebrations and festivals throughout the year. Even the birds whistled gleeful tunes. That was what he loved about his childhood home: the people masked their pain masterfully.

But it only took a glance at a local newspaper to see Nysa's truth. He grabbed one as he walked past the bookstore, dropping an uncut diamond chip on the counter. Some nonsense about an imminent Agarthan strike was plastered all over the front page again, and it took him seventeen pages to discover a single drop of real news.

Today, he learned that the Atlantean mermaids had determined their new pharaoh: a woman who had served as interim since the passing of the last. The Lemurians had also elected their new president: some radically progressive magick who had lived among the soulless in Tokyo for the last three years.

He flipped back to the front page, intent on dropping the paper into the garbage, until a particular sentence caught his eye.

...A spokesman for the Crown says that an unnamed Agarthan diplomat is temporarily residing in the castle. It appears the Crown and Agartha are entering into peace negotiations...

Agarthan diplomat? he thought with a frown. *Since when has el Alcázar been allowing guests?*

He did one last pass through the paper, ensuring there were no other hidden stories, then tossed it into the can. At this level of isolation, it was amazing that Nysa had any sort of diplomacy—or economy, for that matter. Despite the Crown's adamant disdain for the Soulless Realm, somehow, they still managed to trade glassware and ceramics for soulless food; the soulless, of course, had no inkling of how the products were made. But, the queen absolutely refused to deal with other magick nations. *Which makes this bit of news all the more interesting.*

He continued his walk through town. There was no question that isolationism had taken its toll. The public's fashions hadn't evolved from simple dress, and the architecture of the stores was archaic: the roofs were flat, the railings iron, windows and doors large and arched, and no shop stretched more than three stories high. Even the landsailers, though native to Nysa, were of an ancient design, using a handlebar instead of a wheel. Since his return, he'd realized the only significant progress made in the last four hundred years had been in the navy and its ships.

And, considering how few Nysans even knew about soulless technology, cutting off the rest of the Magick Realm had only exacerbated the problem.

There was only one real solution. The queen had to go.

He stopped in front of a yellow shop, lured by the assortment of lilies and orchids displayed in the windowfront.

The girl comes first.

An intense floral aroma hit him, then a cacophonous collection of hues. Were it not for a ceiling, the shop could have been a jungle, and he would have never been the wiser.

"Welcome in, Señor," said the chummy older man behind the counter. "Let me know if there's anything I can help you with."

"Will do," Kiva said as he delved into the hibiscus aisle, but he needed no help at all. He had thought long about this decision and was sure the hibiscus would be perfect for charming a woman. The jasmine was too dull. The rose too serious. But the hibiscus was bright with large purple petals—pretty and he wouldn't come across as too forward. He picked his three favorites and turned the corner near the front of the store.

"Oof!" He doubled over.

"Sorry, Señor," said the teenage boy that collided with him. The boy bent over, reaching for the cloth he'd dropped.

Kiva held his abdomen. "It's okay—"

The teenager lifted his head, his pointed ears on full display.

Nymph blood.

The boy hurriedly retied the fabric around his head and stepped several paces back.

Kiva forced himself to take a breath. The kid was clearly mixed, and given he looked only to be about sixteen, he'd been, at most, nine when the nymphs had attacked. *He couldn't have killed the alloys*, he thought, though that logic hardly calmed him.

"You dropped your flowers, Señor," the teenager said, holding out the hibiscuses.

Kiva grabbed them. "Thanks."

"Sorry again. I was distracted."

"Forget it." He looked to the counter, but the kid still blocked his way. "If you'll excuse me."

But the boy stepped in front of him, cutting him off. "You know, Señor, I'm in town a lot, and I've never seen you before."

Kiva frowned. "I don't believe we've met before."

"Yeah, I know, but I've never *seen* you before."

"And you've seen everyone on this island?"

"Most of them. When did you get here?"

He eyed him. "I was born here."

The kid narrowed his eyes and scrunched his nose; he apparently didn't like that answer.

"It's true," Kiva said. "I'm in the suburbs. Sister is near town. My family has lived here for generations. Oh, and you know Valentina?"

"The bookstore owner?"

"That's the one. Ask her. She'll vouch for me."

The boy's expression didn't change, but he pressed his ear as if he was blocking out some unheard noise.

"Look, kid," Kiva said, "I've got things to do, so if you could please move out of my way."

The boy stepped in front of him again. "Who are the flowers for, Señor?"

Motherfucking... He didn't have the capacity to find this woman, identify the assassins, *and* entertain some nymph-spawn. He pushed again.

The boy pushed back. "Who?"

Kiva gritted his teeth. "A girl."

"A girl you like?"

"Yes."

The boy's nose scrunched up again. "Why would you give flowers to a girl you don't like?"

Kiva threw his arms and flowers to the side. "I just told you I liked her."

"I know."

"Then, why won't you leave me alone?"

"Because you're lying, Señor. But what about or why, I haven't figured out. Most Nysans don't lie like you do."

He growled. "Move out of my way so I can get on with my day."

"What is it that you're planning on doing with that girl?"

"What?" Kiva said a bit too loudly, and the man at the counter glared at him. He lowered his voice. "What are you talking about?"

"The girl those flowers are for. You're not planning on hurting her, are you?"

"Oh my gods, no!" he whispered. "I'm not planning on hurting anyone."

The kid scrunched his nose and pressed on his ear again. "Uh-uh. I do not like the sound of that."

"Sound of what? I told you I like her!"

The teenager continued pressing on his ear and making a face. Kiva turned to the cashier whose red face looked near bursting.

"Get out," the man said through clenched teeth. "Now."

Kiva's jaw dropped. "You're not serious. You're going to take this *nymph's* word over mine?"

"*Now!*" The man pounded the counter.

"Fucking green-blood sympathizer," Kiva grumbled, throwing the hibiscuses on the ground. He then stormed out of the shop, catching a glimpse of the kid's smirk as he left.

Who the hell was that brat? he thought.

And how the hell did he know?

CHAPTER II

EMBER

I need you to help me escape.

Ember refocused her attention on the magic in her fingertips. Profe Ozamiz had already ended this morning's session, but she was desperate to nail at least one spell. She sat in the grassy courtyard, grasping a handful of sand. *This should be enough to make a knife.*

"*Telum,*" she said, focusing her energy into her palms. *Come on. Give me an edge. Give me a handle.*

The sand gave her nothing.

"*Telum,*" she said again but with more force. This time she squeezed the sand, getting as close to it as possible, so as much of her connection would transfer to it as possible. She had enough sand for a knife. She had enough magic for a knife. All she had to do was shape it.

And still, it wouldn't shape.

Maybe Profe was right, she thought, chewing on the inside of her lip. *Maybe I'm not ready for that.* But if she couldn't manipulate the stuff regular kids built castles out of, how was she supposed to manipulate wood or rock or anything else the estrellas used? Hell, Sombra and Nieve could apparently levitate *people.*

I need you to help me escape.

Ember shook her head wishing she could shake the voice out of her mind.

No, she told herself. *I need to control my magic.*

She released the sand and dropped to the ground, but that only brought the princess front of mind. The princess who she'd known nothing about until two days ago. The princess who should have had a vested interest in seeing her become an estrella. The princess who had to be lying because why else, with something so serious, would she go to the magick who knew nothing about magic. Why couldn't Ember let go of what she'd said?

Because it's what Daphne said.

Ember rolled to her back and stared at the cloudless blue sky, those same seven words resounding in her head.

I need you to help me escape.

I need you to help me escape.

I need you to help me escape.

"Señorita Slade, are you alright?"

She sat up.

A teenage boy with a sunken face, wearing a kitchen rag around his mop of hair like a headband and a stained apron over his shirt, leaned over her. "Shall I get you some water?" he asked.

"Thank you, but I'm fine. I was just thinking." She pushed herself off the ground. "Damian, right?"

He nodded. "I figured I'd stop by since our conversation the other night was cut short."

"Oh? What were you wanting to talk about?"

Curiously, he turned his head, as if he was trying to better hear her, though she was completely silent. "That."

"What?"

"Shh. I can barely hear it now."

She remained quiet, straining to listen, but other than the singing birds and rustle of the nearby forest, there was nothing to listen for. "Hear what?"

"Your rhythms. Just fascinating."

How all women love to be described: fascinating, she thought. "I don't hear any rhythms."

"I expect you wouldn't. But they're there." He made his way across the green lawn, then climbed up the gazebo's perimeter spindles, and walked the structure's waist-high railing as if it were a tightrope. "So what has you so mad, Seño? Did I say something wrong?"

Ember furrowed her brow, both at his acrobatic maneuvers and the question he posed. "I'm not mad. Why would you think that?"

"Your rhythms, of course. They sound an awful lot like the queen's. I just assumed."

She was stationary again, listening for whatever "rhythms" were, and still, she heard only silence. "Why can't I hear them?"

"Because you haven't been trained to. Nothing to be ashamed of—few humans have."

She moved closer to the gazebo, watching him as if she were watching a theater performance—the way he effortlessly walked on his hands and swung about the ledge of the roof and the five structural posts like they were a set of uneven bars and a pole. "And you're one of those humans?"

Damian smiled wryly before swinging himself on top of the gazebo's roof. He pushed up the rag that held together his mop of hair, revealing his ears—his *pointed* ears. "Depends on what you mean by 'human'."

"Elf?"

He scrunched his nose. "Nymph. Well, half. Mom lives in Nyseion with the others." He pointed toward the forest that outlined the edge of the northern courtyard. "Dad used to work in the castle before he died. I'm supposed to take over his role." He glanced back at the castle behind him. "I'm training to become an estrella, just like you."

"Yeah, well, hopefully, you're nothing like me." She climbed the steps of the ivory edifice and spoke to the underside of the roof. "So what are 'rhythms' then? And why are mine so fascinating?"

Damian peeked his head over the top while holding tightly onto his rag. "Rhythms are the sounds of feelings, the cadence of emotion, the music of the soul. Sadness, contentment, joy, love—they all have songs that, from birth, every nymph is taught to hear." He lowered his voice. "And the estrellas cannot know about them."

"But you're an estrella."

"There are few things you could say that would offend me more." He rolled into the underside of the gazebo like a gymnast, landing on two feet with both arms outstretched. But he quickly lowered his arms and crossed them, and kept his voice at a whisper. "I'm training to be an estrella. I have no intention of becoming one."

"Why not? Didn't you say your dad was one?"

"My dad was not *them*." His eyes flicked to the castle. "And I won't be them either."

"But you know that I'm supposed to be, right?"

He laughed. "I wouldn't have told you about the rhythms if I believed that for even a second. You could never be an estrella. You lack the...intensity."

"Oh, do I? That's news to me."

"Well, if you could hear your rhythms, it wouldn't be." He stood on the gazebo's railing.

Ember climbed up beside him, holding onto the roof for balance. "Damian, talk to me like I'm five. I don't understand these rhythm things. How do they tell you what you need to know? What exactly are you hearing?"

"I don't know how to describe it, really. I can tell you that when someone is happy, the rhythms sound plucky, staccato, and high-pitched, and when someone is sad, the rhythms are slower and slurred. Just now your rhythms were offbeat and out of tune, which usually indicates anxiety—often the sound of a liar. You had the same rhythms at the welcome dinner when you told Estrella Bailón you would fight." He gave her a knowing look. "That was when I knew I could trust you."

She thought back to the welcome dinner.

You're slow, he had said. *Why are you slow?*

"What about when someone is angry?" she asked. "What does that sound like?"

"Anger is a monotone, thunderous drumbeat. It's very different from the other rhythms. Other rhythms hasten when the emotion intensifies. But when someone becomes angrier, the drumbeat actually slows instead."

"And the other night—you were there the whole time?"

"I was mostly in the kitchen, but yes, I heard the entire thing."

"What did my rhythms sound like then?"

His eyes drifted to the hand that played with her locket, and he seemed to swallow whatever his initial thought was before looking back up.

"Silence."

She stilled.

She hadn't been that angry, had she? She'd left before she'd blacked out. She could've been angrier. She *had* been angrier, many times.

If that night brought a rhythm of complete silence, then

what would several nights ago have brought? What would six years ago have brought?

And what made her that angry to begin with?

I need you to help me escape. Exactly what Daphne had said to her.

But what had happened after that? She'd relived the days before and after hundreds of thousands of times. And every time she'd gotten to Daphne's pleading, she could feel the prickle at her neck and—

"Señorita," Damian said. "Your beats are slowing down fast."

She looked at him. She hadn't noticed how much her vision had blurred or how much fire blazed through her body. He was right; she was furious.

Raindrops. Race the raindrops. The heat receded from her chest, then her arms. Her sight cleared. Her balance steadied. All that remained was the usual heat in her palms.

"Whoa," he said. "How did you do that?"

"Years of practice." She let go of her locket and sat down on the ledge. "I still don't get it. It's not like I can use the rhythms to any advantage. Even if you think I'll never become an estrella, why tell me about them?"

He sat next to her. "Because there's a war on the horizon."

She rolled her eyes. "I'm aware."

"You need to stop it from coming."

"What?" She looked at him. "Why is that my job? How could I even do that?"

"Nysa isn't strong enough to defeat Agartha without you, so the war won't happen if you're not a part of it. So don't become a part of it. Don't become an estrella."

"You seem to already know that I won't."

"I know that you don't want to, but you haven't seen the real estrellas, yet, Señorita." He dropped down from the ledge and sat on the bench at the gazebo's center. "I know you're not them. But that won't stop them from forcing you to act like them. You can't let that happen."

Shaking her head, she said, "I don't understand. How can you know that? Why do you care?"

"Before you, Seño, it was me. I was the chosen magick who would lead the righteous Nysans to victory over the dastardly Agarthans." He didn't meet her gaze, but she saw the bobbing of his foot, the tapping of his fingers. "It's a lie. The war. The 'savior.' The Agarthans. All of it. But they will do anything to keep the lie alive. My advice: as soon as you get a chance, get off this island."

She sat on the bench next to him. "And how do you know they don't already know about the rhythms? Aren't the twins oracles? Surely they'd have seen us out here by now."

"Don't worry about them."

"They'll know something is up."

"They won't. They haven't seen anything."

She narrowed her eyes but didn't question his peculiar amount of confidence. "And you don't think anyone has heard us? You've been shouting about the rhythms for half an hour."

His smile fell, and he bit his lip. "An oversight. But we're fine. I'm pretty certain all the estrellas are in their quarters far away from being able to hear us." He then turned his ear toward the castle and nodded. "Yeah, we're fine. Nothing to worry about. Any other questions?"

Her eyes widened. Of course, she had questions, not the first of which was: *Why did you not check no one could hear us* before *trying to conspire with me?*

But she asked instead, "If it's so bad, why are you still here? Or actually, why would they let you stay here?"

"The twins are a bit too proud to admit that I'm their failure, and I have some loose ends I need to tie up."

"Loose ends like...?"

"Like making sure you never become one of them." He folded his hands together as if he were praying. "Seño, I saw you the other night. I know you have no desire to become a part of this. And I have a magic that no one on this island even knows about, much less does anyone know how to fight it. Not to mention, I've been training as an estrella for two years now. I can help stop you from becoming a part of this, if you simply trust me."

In their silence, the birds chirped. The leaves rustled. The wind whistled.

His neon green gaze didn't waver.

First the princess, and now him. Twice in two days she had been asked to leave. She was starting to wonder if maybe she should heed the message.

But what will happen if I go now? she wondered, flexing her wrist, pulling at the tightly healed skin. *I won't learn control, and it'll only be a matter of time before...* She outlined the scars.

But if I stay, there's a chance I keep them to three. There's a chance I see Daphne again.

"I don't trust you," she finally said. "For all I know, you're about to turn around and tell Bailón I'm a lost cause, and I can't hear any rhythms that would tell me otherwise. Besides," she rubbed her fingers together, "I have to train." *And when I can control my magic, I'll leave—it's not like I haven't done it before.*

Surprisingly, Damian nodded, as if he already knew what she was going to say. "I wouldn't believe me either. I *didn't* believe me." Sadness flickered in his eyes. "But you will. And I'll be around when you do. Let me know when that is, Seño."

As he started for the castle, she clutched her locket, deciding whether to ask the question that had gnawed at her since the moment he'd come out here.

"Wait."

At the gazebo's entrance, he turned. "Yeah?"

"You said before that my rhythms sounded like the queen's. Does that mean…," she exhaled, "does that mean I'm like her?"

His eyes widened with seeming realization. "I'm sorry, Seño, I was both rude and very mistaken. You're not like Su Majestad."

Her grip loosened. "I'm not?"

"Not at all," he said, shaking his head. "Apparently, your beats come back. Hers never do."

CHAPTER 12
ADEMURE

Ademure stretched the black fabric across the length of her vanity, lining the folded edge with the edge of the table. The opposite edge she smoothed flat with the back of her hand. This way, she could better feel the connections bonding the threads, the ones that made the fabric, taffeta.

She wanted to make it gold.

Most other fabrics she could manipulate into the metal in a heartbeat. Cotton, silk, wool. These were all natural fabrics—fabrics taken from the living, from the Earth—where the magic remained strong.

But polyesters were difficult. The dozens of processes the fabrics had undergone in the Soulless Realm eroded their connections significantly. She could hardly feel the magic inside the taffeta now; it flickered like a flame at the end of its wick. She pressed on it.

The flame strengthened, the threads softened, and the bonds grew malleable. She touched a single corner of the fabric, feeling its desire for molding, its desire for change. Still, it was surrounded by tougher, more rigid bonds, and they didn't want her to mold any of them.

"*Chrysum*," she whispered, keeping her finger pressed to the corner.

The fabric resisted her.

"*Chrysum*," she tried again, laying two fingers down. She was delicate in doing so: any more touch and she risked melting whatever gold she might produce.

Again, the fabric resisted her.

She could sense the malleable bonds attempting to change, but the rigid ones continued to frustrate their efforts and herself. This time, she lifted both fingers and added a third, but kept all three hovering over the black edge, rather than touching it. The distance should have been enough to reduce the risk of melting while still giving the taffeta an extra zap of power.

"*Chrysum*," she said a final time.

The fabric yellowed.

"Engineering charms again, Princesa?" a voice said behind her.

Ademure jumped, and the taffeta snapped back to black. She groaned, then whipped around in her seat. Her plush jade chair creaked under the shift in weight.

"You could stand to make a little more noise when you enter through my window," she said. "I nearly had it this time."

The balcony doors clicked shut, and Damian retied the kitchen towel about his head. "If you want gold, why don't you start with steel? Or copper? Or sand? Pan knows we have more than enough sand."

"Because I'm not trying to reinvent the charm for sand to gold. I'm trying for something new."

"But why? When would you ever need to rely on..." He

picked up what draped over the side of the vanity. "Is this a dress, Princesa?"

She yanked the fabric back. "It was. Now it's an experiment. I'm testing soulless-made fabrics. If I can learn how to turn polyester into gold, perhaps I can learn how to turn gold into polyester."

"And again, I ask why? How is that useful?"

"Does it matter that it's useful? It's new." She returned the fabric to her vanity. "And I'm quite bored. I need something to keep me occupied until my execution."

She said it casually, but her breath betrayed her terror, becoming ragged and short. She glanced at Damian who had his head tilted and eyes wide and sad.

She cleared her throat. "So were you never going to tell me about the rhythms?"

"Shh, Princesa. Cadeña is outside your door. He can't know."

"He wasn't *always* outside the door. And you told her without hesitation." She gestured her head to the courtyard below.

Damian plopped onto the bed as if it were his own, resting his head against the dark green bedpost and inadvertently knocking off several viridian pillows. "I did that to improve your situation with her."

"I should have never asked her," she said.

"It was fine to ask. A bit aggressive to beg."

"Well, I am about to die. I believe the circumstances warranted a bit of begging."

He tugged his ear and adjusted himself on the bed. Another pillow fell to the floor. "I know you're frightened, Princesa, but you must be calm."

With a slow, shaking hand, Ademure grasped the tiara from her head and set it on her vanity. She closed her eyes, breathing in deep, but unsteadily, as she attempted to hold back tears.

"I am calm," she stuttered. "But I'm finding it hard to remain so." She pulled at the edges of her frayed brown hair. "The alloy is a lost battle. Surely, there is someone else who would help? Do you use your rhythms on everyone? Tell me who else is fit."

He bobbed his head from side to side. "Bailón is a possibility. Her rhythms are unlike the others, but I haven't yet decided what they mean." He then shook his head. "Princesa, the alloy is your best option. She is tied to something else, I believe, but she is not in any sense lost. She simply doesn't trust anyone, including the Delfinos. I can hear it."

"Did she throw a tantrum with the Delfinos, too?"

He raised his chin as he considered his next words. "I don't believe so, no. But perhaps you caught her at the wrong time. I spoke with her. She listens, Princesa. I believe that you should give her another chance."

"Why?"

"Because what other option do you have?"

"You."

She stared at him for a moment, looking for answers in his distinctly nymph-green eyes. Like usual, he gave her none.

"You need the help of an estrella or an alloy," he said. "I am neither."

They'd had this argument a dozen times since his father died seven years ago—when this entire debacle started spiraling. And he had given her the same excuse every time. She still didn't understand it. Damian was nearly as strong as Estrella Rodriguez or Maduro. He had capabilities other magicks didn't have. He had the ability and desire to protect her, and yet he wouldn't.

There was something else he wasn't telling her, she knew.

But she had long ago decided to let him disclose it when he was ready.

"How do I gain the trust of someone who trusts no one?" she asked finally.

Damian smiled, then hopped off the bed and made his way toward her balcony, gesturing for her to follow. Its doors were shut, but through the window, they could still see the courtyard below. And in the courtyard, there was something new.

"The Delfinos apparently granted the alloy's request. Have you ever played basketball before?"

"I've read about it," she said, standing on the tip-toes of her ballet slippers, peering out at the newly paved asphalt and pair of baskets. "You're telling me I should learn to play?"

"I'm telling you to find some common ground, Princesa. Make her feel comfortable. Talkative. Plus, the alloy feels some guilt. Whether that's for you or something else entirely, I have no clue. But I also don't believe it matters. Exploit it."

She glanced at her bedroom door. "What about Cadeña? I'm no longer able to move about el Alcázar freely."

"Will they not let you go outside?" he said. "Ask to go for a walk. Take him with you—I think he has a strange admiration of her anyway. Then, let the alloy strike the conversation. At worst, she ignores you, and you gain some sunlight."

She considered this. He was right, she was certain, about the alloy's tendencies and the length of Cadeña's leash. But the alloy's words from the other morning still sat fresh in her mind: *not by my hands.* That had been a pretty clear no, right?

Then again, what else could Ademure do? Try Bailón? The captain of the same estrellas who had locked her up in the first place?

Not in this millennia.

"Fine," she said. "Better ignored than dead."

CHAPTER 13

EMBER

No oracles. No princess. No nymph, Ember thought with a contented sigh. The ball swished through her new graffiti-free hoop. *Finally, something normal.*

It wasn't all normal, of course. Now that she knew what the sensation was, she couldn't ignore the electricity humming beneath her skin, ready to discharge from her fingertips at a moment's notice.

Not this moment, she told herself. *Raindrops. But how long until the raindrops run dry?*

Another swish.

She glanced at the castle entrance—or, more specifically, the dining room doors. Three nights ago, she'd been sure the raindrops had finally gone. Damian had been sure of it, too.

Not that she completely believed his story yet, but she suspected that at least on this point, he was telling the truth. And that forced her to reconsider the severity of the princess's plea. Because although Ademure had been quite dramatic, the truth in her expression had been unmistakable. She was scared.

She's fine, though, Ember tried to convince herself. *Her mom sucks, but she's not going to kill her only heir.*

She shot the ball, and as the rubber hit the asphalt, she wondered if she had made a mistake by agreeing to stay on this island at all.

"Hello, Alloy!"

Her breath hitched.

From the dining hall doors walked Princess Ademure and the plump estrella with the monocle—Oscar Cadeña, the latter of whom waved with the enthusiasm of a teenage girl meeting her pop idol. For a moment, the princess frowned at his odd behavior, but she quickly disguised her apparent discomfort with a laugh.

"Good morning, Estrella Cadeña." Ember bowed to avoid the princess's gaze. "Your Highness."

"Good morning, Alloy," Ademure said, her pale blue dress catching the breeze. "Good to see you're enjoying the court."

Her easy smile only made Ember feel worse.

"It's great," she said, eyes still averted. "I appreciate y'all building this for me."

"All the Delfinos' doing, I assure you." Ademure turned toward her guard who still seemed a bit starstruck. "Have you played before, Cadeña? I know you have a curiosity for such soulless things."

"I haven't," the estrella said eagerly, "but I've heard about it. You're aiming to put the ball into the hoop, right, Alloy?"

Ember tilted her head. She'd never really thought to explain basketball before. "Um, yeah. And to move on the court, you dribble." She grabbed the ball from the grass and bounced it on the pavement twice. "When you pick the ball up, you have to stop. Here, try it."

She handed it to Cadeña, and the man used both hands to bounce the ball, not only higher than himself but the basket, too.

"Like this?" he said, his head bobbing down and up with each "dribble."

Ember stifled a laugh. "Something like that." Her eyes drifted to the princess, who held a similar amused expression.

You don't owe her anything, she tried to remind herself. *She's given you nothing.*

But then...

I need you to help me escape.

Someone cleared their throat, and suddenly, Ember realized both the princess and estrella were staring at her. She rolled back her shoulders and gestured to the hoop. "Would you like to try, Your Highness?"

Ademure looked back at her, her soft smile unfazed. "I wouldn't know where to begin."

"That's fine, I can teach you," Ember said, her forehead sweating a bit more than it should've. "Estrella Cadeña, would you mind? I, uh, need the ball back, please."

The estrella caught the ball mid-air and whipped his attention to the princess. "She cannot participate."

Ember frowned. "I promise she'll be safe."

He eyed Ademure with a strange, furrowed brow, as if only just realizing she stood next to him. "It isn't about safety."

"Then what's it about?"

She and Cadeña both looked at the princess then; Ademure stood calm with her head cocked and questioning eyes fixed on her guard. He pulled the monocle from his pocket and spun it around as his own gaze alternated between his royal charge and the castle doors.

"It must be quick," he said at last.

Ember nodded. "Five minutes tops."

He held a hand to the pulsing vein in his forehead. "Remember the rules, Alteza."

"Of course," the princess said with a small curtsy. "Please, Ember. Go on."

But Ember took a second longer because something had just happened here—something she had witnessed a thousand times. *Someone just got played.*

She respected that.

Failing to suppress a grin, she handed the princess the ball. "Maybe we work on shooting first?"

"Shooting?" Ademure said, wearing her own sly but plausibly innocent expression. "Like a gun?"

"It's what the soulless call throwing this into the hoop. You'll hold the ball in one hand, punch up with this arm, and aim at the basket. Here." Ember balanced the ball on the princess's uncalloused palm and bent her thin arm at the elbow. "Go for it."

Ademure obeyed—sort of. She less punched and more straightened. The ball hit the blacktop just three feet away.

"That was horrendous," she said. "This seems incredibly inefficient. Why wouldn't you use both arms for power?"

Ember retrieved the ball. "Because one hand is way more consistent than two. C'mon, try again."

She did. This time, the ball went five feet and almost cleared the top of the rim.

"See?" Ember said. "Already better."

"It wasn't even close."

She laughed. "You need to use your legs more. You're too small to not. My sister had the same problem."

"Well, good to know there are others out there who face the adversity of height." Ademure plucked the ball from the grass. "Do you and your sister play often?"

But Ember was already lost in a kaleidoscope of memories.

She thought of basketball, yes, but also bus rides to school, movies with friends, walks to the park, and chatting...just chatting. And then she remembered the colors black, blue, and purple, and the makeup that concealed them.

I need you to help me escape.

"Alloy?"

She snapped back to the present, clutching her locket and tugging on the chain. "No," she said as her skin started to break. "We don't."

"A shame," Ademure said, lifting her inquisitive eyes from the jewelry. "But I suppose that's how it goes as you age. I rarely see my brother either."

Ember lessened the pressure on her chain but left her hand on the pendant. "You have a brother?"

"He and my father rule Agartha together. It makes for quite interesting family reunions, I must say."

But the princess's laugh rang hollow, and Ember didn't miss the furtive glance she gave Cadeña. Nor his own to her.

What is she not allowed to tell me?

"Anyway," Ademure said, "I appreciate you teaching me something new. There are surprisingly few things to do around the castle."

"Really? What do you do all day, then?"

She tapped her chin. "Up until recently, I spent most of my time in the library—" another side-eye from the estrella "—but currently, I'm attempting to develop a charm."

Ember raised her brows. "Like a manipulation charm? I didn't know you could make those."

"It's more like discovering them, though I do tinker with the connections a bit."

As she toyed with her necklace, she felt the low hum beneath her fingertips, the electricity under her skin. "Do you think I could make a charm for producing lightning?"

"Hard to say. Most magicists believe manipulating lightning to be impossible. Of course, you've already proven to do the impossible. But if you don't already know the charm, I don't know how you did it." Ademure's eyes lowered to the locket again. "So, though there may be a charm for producing lightning, I don't think *you* need a charm to produce it."

Ember nodded, pondering this as she continued to zip her metal heart back and forth along the chain. All these questions brought her to another one that had bothered her all her life. "Can I ask you something else?"

"Certainly."

"Why doesn't this come off?" She hooked the locket with her thumb, holding it away from her chest. "The clasp doesn't work. Nothing breaks the chain."

Immediately, the princess moved closer as if she'd been waiting for her to ask.

"Hm," she said, fumbling with the clasp. "It doesn't look particularly strange. Perhaps it was manipulated in such a way so that you could never remove or destroy it. How long has it been that way?"

"My entire life."

She held her chin. "I don't know, then. Manipulations usually don't hold for that long."

"I'm sorry, Alloy," Cadeña interjected, "but we are well beyond five minutes. Su Alteza must return to her room."

A soft, sad smile fell back on the princess's lips, and she stepped back to the estrella's side.

"Yes, it's been quite a while, hasn't it?" she said. "I should go." Hands folded, she looked at Ember. "Thank you again for the lesson. And the mystery. Now I have something new to occupy my time."

And without a chance for Ember to return the gratitude or even a goodbye, the estrella and princess left.

She dribbled the ball as she walked aimlessly, her mind replaying the conversation, the lesson, the laughter. In theory, it had all been pleasant. In practice, it had been a front.

I need you to help me escape.

She glanced over her shoulder, where the two had already disappeared from the path and entered the castle doors. *From what?*

CHAPTER 14

ADEMURE

The door to Ademure's bedroom slammed shut. She gripped tightly to the armrests of her chair, and Cadeña stood stiff as a board next to her.

"Just what do you think you were doing?" Sombra shouted from the threshold.

Refusing to look at anything but the estrella's stark white boots, Ademure said, "The alloy was only showing us how to play basketball."

"Oh come, Alteza, you don't expect me to believe that, do you? You found her. You approached her. Could you make your intentions any more apparent?"

"Sombra," Cadeña started, "I was with Su Alteza the entire time. I assure you that there was no talk of anything other than the game."

"Then you must be even denser than I thought," Sombra spat back. "Because our princess is not dense at all. Let us not forget that it was her ability to speak that put Nysa in the position it resides. On the brink of war without a defense."

I was fourteen, Ademure argued to herself. *I didn't know.* But she also didn't dare reopen the issue of her guilt aloud. Not with the twin who'd decided it long ago.

"Letting her run her mouth does not put only your career at stake, Oscar. Or, do you not remember what happened to Cristian?"

Cadeña looked down at the monocle he twirled in his hands. "I remember."

"Then do not forget it. We have few loyal estrellas as it is."

Ademure boiled. *Cristian was loyal*, she thought. *You are not.*

"And as for you, Alteza—"

"What?" she hissed as hair fell in her face. "You're going to kill me and be done with this already?"

But instead of a response, the white boots moved closer to her, each step slow and steady until they were almost on top of her own slippers. Then, they stopped.

"No," Sombra said. "We're not. And for the love of Pan, I cannot understand why. That being said..." A cold, sharp nail lifted Ademure's chin, and she met eyes lined in black but so incredibly green. "Do not seek her out again."

CHAPTER 15

EMBER

Over the next several days, Ember returned to her room each morning and each night sweaty, sore, and tired. Her fighting stances improved, but she still had yet to add any magic to her attacks. On her seventh morning in pain, she lay in the grass in the courtyard, too weary to move.

And yet, she was strangely proud of it. She hadn't so fully committed to something since high school basketball, and she'd forgotten what it felt like to see progress from hard work.

"You fight hard, Alloy," Ozamiz said, regaining her attention. "But you still hesitate to throw a punch. Why is that? What are you thinking about?"

"I don't know," Ember said, though she could feel what made her hesitate in her fingers this very moment.

"You're not going to hurt me if that's what slows you. Students have tried. They all failed. You're no different than they are."

"I'm not trying to hurt anyone."

"I know," Ozamiz said. "That is what makes you unusual."

Brows raised, she sat up.

"Alloy Slade."

Nieve strolled from the dining hall, alone, snow-colored hair floating behind her. "I see you've taken to training well."

"Profe Ozamiz is quite demanding," Ember said, "but I'm surviving."

"I trust she's advancing," the twin said to the tutor.

Ozamiz nodded. "She has more determination than the last set you gave me combined. Though, she's still much weaker than they were."

A sliver of light glinted off Nieve's eyes, and both corners of her mouth upturned. "Good. We can do more with determination than with brute strength. I gather it won't be much longer before the alloy gains a grip on her abilities anyway. Let's skip this evening's lesson. I'm sure both of you could use a recess."

The tutor nodded and gathered her things.

"I'll see you tomorrow, Alloy," Ozamiz said as she left the courtyard.

Then Ember, with much effort, pushed herself to her feet. "I'm getting a break? It's only been two weeks."

"Despite your first-day objections, you've acclimated quite well," Nieve said. "I'm impressed. As a show of gratitude for your diligence, I'm offering you a change of pace. You may do with your time whatever you please. I suggest a venture outside these walls, to see the paradise we ask you to defend."

"*And* you're letting me leave the castle?"

She chuckled. "Your schedule is strict only because you are underdeveloped. As long as you return for dinner and continue your training, there is no reason you can't roam the world."

The world, Ember thought. *I've only ever been to Dallas. I would like to see the world.*

"I'll see you at dinner, then."

"I'll see you then, Alloy."

After lunch, a shower, and a change into common clothes, Ember crossed the front lawn through the wrought-iron gates, hiked the boardwalk, and slid down the sand dunes before finally reaching the sea. From there, she walked the shoreline and headed for Ademure's fabled harbor.

She inhaled the ocean air. The sky was a beautiful baby blue, not a cloud in sight. The sun warmed her skin without making her sweat, and a breeze tugged at her curls without pulling them apart. She dragged her hand in the cool water, watching the minnows scatter back to the deep blue beyond. The view from her window didn't do this place justice—it was perfect.

Except, perhaps, the harbor. After the two hours it took to get there, she expected to be greeted with a thousand grandiose ships—so the eight she saw docked were hardly impressive. She knew the country was small, but could this truly be the entire fleet?

Several men and women in gray uniforms patrolled the entrance, and a sand-made building that stood behind them looked like the only pathway to the dock. Curiously, there were no walls, gates, or other barriers as one would expect for a harbor used by the queen herself.

She walked up to the tall, attentive man who stood at the building's lone door. He held no weapon, but as she learned in her lessons, discovering the preferred weapon of an opponent was part of the fight. Any material could be manipulated into whatever armament one chose, and sand happened to be particularly easy to mold.

"Declare su razón para estar aquí," the man said to Ember.

Okay, reggaeton only teaches so much.

She smiled sheepishly. "Um, sorry. English?"

The man raised a brow. "State your business."

"Oh, tourism."

"We don't have tourists here."

"Um, official business, then?"

He lowered his chin. "The people of this island are not many, and I've not seen you before."

"I'm not from here. Like I said, I'm a tourist."

"*Colora reditio.*" He waved a hand in front of her face.

Her pulse skyrocketed, and she patted her cheeks and forehead. "What did you do to me?"

"You don't know a simple return spell? But your eye color didn't change. You're of Nysan blood." His brows raised higher. "Who are you?"

"Change my eye color? You can do that?"

His brows danced with his hairline.

"I came here the other night," she said, "with the estrellas."

He snapped his fingers. "Ah, the admiral did tell us they sailed you in from the Soulless Realm. My apologies, Alloy. You are welcome to tour as you see fit."

Damn straight, I'm welcome. She nodded a bit too proudly as she entered.

"Alloy," a booming voice said.

Across the office floor, near the dock-facing windows, a man a foot taller than her, with broad shoulders encased in a dark gray uniform and five medallions pinned to his chest, held out a hand.

She took it with grace. "Sir."

"It's good to see you awake, Alloy Slade. I trust the Delfinos have recovered as well."

"They have..." she trailed off, realizing she didn't know his name.

"Admiral Guerrero," he said, then bowed. "How can I be of service to the Crown today?"

To the Crown? she thought. *Oh, right. I'm with the Crown, now.*

"The princess said I might be able to walk around the harbor. If that's possible, I don't want to intrude."

"Of course, that's possible! Come this way—I'll give you a tour." He held open a door at the back of the office.

She followed him onto the wooden dock. On either side of her, several seamen loaded cargo or made repairs or washed down the decks of the several ships. Behind her, others shouted out the windows of the office, giving commands or updates or news.

And out in front of her, the open sea.

"Thank you," she said. "I'm, um, intrigued by the really small fleet you have."

"Small?" The admiral chuckled, though even his chuckle reverberated in the air. "Oh, yes. I hear the soulless have hundreds of ships docked at once. Upkeep must be difficult."

"I think they have large enough forces to handle it."

"Yes, but they'd have to feed and house and pay all those men and women. Not to mention train and handle them. We simply don't have that manpower here. Not that we need it, of course. Our magic makes us quicker, more efficient, and there-fore deadlier on the seas if it came to it. In the time a soulless navy could sail out of their harbor, we could sail across the Caribbean."

So modest, Ember thought. But she didn't doubt the Nysan navy to be fast, considering how far she and the twins suppos-edly sailed in one night.

She looked at the ships to her left, the large ones. At least three metal masts and cloth sails attached to the center of each—a combination she believed would be both difficult to control and completely out of place in the fleet of any modern country.

"How do you sail these?" she said, looking for an engine or oars.

"Perpetual manipulation of the water and air. We flatten the water for smoother travel and push air into the sail. Some use the water to push as well, though, that tires even the best of us magicks out quickly."

The smaller ships floated to her right, each one streamlined like it was meant for racing, as if the finest welders took half a lifetime to craft each edge. They each had one mast and sail. *Much more manageable.*

"How often do these ships get used?"

Guerrero rubbed his chin. "Depends on the ship. Two of the larger ones leave almost daily." He gestured toward two barges, packed end to end with containers. "They're commercial ships that import and export to the Soulless Realm. But the *Maldojo* over there, that one's used solely for the queen and princess's passage. And that one hasn't left in quite some time." He pointed to the largest ship, bigger than either barge, with decks upon decks constructing its height.

"Three of the smaller ships are meant for the estrellas," the admiral continued. "Those are gone regularly. The last two belong to two private citizens. They leave on occasion."

They rounded out the end of the dock and headed back for the building.

"I appreciate your tour, Admiral."

Guerrero bowed before opening the door. "Anytime, Alloy. I can't thank you enough for coming to our nation's aid. If there is anything else I can do for you, anything at all, please ask."

Ember remembered what Damian had told her. *As soon as you get the chance, get off this island.* And, of course, Ademure had told her something similar.

But Nieve had thus far kept to her word. Ember was learning magic, and she hadn't been asked to do anything more. And in fact, since that dreadful dinner the other night, the subject hadn't come up once.

Still, she wasn't yet willing to believe it never would again.

Through the window, she eyed one of the smaller estrella boats. *I do need an exit strategy.*

"Actually, Admiral, would I be able to sail one of the estrella ships on occasion? It'd be nice to get out of the castle from time to time."

He stroked his chin. "I don't see why not. It's good to get your bearings early on. I remember when the Delfinos first learned to sail. Their cheeks matched the color of their eyes."

"Perfect," she said, grinning. "Well then, I'd better get back to the castle. Thank you for all the help."

He shook her hand. "Truly. The pleasure is all mine."

The sun kissed the horizon, and the breeze picked up, gently tousling her hair. Several birds chirped a melody (a seemingly familiar one, though she couldn't name it) whilst others dove into the ocean, surfacing with their meals. She dipped her toes into the cool water before taking a seat in the sand.

It does look like paradise, she thought, recalling what Nieve had said.

She put her hand down beside her.

"Ouch!"

She ripped it back, then searched her surroundings to find the culprit. A pink shell with a pointy edge glinted in the sunlight. A drop of blood colored it.

Half a second before pitching it into the ocean, an idea came to her, and she waved her right hand above it.

Nothing.

"What was it that harbor guard said? *Colora reda...?*"

She tried waving at it, then snapping at it. She turned it over a few times, then whispered at it. Still nothing.

"What are you trying to do?" a voice said behind her. She jumped, flinging the shell out of her hand.

Over her shoulder stood a tall, lean man, chestnut hair blowing across his forehead. He had to have been around her age, maybe a few years older. Next to him was something that looked like a scooter but with a ski for a bottom and a sail attached to the seat.

"Sorry, I didn't mean to startle you." He knelt and grabbed a handful of sand. "Here's your shell back."

She slowly took the shell from his hand. "Thanks."

"I'm Kiva by the way."

The hairs on her neck rose as she realized that he'd immediately spoken to her in English. Still guarded, she said, "Ember."

"Ember. Very pretty. Mind if I sit down?"

She surveyed the beach, looking at all the empty real estate she already knew was there.

"I'm going to take that resounding silence as a yes, then," he said.

He doesn't have an accent either, she noticed—unlike every other Nysan she'd met so far. *Not a Spanish one, at least.*

The man sat much too close to her, greeting her with bright green eyes and an unwavering smile. He unfurled his legs like the sand was his couch. He then brushed back his hair in a way that led Ember to believe it was never in place. *He's a serial killer for sure.*

She scooted away. "Is there something I can help you with?"

"Nothing I can think of. Maybe a little conversation?"

"With a complete stranger?"

"Is there something wrong with that?"

"There's no one else out here."

"I know. Isn't it great?"

"That's a little weird, don't you think?" She scooted further.

"Ah," he said, leaning back. "You think I've got some ulterior motive?"

"Do you?"

"I don't," he said, then pursed his lips as he considered her. "But I see that it'll be difficult to prove that."

She narrowed her eyes.

Kiva closed his own and let his head drop back, as if he were soaking in the sun—as if whatever exchange they'd just had didn't matter in the slightest.

"So, you're looking for 'a little conversation' in a deserted location?"

He peeked one eye open. "Yes."

"I don't believe you."

"I don't know what else to tell you, then," he said, leaning his head back once more. "You can continue to sit there in silence, you can leave, or," he smiled, "you can talk to me."

She chewed the inside of her cheek. Perhaps, she was being too cynical. The man had walked up to her in broad daylight, and it wasn't like he'd brandished a weapon when doing so. Maybe he really was looking for what he said he was.

After all, she hadn't had a guy genuinely interested in her since she'd been sixteen. It wasn't like Ethan had ever cared about what she'd had to say, or Garrett before him, or Derek before him. Maybe she had forgotten what it was like. Kiva's approach *was* familiar: uncomfortable and weirdly assertive. Her homecoming date had been the same.

"So, you never answered my earlier question," he said. "What were you trying to do with that shell?"

He speaks so casually, though, she thought. *No nervousness, no hesitation. Is it really flirting or is it something else?*

"I was trying to change its color," she said.

He sat up. "That's easy enough. Mind if I have a look at it?"

With a raised brow, she handed him the shell.

"*Colora caeruleus*," he said.

The change started from the tip he held with his fingers. The edge deepened, pinked. Then gradually, the pink purpled and blued in spiral fashion along each ridge of the shell until the color reached the top—until finally, the shell donned cerulean. He threw it up, snatched it back out of the air and, when he handed her the shell, glanced at her expectantly.

She frowned.

"What?" he said. "Not impressed?"

She eyed the shell, and then him. "Should I be?"

"I guess not for a simple coloration spell, no."

She studied the shell further. It was perfectly blue, no doubt. He'd even gotten the cracks in the inner wall. *And damn did he do it easily.*

And *damn* had she been itching to complete a spell. Almost two full weeks of training and, still, she had nothing to show for it. Sure she could shoot, but she wanted to do something magical. Just one charm—any charm—and she'd be satisfied.

"How simple?" she asked.

"Want me to show you?"

The look he gave her sent a flutter to her chest, however reluctant, and a tightness to her jaw. "Sure."

"Hold the shell in your hands, and hold your hands out for me."

She complied.

"What's your favorite color?" he said.

"Green."

The corner of his mouth upturned, and when her cheeks flushed, a twinkle caught his eye.

Damn it, Ember, you are not twelve. Stop acting like it.

"Okay, I want you to hold it like I did." He formed her hands around the shell accordingly so that she only held it with her fingertips.

"Now repeat after me," he said. "*Colora viridis.*"

"*Colora viridis.*"

A warmth—a friendly warmth—rushed from her palms toward the shell. And then, where her skin met the apex, the blue lightened, yellowed, greened, and the warmth—the green—swirled about the shell's spires until the blue was completely overwhelmed. Despite holding only the tip, she could feel every edge, every lip, the entirety of the inner surface and the outer. She was connected. And then the shell was green, and her connection faded.

She flipped the shell over and over again, searching for the trick he had played on her, but there was none to be found. It really had changed.

"I made this happen?"

Kiva laughed. "Yes, you did."

She stared at it. Though it was simple, it was surreal. Watching it was one thing, but to create it... It was like pulling back the curtain, revealing the mechanics of the theatrics. And it was relieving. The first time she had ever produced magic... while completely in control.

"Wow." She looked up to see him beaming, and she couldn't help but smile herself. *Maybe I judged him too soon.* "Thank you."

"Anytime. We all start somewhere after all. Some of us later than others."

Her smile disappeared. *Or not soon enough.*

"It's that obvious?" she asked.

"That you're completely unaware of magic? Extremely."

She tucked the shell away into her pocket and pulled her legs into her chest. What else was so obvious about her?

"So, where are you from?" he said.

"Would you believe me if I said Nysa?"

"Not for half a second."

She kept her eyes on the sand. "I'm from Texas."

"Texas? As in the Soulless Realm?"

Ember stared at the horizon and played with her necklace. *I should probably get back soon.*

"I've never heard of a magick growing up in the Soulless Realm before," he added. "I wonder why someone would risk exposing the Magick Realm like that."

She cocked her head. "What do you mean? I think most 'soulless'—" she feigned quotation marks with her fingers "—would love to know that magic exists."

"I'm sure they would," he said, chuckling. "That's *why* they can't know. They're always after our power. We only expose ourselves to them for strictly economic purposes, and even then, it's discreet. They're more capable than they seem."

Something about that assertion didn't sit right with her, but she knew he wasn't exactly wrong. Her foster father, Richard, would've been after this power. And had she not seen for herself its consequences, she would've been too.

"It's incredible you've made it so far in life to only now be found," Kiva continued.

"Found?"

"Educated guess. I assume you didn't wander here on your own."

She gave him a sidelong glance. "Good guess."

"So, where are you staying now that you're here?"

"With some distant family of mine," she lied, returning her

gaze to the sea. "I have a curfew. On a tight training schedule. They're pretty strict."

"Oh, well that doesn't sound like much fun."

"Yeah, well."

The rush of the ocean filled the dead air. Her mind wandered, piecing together who this guy was, why he was here. But she felt as if she was missing a large portion of the puzzle.

At the same time, a part of her was willing to overlook it.

Well, if he was volunteering lessons in foreign relations, she might as well learn some culture, too.

"Why are spells in Latin?" she asked against her better judgment. "I thought you worshipped Greek gods here."

"Hm. I guess it's a remnant of the Spanish Empire," Kiva said. "The nymphs and indigenous magicks declared independence, the Spanish left, and the island made sure the Christian god did too. Kinda hard to unlearn a language, though." He brushed back his hair. "Or it could be older, from Ancient Rome, when Nysa resided in the Mediterranean."

"The Mediterranean? But I thought we were in the Caribbean?"

"We are, for now, until the nymphs decide to move it again. They like to do that every half-millennia or so. Keeps the soulless on their toes. By the way, not all spells are in Latin. Only about half of the Magick Realm uses them. And even then, since the royal divorce, a lot of older Agarthans have reverted to using Old East Slavic."

"Huh. Cool." She glanced over at the contraption he had at his side, the scooter with the ski and the sail. "What's that?"

He looked over his shoulder. "The landsailer?"

"Landsailer?"

"You don't think we walk everywhere, do you?"

She looked north at the shoreline in the direction of the harbor. *That would've been good to know.*

"How does it work?" she asked.

"Manipulation. Undulate the sand, put wind in the sail. I can show you if you want."

"Some other time, maybe. When I can come back to the beach." Landsailer lessons could be fun, but judging by the sun, she didn't have much time left out here. Nor was she sure she wanted to be with this guy after dark.

"We don't have to do them here," he said. "The beach is pretty, but there's so much more to see. What parts of the island have you explored so far?"

She pressed her lips together, deciding what to tell him. "The harbor. And the beach."

"That's it? Not the forest or cliffs? The stadium? The town?"

"No."

"Well then, we'll have to plan for a night around the town soon."

"We?"

"You'll need a guide, right? Unless you have someone else in mind who can navigate this island with their eyes closed."

She dug her fingers further into the sand, thinking. There was no one else on this beach. If Kiva wanted to kill her, he would've done so. And if he kidnapped her, well, the last kidnapping had panned out alright.

Plus, she had the strangest feeling that he wasn't actually a threat, a feeling she didn't often have, but was quite often correct.

Or maybe, she was just horny.

"Fine," she said. "I don't know when I'll be free next, but when I am, I'll be here."

"I'll be waiting." He grinned. "But right now, I had better get going." He stood up and held out a hand.

She let him pull her out of the sand. "Thanks for the help," she said, tapping her pocket that held the green shell.

"Of course. It was a pleasure to meet you, Ember. Hopefully, I'll see you around." He lifted his landsailer from the ground, sat down, and cruised into the distance.

And Ember stayed there a moment longer, watching him sail away. *Weird.*

CHAPTER 16

EMBER

After her conversation with Kiva, Ember realized in the more than two weeks she'd been here, she'd not once explored the temple—despite it being right next to her new court. So today, instead of her daily basketball routine, she stood across the grass, in front of the columns that formed the outer architecture of the Greek structure.

The temple looked exactly as how she'd pictured one of these things. Nearly fifty columns formed the perimeter; each column was probably ten times her height and four times her width. And the bright white sand from which it was molded reflected the beaming sun, only intensifying its radiance.

Ember had never really held much faith in anything, but if it helped her learn control, she wouldn't turn down some divine intervention.

She pushed open the door. Inside, it was reminiscent of the castle, entirely made of sand with no shortage of green stained-glass windows. Instead of ornate walls, however, the temple opted for a massive painting that encompassed the entirety of the ground beneath her feet. It was difficult to fully appreciate the work from her vantage point, but after a moment, she realized that she stood at the roots of an elaborately painted tree. As she looked forward, she spotted a few branches, then a few branches more, each decorated with fascinating greenery that didn't look quite like normal leaves. Nearing the front of the temple, the branches grew denser and more complex, entangling themselves into what looked like a point at the top of the trunk. From there, the greenery overtook the floor-bound mural, but Ember was suddenly distracted by the non-painted, very real young woman who knelt on top of the tree's crown.

Ademure.

And at her side, Cadeña. He lazily twirled his chain in his hand before replacing the attached glass about the bridge of his nose.

"Good to see you this evening, Alloy Slade," he said cheerfully. "Su Alteza is nearly finished with her prayer hour. Give us a moment, and we'll give you your privacy."

The princess looked over her shoulder as he spoke. Her eyes were reddened and puffy, but she didn't make a sound.

Ember's chest tightened. *Something's happened.*

"Thank you, Estrella Cadeña," she said softly, "but that won't be necessary. Actually, if the princess doesn't mind, I'd like to pray with her."

The once bubbling bald man frowned. "Truly, Alloy, it will only be a little longer."

"Oh, I don't mind. Unless I'm bothering you?" She looked at Ademure. "I only wanted to share the space. Is that okay?"

The princess's eyes narrowed, by anger or confusion she couldn't tell. But then Ademure nodded, and Ember didn't really care to know the reason. She immediately knelt, mimicking the other young woman's pious position. Cadeña let out an irritated breath and resumed twirling his monocle.

"You didn't strike me as the religious type," the princess said out of the side of her mouth.

"Really? With a life like mine?" Ember laughed. "No, I refuse to believe I've been made miserable by chance."

Ademure didn't smile.

Alright, no jokes. Ember rubbed over the engraving of her locket, wondering how she was going to talk to her. Even if she thought the princess's fears were a little overblown, she had seen Bailón throw a knife. The estrellas could be scary, and Ademure didn't deserve to be dismissed for simply worrying.

Maybe I start with an easier subject, she decided.

She turned toward the front, facing the statue of a goat-man who stood nearly as tall as a column. "Who's he?"

The princess followed her gaze. "Pan, the god of nature. He's our patron."

"He's so big." Ember gestured toward the temple. "*It's* so big."

"It's been modernized. It used to be open to the public, like the library and the courtyard." Ademure glanced at Cadeña. "The queen has since restricted such use."

"Where do the other Nysans go, then?"

"I'd imagine they'd return to the original temple in the south. It's as old as the island itself. Built by the nymphs."

"I thought the nymphs lived in the north?"

"They do now." She inhaled deeply. "But the nymphs have been here much longer than any of us."

Ember considered that a moment. "Do you know Damian?"

Ademure's eyes flicked to Cadeña again. "Of course. He's an estrella-in-training."

"And part nymph."

He stopped twirling.

She looked back to Pan's statue. "Yes."

"The queen mentioned the nymphs at that dinner the second night I was here. She said I eluded them. Do you know what she meant by that?"

Ademure was quiet for a moment. "I believe—"

"I believe it would best if I answered that question, Alteza."

She bowed her head. "Of course, Cadeña."

The estrella leaned against a column, arms folded and his chain still in hand. "Su Majestad was referencing an altercation we had with the nymphs a few years back."

Ember quirked a brow. "What kind of altercation?"

"A massacre. Seven years ago. It was an ambush."

"That's awful."

"Horrible," he agreed. "The nymphs killed all of the alloys who were part of the estrellas. Over two hundred in total, our strongest warriors. And our princess helped."

Ember blinked.

"What?" she asked as she looked at Ademure, who seemed to shrink in size.

"Sadly, that wasn't even the worst of it," Cadeña continued. "Originally, we thought the attack was solely against us, in Nysa. We rounded up the rest of the estrellas—there were about fifty of us back then—and pulled together our navy. We were set to go to war. Then we learned that every alloy from Nysa to Lemuria had been found and poisoned. Thousands of men, women, and children across the globe had all died a slow death. Every last one—except you, of course." He pointed his glass at her.

"Across the globe?" she repeated. "How is that even possible?"

"Our young princess acquired a list of all the alloys in existence. Stole it from the Delfinos. Of course, you weren't on the list, but the others were. She schemed with another traitor and he gave the list to the nymphs. The massacre was finished within two days."

Ademure trembled in silence, seemingly avoiding everyone's gaze.

She *killed thousands of people?* Ember thought. *The same princess who can't shoot a basketball ten feet? There's no way.*

But she thought on it longer. Thousands. *Thousands.* From a mistake? Was such a mistake even possible?

And they were alloys—like me.

But then, that had to mean that this, right now, was an act. The begging that morning was...an act.

But Ademure had stood up for her before then. Or had she meant to elicit sympathy from her, before Ember had known the truth? Had she only wanted to soften the blow? Was that day on the basketball court all an act too?

It didn't feel like one.

"I didn't mean to, Alloy," Ademure whimpered. "I swear."

Except, Ember wasn't convinced.

"Is that why y'all came after me?" she asked Cadeña. "I'm the last one?"

He nodded. "The traitor was dealt with accordingly. But we never sought anything further from the princess or the nymphs. We realized we didn't know the nymphs as well as we'd thought. Not that we couldn't win a war against them, but it would've been a brutal battle, and for what? Revenge?"

Ademure sniffled. "It was one of my mother's last sensible decisions to back off and leave them alone."

"Alteza!" Cadeña snapped.

The princess shrunk away from the estrella, clasping her hands together and shutting her eyes tight. "Perdóname."

Ember rubbed her wrist, brushing against her three scars, again considering the chances of making such a costly mistake.

It hadn't taken much for herself to kill two. *Maybe thousands isn't so extreme.*

"Do you know why the nymphs would attack?" she asked.

"The nymphs are cold-blooded, evil creatures," Cadeña said. "They don't need a reason."

Though Ademure kept her head down, Ember could make out her side-eye. *She doesn't believe that.* And after meeting Damian, Ember wasn't sure she should believe that either. So she nodded, but let the conversation fall silent.

The three of them remained silent for a while. At some point, her knees ached, and she shifted to sit cross-legged. Cadeña yawned as he returned to twirling his monocle.

But Ademure stayed still, her eyes fixed on Pan.

"Alloy," she said, her voice no longer wavering, "what is your family like?"

Cadeña caught his glass, eyes narrowing.

A bit skeptical herself, Ember lifted her head. "Er, I don't really have a family, Princess."

"I thought you mentioned a sister before. Was I mistaken?"

She tucked her palms into her folded arms. "I had one. She left me."

"Oh. I'm sorry."

"Don't be. You didn't make her leave."

The princess sat a bit higher. "Even still, I am sorry. What about your parents? Are they still around?"

Ember shook her head. "My foster ones passed." Her locket danced between scalding fingers. "I'm not certain I want to know about my birth ones."

"Why wouldn't you?"

She shrugged. "Allegedly, they're pretty infamous."

The corner of Ademure's lips turned up, and she whispered, "Allegedly, mine are, too."

"*Alteza!*" Cadeña shouted.

And for the first time all evening, she laughed, though it was not the type of laugh that came from joy. "Only teasing, Cadeña. No one's infamy rivals my own."

She then wiped away a straggling tear, bowed her head to Pan, and ambled down the trunk of the painted tree. Cadeña followed closely behind her.

And Ember didn't know what to make of any of it.

CHAPTER 17
ADEMURE

Ademure's fabric sat on her vanity table untouched for the third day in a row. And she lay in her bed, staring at the ceiling, praying to Pan for a fourth. She didn't usually spend so much of her days worshipping, but the more restrictions she'd had put upon her, the more disconnected from her magic she had become. Now that she was no longer allowed in the temple or the courtyard, her connection was the weakest it had ever been, and she had to rely on the god of nature to keep it alive.

"You're not working on your charm anymore?" Damian asked, quietly shutting the balcony door behind him and walking to her bedside.

She didn't move. "Why would it matter? I'm not going to have time to perfect it anyway."

"Princesa, there is still time. Agarthan, Nysan, and Nyseionian people still need a leader."

With a snort, she said, "Nyseion despises me, I'm positive. And in what timeline would I be able to return to Agartha without issue?" She fell quiet for a moment. "Besides, if this predicament has taught me nothing else, it has taught me that I can lead no one. Not the estrellas, not the alloy. Certainly not three entire nations."

She closed her eyes. Several tears escaped her lashes, retracing the rivers that must now have been etched into her face.

"I don't know what to do anymore," she said. "The alloy isn't coming around. My mother isn't coming around. No one is going to save me."

Damian sat in her plush green vanity chair and pulled his legs tight to his chest. "It will happen, Princesa. It must."

CHAPTER 18

EMBER

A week later, Ember sat at her mirrorless vanity, one hand underneath her chin, the other holding sand.

"Telum."

A warmth shot down her forearm and into the small pile, connecting her to every single particle within. The power of her charm followed, organizing the particles, demanding they reshape, restructure, smooth and sharpen, until they were in their proper place. A second later, the connection broke, the warmth left, and she was left holding a letter opener.

"Reditio."

The warmth returned. She reconnected. And the particles of the blade, as if they had muscle memory, snapped back to their true form. She held sand.

"Telum."

Again, the sand obeyed her command, forming into a letter opener; but her mind went astray. *I need you to help me escape.* Nearly three weeks and the plea still hadn't left her thoughts. Rather, it played constantly, increasingly so as of late, especially now that she could do this.

"Reditio."

Why do I care? Ademure was a traitor, right? Her actions led to the death of thousands. She'd said she hadn't meant it to happen, but as far as Ember could tell, morning, noon, or night, Cadeña never left the princess's side. Would the estrellas put so much effort into guarding someone who "hadn't meant it to"? No, they wouldn't.

And anyway, she owed her nothing.

"Telum."

But why did she kill them?

She remembered how frightened the princess had looked when she'd knocked on her door. How sallow her face had been and how loosely her gown had hung about her frame. She had sounded so desperate, so real when she'd said: *I need you to help me escape.*

"No, you don't!"

With a near-growl, Ember shot from her chair and stabbed the wood of her vanity.

A moment later, when the fire-hot sensation receded from her arms, she forced her shoulders to loosen and took a deep breath. *Raindrops.*

Then she tied up her curls, smoothed her skirt, and made her way to dinner.

At the sight of Ademure, Ember considered turning around and skipping tonight, but per Nieve's request—and only because of that request—she took part in the meal. Still, she couldn't help but notice how as the days wore on, the princess rarely looked up from her plate and hardly touched her silverware. Often, the kitchen staff removed her meal with scarcely a few bites taken from it. And, in seven days, she hadn't talked once. Each meal, she sat as still as stone while the estrellas and the queen chatted over her, and tonight's dinner was no different.

Until it was.

"I suppose people don't change," Esmerelda said. "You were always a troublemaker."

The room's chatter died down as Her Majesty spoke, and all eyes, including Ember's, were on the princess. Ademure took a single, mute bite.

"Remember when you stole the crown from my head?" the queen snarled. "And you gave it to your father. Said it belonged to him. I should've seen it then, the traitors you'd all become."

Ember looked to Cadeña who sat to the princess's left, casually twirling his chain.

"As if I needed more proof," the queen continued, "my only son had the audacity to tell me that I was a tyrant. That I never cared for him. Yet it was *I* who sacrificed *my* political power in the Magick Realm to raise you both!" She slammed the mahogany—unfortunately, something Ember had become accustomed to.

But she wasn't accustomed to the soft, resentful laugh that followed.

"*Raise* us. Imagine calling it that."

The entire room turned to the princess at the other end of the table.

"I'm afraid I didn't hear you, daughter," the queen said coldly. "Could you say that again?"

"I apologize. A princess should speak with clarity." Ademure met her mother's glare with a humorless smile. She cleared her throat and spoke slowly. "Neither you nor Apá actually raised me. In fact, I think I was about eight when you both abdicated the role of parent entirely."

"You thankless, heartless, leech—"

"I wasn't done." And now, she held no smile at all.

The queen silenced, but her fury was loud—the only sound Ember could perceive, other than the sound of her own heartbeat.

"I find it funny," the princess continued, "that you are so set on winning over your people and country, but you don't even try to win over your heir, your *daughter*. You hate my father with such a passion—such an obsession—for taking things you believe to be yours, and still, you give him all your time, mind, and energy. And leave none of it for you. And none of it for me." She glowered, her eyes puffy and red, but she shed no tears. "So no, you didn't raise me. That would require a mother, and I no longer have one."

Smack!

Ember barely heard the queen hiss, *"fringo,"* before a spindle broke free of its chair and, of its own accord, whipped Ademure's shoulder like a switch. Heat surged to Ember's spine as she threw back her chair.

"Sit, Alloy," Sombra warned.

The twins both gripped the wood of the table, like they were ready to manipulate it into blades. Bailón levitated an arrow. Even Cadeña had stopped spinning his chain. Every single estrella now stood, waiting, watching for what Ademure would do next.

Ember's gaze flicked to the princess who, despite the redness in her eyes and the heat in her cheeks, stared back at her with an air of confusion.

I need you to help me escape, Ademure had said.

But she was acting when said it, Ember told herself. *She's acting now.*

And so she heeded Sombra's command and sat back down.

Esmerelda raised her chin. "It saddens me that my own blood would accuse me, the queen who has given her a luxurious room, a full belly, and a wealth of knowledge, of such cruelty. I gave you *everything*."

"What about love?" Ademure shot back. "Do you even love me?" She held her arm with care, but the bruise didn't slow her words. "I know you did once. I remember the feeling. But it has been quite some time since I've felt it."

"What an absurd question."

"Is it really? Tell me that if you could, you would give up all the niceties of this world—your dresses, your crown, your ridiculous quest to prove something to my father—to have me by your side forever. Tell me you love me more than all of that combined."

"That's enough," Bailón said as she dropped her aim. She looked at the princess. "I think it's time for you to return to your room."

Suddenly, Ademure turned her attention to Ember with an expression that begged, *help me.*

But Ember could only shake her head as she traced the three lines on her wrist, trembling from the furnace inside her. *I can't.*

"Fine," the princess said to Bailón. "But I think it's time for a new queen."

And without another word, she left.

"That ungrateful bitch!" the queen screamed when the doors closed. "I cannot wait to be rid of her!"

"In due time, Your Highness," the estrella captain said. "It is not yet the right moment."

"I'm tired of this, Bailón. When will be the right time?"

"When we have cause for celebration."

"I don't understand you."

"But you trust me, right? That's all I need."

Bailón and the other estrellas in attendance stood by the

queen's side, leaving Ember and Esmerelda the only ones left sitting at the table. Ember joined the estrellas.

"Come, Majestad," Bailón said. "Let the Delfinos and I escort you to your room."

Still muttering complaints about her daughter under her breath, Esmerelda stood. Each twin then took a door and held it open, waiting for their captain and ruler to step through.

And that night, Ember dreamed of Daphne.

"Alloy Slade." The snow-haired oracle appeared around the corner of the corridor.

"Nieve," Ember said, putting a hand on her hip, and leaning against her closed door. Her breathing hadn't yet slowed from training, and her hair stuck to her neck.

"Concerning our dinner yesterday…"

Her palms heated at the memory. She tucked them into her arms and braced herself for whatever the oracle had in mind for her. "What about it?"

"You did well." Nieve smiled. "You have the afternoon off."

Somehow that only made the heat hotter.

"I did nothing."

"And you did it exceptionally well. Had you done anything else, I promise we'd be having a different discussion this morning."

Ember put a hand to her temple. *Raindrops.*

"Nieve, what is our relationship with the princess? Isn't she royal? Isn't she under our protection?"

"The princess is an Agarthan sympathizer. She is a royal, unfortunately, but we protect the queen, not her."

"Why keep her around, then? Don't you worry that she'll

leak information to the nymphs again? Or Agartha? Don't you worry she'll have me killed?"

"She's under tight restrictions that grow tighter as time passes. We have it under control."

"But isn't that more work than it's worth? Why not banish her from the castle altogether?"

"Trust me, Alloy, it will pay off in the end." Nieve lowered her voice. "The princess is an excellent player, you know. You shouldn't feel foolish for falling for her act. She's had more than seven years to perfect it."

Ember's face heated. The way Ademure had looked at her last night. The disappointment, the fury. Every single time she interacted with the princess—it *was* all an act. *Right?*

"I know you spoke with Cadeña before," Nieve continued. "Did he tell you how she acquired the list of alloys?"

She shook her head.

"Acting," the twin said simply. "Pretending to befriend my sister and me so that she could access our records. She gave them away the next day. It's all a part of her ruse. As I said, don't feel foolish for believing her. We've all believed her at one point or another." With that, the estrella patted her on the shoulder and continued down the hall.

But unable to let it be, Ember blurted out from behind, "But why? What does she have to gain?"

Nieve turned. "Power, Alloy. What everyone desires to gain. Princess Ademure is loyal to her Agarthan half, and she does not hide it. She is the successor to Agartha's throne. She defies the queen's wishes to strike. For Elysium's sake, she remains friends with the *son* of her *co-conspirator*."

"Wait." Ember held the bridge of her nose, trying to recall the conversation at the temple. "Who was the co-conspirator? Who's their son?"

"I believe you met Damian at the dinner?"

Her breath stilled.

The oracle nodded solemnly. "After his father Cristian Estrada was put to death, Damian pledged his loyalty to us." She sighed. "It hurts to learn how much someone's word is actually worth, but I digress."

Ember still couldn't process any of this. *Wasn't Damian's dad an estrella himself?*

"When the nymphs struck," Nieve continued, "Nysa was devastated and exposed. Luckily, the Agarthan attack never did come, but had the princess's plans come to fruition, her brother and father would be ruling this island today. She would be acting queen. And the rest of us would be resting on the ocean's floor.

"I won't lie to you, Alloy. The connections at Su Alteza's disposal are terrifying. I understand why you don't believe it wise to allow a couple of traitors to remain in el Alcázar. But trust us. Trust Fate. It must be this way for the time being."

This time, Nieve walked away for good, and as Ember entered her bedroom, she thought of Damian coming to her, asking her to leave the island, just as Ademure had. *It wasn't a coincidence, then*, she thought.

The only question was, were they working together for Ember's benefit—like they had said—or for theirs?

CHAPTER 19

EMBER

With the sun mid-sky, Ember found herself digging her toes in the sand once again. It had stormed a few nights back and the waves still seemed agitated. But the sand was soft and powdery, as if it had never been disturbed by rain or anything else. As she sat on the shoreline, her mind drifted to her last day in Texas. She remembered the train crashing. A smattering of lights. Shouting. A storm brewing.

But the twins? Hardly. Agarthans attacking? Maybe. Lightning?

Nothing.

On the horizon, the clouds darkened, and she rubbed at the back of her neck to ensure there wasn't a spark.

"Long time, no see," a familiar voice said. "I was beginning to think you wouldn't show."

Heart fluttering, she looked over her shoulder and spotted a tall, chestnut-haired man looking down at her with a mischievous grin.

"I told you my family was strict," she said matter-of-factly, annoyed at how quickly her face flushed. "This is my first afternoon off since I last saw you. I'm surprised you waited."

Kiva shrugged before sitting down next to her. "Eh, it wasn't too bad."

"Really?" She raised her brows. "Waiting for hours every evening for over a week, not sure if I'd even come back, *not too bad*?" *Is that endearing or horrifying?*

"I knew you'd return at some point."

"And how'd you figure that?"

"I have that effect on women," he said with a wink.

She squinted at him as she determined how to respond. Usually, a comment like that would've set her entire body ablaze—and even now, her palms simmered as she fought the urge to roll her eyes. If the circumstances were at all normal, she would have left him in the sand, then and there.

But then, nothing about the last few weeks had been normal. And she so craved a casual, low-stakes conversation, untainted by politics and tragic family quarrels, that she was willing to ignore...well, all of it.

So she played along.

"Oh, yes," she said, a smirk tugging at her lips. "Since the moment I met you, you've all but consumed my every waking thought."

"See, I told you," he said, and the way his mouth turned triggered another rebellious flutter in her chest. "Cruising up on a landsailer to a completely unfamiliar woman all alone on the beach and telling her I'll be stalking this spot until I see her again. Works every time."

She failed to suppress her smile.

"Come on," Kiva continued. "I don't know when I'll see you again, so we've got to make the most out of the time we have."

Smile faltering, she sat for a moment, staring at his outstretched hand, wondering if she should take him up on the offer. Then she looked at his magical contraption. *I wouldn't mind learning to use that thing.* And she turned to the ramparts that peeked over the dunes. *And I could use a vacation from my vacation.* And then her gaze returned to him.

She took his hand, letting him pull her out of the sand, and followed him to the landsailer. He swung one leg over the seat and tapped the empty space behind him, and slowly, she slid into the space. He handed her a pair of goggles before putting on his own.

"Are there handles or something for me to hold onto?" she asked as she slipped them on.

"Just hold onto me."

She grabbed the loose fabric of his shirt.

"You're going to fall off," he added.

"I'll be fine."

He chuckled. "Have it your way."

Then he whispered something unintelligible, and the landsailer jolted forward. With a yelp, she grabbed at his waist, pulling herself tight to him, head tucked into his back and pink rising in her cheeks.

Wind flew through her hair, sand at her face. The vehicle wasn't buoyant like a jet ski; it felt like it nearly sunk into the sand. But it also wasn't caught in the friction of the pavement like a car. It was more like riding a motorcycle through water, if that made any sense. It was simultaneously awesome and nauseating.

Her stomach flipped as they climbed the first dune, and again as they cruised down the other side. At one point, she could've sworn they would topple end over end. At another, they nearly earned themselves road rash. Kiva cut into the sand like he was racing, like he had something to prove.

And though it was just ten minutes, the ride felt like an eternity. Only when the smattering of buildings appeared and they returned to flat land did she feel any sense of relief, and she could finally focus on what was in front of her—on the pastel-colored shops and the sand-paved streets and the linen-clad, common-dressed, men, women, and children that walked them.

This was a real town, with real citizens. No estrellas or queens or princesses. *People.*

I never thought I would miss normal-ass people.

Kiva slowed the landsailer next to several similar contraptions, all varying in size and color. He parked, lifted his goggles, and helped her off the seat.

She fell to her knees.

"Oh my gods, Ember. Are you okay?"

She held her stomach and covered her mouth, taking in deep breaths through her nose. Sweat formed at her temples as the color drained from her face.

You will not puke here, Ember Slade. You will not.

"Do you have a bottle of water?" she asked meekly.

"I have an empty flask. I can run and fill it for you. I'm sure one of the restaurants in the plaza will let me."

"No, please don't. Just give me a moment." She rolled onto her back, letting as much air fill her lungs as possible.

He lay on his back as well.

"What are you doing?" she said, gulping down what wanted to come up.

"Talking your ear off while you figure out when to puke and get it over with. You'll hear me better from down here."

This man was aggravating.

"Fine. Fill up your flask for me, please. But hurry, or I won't be here when you get back."

"It's a small island. I'll find you." Then, he was gone.

I wonder if he's trying to ann—

Her gut betrayed her. She rolled over and retched as her

stomach emptied of all its contents and perhaps the stomach itself. Mortified, she wiped her mouth, eyes darting around to see if anyone was watching. A few people were close by, but to her relief, none paid her any mind.

She had to get rid of this before Kiva returned. Unfortunately, the catalog of charms she knew was still limited, and her current state of panic did nothing to stir her creativity for the ones she did know.

So she dug, trying to conceal the refuse of her stomach with her bare hands. *Goddamit, I just wanted to learn how to drive a landsailer.*

"I thought you'd last a little longer."

She froze, sand and vomit partially buried, and looked up. Mouth quirking, Kiva held out his flask of water.

She shot to her feet, ripped away the flask, and jabbed a finger into his chest. "Not. A. Word."

"Not even one to bury your mess?"

She narrowed her eyes.

"At least take this," he said and pulled a hand towel from a compartment in his landsailer. "Dust off the sand."

With no shortage of grumblings, Ember brushed off her arms and knees while Kiva recited a spell that cleared the rest of her humiliating handiwork. When he was done, the sand looked untouched.

"Thanks," she muttered, returning the towel and opening the flask.

"Of course. Everyone gets a little sick the first time. Though, I can't say many people clean it up by hand."

She thrust the water back into his chest, her palms hot enough to boil it. "I cannot stress this enough, Kiva. Shut. Up."

He grabbed her outstretched wrist with a grin. "C'mon, let's go to the plaza."

Like the castle, the buildings they passed were made of

sand. And they were colorful, each painted a pastel blue, green, or yellow. There was no red—Nysan law—and the only beige to be seen belonged to the unpaved roads that wove between the shops. As they drew closer to the center of town, Ember could just make out a tune, a familiar tune—the same one the birds on the beach sang.

They stopped in front of the fountain which, upon further inspection, she realized was actually a statue with water cascading down its sides. Even closer, and she could make out the person it depicted. He was tall and lean, hair falling to his shoulders, and he wore a tunic with a flower pinned to his chest. In his hand, he held a spear.

"Who is he?" she asked, looking for a plaque.

"I'm not sure exactly," Kiva said. "But the statue's been here as long as I can remember. I'm assuming it was a gift from them. They used to give us a lot of gifts."

"They?"

"The nymphs." He pointed toward the distance.

Ember squinted. Above the cityscape was a strange-looking object. Almost like a mushroom, with a stalk and a large cap. But it was darker than a mushroom, perhaps a deep jade, and of course much, much larger. At least the size of a mountain. It stood alone, though. It wasn't a part of any range...or forest?

"Is that a tree?" she asked. It hadn't been visible from the castle at all.

Kiva nodded. "Nyseion. Their capitol."

"That's a city?"

She looked back at the statue. Ears poked through his hair, but aside from that, he seemed so human. After learning that Damian was a half-nymph, she'd assumed the difference between the species would be more remarkable, but the statue looked exactly like the teenager.

"They were never kind," Kiva said. "But they were never hostile either."

"You mean before they killed the alloys."

He nodded.

"Do you know why they did it? And why just the alloys?"

"That's the million-chip question. As far as we know, there was no reason." And though his answer was matter-of-fact, he stood stiffer than she had seen him yet, lacking his ever-present smirk and continuing to stare at the statue, fist clenched.

"Is there something wrong?"

The question pulled him from his trance, and though discontent hadn't yet left his face, he said, "No."

She nearly asked him more, but the familiar music grew so loud she could no longer ignore it. She searched the plaza for its source. "Why do I know that song?"

"The National Anthem?" Kiva asked. "Nysans are a strangely proud people. You've probably heard it uninterrupted since the moment you arrived."

But I heard it before coming here, Ember realized. *Way before.*

"I'm surprised your family hasn't taught it to you, yet," he said. "You need it for clocking."

Her brows knit together. "Clocking? Like telling time?"

"No, *clocking*." He gestured toward what she supposed was invisible self-evidence. "You know, the green-eye innate?"

"Was that English?"

His mouth fell open. "I know you haven't been here long, but you really don't know? Your family hasn't said a thing to you about it?"

"I'm sure I would remember something like that."

"Hmm," he hummed, his forehead creasing. "I guess it is a somewhat complex magic, though it's a fundamental skill. Maybe they'll teach you later, when you're more practiced."

"Well, can't you teach me now? Like you did with the shell?"

He cupped his chin with his finger and thumb. "No."

"What? Why not?"

"Doesn't feel right." He shrugged. "If your family didn't tell you yet, they probably have a reason for doing so. Maybe they want to bond with you over it or something. I know a ton of families who do that with their kids—they have whole ceremonies and everything. I don't want to ruin that." He walked away from the statue and headed for the west side of the plaza deeper into town.

Ember frowned at the back of his head and followed him. *I sincerely doubt there's a party in my future*, she thought. *But maybe I'm rushing things. Maybe it's next on Ozamiz's curriculum.*

The music grew louder as they walked, and surprisingly, she realized she could hum a few words, but they weren't English. Or Spanish, though it sounded a lot like Spanish. "Is the anthem in Latin?"

"Greek," Kiva said. "Legend says that the gods used to sing it to the nymphs when they got it on to, you know, make the night—and other things—last a little longer."

"So it's mood music?"

He laughed and grabbed her hand. "Come on. This is my favorite shop on the island. They have the best cucuruchos."

Feeling like she had mild whiplash, Ember let him pull her inside a blue building, small and smelling of cinnamon and sugar. She found a table while he ordered for the both of them. He dropped several diamond chips onto the counter and returned with two cone-shaped desserts.

She pulled out her own triangular chip—it was supposedly worth ten times the uncut ones he had paid with. "You know, anywhere else in the world, diamonds are worth a fortune. And you Nysans treat them like they're trash."

"But diamonds are so common," he said as he sat across from her. "And they're extremely difficult to manipulate, so it's difficult to forge them." He handed her a cone. "Hope you like coconut."

She unwrapped the palm leaf and took a bite. The dull brown treat melted into a rainbow of flavors: baked sugar and coconut, orange and pineapple. Sour and sweet bliss.

"Good, right?" he asked.

"Wow," she admitted. "Something this delicious must be sinful."

"Then I'm destined for hell." He smiled before devouring the rest of his cone. She couldn't help but devour hers in turn. When she finished, she found herself a bit sad it was gone.

Then the faint melody resumed, and though the music played without lyrics, she could feel the words at the tip of her tongue. She was certain she knew it. But how?

"So that clocking thing you mentioned..."

"Mhmm?" Kiva responded, mouth full.

"What does it do?"

He swallowed the last of his cucurucho. "Clocking is the ability to slow down time."

She cocked her head. "But I thought you couldn't manipulate time. That objects of manipulation needed mass." That's what Ozamiz had told her. The volume of your target couldn't be changed, so things like time, light, sound, space, emotions, thoughts—things without mass or volume—couldn't be manipulated.

He balled up the palm leaf. "For charms, you're correct. Objects need mass, and you need a spell. But innates aren't charms. Each innate has a different requirement, and none of them require spells. For green-eyes, that requirement is the song."

She frowned, plagued with the same thought from earlier:

why hadn't Ozamiz told her this? For how much the estrellas insisted on her learning to fight, it didn't make sense not to teach her. The way she saw it, slowing down time could only be an advantage. *Nieve must have some explanation.*

But she had other questions first.

"Why do you say 'green-eyes' instead of Nysans?"

He shrugged. "Not all green-eyes are Nysans. Green-eyes in other nations can clock as well."

"Other nations?"

"Seriously, has your family taught you anything? There are magicks in settlements all over the world. They aren't officially recognized like the big four nations, but they're cut off from the Soulless Realm like we are. They mostly reside in places like Antarctica, Siberia, the Sahara. Places where the magic is strong and the soulless can't easily access them. But c'mon, we're not here for another lesson."

He stood and offered his hand, and she stared at it, but for a much briefer period of time than before. She put her hand in his, and he pulled her out the door.

They passed several restaurants, a florist, and a jeweler. Then there was the daycare, royal training facility, and hospital. Finally, there was a landsailer repair shop—Kiva seemed especially taken in by that store—and the bakery. Each building sported a lively non-red color, unlike the dreary expanse of sand they entered next.

"We're at the edge of town already?" Ember asked as they walked out from behind the bakery.

"Yep," he said. "Look."

He pointed to his left. The stadium was enormous, far larger than her high school's football stadium. Possibly larger than her local college's. And, like every other building here, it was made of sand, making it all the more astonishing.

"Let's go inside."

He led her to the entrance and up several rows of bleachers, her hamstrings on fire from the climb. At the top, she put her hands to her knees to catch her breath, but the stadium took it away.

There had to have been tens of thousands of seats, all doused in green. Enormous orbs hovered in the sky above, lighting each and every one of them. And instead of stairs, platforms scaled the hundred feet of height in the bleachers, manipulated in such a way that they never stopped moving.

"We couldn't have used those to get up here?" Ember asked, still panting.

"What, and forego the cardio?" he said with a laugh.

From this height, she could see bits of the town, namely the open plaza and a tiny figure she assumed was the statue. She could see the stores that lined the streets and el Alcázar overlooking them. If there were any other people in the square, they were only specks in her eyes.

It was the track, however, that was the real showstopper. Marked by a dark green hue, it started from the very center of the arena, then weaved up *into the seats* and back down to the center. That path repeated all around the stadium until it eventually finished where it started. From where Ember stood, it looked like the outline of a massive flower.

"I've wanted to landsail here for as long as I can remember," Kiva said, a wondrous look in his eye.

"Why don't you?"

His smile disappeared. "I don't have the time."

"You spent hours every day on a beach for a week just waiting around for me to show, and you're telling me you don't have *the time?*"

"I know, unbelievable. But I have other priorities." The look he gave her—a twinkle of the eye and small simper—made her blush.

But when his gaze grew distant and turned to the track, she knew. *You don't mean me.*

The realization stung, but the embarrassment stung worse. *Of course, he didn't mean me*, she reasoned with herself. *Why on earth would I think he meant me? We don't know each other. He owes me nothing.* Thankfully, the wind blew a bit harder up here, cooling the heat she felt in her cheeks.

Desperate to fill the silence, she asked, "Do the other colors have quirks?"

He tilted his head. "Innates, you mean?"

"Yeah."

"So clocking is the colloquial phrase for time warping." He counted off one finger. "There's also time travel, known as hopping; space warping, known as stretching; and space travel, known as mirroring." In the end, he held up four fingers.

Ember remembered her mirrorless vanity. "How does mirroring work?"

"Mirroring requires a reflection, a clear one, both where the traveler is at and where they're going. Most red-eyes use mirrors that they've manipulated. Considering its use in glass, sand is the easiest to use. But Agarthans usually use the naturally occurring obsidian found in the city, what the first mirrors were made of." He grabbed a fist full of sand from the bleacher below. "If I were to manipulate this into a mirror right now, any red-eye anywhere in the world could enter the island for the first time in over a decade."

I suppose that's a good enough reason for the queen to make me put my mascara on blind, she thought. "I take it most Nysans don't create mirrors often?"

"Never. Not with the estrellas around." He let the sand sieve through his fingers.

She watched it fall into a neat pile before looking back up at him. "How does stretching work?"

He raised his brows. "Good question. I'm not exactly sure, but Lemurians are always chewing gum or wearing rubber bands about their wrists." He wrapped his forefinger and thumb around his left arm. "It has something to do with that."

"And hopping?"

"Also couldn't tell you. But Atlanteans have a strong affinity for magnets."

She stared at him a moment before saying, "Have you been to Agartha?"

He stared right back. Then blinked. "No, I haven't." Then he walked toward the edge of the bleachers and pointed to a blue shack that sat outside the arena. "Here, see that building? You can take landsailing lessons there. Want to check it out?"

Shaking off the new bout of whiplash, she followed him to the edge. "Some other time."

"I'm holding you to that." He grinned, and sunlight sparkled off his emerald eyes. Though this instance, she couldn't get past the emptiness of his words, and she was reminded of her initial feelings about him—that he was so *weird*.

You're overreacting, she told herself. *This is why you don't do emotions.*

They took a platform down the bleachers in silence. The moment they touched the bottom, he turned back toward the town, leaving her behind.

She let out a breath of disbelief. "Kiva, where are you going?"

"To my favorite shop on the island!" he shouted over his shoulder.

She scowled. "I thought the cucurucho place was your favorite?"

He let her catch up to him, weaving between buildings, until they ultimately found themselves back in front of the nymph statue. But this time, Kiva had his back to it, facing instead a pale green shop with the name "Valentina's" scrawled across the top.

"A bookstore?" she asked. "I wouldn't have pegged you as a reader."

"I'm not sure if I should be insulted, though you happen to be right," he said. "But my friends basically live in libraries, so I've learned to like a book here or there. I have a soft spot for this store in particular."

A bell chimed as he pushed open the door. The dim room was bathed in gentle, comforting candlelight. Stacks of books covered the entire floor, save for where there sat two desks and a couple of sofas. The smell of parchment was staggering.

A small bespectacled woman with her hair tied in a bun and a stack of books in her hand greeted them with a nod. They nodded to her in turn as they entered the cozy shop.

"This is quaint," Ember said.

Kiva took a deep breath in. "It's like a second home to me."

A thought came to her. "Where is home for you?"

"In the suburbs." His brows furrowed. "Why?"

"No reason." But it was curious that he'd sounded so honest about his second home and not at all about his first.

Now you're just looking for problems.

"Sofia Valentina, the owner," he said, "has collected texts from all over the world. There's information in here I don't think el Alcázar has. Maybe even the Library of Congress." He walked past the first stack. "On second thought, that might be a stretch. Half of the Library of Congress is dedicated to the Magick Realm. Still though, Valentina has a lot of information."

"Wait, what?" she exclaimed, trailing him. "You think the U.S. government knows about the existence of the Magick Realm?"

"You don't?"

They did hide those aliens for a long time. "Okay, yeah, that makes sense."

He tapped the shelf next to him. "Find something you like. I'll buy it for you."

She followed him toward the back of the store. "You don't have to do that."

"I know, but I want to." He dragged his hand along the shelves, eyeing each title they passed.

"Why?"

"Why?" he repeated as he turned around and put his hands on her shoulders. "Why do you need a reason for a friend to give you a gift?"

She brushed off his touch. "We're not friends."

"You wound me." He put his hand to his chest. "I thought for sure I'd finally won you over."

"What, because you ran me all over town?"

"Ember, please. May I simply buy you a book?"

She thought of Rachel, of how similarly insistent she'd been about them going out together. There couldn't have been that many people in this world who couldn't take no for an answer, yet she'd lucked out on finding two. She folded her arms. "Fine."

"Thank you." He continued to drag his fingers along the many books, even stopping to make them all flush with one another. "Seems that what I need isn't here, so I'm going to the other side of the shop. Meet me at the front when you're ready. Anything you pick up is on me."

She watched him leave, still unsure what he thought their relationship was, but she did as he said and turned her attention to the shelves. Fairytales, history, picture books, encyclopedias... The store had it all, and in a variety of languages at that.

Her fingers danced along the spines of several books, coming across one that stuck out much further than the rest. She grabbed it, intending to set it flush with the others, until a single word caught her eyes: *Slades*. She pulled out the book and took a closer look.

Magick Martyrs: The Slades by Liliana Caldwell. The name was embossed in gold along the spine.

Her stomach dropped. She wiped the sheen of dust from the cover, revealing a picture of a man and woman, smiling… and cracked it open.

The first few pages had more pictures of the couple. Some with friends, some alone, all in full color. The man wore his black hair shaggy, his skin pale. The woman's skin was golden, as was her hair. The last picture was a portrait of the woman, alone, eyes green as emeralds. And at her neck, there was a silver locket. Heart-shaped.

Ember reached for her own.

"Grab something interesting?"

She jumped at the sound of Kiva's voice. He was back at her side, peering over her shoulder.

"I thought you were looking for your book?" she asked.

"Found them faster than expected." He raised the two books in his hands and nodded at the open-faced tome in her hands. "So? What's that?"

"I don't know yet," she said before flipping the page, afraid her fingers might burn the corner.

In memory of my dear friend, Ana Slade. Your love and smile are missed.

"Oh," Kiva said mournfully. "Ana Slade. She and her husband died in a fire years ago."

"Fire?" Ember looked at him with a frown. "Weren't they magicks? How could they not fight a fire?"

"I don't know. I was a baby when it happened. Is this the book you want to get?"

She pressed her lips into a line. Was it? She had accepted that her parents were dead so long ago, but to have proof that they were gone forever, that she could never confront them for leaving her... Did she really want to know more than that?

"Yeah."

She closed the book and followed him to the front where he stacked all three of their books on the counter, hers on top.

The bespectacled woman scuttled toward them, grabbed *The Slades,* and paused. Then she looked at Ember and straightened her glasses.

"Wow," the woman said. "You look remarkably like Ana, dear. Any chance you're related? A niece perhaps?"

Ember didn't expect the remark to sting as it did: it felt as if flames surged up her forearms, licked her shoulders. But through her wrath, she forced a smile on her lips. "I doubt it."

Kiva doubled over. With a reddening face, he held his shoulder tightly, biting his lip as his breathing grew labored, hastened.

Ember thought he might scream. And as her worry grew, the heat fled her arms.

"Kiva?" The woman rushed out from behind the counter. "What's wrong?" She attempted to lift his sleeve but couldn't maneuver around his grip.

However, soon enough, it didn't matter. He took in a deep breath and let go of his shoulder all on his own. "I'm fine, Señorita. Thank you. Just a fleeting ache."

"At least let me have a look."

He massaged the area. "I swear the pain is gone. There's nothing to worry about."

Señorita Valentina didn't seem to agree. Though she spat at Kiva in a Spanish too rapid for Ember to understand, when he didn't respond but eyed the woman, Ember was pretty certain she got the gist.

"Are you sure you're okay?" she asked, hoping to ease the tension. "That didn't seem like just an ache."

Both the woman and Kiva broke away from their staring contest.

Kiva threw on a smile. "Yeah. I'm sure," he said, glancing out the front window. "It's getting late. I should get you back to the beach."

Ember didn't believe him, but she nodded anyway. "Okay. You're right. I should get back."

He dropped two square diamond chips on the counter—Señorita Valentina narrowed her eyes as he did—and grabbed the books. Ember then followed him out the door, and they traversed the short walk to the landsailer in silence.

When they returned to the beach, she stumbled off the contraption, praising the solid ground as she held back her cucurucho. She spent minutes on her hands and knees, taking deep breaths until she felt like she could speak without anything but words coming out of her mouth. Kiva sat beside her, hand glued to his arm.

"Are you okay?" he asked at last, no hint of the playfulness from earlier.

"Yeah." She moved to sit cross-legged. "What about you? You haven't said almost anything since the bookstore. And you haven't stopped rubbing your shoulder."

He looked at his shoulder, then put his arm down. Then, he

pushed himself out of the sand and held a hand out for her to do the same. She took it this time without question.

"I don't know what that was, honestly," he said. "But I'm fine. I promise." He uselessly brushed back the hair out of his eyes and grinned. "I appreciate you looking out for me, though."

To hide her instinctive eye-roll, she looked away, but when she looked back, his gaze was distant, worry lined his forehead, and his hand had returned to his shoulder. He was scared.

I want to see him again, she decided.

Not because she wanted to see *him*, necessarily—*no,* she told herself, *not at all*. Rather, she could only chalk up his odd mannerisms to *weird* so many times. If this whole ruse wasn't because he was interested in her—and after the arena bit, she knew it wasn't that—she had to know why he was so persistent on seeing her. Why take her around town? Why wait for her on the beach? Why approach her in the first place?

Why are you being nice to me?

There was something he wasn't telling her, and she simply did not do deals with secrets. If he was going to continue to insist on seeing her—for whatever reason that might be—she needed to make sure the transaction was fairly negotiated.

"So where will we go next time?" she said, hating herself for it.

He lifted a brow. "You're not pitying me, are you? I won't settle for a pity date."

"I don't think I'm capable of pity."

He laughed. "My charm actually worked then?"

"Let's not get carried away."

"Oh, before I forget." He opened the compartment of his sailer and handed her *Magick Martyrs*.

Ember stared at the cover. *My parents.*

"You do look a lot like her," he said. "She's stunning."

A tear formed at each corner of her lashes, and she chided herself for having them. Regardless, when she closed her eyes, they rolled.

"I'm sorry, I didn't mean to upset you," he said, placing a hand on her shoulder.

She could've screamed. *Why are you being nice to me? Why are you here, Kiva?*

She opened her eyes to him gritting his teeth, and her tears dried. *Why are you hurting?*

"You didn't," she said. "Thank you for taking me around town today."

And then, seemingly without pain, he nodded. He swung his leg over the landsailer. "I had a great time, Ember."

She forced a smile. "Yeah, me too."

Then he whispered a charm before taking off, and she watched him sail toward the town before starting her trek back to the castle. Keeping the book tight to her chest as the tears fell harder, she told herself, *You're overreacting...*

Am I?

CHAPTER 20

KIVA

The bell rang as Kiva closed the showroom door behind him. He then locked it and extinguished the light before heading toward the back of the bookstore.

He met another door. He brushed the back of his hand over the wood, and the wood shimmered, then faded into a freshly deglamoured glass front, revealing a lit room behind it, no bigger than a closet. In the room sat cardboard boxes full of well-worn books and a plastic table with two chairs, as if the room were just the back room it purported to be.

But when he pulled the handle up and let go, the cardboard boxes shimmered too. The room stretched at least ten-fold. The boxes grew into dozens of ceiling-high metal display cases that reached into oblivion. The plastic table and chairs were replaced by a grandiose round table and thirteen intricate chairs, all antique in design.

At one of those chairs sat a young man with cropped black hair in a tailored black suit, leaning back with his arms and legs crossed. His skin was a deep ebony, and his eyes...a deep red.

And when he pushed his chair back and stood, he met Kiva with laughter.

"You look strange with green eyes," Alden said. "Kind of a sexy look though."

Kiva laughed in turn. "But we all know I'm sexier with red."

"Agree to disagree."

His lifelong friend pulled him into a hug that Kiva was convinced was a show of strength more than brotherly love.

He hugged him back harder. "Where's Profe?"

On cue, the bespectacled woman turned the corner and scuttled toward her seat. Her legs dangled from the chair and her torso hardly met the tabletop.

"Right here," she said, grinning. "How's your shoulder feeling?"

Alden's smile fell. "Shoulder? The injured one?"

Profe Valentina frowned, too. "You didn't tell me you were injured."

Kiva waved them off, pulled back one of the thirteen ornate chairs, and plopped down, setting his feet atop the table. "It's nothing to worry about."

Valentina swiftly pushed them off, forcing him forward with a jolt. "Your scream sure didn't sound like nothing."

"You screamed?" Alden said. "Why?"

Kiva couldn't think of a worse way to be greeted after such a wreck of a night. But if he didn't answer them, they'd only continue asking.

"I did *not* scream," he said. When Valentina eyed him, he added, "But I did come close. And I don't know why; the pain came from nowhere. But it's gone, really. Don't worry about me."

Alden jutted out his chin in the way he did when he was

solving riddles—when he tuned the rest of the world out. "What kind of pain?"

"The throbbing kind," Kiva said.

"And it was just the one time?"

"Yes. Well..."

"Well...?"

He gave an exasperated sigh. "It returned just now, when I was on the beach."

"Why?"

"I don't know. But both times the sensation was fleeting. It's better now, I swear." Although, Kiva wasn't so convinced of that himself. The pain was as searing as that day in the Soulless Realm, when the alloy had electrified him.

Alden's eyes narrowed. "I don't buy it."

"Thank you!" Valentina said. "I knew it wasn't nothing. Kiva, don't you ever brush me off like that again—"

"Enough." He held up his hand. His former tutor huffed, but he ignored her. "Tell me about you, Alden. I haven't seen you in three weeks! What happened with the latest job? Was it dangerous? Where'd you go? Was it just you, or was it a team?"

Alden took the seat next to him. "You know I'm sworn to secrecy."

"It would kill me to keep the number of secrets you do."

"Which is why I keep them from you."

Valentina snickered.

"Can you at least tell me why I can't know?" Kiva asked.

"Plausible deniability," Alden said. He closed his eyes and leaned back—a signal which meant he would be volunteering no more information for the night.

Kiva groaned, but after two decades, he knew his friend was only looking out for him, in his Alden sort of way. "You know, I could use your help with the girl," he said.

"He's right," Valentina chimed. "He could."

Kiva shot her a look.

Peeking through one lid, Alden asked, "So, you found her?"

Kiva nodded. "She's poor and essentially a foreigner. I would've never guessed the Crown would let her reside in the castle. But apparently, the queen's been more hospitable as of late." He pulled out today's copy of the paper and laid it on the table. "Speaking of, have you seen this news about an Agarthan diplomat? Do you know anything about this?"

Alden grabbed the paper. "I don't," he said, skimming the page. "I can ask my father about it."

"No, don't waste your time. I'd rather focus on the girl, now that I know where she is. Had I been in better shape, I could've easily taken her." A phantom pain pulsed in his shoulder.

"Arrogance runs in the family, I see," his friend said, shaking his head. "I'm only here for another hour or so. I won't be able to help with that."

"Only an hour?" Kiva said. "Your father has you working to the bone. You need a vacation."

"And you think my ideal vacation would be to assist you in kidnapping one of the most powerful magicks in recorded history?"

"That's a little overblown, don't you think? She can hardly ride a landsailer without getting sick."

"She shot you with lightning, Kiva. *Lightning.* Sensitive stomachs can be compensated for when you can control electricity at the speed of *light.*"

"She did what?" Valentina exclaimed.

"Alden's exaggerating," Kiva said. "Lightning doesn't travel anywhere near the speed of light." He side-eyed his friend before looking back at his tutor. "It was nothing more than a little shock. Like I told you before, I'm fine."

"You're lying," she said, and Alden nodded in agreement.

"But, considering he's short on time, I'll catechize you some other time. Don't think I'll forget."

"I wouldn't dare," Kiva said. He turned to Alden. "But you're right. She's strong. Which is why I could use your help."

"What's wrong with the approach you're using now? Things will go over much easier if you can convince her to join you instead of forcing her. General Hesson in particular would much prefer a willing soldier."

"Theoretically, you're correct. But in execution—"

"Kiva's a terrible flirt," Valentina interrupted. "Made her cry on the first date."

"My gods, Kiva. Really?"

"I didn't mean to!" Kiva shouted. "I only wanted to poke holes in whatever nonsense the estrellas were feeding her. She never even knew her parents' names. I didn't think she'd get so emotional by simply reading about them!"

Valentina sighed. "Only you would think a woman wouldn't care about her dead parents."

"Yes, not your brightest moment," Alden added. "But perhaps, despite your fumble, her curiosity will outweigh her emotions, and she'll take an active role in her unlearning. Did she take the book with her?"

"Yes," Kiva said. "But I'm not sure that there's that much unlearning left to do. She doesn't know much about anything relating to the Magick Realm, so she's not well-versed in propagandized Nysan history. Oh, and she lied to me. Told me she was staying with family. The woman doesn't trust anyone as far as she can throw them. I doubt that she'd be so easily duped by the Crown in a matter of weeks."

"Well, isn't that overall good news?" Alden said. "She'll learn a little history, and if she hasn't yet been brainwashed, she'll be much easier to persuade. A bonus."

"I guess." Kiva ran through the night in his head, then held the bridge of his nose. "I hate this. You can't at least play my wingman?"

"Sorry. My father has us working nearly every night now. I think he's working on something grandiose, though I haven't had the nerve to ask him what. But I know I'll have to stay in Agartha for the foreseeable future. You're on your own."

"But I've already been chasing her for a month, looking for her for a year. What will *my* father think?"

Neither Alden nor Valentina responded, but they didn't have to. Their faces said it plain as day: *Stop caring about what your father thinks.*

Kiva shot them a look equally as telling: *Believe me. I want to.*

After a moment of quiet tension, Valentina wandered away, and Alden rapped his fingers on the table.

"I wish I could see my mother," he remarked.

"Why don't you?" Kiva asked. "You can take a landsailer most of the way."

"You've heard the rumors. It may not be a warm welcome."

"I could go with you."

"No," his friend said quickly. "It's too much of a risk. Being seen by the twins would compromise my mission."

Kiva snorted. "I risk being seen all the time."

"Yes, well, that's a whole other discussion." Alden rolled his eyes. "Anyway, I don't have time for the trip."

"Sure, you do. Your father can't keep you on your leash forever. Once the job is done, come back. Valentina will always be here."

Alden narrowed his eyes on him. "You know we put her at risk every time we come here, right? Especially me."

"Your mere presence in Nysa doesn't set off alarms," Kiva said, laughing. "Besides, she's fine. She's Sofia Valentina! If the estrellas were going to come after her, they would've done so a long time ago."

His friend was quiet for a moment, probably pondering whether to voice his concerns. He was meticulous in that way. Everything he ever said or did, he had thought through a dozen times, and then a dozen more.

At last, he said, "I worry about you."

Kiva shook his head. "Alden Caldwell, you are not worried about me. That's Valentina's job."

"You're getting reckless again. Jumping into missions head-on without heeding warning, choosing to fight the estrellas of all damned people—all for this lie that you can win back your father. What is wrong with you?"

He frowned. "I'm not getting reckless. I lost my reputation. My future. What would you have done?"

"You have no need to be above the protection of the Black Sky, yet every opportunity you have to mirror out, you not only leave but throw yourself and others in harm's way."

"It's not my intention to throw myself into harm, but I will do whatever it takes to get what's mine. Besides, if the alloy isn't on our side, how else do you expect us to defeat Nysa?"

"You know you can't bring them back, right? They died seven years ago—it's time to accept that and move on."

"I *have* accepted it. I *have* moved on. I'm only trying to get my life back."

"Our friends died on my watch, too," Alden said, massaging his temples. "Frederick died on my watch, too. It wasn't your fault."

"It *was* my fault!" Kiva snapped. "And I put all of Agartha at risk by not protecting them."

He stood, nearly knocking over his chair, and stomped toward Valentina's wall of treasure. But rather than study the collections of art, his mind replayed the memory of the twelve-year-old Frederick laughing at the dinner table. Then leaving the dinner table. Then Kiva wandering off after him and finding him...with a belt around his neck.

If only Kiva had found him sooner or asked him where he'd been going. Or if he had spotted the nymph faster. He could have killed it! And then—

"Is that what your father told you?" Alden asked.

He remained silent.

"Hey," Alden said from the table, "I miss Frederick, too. I miss them all! Every day. But—"

"But what?" Hot tears formed at the corners of his eyes. "But if only I had done my one job, Agartha wouldn't be so desperate for an alloy today."

"*But,* we were only teenagers," his friend said calmly. "No one can blame you. Not even your father. Nor mine. Not for what happened then. But now? Now we're twenty-three. And everything we do, or fail to do, that comes down on us. I need you to wisen up before you get yourself killed. Do you hear me?"

Kiva reached for his hurt shoulder, imagining what he had looked like on the concrete in the Soulless Realm. He hardly remembered it, Alden had mirrored them out so fast. And he had so quickly recovered, he hadn't believed the injury was serious. But if his friend was acting this way, Kiva must've been closer to death than he realized.

He nodded.

"Good," Alden said. "And if your being here on this island is actually some nymph revenge mission, I will drag you out of Nysa myself."

"It's not. The location is pure coincidence."

His friend raised a brow.

"You're right about going to see your mother," Kiva added, "as you always are. Forget I said anything."

"You know if you need to talk—"

"*Forget I said anything.*" It came off harsher than he had wanted, but the effect was the same. Alden quieted.

Valentina returned to the room holding a pan of seared sea bass and a bowl of mangoes and pineapple.

"I will need you two to move from the Round Table," she said. "We'll eat on some other furniture I have in the kitchen."

"Round Table?" Kiva asked.

"I hate to do this to you, Profe," Alden said, "but I didn't realize how late it was. I need to get back."

She pouted. "Right after I made dinner?"

He chuckled. "I'll come back for dinner another day. I promise."

"You'd better."

To the right of the wall of treasures was a wall of mirrors, some large, some small, all with different frames. Several were gilded and others could've been pure gold. Some even held large sapphires on every corner. Kiva could only imagine what the Nysan queen would do if she knew.

Alden stepped through the largest one as if it were a pool of liquid glass. The mirror rippled for a moment before returning to a flat reflection of Kiva, his eyes still puffy and green. In the same reflection, a short woman peeked out her head from behind his waist.

"Are you planning on leaving me too?" Valentina said. "Or shall we eat?"

Kiva and his tutor sat in plastic chairs at an aluminum table, marveling at how vast his tutor's ostentatious collection had grown. Paintings, chandeliers, ballgowns, animal skins, small sculptures, large sculptures, among a thousand other things.

The showroom's number of texts was impressive, but this room was where the real value lay.

After he finished his mango, Valentina grabbed his plate and washed the dishes. He took the moment alone to further inspect the so-called Round Table.

On the back of each antique chair was an engraving, patterned among the chairs in such a way that one chair had a sword inscribed on it, and the ones on either side were inscribed with horses. The pattern followed—sword, horse, sword, horse...—for twelve of the thirteen chairs. But on the thirteenth chair, he traced what he thought were the points of a mountain range until he reached the square bottom of the drawing. *It's a crown*, he realized.

He sat back down at the inferior kitchen table where Valentina could hardly stop herself from bouncing.

"That really is King Arthur's Round Table, isn't it?" he said, awestruck.

She squealed. "My new most-prized possession! Don't you just love it? The gentleman who gave it to me was actually from the Soulless Realm. Can you believe that?"

"This wasn't here yesterday."

"I sailed it into harbor earlier this morning while you were out waiting for the girl."

"Was it a gift?"

She hesitated. "A trade."

"And what did you give him?"

"Nothing much. Only some information he wanted to know."

He inclined his head. "What information?"

"Oh, please. It was nothing! He asked me about the four nations in the Magick Realm, so I told him about the four nations in the Magick Realm."

"You did *what*?"

"He already knew! He even knew where they were. I simply provided confirmation. Besides, it's not like he will be visiting anytime soon."

"Profe, please tell me you're joking."

When she didn't alleviate that concern, he dragged his hands down his face, "Well, you didn't tell him anything else, did you?"

She bit her lip.

"What else did you say?"

"I may have discussed magic."

"Profe!"

"It's fine. My gods, must I reiterate? He cannot access anywhere. It is all fine. I know it was a risk. But I have also lived long enough, seen enough, to know that taking risks is the only way to earn rewards. And Elysium knows it is well within my prerogative to claim some rewards."

"But for a table?"

"The *Round Table*, Kiva. Do not pretend you don't know its worth."

He ran his fingers through his hair. The most intelligent woman he knew had willingly sold some of the most sacred secrets of the entire Magick Realm, and she wouldn't stop boasting about it.

"Did you tell Alden?"

She shook her head. "Alden didn't ask. He was only here a few minutes before you walked back in."

"He would've chewed you out."

"It was harmless information."

"Did you ever think about the kind of soulless that would ask something like that?"

"Stop it, Kiva. You shouldn't speak on things you know nothing about."

"I know plenty. Everyone knows plenty. It wasn't that long ago that we were hunted."

"Not all soulless are out to kill us," she said, her voice rising.

"You can't possibly say that with any amount of conviction. People kill people for power. We have it. The soulless want it. Given the chance, they will eradicate us."

"That is a lie!" she shouted, making him still. "They are our other halves to Gaea's balance. Soulless and magicks can and should live together in peace." Her eyes told Kiva not to say anything more.

Feeling ten years old again, he cleared his throat and consciously lowered his voice. "All I'm saying is that you'll be hard-pressed to find even red-eyes and green-eyes together in peace."

His tutor sighed and looked back at her collection. "We aren't meant to be a world divided."

Profe, how can you be so naïve? A woman so knowledgeable about both Realms, so entrenched in history and culture that she kept her own private museum of works, yet so trusting. *The world will skewer you.*

Something near the bottom of a display case caught his eye, a large trunk too normal-looking to be a part of this collection. It was enclosed with a number of locks that covered the entirety of the box, and each lock had a differently shaped keyhole.

"Profe," he said, stepping closer to it. "What's this?"

The bun affixed to Valentina's head bobbled as she scuttled across the room. "The bane of my existence. I've had it for two decades and have never been able to open it."

He knelt down to inspect the locks and discovered that they seemed to be simple clasps. Even without a key, someone should've been able to break them fairly easily. "Do you mind if I try?"

"Be my guest."

He held his palm over the first lock and closed his eyes, letting his mind fill with the image and sounds of shattering glass before taking a deep breath and saying, *"fringo."*

The metal of the clasp heated so quickly, he ripped his hand from the trunk. The entire chest vibrated and a high-pitched whistle screamed from the keyhole. The metal turned red. The base rocked back and forth. The top swelled as if it were about to pop.

Then, it stopped. A burst of steam released through the seven keyholes and the trunk was once again still. He waved off the pungent odor. *You never do get used to that smell,* he thought.

Valentina laughed. "If all it took was a simple destruction spell, it wouldn't have gone unopened for twenty years."

"I'm assuming you don't have the keys."

"I don't even know what those keys would look like. Clearly, they don't have the basic teeth of a normal key."

"What's even in there?"

She shrugged. "I bought it at a storage auction, thinking something with such intricate designs had to contain something unique. But even with a transparency charm, I can't tell what's inside. Whoever manipulated this was fairly paranoid."

"Probably for good reason."

"I'll be able to open it one day," she mused. "Maybe I'll close up the store and go hunt the world for those keys."

"Where would you even begin?" Kiva said, smirking.

"That's for future me to figure out." She jumped up to sit on the Round Table, feet dangling over the edge. So odd for someone who cared so much for her relics. "So, Kiva..."

He took a seat in one of the elaborately decorated chairs. "Yes?"

His tutor smiled impishly—a sign he was not going to like whatever she said next.

"You like her?"

"Like who?"

"That alloy you had with you."

His face heated. Of course, he should have expected this. Profe Valentina was nothing without her gossip.

"Miss Slade is a weapon."

"A weapon that you must date? Is your father worried he won't be able to get you settled otherwise? If that's the case, I'll be sure to give him a list of prospective women in Nysa, pre-screened."

"I can get a woman on my own, thank you very much."

"Oh? And when was your last relationship? Six months? A year?"

He narrowed his eyes. Truthfully, it had been a few years, but she could never know that. She taunted him enough as it was.

"That's irrelevant," he said. "Ember is a target, not a love interest."

"Hmm... Is that so?" She tapped a finger on her bottom lip. "Are the two mutually exclusive?"

"Yes."

"Well, she was very pretty. And seemed intelligent. Pity you have to drop the idea of her so quickly. And that she trusted you enough to go out with you seems to me like you've won her favor."

"That is sort of the idea, Profe. I'm not in any state to be taking her to Agartha by force." He pulled down the collar of his shirt, revealing the purple-gray striated wound on his shoulder, outlined in scorched flesh.

His tutor's eyes widened. "Kiva! What happened to you? It's incredible your shoulder still works with a wound like that."

"I unknowingly flew too close to the sun." He grimaced. "Alden said she was strong."

"*She* did this to you?"

"Still think we should date?"

"Of course! Imagine the children!"

His cheeks went red at the preposterous idea.

Giggling harder, she fixed her eyes back on his shoulder. "But I wouldn't go breaking her heart."

CHAPTER 21

EMBER

"F*ringo.*"

The rock in Ember's hand exploded, along with her connection. The smell was putrid, like the bathroom of a music festival, and she could no longer sense the particles she once controlled. Rather than the warm magic of manipulation, she felt the cold curse of destruction. It reminded her of electricity, the way it lingered on her fingers.

"And now," Profe Ozamiz said, "you will never be able to manipulate that rock again." By hand, her tutor picked up the broken pieces and gave them back to Ember.

"Manipulation and destruction." She held the pieces of rock in her palm, trying to feel for any bit of connection that remained. "Is there a third type of charm? Something to put this back together?"

Her tutor shook her head. "Creation is a magic reserved for only Mother Gaea herself, and thank the gods for that."

She looked closer at her pieces. There were seven of them, equivalent in size and shape, each edge as though the rock had been butter, sheared by a knife. She could put them back together to reform her rock, and there would be no line or crease to reveal its broken nature. Yet, without some physical substance—glue or tape but not magic—it would never actually be whole again. And though it was just a rock, she grieved for it.

"Great performance again today, Alloy," Ozamiz said. "You really are advancing quite quickly. I don't think I've ever had a student who was so in tune with their connection as you."

Ember smiled. "Thank you, Profe. I've had a fantastic teacher."

"Now that we've come to the end of terminating spells, we'll start with perpetuating ones in the morning."

"What's the difference?"

"Where terminating spells end as soon as you're done speaking—like when you're creating weapons—perpetuating spells continue for as long as you focus your energy on them. They're how you landsail and levitate."

That reminded her of another magic she'd learned of several days ago. "Profe, have you heard of clocking—"

"Alloy Slade."

The white-haired, white-clad vice-captain strolled from the castle entrance with a bright white smile upon her lips.

"It is good to see you working hard this morning," Nieve said. "Hopefully, I'm not interrupting anything?"

"We just concluded." Ozamiz set a hand on Ember's shoulder. "Again, phenomenal job, Alloy. Whatever questions you may have we can discuss tomorrow." She then started toward the castle.

"Profe Ozamiz is fond of you," Nieve said when the tutor was out of sight. "And the woman is fond of no one."

Ember shrugged. "I like her, too. She's direct." She looked at Nieve. "So what's up?"

"If it's alright, Sombra and I would like to discuss a number of items with you. There's still several hours before dinner tonight, but I realize if you had prior plans..."

"I don't have plans," Ember said, which wasn't entirely true, but she wasn't yet sure she wanted to try to see Kiva tonight.

"Splendid," the twin said. "Let's go to our office. Sombra will meet us there."

The office was as sharp as their eyeliners. Each piece of furniture had been placed with a delicate deliberateness. Two curtains, exactly each other's length, framed a lone central window, and a sofa sat squarely beneath it. On the opposite wall counterbalanced a bookshelf, itself splitting the room into two halves. The bookshelf held scrolls, papers, and books, and not a single document, either by size or color, was out of place. There were two desks, two coatracks, two rugs—a perfect equivalency.

The only imbalance was the black-haired twin who sat in one chair.

Nieve took the other chair immediately. "You can sit by the window, Alloy."

Ember did as she said, sitting in the very center of the couch for fear that, if she sat elsewhere, the room would have toppled over. However as soon as she sat down, a horrible, familiar feeling swept over her. *I'm in the principal's office, aren't I?*

"So," Sombra said through a strained smile, "how are you?"

Ember furrowed her brow. "I'm fine."

The oracle gave a knowing, distaste-filled look to her sister, but Nieve ignored her.

"What Sombra means to ask is, how are you feeling, Alloy? Have you explored Nysa? Met the locals? Experimented with magic?"

Ember frowned. *So I'm not in trouble? This is just a mid-year meeting?* "Um. I'm alright. I've explored. Met a few people. Tried a spell or two."

Nieve's eyes widened. "Your lightning?"

Oh.

"No. Not lightning."

Nieve drew her lips tight and nodded as if she'd expected the answer. Meanwhile, Sombra returned to her sour demeanor, and Ember was relieved to have back that sense of normalcy.

"I wish you would work on it," Nieve said. "When the war comes, it will be an invaluable asset. We have been preparing for over twenty years, and I would be disheartened to see the end of Nysa's reign come about merely because we didn't exhaust all of our resources."

"I've told you—"

"I know," she said softly. "I know. And I commend you for your stance. It's just that when the war comes—"

"How can you be so sure the war will come?" Ember asked, her hands fidgeting in her lap. "I'm sorry, but from what I understand, no one, Agarthan or Nysan, has attacked, right? How do you know that there will even be a war?"

The estrella raised her brows. "We know it because we've foreseen it."

Ember paused. "And what exactly did you see?"

In response, Nieve looked at Sombra with eyes wide and lips at a full pout.

Her twin grimaced. "Why do I have to say it? You read the prophecy as well as I."

But when Nieve didn't drop the puppy-dog eyes, Sombra rolled her own, groaned, and turned to Ember.

"The gods told us that Nysa will be haunted by an evil we thought dead, namely, the Agarthans, who have been our enemy for all of history, save the last thirty years or so." She took an irritated breath, as if speaking were a phenomenal burden. "The gods also told us that in order to overcome that enemy, we would have to seek what the soulless took. That would be you. You and your lightning magic will be how Nysa reclaims her legacy." She shot a look back at Nieve. "Happy?"

Her sister smiled. "Quite." The more amiable twin then returned her attention to Ember. "So you see, the war is fated, and your lightning will win it in our favor."

Ember leaned back into the sofa, crossing both her legs and arms. Her locket weighed heavy about her neck, and she played with the jewelry, flipping it over and over again until the chain was tight enough to choke her. Then she let her locket go, freeing it to twirl on its own.

Her gaze drifted to her wrist.

"I can't."

Nieve's smile grew sad. "You know, neither the pain nor power goes away by ignoring it. You will conduct lightning again, whether you desire to or not. It is who you are. We only want to help you control it. Fate wants you to control it."

Ember flicked her eyes between the two of them, the smile and the scowl. Neither felt disingenuous, but still, something didn't feel right.

"What if we make a deal instead?"

"A deal?" the twins repeated in unison.

"Yes, a deal," Ember said. "If you want me to control my lightning, I'm going to need something from you. Otherwise, practicing will be way too dangerous, and I won't even try. Sound good?"

"You're not really in the position—" Sombra started.

"Depends on what you want," Nieve said, holding a hand up to her sister. "We can't give you the world."

"I wouldn't know what to do with the world." Ember pulled at a stray curl. "No, first, I want to talk to the princess. *Without* her bodyguard."

"What could you possibly want to discuss with her?" Sombra demanded.

"If I told you, it would defeat the purpose of what I'm asking for. I promise I'm not conspiring with her."

"Odd statement for someone not conspiring with a traitor to make." She turned to her twin. "This is ludicrous. I know you promised Su Majestad—"

Nieve shot her a glare of daggers.

But Sombra didn't back down. "Nieve, be reasonable. We can't possibly agree. Please, tell me you're with me."

Her sister's glare remained sharp and still for another moment. Then a muscle twitched in her jaw, and her attention softened, fixed on Ember.

"You do remember our conversation the other day?" Nieve asked. "The princess may want to hurt you. We can only get to you so fast if she does."

"That's fine," Ember said. "It's not negotiable. I won't be able to conduct lightning without a clear mind. And I won't be able to clear my mind without talking to her."

"Nieve..."

"Shh, Sombra. You worry too much. The alloy has done as we've asked. She's attended every dinner and training. Only once tardy. Hardly a complaint." If possible, her eyes were greener, eyeliner whiter, and she peered at Ember with a stark intensity. "And the threat Su Alteza presents has been greatly diminished over the years."

"But it's not gone," Sombra argued. "And it wasn't the

princess's own ability to kill that was the problem. It was her ability to convince others to do it for her."

"True." Nieve looked at Ember. "You're certain this isn't negotiable? That the only way you can progress is if you talk to her?"

"Yes."

The oracle was quiet a moment longer. "I'm inclined to allow it."

"You're joking," Sombra said.

"I'm not." Nieve met her sister's eyes. "But I won't make the decision alone. If you believe the request is inappropriate, I'll concede to your judgment."

Sombra bit back whatever she first wanted to say and instead took her turn to interrogate Ember.

"Alloy, do you fully comprehend what you're asking for? Your association with the princess does not do yourself any favors. And your discussion could thwart our cause."

"I won't be discussing any cause with her, Nysan or Agarthan."

"But what if she sways your position? What if she persuades you to do otherwise?"

"She won't."

"And you know this, how?"

Ember outlined the raised skin on her wrist. "I just do."

Sombra thinned her lips tight, then looked back at her sister. "Do as you want, Nieve. But might I remind you that if she doesn't—"

"I'll take blame for it." Nieve smiled warmly at Ember. "Though, please do keep this meeting hush. I will talk to Cadeña, and the princess will be in the courtyard following tonight's dinner. Is that acceptable?"

Ember nodded her head vigorously. "Yes, very. Thank you both. I'll keep you updated on the lightning."

The sky was painted yellow with a dash of orange, a stroke of purple, and a tinge of blue. The stars began to fill the canvas, sprinkled in like dusted sugar, and the air filled with the sounds of wind, water, and the dribbling of a basketball.

Ember swished the basket. Just like usual.

And her fingers tingled. Just like usual.

Each shot, she could feel her connection to the ball grow stronger. She touched every seam, every raised pebble. She sensed the air on the inside, the orange on the outside. Like her arm, leg, or head, this ball was a part of her, and she controlled it as such. *Swish.*

The ball rolled into the lawn, but she hesitated to pick it up. Even now, from a distance, she felt the ball, felt the gravelly sand and plush grass that touched it. She was still connected.

At the sound of footsteps, she turned.

Ademure swiftly sat down on the bench of the gazebo, setting her chin in her hand. And she kept her gaze at the trees so that when Ember followed her into the structure, her face was hidden from view.

"Hey," Ember said from the stairs.

"Hey," the princess said about as enthusiastically as she'd expected.

Like a broken record stuck at top volume, the seven words thundered in her head. *I need you to help me escape I need you to help me escape I need you—*

"Mind if I sit here?" she asked as she moved to the princess's side.

Ademure looked up. Her eyes were sullen, her face gaunt. Her brown locks were poorly kept, and the simple pale blue dress she wore didn't fit as snug as it should have. "Sure," she muttered.

Ember sat down carefully, not wanting to disturb even a hair on the young woman's head. "What are you thinking about?"

"My mortality."

A breeze rustled through the trees.

"Did you enjoy dinner?"

"I didn't eat tonight."

Another silence. Ember tugged at her locket like it was strangling her, and for a moment, she considered whether to let it.

"I guess I should start with thank you. For agreeing to meet with me."

Ademure's laugh rang raw, hollow, and chilled the air more than the wind had. "I did not *agree* to meet with you." She looked back at the northern forest. "Why am I here?"

Ember wrapped her free hand around her burning scars, gripping her wrist so tightly, her fingers throbbed. She shut her eyes, hoping it would shut her ears, but nothing silenced those seven words. *What was I thinking? This was a mistake.*

"I'm sorry. I shouldn't have bothered you."

And with a dropped head, she dragged her feet toward the stairs of the gazebo.

"Oh, fuck off."

At the threshold, she whirled. "Excuse me?"

"I'm sure I don't have to repeat myself," the princess said, inspecting her nails like they were the most fascinating things in the world.

Heat exploded in Ember's hands, but she was able to mask her fury behind "*raindrops*" and a derisive grin.

"Interesting proposition, Princess, considering *you're* the one who begged for *my* help. Or did you forget?"

Ademure shrugged. "As I said."

Surely, she was mishearing all of this.

"Do you know that I'm not even supposed to talk to you?" she said, her grin falling. "Do you know that I don't even *want* to talk to you? And yet, despite you failing to mention that you're the reason all of the alloys—people like *me*—are *dead*, here I am. Don't you think you could afford to be a little bit nicer to me?"

Ademure's attention snapped to her, and her pupils shrank to pinpricks. "Fuck. Off."

"No."

The princess shot to her feet.

"The estrellas are fantastic storytellers, aren't they?" she said, closing the space between them. "Turning hubris into heroism. Victims into villains. And even still, they are honest about their positions, about their true loyalties. Even my mother is unabashedly cruel. But you?" She scanned Ember from toe to head, ultimately landing her scathing gaze on her eyes. "You go on pretending like you don't see any of it. Like this magical little island is your heaven on earth. And you know it's bullshit."

"And what about you, huh?" Ember's palms simmered, and she felt the same heat reflect in her glare. "You killed *thousands* of innocent people and act like you were too naïve to know? Play basketball with me like if given the chance, you wouldn't have killed me, too? Spare me, Princess. I was fourteen once. You're not the victim you say you are."

Ademure looked as if she could've lit the forest on fire. "You're a monster, Alloy Slade. So kindly, fuck *off*."

At that, Ember couldn't help but chuckle.

"You're right," she said as smoke filled her nose and electricity stung her fingertips. As she heard the screams from all those years ago. "But for all the wrong reasons."

With a hot palm, she yanked Ademure's wrist, hauling the leaving princess back into the gazebo.

"How dare—"

"Yes, how dare I," she said. "How dare I ask the princess who begged me to rescue her for an explanation. How dare I try to understand why I should save the life that took so many others."

"Then why am I here?" Ademure screamed, ripping her arm back, tears breaking free of her lashes. "If you've already judged me to be so unworthy, then why are you wasting my time? You've made it *abundantly* clear that you won't help me!"

"But I still want to!"

The princess went as still as the forest, with only the sounds of wind and ocean, and her and Ember's breaths, carrying in the evening air.

"What?" she said, her chest still rising.

Grimacing, Ember closed her eyes, praying she wouldn't regret the next words that escaped her lips.

"I still want to *help* you. And for the love of god, I can't understand why. I just... I need to know what actually happened." She sighed. "I know how I became a monster. How did you?"

Ademure blinked, furrowed her brows. Then she dropped onto the bench. Her gaze returned to the northern forest, and a mournful laugh escaped her lips. "Do you actually want to know?"

"Please," Ember said, nodding. "What did you do?"

"I made the mistake of being young and alone."

She took a seat next to her. "What happened?"

"The oracles happened," the princess answered with a scoff. "It'd been four years since I'd seen my brother and father, and the twins were so kind to me. I looked up to them. They showed me everything about what it meant to be an estrella. The ships at the harbor, the tailor for their uniforms, and the soulless computer they used to store the alloys' data."

She focused on the skirt she twisted between her fingers. "When Estrella Estrada stopped me in the hall and asked me what I knew of the alloys, I told him I only knew what he did, which I assumed must've included whatever was on the computer.

"Of course, I assumed incorrectly. Cristian had no idea of even the existence of the database, and he asked me to show it to him. And I didn't think twice." Her voice cracked. "Forty-eight hours later, I was labeled a traitor, and my mother banned technology from the rest of the island in no small part due to my misjudgment."

Ember glimpsed the forest and thought of her own misjudgments, brushing a thumb over her scars. She took in a long, deep breath. "Princess, why me?"

Ademure sniffled. "You are one of the few in this castle with the strength to fight off the estrellas and help me escape. And you are one of the only ones who could do so willingly. Because you know the truth. You've known the truth."

Ember shook her head. "But why is it up to *me*? Sure, I might be strong. But I'm not trained. I can barely control... anything. Even you said that there are others who would do it. So why does the person who has to save you, a princess, need to be the girl that learned about magic yesterday?"

Ademure let out a laugh of bewilderment. "And why do you refuse?"

"Because I don't know you!" Realizing her mistake, Ember lowered her voice. "And I don't owe you."

"Incredible." Ademure eyed her up and down, ire returned to her stare, disgust returned to her lip. "You're so gifted, so powerful. And so heartless."

"I am not."

"Please. You've seen the way they speak to me. The way

they treat me. You've seen who they really are, and still, you're desperate to become one of them."

"I am not!" Tears formed at the corners of Ember's eyes. "I am not," she repeated, quieter this time. She placed her elbows on her knees and rubbed her wrist. Then she closed her eyes and felt as if it would take the strength of Zeus to reopen them.

It took only the voice of a weeping young woman.

"I'm not strong enough," Ademure said. "I'm not smart enough. If not you, then who?"

She hiccuped and rubbed mascara across her cheek, black pooling below her puffy, inset eyes.

It's an act, Ember told herself for the thousandth time, and she wondered when she would begin to believe it.

"It can't be me, Princess."

Overwhelming silence. The clouds on the horizon grew dark, the winds picked up, the last bird quieted. The locket about Ember's neck grew heavy, and she couldn't seem to stop the tears from falling. She gripped her own hands so hard they shook, her knuckles white, and despite focusing her sight on the trees, she couldn't erase the purple-blue-faced little girl from view.

"Ademure," the princess whispered.

Ember blinked. "What?"

"Ademure. Call me Ademure." She sat her chin in her hands and stared at the trees. "Not princess."

"Okay," Ember said before wiping her eyes. "Well, Ademure, you should know, the last time I tried protecting someone, I hurt them instead."

"Your sister."

She glanced at her, then nodded once. "Yes."

"She's not dead, is she?"

Slowly, she shook her head, fearful that if she moved it faster, she'd shake the memories free for Ademure to see. "But others are. And I've hurt hundreds more. I don't want to add to either list."

"I'm already marked for death, Ember. I don't know how to make that plainer to you."

"It's not just you I'm worried about. It's everyone else."

"I don't understand."

Ember kept her hands at her lip. Her breath was warm, shaky, and her palms were hot.

"If I helped you escape, I…" She exhaled and closed her eyes. "I might level this castle and everyone in it."

Ademure's sob came out as a gurgled laugh. "You're exaggerating. You couldn't—"

But the look Ember gave her cut her off.

She tried to laugh again, though this time, it was replaced with cries. "But that's why you're training. You're learning control. You've learned control!"

Ember shook her head without meeting her gaze.

"Stop lying to me, Alloy. You have! I've *seen it*."

"I haven't," she said curtly. "I have more control than I did before, and it's nowhere near enough. I need more training. I want to help you. Believe me, I do. But if I tried to save you now, so many more would need saving." She winced at the sound of her own words. "It's nothing personal."

Ademure stared at her, quiet, tears still dripping down her cheeks like raindrops down a windowpane. And then she cracked a wet, broken smile.

"Nothing personal." She looked down at the skirt that she'd pulled so taut, the threads began to fray. "That clears this all up then. It's not that you're cruel or heartless or incapable. You simply don't do personal. Perfectly sensible."

"I *can't* do personal. I want to, but I can't. It's too risky. I don't even have friends."

"I'm certain that has nothing to do with the risk you claim to present."

Suddenly, Ember was a teenager again, talking to her younger sister. Daphne made a snide remark at her expense, a cruel one but true. And Ember prepared some equally nasty but witty retort. She spit it back and they laughed and laughed. So much so, Ember's stomach cramped from the cackling, her cheeks wet with tears. How she had missed the honesty they had shared. Always brutal but always from a place of love.

The moment was fleeting, however, as Ademure sat in Daphne's place, staring at the tree line.

"I want to have friends," Ember said. "I want my sister back. I want to help you. But none of that can happen if I don't stay to train, if I leave too early."

Ademure looked back at her with a half-curled lip, as if she found the statement amusing, and shook her head. "And what happens if you can't leave at all?"

CHAPTER 22
EMBER

Ember's eyes drifted to the tree line that bordered the northern edge of the courtyard where Damian had told her the nymphs resided.

Cold-blooded killers, she thought. *Only a hundred yards away. And yet, I'm still here.*

Sparks followed the ball into the basket, but they wouldn't leave her hand any other way. She'd tried snapping her fingers, spinning in circles, imagining storms. She'd even tried praying —or at least, sitting in silence with her hands together—but nothing conducted lightning like shooting a basketball.

What was worse was that she could feel the lightning's presence. It was definitely there. But it was as if there was a blanket of something inexplicable dampening her ability to reach it.

She lowered herself on the ground and put her head between her legs.

Ugh. I need a how-to video or a manual.

She remembered the book that had sat at her bedside for a week, untouched. Since that night with Kiva in the bookstore, she couldn't bring herself to touch it again. But she also couldn't ignore the possibility that it might have had the clues she was looking for.

Her hands heated at the thought, and she turned her palms upward. That magic was consistent at least, even if she had no idea what caused it. The heat didn't feel related to the lightning, though the two did seem to coincide. But when she practiced her shooting, there was a rare moment where her hands cooled, even as sparks danced about her fingers.

She sat cross-legged on the asphalt, clasped her hands, and balanced her head on top of them. *Why didn't my parents tell me anything?*

"Sulking much, Seño?"

Damian climbed down from the rafters of the gazebo. Once on the ground, he retightened the rag around his head and shot her a deviant smirk.

"How long have you been there?" she asked.

"How long have you been out here?"

She pursed her lips. "I wasn't sulking."

"Ah. Brooding."

"Thinking."

"Sure. Thinking." He wandered closer to her. "Well, have you *thought* about believing me yet?"

He's acting too, right? she thought. *He's the son of a traitor. Whether Ademure meant to help him or not, his dad got thousands killed.*

But Damian didn't.

"Not yet, then," he said. "But you're closer."

He took a seat on the asphalt a foot away from her. Under the midday sun, Ember thought she could see strands of green hair peeking through his mop of mostly brown, and his sharp neon eyes glinted. This close, it was easier to see he wasn't fully human.

She dropped her voice to a whisper. "For the record, I'm not sold on the estrellas' story either."

"So what do you believe?" He mimicked her whisper. "If you don't believe the estrellas, then you know they intend for you to become their weapon. If you don't believe me, then you don't think they can force you to do that. So do you believe you're stronger than them? That you can overpower them before the seven of them overpower you? That you won't break first? Because I can assure you, you will."

His words didn't sound like a threat; rather they were tinged with pain. True pain. As if he had experienced such a misfortune himself.

It's an act.

"I have to train," she said.

"Each day you train for them is a day wasted for you. You don't honestly believe they would teach you a magic that you could use to escape them? Have they even taught you clocking?"

She frowned. "I don't want to escape. I want to learn control."

"What you want is to never kill."

"Same thing."

"They are not." His irises flared greener, more intense. "You can learn control from most other magicks you meet. Perhaps even I could teach you. Later. But if you don't want to kill again, you'll only do so by leaving. Now."

Heat trailed up her arm, and she met his eyes with her own green gaze. "If I leave now, I could kill everyone. I'm a danger."

His attention drifted to the castle, and his neck grew tense. "My dad always told me you shouldn't let fear rule your life."

She knit her brows, wondering if she should fear him. She didn't.

"That's why I'm training," she said. "If I can learn to

control my powers, then I don't have to worry about unintentionally hurting someone ever again. Then I'll go, I swear."

"And 'then' will be before the war? Before they'll use you?"

"How can they force me to kill for them, Damian? Honestly? I'm the one holding the trigger."

He pressed his lips into a thin line. "I can hear your truth, but I don't know why you believe it to be true."

She thought of the twins, of how they'd asked for only lightning, not killing. Of how they'd held up their end of the deal. And how she hadn't yet held up hers.

She reached for her locket, flipping it side over side, *Ember* to *Slade*. She'd spent so much time trying for lightning, yet the prickle, like static electricity, that played at her fingertips was all she had to show for the skill. And she was sure she knew why.

"Ademure," she said.

"What about her?"

She looked to the empty balcony with a tight chest. It had been a week since the princess had screamed obscenities at her, and she felt no lighter. "The estrellas will really kill her?"

"Most likely."

"Why? She's not a threat. And even if she did what they say she did, what does it change to kill her now?"

Damian furrowed his brow. "Seño, with due respect, I think you still misunderstand the situation."

"Explain it to me, then."

"The truth? It doesn't matter." He shrugged. "It's a ruse. They were always going to kill her anyway."

"That's ridiculous," she said. "The queen is—well... But Nieve is fine. And Sombra is a bitch, but a killer?"

"The princess will die here."

Ember frowned. He seemed so serious.

"Okay," she said. "Assuming you're right, what can I even do to stop it?"

He inclined his head as if the answer was obvious. "Take her with you."

"You think Ademure can fight against the estrellas? You think I can?"

"Make it to the harbor before they know either of you are gone. There's a roughly thirty-minute gap from when Cadeña leaves her room at midnight to when Rodriguez takes his place. The twins are always asleep. Take her then. I can help you."

"I don't know how to sail. We'll be worse than sitting ducks."

"Don't give me your excuses, Seño. You have the freedom to go about the island, correct? If you truly want to rescue her, you will learn how to sail."

She knew he was right; she could learn to sail on her own. And judging by Ozamiz's comments of late, there was even a chance that with her alloy powers she'd actually outrun the estrellas. But she couldn't bring herself to say so.

"You can leave," Damian continued. "You can make it to the harbor. You can sail far away from here and never have to hurt a soul. The only one stopping you is you, Seño."

"I'm not rescuing her," she said with a tone of finality. "And don't tell her I asked about any of this."

His eyes widened, and he shook his head quickly. "I don't speak to the princess."

Her eyes nearly rolled out of her head. "Don't play dumb, Damian. Not with me. I can't read rhythms, but that plan you came up with sounds an awful lot like hers."

He averted his gaze.

She ignored him and looked back to the balcony. "I guess I just don't get it, why you're asking me to leave. Like, what's in it for you? Is getting me to leave a trick? Are you trying to get me killed so you can finish what your dad started?"

"I have nothing against you, Seño. I only want you gone so that the queen doesn't have a weapon—so she can't go to war."

"But how does a Nysan-Agarthan war matter to you? How does getting Ademure out matter to you?"

"It's the queen who *wants* the war with Agartha," he said. "A war that will destroy my home. She will use Princess Ademure's death to start it. She will use you to end it. She cannot be allowed to have what she wants. You or her."

But how does Ademure's death start a war?

"I don't believe you," she said.

He grimaced. "I know."

And they fell silent for a minute. She picked at the grass that lined the asphalt's edge, wondering how much of Cadeña's, the Delfinos', and Ademure's stories were actually true. *She seemed so honest.*

"Your dad was an estrella," Ember said.

"He was."

"You watched your father be put to death."

"I did."

"So is this really about payback, then? You're helping both the queen's weapon and heir escape so that you can get her back for what she did to your dad."

The pained look returned, and Ember could've sworn there was a glisten at the corner of his eye. But he didn't look at her. Only at the balcony.

"Payback isn't the word, Seño."

A breeze passed through, flipping down his rag so that she could make out the tip of his pointed ears. The birds chirped and she wondered if that was what the rhythms sounded like to him, what her own rhythms sounded like now. And the sun shined down, highlighting every bit of anxiety in his face.

"Why don't you help her, Damian? If Ademure's in as much trouble as you say she is, why aren't you trying to protect her yourself?"

At last, he looked at her. "I'm doing all that I can."

He pushed himself off the ground and held out a hand. Tentatively, she took it, but when she stood, he didn't immediately let go.

"I hope you decide to leave soon, Seño. For your sake," his eyes flicked to the balcony, "and hers."

Guilt was a gluttonous creature. It ate at her relentlessly—from her morning break through her afternoon training—and still, it was hungry. So the moment Ozamiz ended lessons was the moment Ember began her trek toward the harbor. She'd only have an hour or so before dinner, but she had to feed the beast.

It was a sweaty walk, and she was sure her cheeks were flushed, but her hamster wheel of a brain at least made the walk short.

"Alloy Slade," said a booming voice. The giant in all gray stood from behind his desk.

"Admiral Guerrero." She crossed the building to shake his massive hand. "It's good to see you again."

"And you! I was wondering when we might see you next. How is el Alcázar? And how are you enjoying the island?"

"Both are incredible," she said as she plastered a false smile. "But I've been itching to get out to sea. You mentioned before that I might be able to sail once in a while. Is that offer still on the table?"

"Of course!" He gestured toward the door on the opposite side of the base. "Do you know how?"

She nodded. She didn't, but she didn't need any extra eyes on her.

"And you remember which ships are the estrellas'?" Guerrero asked.

Another nod.

"Then all you need to watch for are the skies," he said. "The weather is quick to change, and you don't want to face a Nysan storm." He sniffed the air. "Though, I believe today you'll be fine."

She removed her hand from her neck, realizing she didn't remember placing it there. Then she nodded again and pushed through the door.

Though she had never done particularly well in school, she could see the ships were an engineering marvel. For one, they had to have been baking in the sun all day, and yet when she stepped aboard the middle ship, the metal was not even warm. For another, the structure was incredibly streamlined. She walked the deck—at least three football fields long—dragging her hand about the molded railing, noting how each end came to a point so sharp it could prick a finger, yet the slim design didn't curb the space on deck. It was still wide enough to carry large cargo if ever the need be.

At the top of the ship was the helm, then a set of stairs, then a covered seating area, and, at the center, a large mast and sail. And between the seats and the sail was a hatch that Ember was too curious to ignore. She lifted the hatch and dropped below to find four compartments with eight separate mattresses, each room stocked with a bathroom, a porthole on one side, and a kitchenette.

She looked out the porthole at the other two ships. They were identical in every way but color: her ship was silver with a green rose insignia painted on the sides, and the others were just the inverse. Clearly, these ships were all the product of manipulation—there were no visible attachments anywhere. But that didn't take away from the level of artistry it must've required to craft the sleek railings, mold the sturdy helm, or even paint each petal of each flower on the hull. The modernity was unmatched by anything else she'd seen on the island.

Realizing she'd already spent twenty minutes fawning over the ship, she quickly made her way back above deck and behind the helm.

"*Maior*," she said in the direction of the sail.

A gust of wind knocked her into the wheel. Once the wind passed, she looked back. The rope anchoring the boat to the dock hadn't even become taut.

Why didn't that work? she wondered, and then she remembered her lessons. *I need a perpetuating spell, don't I?*

"Ugh," she said aloud, before dropping to her knees. She had only begun perpetuating spells a week ago, and she was terrible at them. It was the first time Ozamiz had been unimpressed with her magic since she'd gotten here. She couldn't keep a breeze blowing, much less the windstorm needed to move this thing—and that assumed that a windstorm was the only magic it took to move this thing.

She set her forehead against the bottom of the wheel and looked at the deck below. *Awesome. I feel* so *much better.*

Then she turned to the purpling sky. The sun would be below the horizon in a matter of an hour, and she would be late to dinner. After what Nieve had done for her last week, she wasn't yet willing to make the estrella upset.

I'll come back, she decided, toying with the chain around her neck. *I can't guarantee anything will come out of this, but I'll be back.*

Ember stepped outside the naval base and stared at the turrets that hardly peeked over the dunes in the distance. The muscles in her legs twitched at the thought of a six-mile walk. Her stomach growled its protest.

This is gonna suck.

With all the mental strength she could muster, she put one foot forward. Then another. Doing her best to keep all thoughts of the sweat dripping down her back, her face, and her stomach, out of her mind. Instead, she imagined herself in a steaming shower, drying herself off with a plush towel, and burying herself deep beneath the covers—

Sand spewed in her face.

"What the fuck!" she sputtered.

"Ember?"

Her heart thumped. She wiped back the sweat on her forehead into her sweatier curls and cleared her eyes as best she could, enough to confirm she was right about the culprit's identity.

"Kiva."

The man stood with one leg over his landsailer, fresh ski tracks carved behind him. The trail looked like it had come from town, exactly in the direction she was heading.

"What are you doing out here?" he asked.

"Trying to regain my sight." She plucked a few stray grains out of her tear ducts.

"Oh my gods." He hooked his goggles over the handles and stepped away from his sailer. "I didn't realize. I'm so sorry. I didn't expect anyone to be out here. No one ever really is at this time of the day."

He reached for her face, but she pushed away his arm. He frowned. "How can I make it up to you?"

"I'm fine." She shook out her hair so that her curls and the sand caught in them fell loose about her face. "Don't worry about it. I need to get back home soon anyway."

He followed her gaze to the darkening sky, then to his land-sailer. "Let me take you back."

"No," she said quickly, her face flushing at the memory of last time. "No, thank you. I can walk fine on my own."

"You can't be serious. It's a two-hour walk at least. C'mon, please, let me take you home."

"No," she said louder. "Getting sick doesn't appeal to me tonight."

"You won't get sick if you're behind the handles."

"I don't know how to landsail."

"I can teach it to you."

With the fading sun came stronger winds, blowing her hair across her face and drawing back his hair from his twinkling eyes. The air around them grew cool. He smiled softly, and her heartbeat quickened.

"Fine," she said. "But I'm on a time crunch."

"We'll be back before you know it."

He pulled another pair of goggles out of the compartment beneath the seat and handed them to her. Then he lifted the sailer upright and tapped the space in front of him. Ember chewed the inside of her lip, looking at him a moment, again wondering:

Why are you being nice to me?

The moment she thought it, she shoved it away, because in this moment, it didn't matter why. Right now, he could keep whatever secrets he wanted. If she intended on coming to the harbor more often, it would only benefit her to learn how to landsail. So she stepped over the ski and sat down, placing her hands on either handle.

But when Kiva set his hands on hers, she jumped.

"First," he said into her ear, making it difficult for her to regain control of her pulse, "you'll want to open the sails."

He turned her left hand over the handlebar. With a click, the sails unfurled behind them, catching the wind and forcing her to strain her legs so that the ski wouldn't topple over.

"Then," he continued, "you'll need to manipulate the sand. Can you do that without sinking us?"

She nodded, focusing on the beach just below them—a difficult task, considering. But she said, "*Undu*," and the area became fluid.

And her foot sunk.

As she struggled to pull her leg from the sand's depths, her knee buckled, and the ski tilted. She yelped as she slid sideways, gripping onto the handles for dear life, while more and more of her calf dropped below the white surface. But before she fell off the vehicle completely, something wrapped around her waist and hoisted her squarely back onto the seat of the ski, freeing her from the quicksand's clutches.

"You will do anything to get out of landsailing, won't you?" Kiva said, still holding onto her.

Her face burned hotter than her palms ever had. "You can let go of me now," she said. "Let me dive in head first this time."

He laughed. "Not yet. You nearly had it. Your charm was just a little wide."

Huh. That's interesting. Ozamiz had never said that to her before.

"What do you mean, 'wide'?" she asked. "Not to brag or anything, but I'm pretty good at hitting a target."

"You did hit your target. And everything else around it." He tapped the surface around the ski with his foot. "It's not an uncommon problem, though most magicks don't have the natural strength to sink *all* of it. But I've shrunk the manipulated surface area to only what's below and in front of us. We should be fine now."

She raised a brow. Then with her foot, she too tapped the same surface, just to be sure. The sand was solid.

"What?" he said. "Don't trust me?"

She turned back to look at him—his unkept hair, his oh-so green eyes. Her own eyes dropped to his lips. They were drawn up into a mischievous smile and so close, she could've...

"What's next?" she asked, clearing her throat, and returning her gaze to the open sand.

He pulled her curls off of her neck and over one shoulder, sending chills across her back and more heat to her cheeks.

"What are you doing?" she said.

"Preparing myself. After that bit of manipulation, I'm afraid of what you'll do to the wind, and I'd rather not have a mouthful of hair for dinner if that's alright."

She rolled her eyes and nodded—mostly in an effort to distract herself from his touch. "Why can't I push the ski with the sand?"

"You can, but it's inefficient. It takes a lot of magic to use only sand or only the wind. The best magicks use both. You get twice the output for as much of the magic. But using both can be a lot to handle. So, before you manipulate the wind, focus on liquifying only the sand in front of you and manipulating only the breeze that blows into your sails." He set his other hand on the center of her handles. "I'm ready when you are."

Ember looked at the sand ahead, her eyes zeroed in on the castle in the distance. With a deep exhale, she leaned forward, and shouted into the wind "*Maior!*"

A mammoth gust shoved the landsailer, and they were off.

For about ten feet.

They skidded to a stop.

"What happened?" she asked.

Kiva wet his finger, then raised it in the air as if he were testing the breeze. "Perpetuate the charm. Don't let it terminate. Try again."

She did as he said and tried again. They made it twenty feet more.

"Ugh," she said. "I can't perpetuate charms. This will take us forever."

"The price you pay for not letting me take you back."

"I've changed my mind. Take the wheel. I'll survive."

He shook his head. "Offer's expired. Besides, even if you terminate every spell on the way back, you'll still arrive there in half the time than if you had walked. Keep going."

She groaned, but she tried again. And again. And again.

And annoyingly, he was right in the end; the beach on which they'd met finally came into view. The moment she spotted it, she parked the contraption—she could walk the rest of the way. She slid from the seat and let Kiva reclaim the handles, and it was then she realized just how much her core burned with all of the connections she had tapped and the magic she'd used. She would be more than a little sore tomorrow. Training would be brutal.

"You're getting better," he said as he stepped off the sailer and removed his goggles. "You've obviously been working hard at your lessons."

"Thanks," she muttered, already dreading putting her aching body through Ozamiz's conditioning.

"When will I see you next?"

Her heart stopped—or maybe it was her breath—and she began searching his face for...well, anything.

Jesus, woman, she told herself, *hold it together.*

"I don't know," she said. "Maybe in a week?"

He stepped closer to her, and her heart jumped into her throat.

"Really? A week?" he said, then sighed. "Well, if it's what I can get, I'll take it. I'm looking forward to it." And he smiled.

She didn't.

What do you really want, Kiva?

"You know," he said, tucking his hands into his pockets, "last time we were out here, I made you cry."

She looked into the town, then at his landsailer. There were a lot of things that had made her upset that night, but he hadn't been one of them. "You didn't—"

"I did. I was clearly insensitive about your parents. I'm sorry for that."

That sent a bolt of heat to her palms and tears to her eyes. "They're not my parents."

He looked at her in silence, mouth shrugged, brow raised. She didn't blame him. She didn't quite buy the statement herself.

"Thanks," she said, "but you didn't need to apologize." She turned her attention to the ocean, the sun kissing the horizon. "I have to go."

"Wait," he called behind her, stopping her before she'd gotten far. "I almost forgot."

He reached into his pockets and, with two fingers, retrieved a folded piece of paper. He slipped it into her palm.

"What is it?" she asked.

"The lyrics you need for clocking. Like manipulation, you want to connect with what you're slowing down. Start with humming, and then work up to singing, so you don't wear yourself out. If you don't know the notes, just listen to the birds—they're pretty good. And promise me that if your family does end up throwing you una Celebración de la Innata, you'll act surprised."

She stared at their hands. "Um, I promise. You really didn't have to do this though."

"Yeah, I did. Honestly, I should've given them to you last time. There was really no good reason not to—it's not a secret or anything. Sorry, again."

She took her hand slowly from his, his touch still warm on her skin. Then, she tucked the paper and her hands into her shorts' pockets. "Well, bye, Kiva. See you soon."

He grinned, his chestnut hair perfectly framing his sparkling smile. "See you soon, Ember." Like last time, he swung a leg over his landsailer and was off before she could say anything else.

She pulled out the paper, flipping it over without unfolding it. And not for the first time, she felt strange. Like she couldn't quite comprehend what had happened. Like the entire interaction had been artificial.

He had this on him the entire time? she thought. *Did he plan this?*

CHAPTER 23

EMBER

Despite spending every bit of free time she had at the harbor or in her room clocking, Ember went another week without making progress. And, to add to that frustration, the weather had canceled this evening's lessons and eliminated any possibility she might have had to shoot hoops while pretending to practice lightning.

She dropped the paper for the thousandth time that day and, despite having the lyrics committed to memory, hummed her heart out. It fluttered to the ground without hesitation.

She glowered at the monsoon outside her window before dropping back on her bed, head at the foot of it, and staring at the ceiling. What was she to do for the next five hours before dinner?

You could figure out how to save Ademure.

She focused on the intricate detailing on the frame of her canopy. The little waves and boats and sails that were etched into the wood, like even they were trying to leave the island.

Is it even possible? she wondered. *Assuming she's not acting, and assuming I somehow mastered perpetuating spells and knew where to go and could make it out of the castle undetected...could I save her? Have I learned enough?*

She lifted her hand, wriggling her fingers in the chandelier's candlelight. She couldn't see the electricity, but she could feel it. It was always there, made more obvious by days like today—crawling on her fingertips, tickling the back of her neck, hiding beneath the surface. *And I don't know how to keep it there. Or let it go.*

She dropped her hand. Her attention returned to the etchings in the frame. *No. I haven't learned nearly enough.*

She sat up and looked at her nightstand, where next to an unnaturally green shell rested *Magick Martyrs: The Slades*. The faces of the couple on the front were frozen in everlasting smiles, begging her to learn more. Taunting her to delve into their cheery lives. Mocking her for spending so much time concerned with the lives of those around her— with whether today would be the day she added another scar. All because *they* hadn't taught her anything. She clenched her fists. Just looking at her parents made her palms warm.

But they aren't my parents.

A truth that she'd had to constantly remind herself of since visiting the bookstore. Because they couldn't be her parents. She'd never had parents. Legal guardians? Yes. Procreators? Sure. Parents? Not even a little.

Infamous, the Delfinos had said. Her procreators were infamous. And not for abandoning their child. Not for leaving her behind with nothing. Not for recklessly letting her become who she became.

They left you alone and in the dark, she told herself.

She wanted to believe otherwise. She had believed otherwise, for a time. That they weren't bad people—or good people, even—but neutral. But the older she'd gotten, the harder it became to believe in fantasies.

You don't have to read it.

The real death knell was the lack of documentation. No records of a Slade family in the metroplex and no one to claim Ember meant she'd gone straight to the foster system, where she remained for the next sixteen years, until she finally ran away. The hospital hadn't even known her parents' names when she'd been found. She'd lived her whole life believing she'd come from thin air.

You don't owe them anything.

Now, she not only had names but pictures and a biography as well.

She grabbed the book. Wiped the light sheen of dust off the cover. Thumbed the corner of the first page.

They. Left. You.

Why?

She opened it.

...Ana Isabela Romero was born to Carlos and Grecia Romero, of Romero Raft Enterprises fame. A true Romero heiress, young Ana spent most of her days on the ocean, using her family's various vessels to ride the waves and—as she grew older—explore the world...

Ember flipped forward a few pages.

...Victor Anthony Slade was born to Sandra and Michael Slade in Anqas Picchu, Peru. Because he lived in such an isolated area for years, there isn't much known about Victor's early life before he moved to Tokyo...

She turned a few more.

...After graduating with a degree in magicism at Lemuria-Kumari Daigaku (The University of Lemuria at Kumari), Victor moved back to Anqas Picchu to begin his research on Peruvian spells and magical items. But soon arrived the new girl, and Victor didn't stay for long...

And a few more.

...The couple returned to Nysa so that Ana, now Ana Slade, could inherit Romero Raft Enterprises. But the passing of the estate was less than quiet. The Crown knew Ana was not as bound to tradition as her parents were—in her hands, that wealth was a threat.

Not to mention the souls of the company she kept were less than pure. Except for the Caldwells, her friends were mostly outsiders to the Magick Realm. The Crown was especially concerned with Victor, knowing so little about him...

And she didn't stop. The minutes turned to hours as Ember learned more about the Crown's surveillance of Ana's business and Victor's research. She learned of her parents' friendship with the Caldwells, Leon and Liliana. She learned that Leon was a long-time counselor of the Agarthan king and Liliana was his Nysan-born wife—as well as the author of the book itself. And she learned that the four of them had increasingly involved themselves in the political affairs of their nation. This was especially intriguing considering the simultaneous, drastic change in the political landscape: the Nysan queen and Agarthan king had married, uniting the nations as one Agartha and against a common enemy.

...Surprising no one, the king and queen declared war on the Soulless Realm.

What was surprising was that at the same time, Lemuria had begun capturing and experimenting on Japanese soulless, and the Nysan-Agarthan Crown was backing the efforts.

So Ana started using her inheritance to fund soulless rights protests. And as one would expect, the Crown was not amused...

Ember looked up. *No. That can't be right*, she thought. *Charity work? That's not who they were.*

But then she looked back at the page, sickened. *Right?*

...No one knows who or what started the fire. But when the Slade mansion's flames died down on 12 January, so did the protests...

She closed the book. Stared at the wall. Thought of all the raindrops she could—a deluge to challenge the storm outside her window, a flood on par with the torrent cascading down her face. She wiped her eyes. It wasn't enough. No amount of water could douse this heat.

January 12. Two days after her birthday. One day after she'd been found at the hospital.

"They knew," she said aloud. "They knew they were going to die."

The author knew it too.

How? Why?

And why didn't the author mention me?

She reopened the book, flipping and skimming through the pages to make sure she hadn't missed it. But after three times through, she finally set the book aside for good. She hadn't missed it; she was never mentioned. Ana's pregnancy was never mentioned.

Thunder rumbled, shaking the chandelier, and she looked at the clock on the wall. It was nearly dinner time. In fifteen minutes she was to share a meal with the queen who had murdered her parents. To eat with the Crown that had orphaned her. That had abandoned her. That had allowed *her* to become the murderer.

She left her room, rubbing the prickle on the back of her neck.

Thankfully, Ember was too familiar with her anger to make the mistake of talking, so she sat in silence through most of the meal. Unfortunately, however, she dined with the twins and the queen only, which diminished her ability to remain quiet as the night went on.

"Profe Ozamiz says you've dramatically improved."

She looked up from her mango sorbet to see Nieve looking back at her with innocent eyes. "She says you're the most talented student she's ever had."

"That's kind of her," Ember mumbled. The dessert melted off her heated spoon.

"Something wrong, Alloy? Is your dessert not to your liking?"

She glanced at the queen who sat haughty in her chair at the head of the table, arms crossed and shoulders back, disgust etched on her lip—nothing out of the ordinary, but it still made Ember seethe.

"No." She looked back to Nieve. "It's delicious." To prove a point—and to prevent her from having to talk more—she shoveled a spoonful of lukewarm mango juice into her mouth and smiled.

Sombra pointed a spoon at her. "Are you certain this doesn't pertain to the book you were reading all afternoon?"

"Sombra!" Nieve said.

"What? I'm only asking." She turned from her sister toward

the queen. "Our alloy got her hands on a copy of *Magick Martyrs*. She blew through it in a few hours."

Ember's eyes widened with realization. *So they did know about my parents. They knew what happened to them.*

And to think she had planned to avoid the topic.

The queen's expression grew strained. The muscles in her neck tensed, and she moved forward in her seat, as if she was about to say something but decided against it.

"Am I right, Alloy?" Sombra said. "This is about *Magick Martyrs?*"

The hairs on Ember's neck rose. "Yes."

Esmerelda hammered her fist on the table, sending a fork and knife clattering to the ground. Sombra caught the glass of water before it toppled.

"Majestad, you must understand—"

The queen's raised hand cut Nieve's words short. Her eyes met Ember's, donning a glower Ember hadn't seen since Ademure had last dined with them.

"Well?" Esmerelda's growl of a voice rumbled with the storm. "What did you think?"

Ember knew she shouldn't respond without taking some time to consider the consequences, that whatever retort was top of mind would only throw fuel onto this already sweltering flame, and she absolutely had to avoid that outcome.

But damn. She was tempted.

Raindrops.

"Out with it, Alloy!" the queen yelled. "You must've had some opinion. Tell me, what did you think?"

Lightning cracked. Heeding Nieve's worried look, Ember slowly set down her spoon and spoke softly, though her reserved tone couldn't quite hide her rage. *Raindrops.* "It was enlightening."

"It was a lie," Esmerelda hissed, slamming the table again,

leaning over her plate to ensure Ember heard every syllable that bled off her lips. "Libel against the Crown. You must not believe a word of it."

Thunder rattled the windows, the floor, the table. And when those all settled, the room was laden with tense silence. The queen sat motionless, waiting, the green rose of her diadem seemingly growing thorns. The prickle at Ember's neck grew just as sharp.

She inhaled deeply and clasped her hot palms together. "So, my parents weren't activists?"

"Of course not," Sombra said with a mouth full of food. "The author is a traitor."

"Sombra!" Nieve shouted again.

"What? She was going to learn eventually." She returned her attention to Ember, waving her spoon about aimlessly. "Caldwell wrote the book as a rallying cry, meant to unify all the traitors. It could use some fact-checking."

Ember rolled her neck, but it did nothing to soothe the spark. "Traitors," she repeated. "Like Princess Ademure?"

"Worse," the oracle said. "Traitors to magickkind itself." She took another bite of sorbet.

"They were renegades," Esmerelda followed. "Soulless sympathizers who spread heinous rumors about our former allies. They also curiously failed to acknowledge just how many magicks had their livelihoods *destroyed* by the magic-less creatures. Regardless, they revolted against us, planned to burn the Magick Realm to the ground—and your parents captained them."

Ember lowered her brow. *So, that's who they really were*, she thought. *That's the truth. Of course, it is.*

Though she was strongly questioning the queen's ability to properly identify traitors.

Raindrops.

"Is that why you had my parents killed?"

Nieve's glare whipped to her. "Alloy!"

The queen waved off her estrella and scoffed. "Please. We did nothing of the sort."

Heat surged down Ember's back. The vein on her forehead throbbed. Vision blurred as did the narratives in her mind. It didn't make sense. Her parents had been activists. Her parents had been rebels. Her parents had been killed. Her parents had died by accident.

Someone was lying—someone *had* to be lying—but who?

Surely it was the author. Her parents wouldn't have helped anyone, let alone *defy the Crown* to help anyone. They hadn't been those people. They couldn't have been. No, they'd been the people who'd dumped their one-day-old baby in a foreign world with nothing more than a fucking blanket and locket.

Because they were killed.

But what did that matter? They'd known they were going to die, and yet they'd told her nothing. Left her with nothing. They couldn't have written a note? They couldn't have explained who she was or why they left? Why not tell her anything?

Because they knew the consequences.

But the book didn't even mention her. Such a crucial part of her parents' lives, completely omitted. It was an obvious lie. And for what? What could possibly be the reason the book didn't mention her?

Esmerelda took an apathetic sip of wine. Sombra had folded her hands behind her empty dish, and Nieve kept hers beneath the table. Both kept a side-eye on Ember, but neither gave anything away.

I don't know, she thought. *But wouldn't it be wonderful to find out?*

She locked her glower on the queen who was sitting to her

right, and because, for the first time in a long time, she didn't fear the consequences, whispered, "Sure."

Esmerelda dropped the glass from her lips. "Excuse me?"

"Sure," Ember repeated louder. The haze didn't clear. "They died coincidentally."

"Watch it, Alloy," Nieve said from across the table. "You're losing yourself."

"Their deaths were an accident, Alloy," the queen sneered. "Don't get it confused."

The sparks at Ember's fingertips were rampant. *Why not confess? Why continue to lie about something so obviously true? The book said—*

The book also said your parents were good people.

Still, she couldn't shake the fact that what killed them was:

"An accident?" she said aloud. "A fire? Against two well-trained magicks?" She laughed. "Oh, well then. Sorry for my confusion."

"That's enough," Nieve said, now standing.

"No, it's not nearly enough," Ember said, rising from her seat. She turned to Esmerelda whose grip was on the brink of shattering her glass. "My parents are dead because of you. I was robbed of my family, my life, because of you. And you're forcing me to defend you?"

"Alloy," Nieve warned.

"No," Esmerelda said to her vice-captain while she remained seated. "Let her say what she wants to say."

Eyes angry but tearless, chest rising but steady. Her mind was a desert, but Ember forced herself to meet the queen's challenging gaze. *The book could be lying,* she reminded herself. Yet the reminder didn't stop her from saying, "I'm alone because of you."

Even the thunder quieted. The storm became a drizzle. The

winds became a breeze. Breath—mostly Ember's—the only sound in the hall.

The queen ran her finger around the edge of her wine glass. "And you think, that the daughter of two traitors deserves more?"

There it was. That feeling on the nape of her neck. The spark.

It burst.

And it no longer mattered who was lying.

Her vision crisped so that she made out every jewel on the queen's diadem. Her hearing heightened so that she heard every breath Her Majesty took. The smell of wine flooded her nose. The taste of wine stained her tongue. The electricity that usually resided in her hands surged through her limbs, through her stomach, chest, back, head. It had been so long since she last felt this strong.

A month since the train. Since the tree. Since the men in black.

Six years since the kitchen. Since the bruises. Since Daphne.

In this moment, she remembered all of it.

Infamous, my ass.

She raised a hand, pointing two fingers at the queen.

And then, Nieve began to sing a song. The one from in the town, that plagued Ember's memories. The tune she had the lyrics to, that Kiva had given her. The melody she had spent hours upon hours rehearsing, memorizing. The clocking song.

Ember slowed. Or the world around her sped up.

Sombra's movements were quick, her raven hair the only detail she could pick out in the blur. It was a strange feeling, being clocked. Her mind still kept what she thought was proper time, but her senses, her muscles, her reactions were all delayed. And before she could do anything else, she was sitting back in her chair, her hands bound behind her back.

Nieve's song became a hum, then faded, and Ember returned to the present. Esmerelda and Sombra had left the room, and Nieve stood less than a foot in front of her, alone.

"Let's have a chat," she said, smiling.

Ember said nothing. Her muscles were weakened, her senses dulled. The heat fled most of her body, leaving only her palms hot to the touch.

"I thought that by now you would understand." Nieve bent down, hands on knees, to meet her at eye-level.

The pounding in her skull was constant, violent. Nauseating. "She killed my parents, didn't she?"

"She did not. Your parents' deaths were a tragic accident. No more. No less. But if you don't make amends with Su Majestad soon, your death won't be." Nieve sat a hand on her knee and forced herself into her line of sight.

The throbbing, searing ache in her head was making it hard to concentrate, but Ember brought herself to look at the oracle anyway. "You don't actually think I fear death, do you?" Beneath the cloth that tied her arms, every scar pulsed about her wrists. "I know him too well. We go way back."

Nieve's smile disappeared for once, and her eyes were colder than snow—an expression that seemed to come to her more naturally.

"I don't mean to threaten you, Alloy," she said. "Sombra and I are on your side. But truthfully, you belong to the Nysan Crown now. I'm sorry; there is no changing that. The only decision that remains is whether you embrace your future here as a servant, or as a prisoner. Fortunately, that decision is yours."

"Is there a difference?"

"That tongue will get you killed," she snapped. "Had I not stepped in on your behalf, it would've done so tonight."

Ember scoffed. "Give me a break. You're saying I should be thanking you?"

"I'm saying you don't know half as much as you think you do. Keep running your mouth, and I won't always be able to protect you from our queen."

"And why should I worry about her?" Her curls fell into her face as she fought her restraints. "I thought Fate was in control. You said Fate *needed* me."

Frowning at her like she was a disobedient dog, Nieve walked behind her, resting a hand on the knot that bound her wrists.

"You're bright, Alloy. The princess is too, undeniably so. *Reditio.*" The knot came undone, and she moved her hands to the back of the chair, sending a chill across Ember's neck. "I honestly do not want you to face a similar end, whether you fear it or not. Fate *does* need you."

She knelt down behind her and whispered in her ear. "*Evorto.*"

Fuck! Ember dropped to the ground; pain jolted up her spine. She looked over her shoulder to see what remained of her chair—and found nothing. It was completely in pieces. Broken, splintered, blackened pieces. The stench was overwhelming. The odor of a chair that would never be manipulated again.

Destruction magic.

"But I fear that I must also warn you," Nieve said as she bent over the debris. She tossed Ember a piece of charred wood. "Though Fate needs you, do not test her. Her need is not irreplaceable."

CHAPTER 24
EMBER

"Alloy Slade, would you please slow down?" Ozamiz said. "This isn't a conditioning session. You won't last the rest of the morning at this rate."

But Ember continued sprinting alongside the incline of the manipulated hill, then pushing off and jumping to the side of another. Then she changed directions in an instant, cutting back toward the castle, racing between the hills like they were defenders, like she was back in high school—like this was playoffs, and she needed a basket. She had to score. She had to win. *Drive.*

"Did you hear me, Alloy? You're not warm yet. You'll hurt yourself!"

Ember pressed harder, planted harder, using the sand underneath for traction. She treated the elevation as if it were flat ground, not letting up any speed and allowing her ankles to take the brunt of the work. She knew her joints were withstanding impact after brutal impact. It didn't matter. She didn't care.

She ran faster, cut quicker. Breath ragged. She turned the

last mound, the sharpest corner of the drill. Her quads ached as she climbed. Her calves throbbed as she descended. But it didn't stop her. *You can't let anything stop you.*

"Ember Slade!"

Her ankle rolled, and she yelped.

Her hip hit the ground first. Her shoulder pulled as she tried, and failed, to catch the rest of her torso. Finally, her head met the sand, and she lay there. As she regained the breath that had been knocked out, she rolled to her back and stared at the impeccably blue sky. The sun had barely cleared the trees. The birds had hardly begun singing. There wasn't a cloud in sight.

A perfect day in paradise, she mused.

Ozamiz blocked her view. "Just what in Pan's name did you think you were doing?"

Still on her back, Ember pulled a knee to her chest as if that would soothe her throbbing ankle. "Sorry, Profe. I was distracted."

She winced as the tutor grabbed her calf, twisting it to inspect the injury. "Hm. Just a tweak," Ozamiz said. "It will hardly swell." Ember winced again when she dropped the leg. "Consider yourself lucky. Distractions are deadly...and unlike you."

Her eyes fixed on Ember like she was studying her, tracing every twitch in her cheek, every wrinkle of her eyes, trying to read what was underneath it all. Ember shifted under the gaze.

"What has you so preoccupied?" Ozamiz asked at last.

"Nothing," she said quickly. She pushed herself to sit upright and gently squeezed the outside of her ankle, biting her lip. *It's good enough to walk on*, she thought. *I can still train.* She carefully set her hurt foot flat on the sand and moved to one knee—

"Don't you even think about it. We're done for today."

"What? Why? It's fine. I'm fine!" She forced pressure on her ankle and shakily made her way to her feet, shifting her weight between legs. "Seriously, Profe. My ankle is good."

"Your head is not," Ozamiz said. She knelt to the ground, touching her palm to the sand. "*Reditio.*"

The green hills lowered like the swells of a tide ebbing back into the sand-filled ocean of the courtyard. When she was done, the space looked untouched.

"Profe, please," Ember said, stance unsteady. "I can continue to train."

The tutor shook her head. "We can train when you heal. It shouldn't take more than a couple days. And we don't need to aggravate your injury when you're not even an apprentice yet. Was it the oracles?"

Her eyes widened.

Ozamiz dropped her voice. "You're easier to read than a book. If you don't learn to better control your actions, you'll never be able to hide your true intentions from them."

Shit shit shit, Ember thought, but she spoke as naturally as was possible. "My intentions?"

"Well you don't actually intend on becoming an estrella, correct? You only mean to learn enough about your connection to control it, then get far away from here?"

She stood still. Frozen. She searched her mind for when she had told Ozamiz any of this, or even hinted at it, but they never discussed anything but fighting techniques and combative spells. "Are you part-nymph?"

Every one of her tutor's muscles contracted as she threw back her head and laughed. Ember didn't know how to react to that. Her tutor hardly showed any emotion ever, much less pure unadulterated joy.

"Alloy, please." Her tutor wiped a tear from her eye as she caught her breath. "I've worked with you six hours a day, every day, for a month. You think I don't know you? I see how you're slow to jab, to kick. I see how you consider your surroundings before each spell you cast. Your every breath is precise. Every hand wave is accurate. And I hear you're at the docks nearly every hour you're not with me. None of the other estrellas of the last decade train with such passion."

"And you think that means I won't become one?"

"Yes. You've seen what magic can do. Lived it. You would never use your connection..." Ozamiz bit her lip and gestured her head toward the castle "...how *they* want you to."

Ember looked at the castle doors, expecting any moment now for the twins to appear. They didn't, and there was no reason for them to, but that didn't relieve any of her apprehension.

"I'm sorry, Profe. I'm not sure what you're talking about. I'm only here to become an estrella."

"There now, that's better," Ozamiz said. "I almost believed you this time. Although, you might keep your hands in your pockets. You like to fidget."

With heated cheeks, Ember removed her hand from her necklace, not remembering how it got there. "I'm serious, Profe. I want to become an estrella."

"Ah, too much. Now you're too stiff. Loosen your jaw, and look me in the eyes. Like you're telling me a story."

Ember did as her tutor said. She looked her in the eyes, loosened her jaw, and put her hands into her pockets. And when her tutor smiled wryly, she remembered. *Unusual* she had called her. *She's known all along.*

So, with a furrowed brow, she whispered, "Are they why you haven't taught me clocking?"

Ozamiz gave her a single nod. "They want to ensure your loyalty first. Before you learn a skill so formidable."

"And I haven't yet learned it..." She looked away, then

cleared her throat. "Do they know, then? What you know, I mean."

"I suppose they know what you want. But they do not understand why you want it. Even if they pretend to. They do not know that you could leave today."

She glanced at the empty balcony that overlooked the courtyard. Then the empty gazebo that faced the northern forest. There was rain on her skin. Smoke in her nose. Screams.

"But I can't leave today. I haven't mastered lightning yet. I have to keep training with you, at least until something clicks."

Ozamiz narrowed her eyes. "I have no problem continuing your training. You still have much to learn. But I do believe it's disingenuous to say that you need to control your lightning in order to leave."

"It's not." Ember wrapped her fingers about her wrist as she remembered last night. A book and a dinner conversation. With hardly any provocation, without a care for the life it would've cost, she had almost added another scar. Had she been in less powerful company, she could've added three.

She let go, allowing the color to return to her paling hand. "Will you tell them what you know? Since you work for them?"

Her tutor quirked a brow. "I was hired to train you. I'm not being compensated for anything more." She turned her attention to the castle doors and frowned. "And a lot has changed in the seven years since I last trained an alloy. I'm not certain I'm compensated enough as it is."

"What's changed?"

Ozamiz's gaze stayed on the doors a second longer. Then she smirked at her pupil with eyes reflecting the warmth of the rising sun. "It's students like you that make teaching worthwhile, you know. When I see you learn, I see hope. I see an entire future for the Magick Realm. But we all must be of sound mind, equal parts zealous and imperturbable, for such desires to come to fruition." She looked down at her ankle. "Don't go stupid on me."

～

Someone knocked at Ember's door.

"Alloy," Nieve said. "Profe Ozamiz told me about what happened this morning. Mind if I come in?"

Ankle propped on a pillow, covered in ice, Ember wasn't sure she could say no. She hadn't seen Nieve since last night and she didn't want to see her now. Regardless, she knew she had to be nice. She needed the estrellas to let her stay. *As a servant, not a prisoner.*

"Sure," she said finally.

Nieve walked in carrying a bowl of diced pineapple, a cup of mango juice, and a fresh bag of ice. She set the pineapple and juice on the nightstand, then went to her ankle to replace the half-melted bag.

"You really don't have to do that." Ember shifted to sit up straighter and took a sip of juice. "It's a minor sprain at most. I won't need to ice it for much longer."

The oracle finished fixing the new bag in place and smiled. "It's fine. I'm not bothered. Besides," she pointed to her own forehead, "I needed to return the favor." When Ember stared blankly, Nieve asked, "You don't remember?"

Ember shook her head.

"How unfortunate. Do you mind if I sit?"

"Go ahead."

She took a seat at the edge of the bed, near Ember's waist. Ember squirmed what little she could away, but they remained much too close together. Nieve didn't seem to care.

"I'm sorry, Alloy, for last night."

Ember choked on the mango juice.

"I fear I came off as harsh," Nieve continued. "Like a warden and not a sister." The twin set a hand on her knee. "We are your family, I hope you realize. It's not just Nysa, or Su Majestad, or Fate that needs you, but the estrellas and me."

Ember did her best to not recoil at the touch, but she hardly tried to contain her laughter. "Sombra needs me?"

The corner of Nieve's mouth lifted. "She won't admit as much, but it's true. She and the others, like I, want you to feel as if you belong with us, because you do. I know not all of us have been the most welcoming." Her eyes drifted to the nightstand. "And I know we're not your real family."

Ember too looked at the nightstand. *Magick Martyrs* sat on top—she hadn't yet put it away. Then, she looked back at Nieve who seemed...hurt.

Is this is what she wants? she thought. *For me pretend to be part of their family?*

Carefully, she said, "They're not my real family either."

That seemed to lighten the oracle's expression, if slightly. Nieve shrugged. "Even so, I know that you have others in the Soulless Realm. I know we took you from them, and I'm sorry for that."

For an instant, it was like breathing in a vacuum, being reminded of Daphne. But after several *"raindrops,"* Ember returned to the moment with finer clarity. Her sister had been gone a long time now, without a word to her one way or another. Not to mention Ember couldn't approach her again anytime soon—not in her present condition. There was no taking. Not really.

"I only have one family member in the Soulless Realm, and I haven't talked to her in years."

"Her name is Daphne, right? Your sister?"

She nodded.

"Would you like to see her?" Nieve leaned forward, a smile

tugging at her lips, like she was telling her an amusing secret, or a joke.

Shaking her head, Ember said, "She wouldn't want to see me. And even on the off-chance she did, I can't be near her. It's too dangerous."

"Well, if you were by yourself, of course. That's why Sombra and I would go with you, to ensure your sister's safety, as well as everyone else's. If things grew tense, we would be there to clock you, just as I did last night." Nieve's eyes were bright, white eyeliner highlighting her excitement. Ember swore she could even feel the estrella bouncing, subtly, like a child recounting a story. Like how Daphne used to recount her stories.

"You would do that. For me. No catch?"

The twin clutched Ember's wrist and leaned in even closer. "Yes. You're family. I know what it's like to love a sister. I can't imagine what it's like to lose one." She retracted her hand as a frown flashed on her lips, followed by a somber smile. "As long as you remain in this family, contribute to our family, we can escort you to see *your* family as often as you like."

Her smile broadened, and Ember supposed she should've felt warm and fuzzy, or thankful and relieved, or perhaps elated beyond belief—but she didn't. Because she couldn't move past that peculiar word, "contribute."

What exactly do I have to contribute?

"Could we go tomorrow?" she asked.

Nieve patted her hand. "Not tomorrow. But right after you complete your first assignment, I promise, we'll go."

She frowned. "Assignment?"

"It's nothing to worry yourself over yet. You'll have time to fully heal before you need to even consider a plan." Nieve stood up as if she was about to leave her with just that, but Ember would be damned if she let that happen.

"I don't need to fully heal to get started," she said. "What's the assignment?"

"Alloy, you have so much time. You really should enjoy it before you're burdened with work."

"Nieve, please. I haven't seen Daphne in six years. What is the assignment?"

The estrella looked about the room, and then, as if she had lost a game, she dropped her head and slumped back down to Ember's bedside.

"Just know that while I am convinced of your loyalty, others aren't so. Additionally, Fate has made quite the interesting request."

Her gaze wavered, as if she wanted Ember to say something to stop her, to prevent her from laying down all her cards. But Ember waited patiently, unrelentingly. This was no game to her.

Perhaps the oracle realized the extent of her resolve, because after a final pleading look, Nieve sighed. "Fine. You must *end* the princess."

All Ember heard were screams.

Many screams.

A scream.

Her locket was hot to the touch. Or was it her fingers that held it? There was no telling. She couldn't even be sure she was here right now. The room wouldn't stop spinning. And then it filled with smoke, flames, sirens. Then just the sound of a single heart monitor.

They wanted her to kill her.

They wanted her to *kill her*.

"Alloy?"

Ember blinked, barely registering the voice. Her mind was still at the funeral, at the cemetery from afar. The pair of gravestones mocked her, taunted her. Ever reminding her of what she'd done to her little sister.

The heart monitor beeped.

"Alloy?" the voice said louder.

She blinked again. Then, glimpsing the outline of white hair, she said distantly, "No."

Nieve set a hand on hers. "Alloy, look at me. Really look at me."

Ember forced herself to focus, and slowly, the vice-captain returned to her vision with some definition.

"I can't pretend to understand what this means for you," Nieve said, "but I know that it's difficult. Believe me, if this could be accomplished any other way, we would pursue it. But Fate has spoken. She recognizes who you are, Alloy. She recognizes the just woman inside and out. And she wants no other hand to end the wickedness that sits in line for the throne."

"But Nieve—"

"The princess is not like you or me, Ember Slade. She does not abide by the same moral code. Thousands of men, women, and children, completely unknowing that to be an alloy was a sin. A sin where those afflicted could only be cleansed by the spilling of their own blood. A sin that was deemed such a sin by only two people. She thinks you're unnatural. That who you are alone is enough to warrant your death. You think that *that* is someone who deserves to continue a life of luxury?"

"No but—"

"Please, Ember." Nieve squeezed her hand, and she looked to be on the verge of tears. "Please. I beg you. Save Nysa from herself."

But Ember could only shake her head and whisper, "No. I can't."

Suddenly, all of the warmth that had filled the estrella's face for the last half hour—vanished, and the oracle from last night returned, cold and unsmiling. "That's a shame. I thought you wanted to see your sister."

"I-I did," Ember stammered, fighting the heat in her palms, the tears in her eyes. "I do. But not like this."

Nieve shook her head. "Unfortunately, Alloy, if it's not like this, it's not at all. Ever. Do you understand?"

No. She didn't. She wanted to cry. She wanted to run. She wanted to puke. She wanted to scream.

For six years, she had tried so hard to be so good—to not kill anyone else, for *six years*—and she was being punished for it. With more murder.

How could this be the price of staying? How could this be the price of wanting to finally return to her sister?

So she said, "I understand."

But she knew that she would never pay it.

And then, as if the first Nieve had never left, the twin's voice returned to being light and bubbly. "I promise, we will visit Daphne the moment you've accomplished the task. Agreed?"

Ember clasped her hands to stop herself from shaking and gave a single, dishonest nod.

Nieve grinned. "Good."

A bag containing *Magick Martyrs* hung on Ember's shoulder as she stood at the corner outside the princess's chambers. She peered around the edge of the hall. Cadeña hadn't yet left his post, but then, there was still a minute until midnight.

You better be right about this, Damian, she thought.

When a distant bell chimed, Cadeña yawned and tottered off. She wiped away a bead of sweat and knocked on the door.

A heart-pounding moment later, Ademure peeked through

the crack. "It's late," she said. "What are you doing here? Where's Cadeña?"

"Can I come in?" Ember asked, fumbling with the strap of her bag.

Ademure looked her up and down. "The Delfinos will see you."

"Sure, if they're awake." When the princess frowned, Ember added, "Please, I'll only take a moment, and then I'll be out of your hair."

Ademure sighed and opened the door wider. "Come in."

The room's walls stretched wide but were bare. The ceilings were high but painted dark. The bed lacked ornamentation. The furniture was minimal. A few small lamps held green flames that barely illuminated the room.

The princess pulled two chairs together and took her seat in one. Ember took the other.

"Not the courtyard this time?" Ademure remarked. If possible, her face was paler than before, though the skin of her arms was a dark tan. The circles under her eyes deepened. The green of her irises and the pink of her lips dulled. "Embarrassed to be seen with me?"

"If only it was embarrassment I was worried about." Ember pulled the book from her bag and handed it to the princess. "Do you recognize this?"

Holding it closer, Ademure flipped through a few pages. "No." She handed it back. "Where did you get it?"

"The bookstore in town. Esmerelda says this entire book is a lie."

"Then I expect it's one of the most honest books there is. Especially if it's in any fashion about her."

"It's about my parents."

Ademure put an apathetic forefinger to her temple and

rested her chin on the heel of her palm. "Yes, you do look very much like the woman on the cover."

"Your mother had them killed."

She paused. "I'm sorry." She then sat straight in her chair, smoothed out her skirt, and returned her now fidgeting hands to her lap. Her foot, too, tapped along, against the hardened sand floor, filling out the moment of silence.

Ember took note of it all. The heel, the fingers, the shivering. *Either I was right from the beginning,* she thought, *or this girl deserves an Oscar.*

"You never meant to hurt the previous alloys, did you?"

Ademure looked at her with hard eyes. "Never."

"Right," Ember said, nodding. "I want you to escape with me."

This pause was much heavier. The muscles in Ademure's forehead twitched. The corners of her lips lifted and lowered, choosing between joy, distress, confusion. Her cheeks flushed and she clutched the fabric of her skirt, ripping her dress taut with the tension apparent in her face.

At last, it appeared, she decided the appropriate reaction was a frown. "What game are you playing?"

"None. I'm completely serious."

"Then what's changed? You aren't still afraid of hurting innocent people, of hurting me?"

"I'm terrified," Ember said quickly, her palms heating just as fast. "But you'll die if you stay here."

"I was going to die a month ago!" Ademure jumped from her chair before turning to her vanity, squishing her eyes shut and letting out a long exhale. "When I first came to you. When I begged for your help. Why now?"

Ember cast her eyes to her feet. "They want me to be the one to kill you."

The princess's head lowered. She leaned over her vanity,

gripping either side of it, as if she couldn't stand without it, and stared at where the mirror should go, where it once might have gone, in total silence.

"When?"

"I don't know."

Another minute passed.

Finally, she looked back at Ember. "You don't have to take me with you. You can leave me behind."

"No."

"Why not? Wasn't that your original plan?" She threw up her hands, pacing about the space. "Pretend like I never existed and go on about your day?"

Ember shook her head. "I'm not leaving you."

"You don't have to play hero, now. I've made my peace with my fate, and I can see there's no gain in this for you."

"It's not about gain."

"Truly? Then please, enlighten me, because I don't see a fucking difference—"

"You remind me of her."

Ademure went quiet then, tears forming at the edges of her reddening eyes, her face reddening too, and for a moment, her hair was shorter, blacker, and she was much younger. The princess and the girl stood as one, and Ember tugged her necklace hard enough to feel the skin of her neck break.

"You constantly remind me of her," she continued, and only the princess was in front of her now. "I've failed you both enough as it is. I won't leave this island without you."

Forehead creased but eyes emotionless, Ademure slowly walked toward her, maintaining impeccable posture, impeccable regality. She strolled with the grace of a queen—one much more poised than her mother—and she had the air of control. Of demand. She would not be fazed. She was a royal.

And then, her veneer cracked, and whatever composure

she once had vanished, replaced with her holding her head in her hands and whimpering—softly, meekly, truly.

Suddenly, she buried herself into Ember's chest.

Wordless, and a bit stunned, Ember wrapped one arm around the young woman's shoulders, used the other to pat her back, and then, when her whimpers silenced, she stroked her hair. Six years, but it was like she had done the same yesterday.

Ember didn't dare interrupt her. No, she waited quietly, guiltily, until at last, Ademure pulled away and wiped her eyes. Until she returned to her chair and smoothed her skirt.

"So what is your plan?"

Ember held out the book again and pointed to the name at the bottom of the cover. "Do you know who this is?"

"Liliana Caldwell. Her husband was my father's counsel."

"Do you think she still lives here on the island?"

"I wouldn't know. You could check the Archives on the bottom floor of the library. Each entry has been manipulated to keep an updated file on anyone who's ever lived in Nysa."

"Would you be able to help me look?"

Ademure laughed mournfully. "I'm not allowed to leave my chambers, Ember, much less go to the library."

"Please? With you, we'd be quick. In the middle of the night so no one knows you've even gone. But without you, I'll spend way longer down there, and definitely draw way more attention. I'm not even sure I know what I'm looking for."

The princess lifted a brow. "Why *are* you looking for her?"

"Because I've been practicing sailing for weeks and can, at most, float." Ember raised the book. "Maybe there's a chance that she can help us. At the very least, she may be able to teach me about my powers, so we stand a better chance if it comes to a fight. Really, it doesn't matter how she can help. I just know that she knows more than she lets on in here."

"You think a random author not only knows about your literally unbelievable powers or that she'll be capable of helping the Nysan princess and last alloy escape the most guarded country in all of the Magick Realm, but that she'll actually *want* to do so? Just because you ask?"

"I don't think she's random." Ember opened the book to the acknowledgment. "She knew my mom well."

Ademure scanned the page. "That may be so, but I still think you're expecting a lot from a woman you don't know. However, if she really did know your mother this well, I bet she'd be willing to tell you more about her. Maybe that's reason enough to see her. You could finally learn about your parents."

Ember's eyes drifted to the page in front of her, and old doubts resurfaced. *Someone has to be lying.*

If Nieve had been lying about Ademure this entire time, surely she was lying about her parents too. Surely they weren't traitors. Surely they were exactly what Caldwell had said they were: martyrs.

But her parents had still left her in the Soulless Realm. They'd still known they were going to die and didn't even leave her a note. And even if there were plausible explanations for those actions, there was still the fact that...

The book doesn't mention me.

...and she had no reason for that.

"I think I know enough." She closed the book. "But the faster I find the author, the faster I can plan. Will you help me?"

"The twins—"

"I'm the one who's supposed to pull the trigger, remember? This is all supposed to be some kind of disturbing loyalty test, so we have some time. But I don't know when that test ends, and I want to be long gone before we find out."

Ademure eyed her. "Fine. But we do this when the twins are gone on a mission. From what I've heard, that's two days from now." She stood and walked to her vanity, opened the drawer, and retrieved two plain pocket-sized notebooks and pens, then handed one of each to Ember. "I was saving this for something else, but this seems a tad more viable. Keep this on you at all times."

Ember turned it over. "What is it?"

"Our way of communication. We can't be seen talking to one another again. From now on, I will write to you in my notebook. A copy of the text will be manipulated in your notebook and vice versa. Keep it closed when you're not using it to hide the pages from the twins' birds-eye sight."

"Will do." She tucked the notebook and *Magick Martyrs* into her bag. "Two days. I'll see you at the top of the stairs at midnight." Then, she swung her bag over her shoulder and reached for the doorknob.

"And Ember?"

She turned on heel. "Yes?"

"Thank you."

Ademure looked smaller than she had ever before, but brighter, with the beginnings of a smile tugging at her lips.

"Please," Ember said, heat rising in her face and a sickness rising in her stomach. "Don't thank me yet."

CHAPTER 25

KIVA

"Have you read that book, yet?" Kiva asked before burying his toes in the coastline, leaving his land-sailer to the side. He rubbed at his red, flaking forearms—a result of spending endless hours on the beach under the brutal Nysan sun waiting for the alloy to show again—and dropped beside Ember in the sand.

"Sorry, what was that?" she asked. She held her legs close to her chest, arms wrapped around her knees, her blonde curls catching the ocean breeze. "A week ago, some maniac sprayed a bunch of sand at me, and I think my ears are still clogged." She feigned digging in her ears and plucking out several grains.

Kiva fought the urge to roll his eyes. *Every day is a new hurdle with her, isn't it?*

"What an ass," he said playfully. "Hopefully he found a way to make it up to you?"

"As a matter of fact, he did." She pulled a familiar piece of paper from her pocket. "He conveniently gave me exactly what I was looking for."

"A poem? Perhaps the man is actually a gentleman then, who was only acting like an ass."

"You mean a gentleman who *meant* to act like an ass. Or else an ass who meant to act like a gentleman." She returned the paper to her pocket with a scowl. "It wasn't an accident, was it?"

"Is that the conclusion you've come to? That I meant to spray you with sand?"

"Yes."

The wind blew hard then, blowing her hair across her face, though she kept her gaze at sea. He watched her. There was more to this woman than he'd initially assumed.

"So, what's your plan today?" she asked, derailing his momentary train of thought.

He brushed a hand through his hair, debating the myriad of answers he could give, then opted for a question instead. "When do you have to be back?"

"I'd rather spend my free time at the beach, thanks."

"Oh, so you *need* to get away for a bit, then."

She didn't respond.

He pushed himself from the ground, dusted the sand off his legs, and held out his hands. "Need a distraction to take your mind off of things?"

She didn't move.

It's like flirting with obsidian, he grumbled to himself.

"C'mon," he said. "I promise not to spray you with sand this time, intentionally or otherwise."

"Honestly, Kiva. I'm not up for it today."

He raised his brows. "Please? You'll love today's adventure, I swear."

She looked up at him, at his best pair of puppy-dog eyes and pouted lips, then at his hands, as she seemingly considered her options. She dropped her head between her knees.

"Ugh, whatever," she said, muffled. "But my aunt wants me back before dusk."

"You'll be back before four."

She bit her lip before putting both hands in his. Then he helped her up beside him, ignoring the twinging in his shoulder. The sand cascaded around them, though specks remained on their reddened skin, glued with sweat. And she stood nearly as tall as him, her ever-skeptical eyes only inches below his.

"Don't make me regret this," she said.

He swung a leg over his landsailer and tapped the space behind him. "Wouldn't be much of a date if I did."

"I think regret is like ninety percent of dating."

Stifling a laugh, he caught her eye just before it flitted away, and a hint of pink tinted her cheeks.

So she does care—or at least, she cares that I care.

Perhaps obsidian was a bit unfair.

She turned to his ride. "These things make me nauseous."

"This place is on the other side of the island. Would you like to walk there?"

With a glare that could cut glass, she stepped over the ski and sat down. He met her glare with a confident smile.

Though when she wrapped her arms around his waist, his confidence evaporated. And when her head rested at the back of his shoulders, he couldn't ignore the way his stomach inexplicably flipped.

Before she could see his heated cheeks, he pulled down his goggles, leaned forward on the handle, and whispered, "*Undu. Maior.*"

Then he laughed into the wind. He turned a sharp corner at the plaza, spewing sand into the nymph fountain. He skirted by the yellow flower shop nearly (purposefully) clipping the owner that sat outside. He swerved from orange to green to blue buildings. Through alleys. Under awnings and balconies. Around children, their parents, and the occasional pet iguana.

It was exhilarating.

It had been years since he had been able to landsail so freely. Everyone always mirrored in Agartha—there was no need for the contraptions. And he didn't exactly have a schedule that allowed him to ride on his own.

But you missed too much when you mirrored. Mirroring was instantaneous, destination to destination. Efficient, but superficial. No feelings. All business. Landsailing, on the other hand, was all about the journey, familiarizing yourself with the destination and all the places that led to it. Experiencing every landmark, every pathway, every peoples. Landsailing was nothing but feelings.

Of course, there were limitations to landsailing: it would be difficult to get to Atlantis or Agartha with just a landsailer. Then again, with mirroring, women didn't hold on quite as tight.

The rainbow of buildings blurred behind them, and everything turned tan. Dark jade lined the horizon, and the mountain-like tree of Nyseion marked the sky like the North Star. Once the jade line turned into a line of a million trees, then trees with a million leaves, Kiva solidified the sand, and the landsailer came, at last, to a halt. With a deep, invigorating breath, he slid the goggles off and stood up, and quickly realized the alloy's grasp had never lessened.

"Ember, we've stopped. You can let go."

She didn't.

He peeled her off of him so that he could step out of the landsailer. But rather than move, she reattached herself to the vehicle, laying her arms and head against the handlebar. "I'm going to puke."

"Not on my landsailer, you won't." He pulled his flask out

of the compartment—this time, completely filled—and set it in her lap.

"I think your landsailer is the perfect place to puke," she said.

He sighed. How could he ever tire of that snark?

She drained the flask of water.

"Feel better?" he asked through a gritted smile.

"This will be the best I feel for a while." She looked up from the handlebars and at the sand forest and groaned. "Did you torture me that entire way just to look at a bunch of trees?"

Had dating always been this hard? Or had it been so long he'd forgotten the absolute shit a date could be.

"C'mon," he said, finding it harder by the minute to be so effortlessly charming. "Follow me."

Kiva would've preferred to sail all the way into the forest, but all of the different rocks, shrubs, and insects that resided in this environment would be too difficult a task to manipulate simultaneously. Plus, the tree coverage would hinder the sail's ability to catch the wind.

Fortunately, it was a short hike. Though the forest thickened quickly and the vines were stocky enough to swing from, a path of low-growing yellow and green shrubbery reserved enough space above it for the two of them to squeeze through. After that, they entered flatter ground, and it only took ten minutes of wading through the six-inch thick leaf litter to hear rushing water.

"A river?" Ember asked.

"No, but close." He grabbed her hand. "We're almost there."

The forest grew denser. Tree roots thickened into an unseen hazard underneath the brush. The sky, though it was mid-day, had almost completely vanished. Sunlight hardly peeked through the canopy, and in the distance, he could finally see the rush of white.

They stepped into an opening where the sky returned and the sun shined down, where the land was flat and the sand and leaves had been replaced by a rocky edge, and he pointed across the pool of rippling water. "There."

The waterfall was several dozen feet tall, cascading out of a mound of glistening gray stones. The water itself fell white and loud as a freight train, and it poured with a certain asymmetric beauty, jaggedly flowing from jutted rock to jutted rock. And when it ultimately met the pool below, the white turned to blue—as blue as the sky above and not a shade darker. The pool sparkled at the perimeter, but it was otherwise calm, in complete contrast to the source that created it.

Ember stepped up to the edge, inhaled deeply, and closed her eyes. And Kiva made sure that when she reopened them, he'd be right in her line of sight.

"Better than a bunch of trees?" he asked, placing a hand on the back of her elbow.

She shook him off her arm. "I can't yet think what to make of you, but this is not at all what I expected."

He grinned. "I'll take that as a compliment."

Then, he sat down, letting his legs hang above the pool. Droplets misted from the waterfall, and in combination with the little breeze, kept him cool despite the sun's relentless beat-down. Surprisingly, Ember mimicked him.

"Why aren't there other people out here?" she asked. "Surely this is a hot-spot for day trips."

He dipped his hands in the water and washed off the bit of sand left on his arms and legs. "I think most are afraid of the nymphs."

"The nymphs?" she said, her eyes growing wide.

"Don't worry. I hate the nymphs as much as anyone else"

—*probably more*— "but they don't come down this far south. We're perfectly safe."

"And just how do you know that?"

"A lot of exploring when I was younger. You stumble into some stupid situations. Test the limits. Nearly die a few times."

He flashed at her another grin, but she replied with a frown. He guessed his brushes with death weren't as dazzling as he'd hoped.

"Why didn't your parents protect you?" she asked. "Or stop you?"

He frowned too, shaking off the water and patting the excess on his shirt. "Neither really cared, I suppose. I don't worry about it. It built character."

"Hm." She crossed her legs, aimlessly dragging her hand along the rocky edge. "What are they like?"

"Who? My parents?" When she nodded, he shrugged. "I don't know. Mom's a lot. Dad's a lot too, but at least I think I've finally figured him out. But I stay away from the both of them if I can help it."

She looked out across the pool. "Have any siblings?"

He picked up the flattest rock he could find. "Yeah."

"Do you see them?"

It skipped twice before sinking. "No."

"Do you miss them?"

He looked at her, and her at him. *Why the sudden inter-rogation?*

"All the time," he said.

She nodded and returned her gaze to the pool. "Me too."

He kept his attention on her a moment longer. *That was strange, right?* he thought. *Or am I paranoid?* But when she asked nothing further, he leaned back on his hands, pretending as if he was completely unbothered.

"Kiva, how do you know so much about everything?"

Fuck. Not paranoid.

Still, he kept his posture casual, staying back on his hands, and he laughed. "What is it that I already know?"

"Don't do that," she said. "You knew that I grew up in the Soulless Realm. That I'm new to magic. That my parents are dead. How could you possibly know that they were dead when *I* didn't even know? How did you know they were my parents at all?"

Thank the gods. Is that all this is about? "So you did read the book, then."

She shot him another death glare. "You know everything about me, and I don't even know your last name."

"Gordynos. And I disagree entirely. I don't know your hobbies, the music you like, what things you read. I may know a little about your background, but I don't know anything about *you.*"

"Kiva Gordynos, I think you know more than you let on."

"Really? I must be forgetting something then. Care to refresh my memory?"

She opened her mouth to respond, but pursed her lips instead.

He smirked. *Please. I'm dying to learn what I don't know about you.*

"Gordynos, huh?" she said, trying and failing to act like she wasn't irritated. "It doesn't sound very Nysan."

"Neither does Slade."

"Touché. Where does Gordynos come from?"

"Agartha."

"You're Agarthan?"

"On my dad's side, yes."

"And you've never been to Agartha?"

Shit. Forgot I said that.

"No." When she looked at him with her familiar skepticism, he added, "Well, I don't remember going. My parents split when I was really young."

She shook her head.

"What?" he asked.

"Is that why you know so much about mirroring?"

"Everyone here knows about mirroring, Ember. Is that why you don't trust me? You think I'm in bed with the Agarthans?"

She tilted her head. "And what makes you think I don't trust you?"

"The hundred rapid-fire questions about my personal life, for one."

"That doesn't mean I don't trust you. Maybe I'm just nosy."

He laughed out loud. "So you *do* trust me?"

Hugging her legs, she said, "No. But you shouldn't take it personally. I'm just wondering what you're getting out of... this." She gestured between them. "And when you'll leave it."

Narrowing his eyes on her, he asked, "What do you mean? I'm not leaving."

"You will. Everybody does." She tossed a rock into the pool; it skipped four times. "So why did you bring me here? Actually, why did you bring me into town the other night?"

Okay, regardless of whatever that *was, you have to make at least some progress today,* Kiva told himself. *She needs to at least tolerate you.*

He placed a hand on hers. "Because you looked like you needed a break. You think too much."

"How would you know?" She pulled her hand away. "It doesn't seem like you think at all."

"Okay ouch. Are you always so cruel to guys who take you out?"

"Are you always so pushy with girls who want to be left alone?"

"What if I just like you, Ember? Is that so wrong?"

"Ugh. I'm not sure my stomach has completely settled. Please don't aggravate it with your bullshit."

He threw his hands up. "What should my answer be, then? Huh? What can I say to satisfy you?"

"I don't know. Something honest." She played with her locket. "Why did you actually bring me out here today?"

She looked at him. The sparkle of the water reflected off her vividly green eyes. Her windswept hair curled around her face, perfectly framing a pair of soft rounded lips.

But there was something more in her expression. Something sincere and wanting and hoping. It was in the way she saw him—as if she saw *through* him—so much more than he wanted her to see. A part of him though to let her see it all.

Hold it together, he told himself. *Or are you trying to elicit more taunts from Profe?*

He coughed, then said, "I wanted to take you away from your worries. Whisk you away for a few hours and brighten your day." He reached for her hand again.

Again, she pulled away. "So no honesty, then."

"Ember—"

"It's alright. I have my secrets too."

His cheeks flushed. *Fucking hell. What does she want from me?*

"Now who's thinking too much?" she said, gently pushing his shoulder. "C'mon. You dragged me all the way out here, we might as well do something." She scanned the water. "I know. Let me show you what I learned the other day."

As she stood up and took her stance, he took a quiet breath and forced himself to calm down. He hadn't lost yet. This was only a minor setback. She might not have trusted him completely, but she did enough to come out here with him. Enough to show off her magic. There was still a chance to win her over.

On his right, Ember stretched her arms over the pool and whispered, "*Glacio.*"

The few ripples in the water stilled, and the temperature of the air dropped, fast. Where Kiva was sweating, he now shivered, but he continued to stay poolside, watching the blue fade in hue. Crystals formed across the pool's surface, spreading out radially from the point directly beneath her open palm, turning the water icy white. And for a moment, the water *was* ice.

But the waterfall continued to move water beneath the newly formed sheet. Erosion led to cracking, then melting, and another moment later, the ice became water once more.

Her brows knit together. "What happened? It should've stayed."

"You cast your spell too wide again," he said, still sitting on the ledge. "Like you did with the landsailer. But you should be proud of your natural strength. Most magicks with that issue would make an ice sheet so thin, it wouldn't last a second, and yours held for at least ten." He slid his hand over the now frozen cold slickness of the rocky ledge. "Though, you should be careful, ice queen. With strength like yours, you might ice something you didn't intend to."

She looked at him as if she had ten new questions ready to fire, but she asked none of them.

I know you're an alloy. Trust me enough to tell me.

"Why don't you teach me some magic?"

He raised his brows, surprised. That was something, at least. "Sure. What do you want to learn?"

"Clocking."

Of course, she would ask that.

"All the spells in the world, and you want me to show you the magic that doesn't require one?"

With a nod, she said, "And I was told there wasn't going to

be a party or anything, so I'm all on my own." She held her hands up and shrugged.

He sighed. He nearly revealed himself that moment. He wanted so badly to rip off the bandage and deal with the aftermath. After all, it had to happen at some point.

But not now. He needed more time to weigh the consequences before making a move so drastic. If earlier's conversation was any indication, there was little chance she'd react well, and he only had one reveal.

So how do I clock without the innate ability to do so? He tapped his thumb along the edge for a second before realizing: *I don't have to. I only have to teach it. Without a demonstration.*

He had been tutored by an exceptional Nysan after all. One who had clocked him and Alden on more than a few occasions. He could pull this off.

"Okay, I'll teach you."

She smiled. "Fantastic. I'll show you what I know."

The alloy grabbed a fallen leaf, and Kiva followed her as she walked away from the water's edge. Then, she began to hum.

The familiar Nysan anthem resounded throughout the forest, filling their surroundings with loud and soft echoes of the tune. He listened closely as she slowed down the melody. She hit the notes perfectly, every beat in exact time. And when she reached the song's crescendo, she dropped the leaf.

But it fluttered as it fell, neither the breeze nor her song slowing it down. She slowed the tune further, and still, the leaf didn't respond. It simply twirled, oblivious to her magic, drifting with the wills of the wind instead. Finally, it found its place of rest on the forest floor, as gravity had taken its toll.

She groaned. "I thought I had it this time. I almost stopped one two days ago."

He studied her, determining what exactly was the problem.

One of the most powerful magicks alive, yet Nysan toddlers can conjure more than that.

He hadn't thought about his own innate in so long. At this point in life, it was all muscle memory. But, if he remembered correctly, there were three components to properly performing one. For mirroring, it was the mirror (of course), the size of what you were mirroring, and the strength of your soul's connection. Similarly, for clocking you needed to know the anthem, the relative mass of what you were slowing down, and you needed to engage your soul through your magical connection.

She had hummed the anthem perfectly. The item she had slowed was essentially massless. And she was an alloy; her natural magic was strong—he knew that firsthand.

He reached for his shoulder. *What's wrong then?* he wondered.

"Ember, what are you thinking about when you try to slow down the leaf?"

"What do you mean? I'm thinking about slowing down the leaf."

"No, what are you thinking about to engage your soul?"

"I...don't know. I'm focused on hitting the right notes. I want the leaf to slow down."

He shook his head. "Yes, but wanting is not engaging. Engaging is more along the lines of..." How did one describe engaging the soul? "Something of an understanding that you have with yourself and the time you wish to manipulate. When you sing, the magic should pull at your core," he pressed against the small of her back, "and dance with the melody. It's almost like hearing emotion."

"Hearing emotion," she repeated, her eyes fixed on the leaf. She clutched her locket. "Like listening to the rhythms."

Listening to the rhythms? "Sure," he said. "If that's what puts you in the right frame of mind, then go with that."

She picked up the leaf again and narrowed her eyes on it. Then her humming started, and she let go.

The leaf spun as fast as it had the first time, edge over edge, drilling through the air to find the rocky ledge. On the other hand, her hum was louder than the last and more strained, desperately seeking to stop the leaf's descent.

"Understand the magic, Ember. It comes from your core, your soul. Let it speak to you. Let it dance."

The leaf had fallen halfway to the ground now. For a brief moment, Kiva could see her jaw tighten and her arms grow stiff. He again pressed against the small of her back.

And with a few inches left above the ground, that was enough to loosen her shoulders and get her hum to slow further. With his hand still pressed against her, he could feel her stance become firmer. She just had to release—

The leaf slowed.

No.

It *stopped*. In air. Half an inch above the ground.

Ember gasped. "I did it!"

Without the song, the leaf immediately fell, as did Kiva's jaw. In all his years on Nysa, not once had he ever witnessed a Nysan *stop time*.

"Uh, yeah," he said before blinking twice more, trying to process what he had witnessed. "Yeah...yeah, you did."

She picked the leaf back up and held it in her palm like it was a delicate artifact. He wondered if she knew the real marvel was her.

"You know," she said, "maybe it was actually worth dragging me out here."

He quickly recomposed himself. "It definitely was." *Worth seeing what I'm working with, at least.* Turning his gaze up to the canopy, he said, "And just in time, too. The sun is beginning to set. As much as I would love more time with you, I don't want to make you late for dinner."

But instead of moving toward the landsailer as he'd expected, Ember turned to the waterfall. "What do you think would happen if I sang instead of hummed?"

"Most Nysans sing," he said. "Normally, it strengthens your clocking. It's all really dependent on the soul engagement though. You have to release it fully, like you just did."

"Got it. We can go back in a minute. I just want to try it once."

He shrugged and sat down on a nearby rock. Ember stood in place and turned away from him to face the pool.

And she sang.

Impressively, it seemed she had actually memorized the lyrics he'd given her, and her Greek pronunciation wasn't half-bad. Plus, every note, she hit with confidence. She wasn't a professional by any means, but she could carry the tune.

Gradually, the melody slowed, though her voice continued to resonate throughout the trees. Somehow it had grown louder. Or maybe the area was quieter? Actually, now that he focused on it, the area was nearly silent, save for the melody. And he realized, in his periphery, the white rush had disap-peared—a mess of clear droplets poured quietly into the pool... right where it ought to have been.

Wait, is she...?

His eyes widened. She slowed a waterfall.

An *entire* waterfall.

"Holy shit."

There she was, her arms outstretched, stance firm, hair catching the wind. He could actually see the magic pulsing through her veins, a glimmer at her fingertips. And she stayed like that until her song ended; then the white rush returned.

"Damn," she said as she dropped her arms. "I thought I could stop it completely."

"Are you kidding me? That was nothing short of incredible!" He found his way to her side. "Your net is still a bit wide, but a little practice and it won't be long before you can stop oceans." He set a hand on her shoulder.

This time, she didn't shake off his touch. Rather, she smiled as she looked at him, sending the smallest—*meaningless*—flutter to his chest. *Finally*, he thought. *A breakthrough.*

"Thanks for making me come with you," she said. "And for teaching me. Hopefully, that was something along the lines of why you brought me out here."

"I only wanted to bring you out of your slump. Nothing more, nothing less. If learning to clock is what did the trick, then I'm grateful to have been your teacher."

She eyed him. "I almost believe you."

The corner of his lip pulled. "Well, whether you believe me or not, it's true. Though, I wouldn't get too excited over this waterfall magic."

"Why not?"

He grinned. "Because time always stops when I'm with you."

Her gaze dropped. Her smile fell. And Kiva suddenly wished he hadn't spoken. He'd come to like that smile.

She looked back to the white rush with folded arms. "Next time, I'd love to see you clock. I'm sure *you* could've stopped the waterfall."

He glanced at her sidelong and shook his head. "I assure you, I can do nothing of the sort."

CHAPTER 26
ADEMURE

Absent of light, the hallway outside Ademure's room felt cold, as if the glassy walls and icy sand floor were preparing for her death. She wrapped her shawl tighter. It had been too many years since warmth had last inhabited the castle.

It was strange to think now, but she hadn't always feared her mother, and her mother hadn't always hated her. They used to walk hand in hand to the beach and laugh together at the shows in the square. They'd put up the Kronia tree in the Grand Hall, bringing festivity and fun to all the servants in the castle. At times her mother had envied the father that Ademure hardly knew, but the queen had hid her envy by showering her only daughter with love.

That mother was long gone.

In her place stood a shell of a person with eyes for nothing but revenge. The queen fixated on gaining loyalty, power, and control—all things the Agarthan king had that she didn't. Some days, Ademure wondered if some semblance of her mother remained, and if it was at all possible to get her back.

At the top of a flight of spiraling stairs in the very center of the castle, the alloy was waiting.

"Ademure," Ember whispered. "You made it."

"I always keep to my word," Ademure said. "And Cadeña is nothing if not routine. Shall we go?"

She took a heart-racing step down the spiral, Ember following behind her. Moments later, they entered the top of the library, and as the alloy leaned over the railing, she gasped.

"This is incredible."

She was right, of course. The high arches. Floor-to-ceiling shelves of books. The spiral splitting into two staircases that encircled the walls of the entire room before diving into the floors below. To Ademure, "incredible" was the only fitting description for her oldest friend.

"Come on," she said, gesturing toward the glass platform that floated in the center of the library.

"Just how many floors are there?" Ember asked as she stepped onto the platform and looked through the glass beneath her feet. "It looks like it goes on forever."

"Five. We're on the top floor where you'll find modern potion-making, cooking, and self-help books. The fourth floor is the Reference section. That's predominantly used by the alchemists and magicists. The third floor is Modern History and Literature. The second floor is Classic Literature. And the bottom-most floor holds the Archives and Ancient History. Luckily for us, it's the least visited floor of them all by far."

"Really? But doesn't it hold a bunch of public records? I thought at least the estrellas would use it."

"*Demitto*," Ademure said, her palms down. The alloy stumbled as the platform started its descent, but her own stance stayed firm. "The oracles are human Archives of sorts now. And the library is no longer open to the public."

"I can't believe it ever was, the queen is so high-strung."

She frowned. "Amá was a different person once. She still is that person, just ill."

"Ill with what, exactly? Rabies?"

The platform came to a rest on the ground, and she released her hold over it.

"I don't know," she said. "But once we leave—*if* we manage to leave—I intend to find out."

The mahogany tables greeted the women first. There had to be at least two dozen of them, each one outfitted with a chair, a lamp, and piles of documents that looked one breeze from tipping over. The dark wooden furniture encircled the entirety of the railing of the library so that they overlooked the central platform.

The shelves met the women next, reaching twenty feet high and winding behind the tables like a labyrinth. Leather and parchment stuffed every inch of every cubby, and then covered the floors next to them, too. She counted ten different ladders on this level.

Without hesitation, Ember walked over to the table nearest the platform, picked up a loosely bound record, and blew on the cover. The air blackened and she wheezed, tears welling in her eyes as she frantically waved at the dust.

"*Caeli pura*," Ademure said with one flick of her hand, and a small gust of wind wafted toward the alloy, dissipating the particles.

Ember continued to cough but was at least able to catch enough breath to say, "Disgusting."

"I told you it had been awhile."

"It's going to take forever to sort through these stacks. Do you have a spell to find the record faster?"

"I can't manipulate something if I don't know where it is. Though, the shelves are catalogued."

On the side of the first shelf, a poster designated the locations of items in both the Archives and Ancient History. Ancient History sorted their titles by subject and alphabetically. Thankfully, the Archives sorted on name alone.

"It looks like last names beginning with the letter 'C' are in stacks twenty-three through thirty-one," Ademure said. "Let's start there."

"You're kidding." Ember looked up, and Ademure followed her gaze. Each stack nearly touched the ceiling. "That's like a million records to sort through."

"Then, we had better start."

After a long sigh, Ember muttered, "I miss computers."

The women made their way down the extensive rows of records until they came upon the stacks they sought out. Ember tied her hair back, Ademure removed her shawl, and so began a solid fifteen minutes of coughing and papercuts and ruffling through the layers of dust. Most of the documents were sifted through in vain, and when there were only two remaining stacks in the section, the alloy groaned and sat down.

"This is ridiculous," she said, head in hand.

"Indeed, you are ridiculous," Ademure continued to the next stack, "deciding to find a grain of salt on a beach of sand."

"You agreed to it."

"Well, of course, I'm ridiculous too. Ridiculously desperate."

She scanned the yellow folders, the beige ones, the yellow, the beige, the hint of brown all underneath a blanket of gray dusty specks—the slurry of monotonous colors made her head spin. So she reskimmed the same stack, much more slowly, ensuring she didn't skip over the name. And this time, at the stack's apex, something caught her eye.

Blue?

She grabbed a ladder and started to climb.

"Did you find it?" Ember asked, still on the ground.

"I don't know. But I'm appeasing my curiosity."

"Appease it fast."

When she reached the top, she could see it clearly, an arm's length away from her. The book was bound in dark blue leather, hand-sewn judging by the spine. On the cover, *The Will of the World* was embroidered in Greek. Ademure carefully picked up the book and gently blew on the cover, but, unlike the others, no cloud of dust formed. She inspected it closer.

Perched at the top of the ladder, she opened the front cover. The pages were discolored and weak, yet the faded text looked clean and handwritten. She peeled the first two pages back.

The gods created humans and demigods alike to inhabit the world...

Her Greek wasn't the strongest, but she was sure that was what it said, even if it didn't make sense. No one believed that lore about the soulless and magicks anymore. The text insinuated that they were two halves of the same whole, but as far as anyone knew, both parties had always been at odds with one another.

She skipped three more pages.

For their insolence, the world was purified by the sacrifice of Pandora. Her ills poisoned the Earth, and with her death they were once again concealed.

"Ademure, come on. We only have ten minutes or so before you need to be back."

"Just a moment."

She looked back at the text. Another myth. Who wrote this?

What was the point? She flipped back to the first page, then to the end. There was no author to this book at all. *Why is this down here?*

She thumbed through several more pages, skimming them, then moving on, until maybe two-thirds of the way through the book, the text stopped, and every page from then on was completely blank. She flipped back to the most recent text. It was in Spanish this time, then rewritten in English.

Each dawn, she rides, daughter of Hope,
Alone into Pegasus City.

"That's not a myth."

"Myth? We're looking for names," Ember said from below.

The alloy rummaged through the second to last stack. They were still a way off from finding the record it seemed. Ademure needed to get back to searching.

She turned back to the blue book, ready to shut it and return it to its curious home on the shelf, but the text irked her. What did that last part mean? Where was Pegasus City?

She would have to decipher this later. She retrieved her pocket notebook and copied the text down, and as she readied herself to once again leave the book behind, she paused, her mind fastening together its oddities—namely that the book was handwritten and unfinished, and it had no author.

It was no book at all.

But why would a journal be down here? she wondered. *And who would journal about myths?*

She had to know more. Shifting her stance on the bookshelf's ladder, she started from the last page of text and moved backward, skimming the pages for clues as to what exactly this was. These last pages differed heavily from the beginning few. For one, the first few pages had read like a textbook, where these last pages read as poor poetry. For another, in the final texts, there was hardly talk of gods and demigods, but surprisingly, a plethora of talk about the nymphs. And most notably, the majority of these texts were short one or two-lined sentences. Some of them had four.

One had twelve.

She stopped on that page. The bottom corner was dog-eared, and the page had obviously been handled more than the others: oiled fingers affected the crinkles in the parchment. She read—strangely, only in English this time.

Evils dead, evils reborn,
Evils source the Woman's scorn.
Soulless weak, soulless strong,
Soulless take what doesn't belong.
Magic natural, magic perverse,
Magic is the Magick's curse.
Power sought, power blight,
Power will the evergreen slight.
War then, war of late.
War ends the Woman's Fate.

Seek Pandora.
11-01

She read and reread and reread once more before scribbling the text into her notebook. The first text she'd copied could possibly take days to decipher. This one would take weeks at least, and that's assuming she would be able to sneak into the library again. She wasn't even sure she would understand what it said if she could decode it now. But someone with access to this library decided that page was important, and she had to know why.

"I found her!" Ember called out, and Ademure jumped. Realizing her mistake, she reached back for the rails.

"That's great!" she panted, gripping the ladder so tightly that her fingers cramped. She slowed her breath before making her way down.

Ember opened her notebook, but her pen stopped short. "What's this?"

Every word that Ademure had copied from the blue leather journal now reflected on the page.

"It's something I want to analyze later," she said. "I can't remove the book from the library."

"Good luck with that. Is this even English?"

"It could be a translation. I really don't know anything about it, but that's part of why I want to study it." She looked at a nearby clock on the wall. "Five minutes. We should go."

Ember traced her finger down the page as she mumbled to herself. "Huh, November first. I wonder what made that day special."

"November first? Where do you read that?

"This date at the bottom." She pointed to the numbers at the end of the text. "At least, I think it's a date."

"Don't be silly. That's the eleventh of January."

"Really? Nysans write their dates backwards like that?"

"It's not backwards. It's proper. Why would it make sense to write otherwise? Do you ever write the year first?"

The alloy stared further into the page.

"Ember, really, we need to go."

"That's funny then," she said as if Ademure had never spoken.

"What's funny?"

"How old do you think this is?"

Ademure shrugged. "I couldn't tell you. I didn't see any other dates in the journal."

"If I had to guess, I'd say it's almost twenty-three years old."

"What makes you say that?"

Ember held the notebook closer to her face. "The Delfinos mentioned something about a prophecy to me. Do you think that's what this is?"

"I've honestly never seen one of their prophecies before. But if that's what this is, then they were hardly six years old at the time it was written. I don't know how they could've authored it. Who's to say this is about you anyway? Are you able to understand that gibberish?"

"No. But January eleventh is the day after I was born, when I was found outside a hospital."

Ademure clasped her hands together, rubbing her thumb along the edge of her fist. *That can't be a coincidence,* she thought. *But if it is a prophecy, what does that mean?*

"I'm going to do what research I can on it, but without access to the library, I'll be limited."

"Maybe Liliana Caldwell knows more."

"I suppose it wouldn't hurt to ask," she said as she watched Ember finish copying the address she had found for the author. *But you're relying a lot on that woman. I hope she doesn't disappoint you.* "Hurry up with that note. There are only two minutes before Rodriguez starts her watch."

Ember packed away her notebook and returned the record to the shelf. Both women started toward the platform.

"*Sumitto.*"

As they reached the top, Ademure realized how sad she was to be leaving. The library had always been comforting, and even if it was for just twenty minutes, this visit had been almost therapeutic. At least, with this poem to decrypt, she finally had—

"It's quite late, you know."

Shit.

"Hello, Nieve," she said as calmly as she could. "Rarely see you without your shadow. I thought you two were out on a mission?"

"We finished early." The oracle stepped into the moonlight that spotlighted the surrounding staircases. Her green eyes smoldered, highlighting her soft smile. "Don't you love how quiet the library is at this time? It makes it so easy for me to record my thoughts from the day."

"Thoughts?" Ember asked from Ademure's side. "Like a premonition? Is that why your eyes are glowing?"

"Very perceptive, Alloy."

Ember put on an unfamiliar smile—or rather, a simulated smile that conveyed no emotion, no comfort. "Oh, we'll get out of your way then," she said, "so you can copy it down before you forget it."

"How thoughtful of you," Nieve replied. "But fortunately, until Fate speaks to me again, I can't forget. We have some time." She stepped closer to the platform, and though the alloy stood on the glass with her, Ademure felt like she was stranded on an island with nowhere to run. "Alteza, I wonder why might *you* be in the library?"

"That was my fault, Nieve." Ember moved in front of Ademure, subtly shielding her with one arm. "I asked the princess to help me with honing my lightning. She brought me to the library."

The oracle's smile disappeared. "At midnight? In the Archives?"

"Cadeña told me she was busy the rest of the day, and that the Archives was our best bet for finding something."

"And you didn't come to me or Sombra first?"

"It was urgent. Y'all were gone."

"There are other servants who know the library as well as our princess."

"Oh, well, I didn't know that."

Nieve quieted as she considered the alloy's story, and Ademure took the moment to pray to Pan, Dionysus, Zeus, and the rest of the pantheon, that the estrella would buy it.

"I know you're not a fan of Bailón, Alloy," Nieve finally said, "but if my sister and I are absent, please do consult her before making such decisions. She is our captain."

Ember nodded. "I'm sorry. It won't happen again."

The estrella put two fingers to her temple and sighed. "It's fine. Please, go on ahead. Su Alteza and I need to discuss something."

"Actually," the alloy said, unmoving, "is it okay if I stay?"

Nieve stilled, seemingly shocked that she had the audacity to even ask. Frankly, Ademure was shocked, too.

"And for what reason would you think you'd be entitled to stay?"

"To better prepare for my assignment," Ember said. "I'd like to stay well-informed."

"I can promise our conversation will not affect the outcome of your assignment, one way or another."

"But will my presence affect the outcome of your conversation?" She raised her brows. "If not, couldn't I—"

"No." Any softness Nieve met them with had hardened into sharp tension at the corner of her eyes and about her jaw. "Don't toy with me, Alloy. Not at this hour."

In half a second, the room went from frigid to scorching, like a fire had been lit next to Ademure. She looked to Ember to see if she felt it too, but the alloy's face was stone. Her lips were pressed, and her eyes were forward—a demeanor eerily reminiscent of Nieve herself.

Nieve must have sensed it as well because she said, "Your temper…"

"I'm fine," Ember said, despite the sweat forming at her forehead. Or her stance starting to sway. Or her rapid blinking. Or the heat.

"You know the consequences."

"I'm *fine*," she repeated.

"You're not fine," Ademure said, stepping out in front and turning to face her. And though every bit of her wanted the alloy to stay, she added, "Leave us."

"No."

"Yes."

Ember stared hard at her, fight in her eyes, asking for her to change her mind. But Ademure wouldn't. Ember couldn't win tonight, but she could get hurt. And if she was to survive, the alloy needed to be in one piece. She needed the alloy to be on the estrellas' good side.

"That is two direct orders, Alloy," Nieve said, arms folded, no soft smile in sight. "Leave."

Ember looked to Ademure as if asking one more time to stay. Ademure vehemently shook her head. With a strained jaw, the alloy then pushed past Nieve and, as if she were drunk, stumbled toward the stairs. Once she was out of sight, the air around them cooled, and Ademure breathed a small sigh of relief.

"I'm surprised you found it, Alteza," Nieve said, waltzing toward her. "My prophecy diary has been hidden there for well over ten years."

"It was purely an accident," Ademure said, attempting to speak with authority but her voice quivering instead. "You should really consider hiding a blue book somewhere that's not entirely beige."

Before she could react, a metal blade pressed against her rib cage, a half-inch below her heart. The pressure behind the blade sliced the thin fabric that clothed her and a shallow cut formed below her breast. She winced as blood seeped onto the knife.

"Cuidado, Alteza," Nieve said, pressing harder. "We haven't yet prepared for a royal mourning."

She reached into Ademure's bag and pulled out the notebook. With one hand she flipped to the used pages and tore them out, then pushed Ademure to the side and threw her notebook back at her. Ademure fell near the railing, thankful it was this floor and not the next.

"*Delique*," Nieve said. The pages she tore dissolved into ash, and she turned her bloody knife onto Ademure. "It is serendipitous that I was here to stop you before you did something truly stupid. Next time," she paused to lick the blood clean, "you may not be so favored."

"I'm not blind," Ademure said. "My grave may as well already be dug."

"Ah, well, we all have our time. Take solace in knowing that it will be neither my sister nor I who gets to bask in the joy of taking the light from your eyes, though we both so desperately wanted the position."

"I don't understand, Nieve. I'm no threat. I can't fight. I have no allies. You have no need to kill me."

"Then what was tonight about, Alteza? You defied at least two orders outright and seem to have put some idea in the alloy's head that she is bound to you. That she should protect you."

"She isn't protecting me."

"She stood in front of you," Nieve hissed. "Between us. She

lied for you. She has never done that before. You are seducing her into committing treason." The twin bent down to meet her at eye level. "If I didn't think it would only push her further away, I'd have your tongue in my palm this instant. Stop turning our weapon against us."

Ademure pushed herself upright so that she was mere inches from the estrella's face. "You're repulsive. Ember is a person, not a weapon."

At that, Nieve's glare broke into a grin. Then, she straightened, returning to her full height and towering over Ademure's pathetic position.

"Alteza, please. Don't lecture me. You don't even have a good grasp of the lesson. *Everyone* is a weapon." She strolled onto the glass platform, then called it, and it began its descent. "Some simply aren't as sharp as others."

CHAPTER 27

KIVA

"I've been here for over a month now," Kiva said before taking a swig from his bottle. "I can't keep waiting for her to show."

"Why don't you seek her out?" Profe Valentina sat across from him at the Round Table. "You know where she is."

"The oracles? I couldn't take them on even if I had my shoulder back."

"There aren't any mirrors in the castle?"

"Were there any when you worked there?"

She swirled her glass of wine. "No."

"Then I doubt they've added any since."

He leaned back in his decorative chair, searching the wall of animal pelts and neon lights for inspiration. He couldn't keep relying on the alloy to randomly show up at the beach. The longer he stayed, the more he risked getting caught, and he needed to return to Agartha soon.

His eye caught a soulless mailbox. "How well do you know the castle's grounds?"

"Well, but I doubt as well as you."

"Do you know if there are any blind spots on the grounds? Somewhere that the oracles can't see."

"None that I can think of."

Tapping the side of his bottle, he asked, "Well, do you know of any way to get a message to someone inside the castle without raising suspicion?"

"I'm guessing you don't have a cell phone, do you?"

"Please, be serious."

"I am being serious. The soulless have created some nifty technology. You should get your hands on one if you can."

"Profe Valentina," he said, running a hand through his hair, "do you have *any* helpful information on the twins? You worked with them. Surely, you learned something."

"Not that I recall." She finished off her glass, then paused. "Well, their father did tell me an interesting peculiarity about his power once. Maybe it applies to them?"

He set his drink down. "I'm listening."

"Before he died, Arlo Delfino and I were at a party. He'd had a few glasses of wine while flirting with *moi*. When I told him what really got me going was secret information, he offered up a secret of his in exchange for a kiss."

Kiva internally shuddered. "What was this secret?"

"Delfino could see the present for any human, magick or soulless. But for other peoples, he saw nothing. He didn't even notice it until he found himself ogling a mermaid in Atlantis. Non-humans were complete unknowns to him."

"So, you think the twins can't see them either?"

"If the oracles inherited their powers from their father, which I expect they did, then I'm absolutely certain of that."

Now *that* was useful. If this was true, this could turn the tides—not just for contacting the alloy, but for defeating the estrellas altogether. Now, he only needed to find a creature that'd be willing to deliver a letter. Though, unfortunately:

"The only creatures in Nysa are the nymphs."

Valentina poured herself another glass of wine. "Count yourself lucky."

"Lucky? They're terrorists!"

"Well, kiras feed on magicks, serpions are quite hard to find, and mermaids might have a difficult time climbing the stairs. I think you're very lucky indeed."

"How am I supposed to convince a terrorist to help me?"

She raised her brows. "Have you ever met a nymph?"

The creature's green face flashed in his mind, its blood-thirsty eyes burned in his memories. He hadn't met it, no, but he had watched it leer as Frederick took his last breath.

"You would have me march into Nyseion," he said, "home of ten thousand nymphs, who would welcome me with spears at my neck...with a dish full of cucuruchos."

She took another long sip. "Not a terrible idea, you know. But I believe there are easier and more effective ways of gaining allies."

"Like what?"

"Being nice is a good start."

"Nice? To terrorists?"

"Kiva," she chided, "they are not all the same, and they did not attack unprovoked."

"I don't give a damn. No one deserves to be slaughtered for who they are, no matter the provocation."

She leaned back in her chair and held her glass up. "On that, we agree." She swirled the wine. "So, how do you plan to find your creature ally, if not without kindness?"

He fell silent. He would have to think on that one for a while.

$\sim$

The next morning, Kiva sat on the ledge of the nymph fountain, vaguely reading the day's newspaper, skimming for more information about the Agarthan diplomat. The unnamed envoy was being given increasingly more space on the page, dwarfing the routine front-page news about Agartha's imminent threat.

Why is the Crown advertising this? Who is this diplomat? He was sure it was no one that he knew. *I'll ask Alden to find out more once his mission is done.*

He looked up from the paper, watching the townspeople walk by, envying them. To be so oblivious to the oncoming war. Oblivious to the destruction, the death that was around the corner. What a privilege.

His eye caught a boy walking alone, head down, hands in pockets. A rag wrapped around his head. The boy slipped into the yellow building on main street.

The half-nymph.

Would the oracle blind spot work with him?

He ripped out the message he had written to Ember in the margins of the paper and tucked it away before following the boy to the yellow building. When he opened the door, he was met with an overwhelming floral scent.

"You're not welcome here," a voice called from behind the first row of flowers. Kiva turned the corner to see the store owner behind the counter; the nymph brat sat on top, arms folded.

"How did you know it was me?" Kiva asked. No way had that man seen him come in.

The nymph smirked. "You're loud as Tartarus."

"Get out before I make you get out," the owner said.

What an easy fight that would be, Kiva thought, then sadly remembered his shoulder. *I'd better save that for something worth it.*

He raised his hands. "Hold on. I'm not looking for trouble. I just want to talk to the kid."

The store owner looked inquisitively at the teenager whose eyes narrowly fixed on Kiva.

"Interesting," the half-nymph said. "He's being honest."

"You want to talk to him?" the store owner said.

"Is there money in it?" the kid said to Kiva.

He held out three triangularly cut diamond chips. "Thirty chips. All yours if you listen to my proposition."

The boy jumped off the counter and swiped the three diamonds from his hands. He held each close to his eye, inspecting them.

"*Delique*," he said. The diamonds remained the same.

"Satisfied?" Kiva asked. "I have thirty more where that came from. But only if we get some privacy."

The boy rubbed his chin. "Pedro," he called to the store owner. "Can we use the back room?"

"You sure, Damian? I don't like him."

Rest assured, Kiva thought, *the feeling's mutual.*

"Me neither," Damian said. "But he hasn't lied yet today. And I could use the money." He jostled the diamonds in his hand. "Let me hear him out."

"I still don't like it." Pedro shook his head as he pushed open another door. "But it's all yours."

Kiva followed Damian to the back room. Except for the smaller space, it was indistinguishable from the showroom. An array of colors and shapes decorated the edges, vines hanging down. And somehow, the floral smell had strengthened. The door shut behind them.

"Alright," Damian said. "What do you want from me, you psychopath?"

Kiva scoffed. "How am I a psychopath?"

"Normal people don't sneak into an isolated country to stalk some girl they don't like."

"Why on earth would you think that's what happened?"

Damian glared at him. "I hope she's still alive, or I'll have to cut you down right here. I'm a nymph remember? Killing is my specialty." He pulled the rag up from his ears.

It took everything Kiva had not to laugh at him. "You're a half-nymph. So, you're at most, half as scary as you think you are. Have you ever seen the real ones kill? You're not nearly as threatening."

"Oh, and you have?"

His jaw tightened. "Yeah."

The kid frowned, seeming to wrestle with a few different thoughts before saying, "What happened to that poor girl?"

"That 'poor girl' probably wounded me for life, and I *still* haven't laid a hand on her. She's fine. Like I said she would be."

"You're telling the truth." Damian massaged his temples. "I don't get it. How can you both want to hurt her and not lay a hand on her?"

Kiva didn't even pretend to understand. He held up the three diamonds. "Ever been to el Alcázar?"

The kid cocked his head. "I work there."

"Perfect. The girl I'm looking for, she's residing there for the time being. I need you to deliver a message."

"Which girl? I won't help you with an estrella."

"I wouldn't dare. I'm looking for a woman named Ember."

His eyes widened. "I won't let you hurt Señorita Slade."

"I'm not going to hurt her, damn it!" Kiva pulled out the note. "Read it for yourself. I just want to meet with her outside the castle. She knows who I am."

Damian took it from him, eyes quickly scanning it.

"So, this is the woman you don't like?" he asked. "The one you were going to buy flowers for that day?"

Kiva rolled his eyes. "Yes."

Damian groaned.

"What?"

"Your lies are obnoxious."

"I'm not lying!"

"Just stop," the half-nymph said, holding his head. "I can't stand people like you."

"But I'm conceding that you were right! I don't like her and the flowers were for her! How can that be a lie?"

"Poor Seño. Listening to you is exhausting. My brain hurts." He swiped the three extra diamonds from Kiva's hand. "But, I'll do it."

CHAPTER 28

EMBER

Ember sat with Damian in her room after training, the two of them poring over a map of Nysa, sheets of paper that he had stolen strewn everywhere. She hadn't yet had enough free time to go see Liliana Caldwell—the author lived on the other side of the island. Even if Ember was proficient in landsailing, it would likely be a half-day trip, and, after being seen collaborating with Ademure, she couldn't afford to miss dinner. Tomorrow would be her first opportunity to go.

In the meantime, she had enlisted Damian's help. After that trek through the Archives a few nights ago, she hadn't been able to sleep, instead spending every waking hour contemplating the best way to get out of this place and fast. However, the same three problems still plagued her plans: navigation, landsailing, and actual sailing.

"So they expected you to save Nysa from Agartha when you were only eight years old?" she asked.

Damian marked the harbor with a circle and traced a line through the dunes. "I had a mix of powers they had never seen before. Some they still haven't seen. They didn't know what to expect, but they thought it was possible."

"But why did they think a half-nymph would help them? Cadeña said that nymphs and magicks didn't get along even before the..." She couldn't finish the rest of her sickening sentence.

"Because my dad was human. And I was his gullible, will-do-anything-to-make-dad-proud child." He continued to draw. "Plus, whatever Fate told them about the nymphs, they believed them vital to Nysa's success. They thought that I was vital to their success. That's also why they were so reluctant to give me up after Dad died. They thought they could train impressionable young me to be like them."

"So Fate was wrong?"

"I mean, I didn't read the prophecy, but I doubt it. No, everyone likes to interpret Fate's aging vague words to fit their far-off destiny, rather than let Fate just be. That's why I prefer to interpret rhythms. They're here and now, and you have to ability to ask the creator for clarification. They're so much more reliable." He capped his marker and slid the map over to her.

The line he traced went from the harbor to the dunes right through the plaza and up the main street of town, then further up the castle pathway, leading all the way to el Alcázar's front gate.

"That's the most straightforward route off the island," he said. "You know how to ride a landsailer?"

"I'm working on it." She held the map closer to her face. "Okay, what am I missing here? Why did I think this would be harder?"

"I didn't mark the estrellas. Or that you'll have the princess to consider. Or any route out of the harbor."

"Got it. This is the easy part." She stared at the map for a moment longer, wondering how she would accomplish even step one: getting Ademure out of the castle while under the oracles' sight.

Which reminded her of the oracles' sight.

Oh my god, she thought. *I'm an idiot.* She hastily folded the map together, her head on a swivel as she looked for any indication that the twins' had seen her plans. *Maybe there's a hidden camera-like thing?*

"Seño? What are you doing?"

She dragged a hand down her cheek. "Just now realizing we should've done this outside the castle."

He shook his head. "Don't worry about it. They haven't seen anything."

"How would you know? Are they out on a mission again?"

"Just take my word for it. I've got an ear out for them. We can continue without worry."

She looked at him from beneath her palm. *Rhythms wouldn't tell you squat about their sight. You're not telling me something.*

Then she remembered what Damian had said the other day, about payback for his dad.

Actually, you haven't told me a whole lot of somethings.

"Damian, why did your dad kill those alloys?"

After tugging his cloth headband and his shirt, he adjusted himself so that he sat on his knees. "I can't answer that."

"But you know the answer?"

He simply looked at her.

That's a yes.

"If your dad hated alloys, and you want to avenge your father, why help me? Had your dad known about me, the nymphs would've killed me. What do you get from an alloy's success? It has to be more than a free princess."

"My dad hated liars and killers. Not alloys. Can we change the subject?"

"Sure, but I'm going to ask again. Ademure gets you a pass on some things, but I don't know that I can work with someone with too many secrets."

"So you're willing to divulge your own secrets then?" he asked with a healthy amount of snark.

She quirked a brow. "Hit me with your best shot."

"I met this guy the other day. Brown hair, kind of tall. Is really obnoxious to listen to." He sized her up as if deciding whether to continue. "Know him?"

Her face was already burning. "Yes. Why?"

"Oh, come on. You mean to tell me you two are actually dating?"

"Stop reading my rhythms, Damian. Why are you asking about him?"

"Your boyfriend said he wanted to see you." He dug through his pocket and held out a crumpled piece of paper.

She grabbed the note. A simple question was scribbled on the page.

Need an escape?
K

"Why didn't you give this to me sooner?"

"I don't like him, Seño. I can't read him well at all, which usually means he's a liar. I didn't want him to hurt you. But now that I know you know him, if you think he can help us..."

She looked at him. "So, you *don't* know him?"

"No, and I know everybody, at least by face. But I only saw him for the first time like a month ago and then again yesterday."

A month ago was when I got here, she thought, wondering if that could possibly be mere coincidence. "But he told me that Nysa was his home?"

"If it was, it wasn't recently, Señorita. I'm pretty certain about that."

Her chest hollowed. Her palms heated. *I knew something was wrong with him*, she thought, though that didn't make the confirmation of it any better. *But who is he? How did he get here?*

Then another question came to mind.

How did Damian get this note past the twins? She considered that a moment longer. *And the maps? And the supplies? And how has he been sneaking into town? And why is he never afraid to meet me on castle grounds?*

"Damian, how often do you see Ademure?"

He shrugged. "Once or twice a week."

"Even now. Even when she's locked away in her room at all hours of the day?"

"Yes. Why?"

Ember toyed with her locket, her forearms growing hotter. "Is it a nymph thing that the twins can't see you like they see everybody else?"

He raised his brows.

Another yes.

"Alright, then," she said. "And did this guy know you were a nymph?"

With a nod, he said, "Jerk knocked the rag off my head when he ran into me."

She crumpled the paper and slid it into her pocket. The heat moved to her shoulders. "Does he know your secret, you think?"

He shook his head. "I doubt it. I don't even think the twins know about it."

"But he went to you specifically to deliver the note, right?

Even after knowing you were a nymph, something most people on this island fear?"

"Yeah."

She felt her eyes water and heat. *I could not be more of an idiot.*

"I'm sorry, Seño. I didn't think he actually knew you. I shouldn't have agreed to give you the message."

"No, I'm glad you did." She took a deep breath. Her forearms were on fire. "Like I said, I don't like secrets."

After another night of restless sleep, Ember woke up early. She had to nip this Kiva thing in the bud before going to see Liliana Caldwell. It was bad enough to have him stalking her in Nysa. She would *not* have him following her back to the Soulless Realm. Ten extra minutes was all she needed.

On the landsailer Damian stole for her the night before, she made her way to the beach...eventually. The sun had hardly left the horizon. Parts of the sky were still starry. The birds weren't even singing, yet Kiva was there anyway.

"Do you ever go home?" she asked.

He turned his head. "Well, good morning! I didn't think you'd be out so early." He moved toward her.

She stepped back.

"I have things to do, Kiva. Why did you want to see me?" She held his note between two fingers. "And don't give me that bullshit about wanting to spend time with me."

His eyes flitted between her and the note. "You sure you don't want to go to the cliffs to talk? I had an entire day planned out."

She glared at him, and his expression soured.

"Fine. We can stay here today." He gestured to the ground.

"Sit with me for a moment? I'm curious to learn how a single question gave me away."

Reluctantly, she chose a spot a distance away from him, sitting slowly, eyes on him the entire way down.

"Did you read that book yet?" he said as he took his own seat in the sand.

"Why do you keep asking me that?"

He kept his eyes on the ocean, his hair uncaring of the breeze. "We're going to war soon. I'm sure you know."

"I've heard rumors."

"I'm sure you've heard more than that. Do you like it here? In Nysa, I mean."

"It's fine. But it's not like I have a choice. I've told you about my family—"

"What if there was a choice?" he interjected. "What if I could take you away to somewhere entirely different? Would you go?"

The waves crashed in the distance. The waves she would have to endure—master—to get Ademure to safety. *If it was just a mirror ride, in a heartbeat*, she thought. *But it's not just that, is it?* Her palms heated.

"No."

"Why not?" he asked. "Isn't this place hell for you?"

"No." *At least, it wasn't at first.* "I'm treated well here. I'm fed well. My family helps me with my magic. I get to sit on a gorgeous beach and watch the waves all the time until *you* drag me away. This place isn't so bad."

He watched her curiously. "Well, it's hell for me."

Now that sounds like something close to the truth. "Isn't it your home?"

"It used to be. Now, it's just where I live."

"But it's not even that, is it?"

He gave her a noncommittal wave of his hand.

Aggravated by the silence, she crumpled the note into a ball before slipping it back into her pocket. "Kiva, what exactly do you know?"

In response, he combed his fingers through his hair, then pushed himself to his feet, walked over to her and held out a hand.

"I was wondering how long it would take you to ask. But why don't you tell me what you think I know, instead, ice queen?" His mouth spread into a new, mischievous grin.

She ignored the gesture and stood on her own. Unfazed, he placed his hand in his pocket and started strolling south along the shoreline.

The heat soared to her forearms. "Where do you think you're going?"

"For a walk," he said over his shoulder. "Join me if you want."

Son of a bitch. She jogged toward him. Once at his side, she waited for him to speak, but he only continued to walk with that stupid sheepish smile plastered on his lips.

She matched his pace, though she injected a bit more fire into every step. "You know I'm staying in el Alcázar."

"I do."

"You knew you needed to circumvent the Delfinos."

"I did."

"You knew Damian could do it."

"That," he said, "I did not know. But I knew it wasn't out of the range of possibility. Glad to see the brat made it."

"Why?"

He shrugged. "I mean yeah he's annoying, but I'd never wish the twins—"

"Damn it, Kiva! Why did you send me the note in the first place?"

He glanced at her, then back at the sand. "Waiting was

tiring." There was a moment more of consideration, of steps taken, before he added, "And I was running out of time before the war."

She stopped. "Because you're Agarthan."

He stopped as well. "Yes."

"And you know I'm an alloy."

A heavy pause.

"Yes."

"Who are you? Really?"

He ran a hand through his hair yet again, and Ember wanted to shave his head clean.

"I'm an agent of the Agarthan government," he said. "King Nikita tasked me with extracting you from the Soulless Realm. I was supposed to bring you home so that you could train to become our…"

"Nuclear bomb," she finished.

"Well, I was going to say 'weapon' but—" when he met her ire-filled eyes, he dropped his own guilt-ridden ones "—yeah. Something like that."

It was as if flames engulfed her arms, her shoulders, her sight, and *holy hell*, Kiva was lucky there wasn't a storm. He winced and grabbed his shoulder, and she didn't give a damn.

"Ember, I'm—"

"No." She held a hand up and shook her head. "Don't even begin to pretend to apologize."

"But I didn't mean—"

"You 'didn't mean'? You're kidding right? You've followed me around for over a month pretending to be into me when you were really after *my* powers for *your* fight. That is all your *meaning*."

She paced in a circle, her mind racing with what this meant for her, for Ademure. She didn't have just one country to worry about but two, both of them wanting her to annihilate the other. Even if they could make it past the twins and out of Nysa, would it be enough to avoid Kiva? And if it wasn't, what would happen to Ademure? Would she be safe? Could she and Ember ever be safe? The hole beneath her steps grew as deep as her thoughts.

Kiva didn't speak the entire time, but when she threw her arms to her side in a bout of frustration, he flinched.

That stopped her. *Keep it together*, she told herself. *No lightning. Don't become what they want you to be.*

She tucked her hands into her pockets before asking, "Why lie?"

"I had to be sure the oracles didn't indoctrinate you. As much as possible, I wanted you to learn about the Magick Realm from that book and from me so that you had another perspective. If I was going to bring you to Agartha, I couldn't have you believing the Nysan side."

Wait.

He'd brought her to the bookstore. Drawn her to that corner. He'd known they were her parents.

She took a step back. "You planted the book?"

"I needed you to know who the queen really was."

The flames were in her chest now. Hot tears welled in her lash line.

He clutched his shoulder tighter.

Raindrops.

"You used my parents' assassinations to *pick me up*?"

"No," he said quickly, his eyes filled with realization. "That wasn't the point. You were supposed to learn what happened so that you didn't trust the Crown. I wasn't trying to win your affection. I only wanted you to see things for what they were. I knew that the truth was enough to persuade you on its own."

"But did you even *think* before doing that? It's not like finding out my parents were old or had some incurable disease.

They didn't just die, Kiva. I knew nothing of my parents before, dead or alive, and now I find out they were *executed*." Her back was so hot, she thought she might grow wings of fire.

"I understand why you're upset—"

"No you fucking don't! Can you, for a second, imagine what it's like to find out that some crazy-ass government, who I'm supposed to be *working* for now, *murdered* my parents? *Orphaned* me. Can you take a moment to make sense of that?" The flame worked through her lower body, and her balance was shaky at best. She was losing control.

Raindrops.

"I—"

"And to then find out that the someone who claimed to like me was the one who told me this? Not because he actually gave a damn, but because he wanted to use me as a weapon *against* that government?" She should've stopped ranting, stopped working herself up further. She was growing too hot, losing too much control.

She didn't care.

Fuck the raindrops.

Kiva doubled over and fell to his knees, groaning as he dug his nails into his skin. The color drained from his face.

And Ember ignored him.

"So yeah, I'm mad. I'm pissed. Pissed that I'm on this godforsaken island training for someone else's godforsaken war. Pissed that you lied to me for so long when I gave you every opportunity to tell me the truth. Pissed that you manipulated my feelings to get what you wanted. Goddammit, if you needed me so badly, why didn't you just kidnap me like the twins did?"

"*Because you shot me with lightning!*"

She froze. Eyes widened.

No...

No, no, no, no, no.

The flame of wrath extinguished, quickly replaced by confusion, then dread. Then the girl's face. Bruised and beaten and begging. And then the hospital room and the doctor. No more foster parents, no more foster sister.

No, not again. It can't have happened again.

Kiva moved to one knee. He no longer gripped his shoulder but massaged the area, grimacing.

"You're one of the men who tried to kidnap me that day," Ember said.

"Yes."

"I shot you with lightning."

He pulled down the neckline of his t-shirt, revealing the purple spiderweb that decorated his shoulder. The purple spiderweb *she* had created. "Yes."

Tears fell, this time cold. She whispered, "I-I could've killed you."

"You didn't kill me, Ember." He stood tall and put a hand on her arm.

She knocked it off. "I tried so hard. So *fucking* hard. Six years. I thought that if I stayed away from everyone, it would be enough. But it wasn't enough. It won't ever be enough."

"Stop it. You didn't know you had that magic. But now you do and you can train it. Look at me."

She refused. "I almost killed you. You're supposed to be dead, and I was supposed to have..." She brushed over the scars on her wrist. "I *am* a murderer."

"No, you're not," he said sternly, grabbing her wrists and forcing her to look at him. Those fake green eyes seemed so genuine in the moment. "Believe me."

She wanted to.

"You're a terrible liar," she said and broke away.

And laughed.

It was robotic and cold and hit the air like shattering glass. She laughed at the gods, if they were even there. She laughed at herself. Just laughed.

Kiva frowned, reaching for her.

"Get away from me," she spat. "Haven't you learned your lesson?"

"I'm sorry, Ember, for making you upset. For lying to you. I really am."

"I'm not," she said, a smile still on her lips but tears in her eyes. "I knew something horrible had happened that day. I knew everyone only wanted me for my stupid magic. And I knew you were lying. I knew better about everything and ignored it, but it's so obvious now."

Those eyes. He continued to stare at her with those stupid fucking fake green eyes.

She averted her own and kicked the sand. "Oh, don't waste your pity on me. You're the one who got hurt."

"Am I?"

She huffed as she dug her hands into her pockets to find the crumpled note, then threw it at him. "I'm leaving."

"The offer stands."

She whipped back around and glowered. "Offer?"

"An escape. I can mirror you off of Nysa."

"Yeah, to Agartha. The other nation that wants to use me as a superweapon."

"Agartha is more stable than Nysa. And only people who use mirrors can get in, so you won't have to worry about the twins."

"I'd be trapped, then. How is that any different than here?"

"I'll take you anywhere you want to go, whenever you want to go."

"And I'm supposed to take *your* word on that?"

"I wish you would."

She laughed again, but when he didn't do the same, she said, "You really think that after all of this, I'm going to willingly leave with you to another version of the same hell?"

"Agartha is underground. It's actually a lot closer to hell." He winked.

Her palms heated again. "You're an overconfident dipshit who can't understand when you've lost."

"And you're an obstinate ice queen who doesn't understand the game. So, you coming?"

CHAPTER 29

ALDEN

"*Telum*," Alden said.

The topmost layer of the waist-high block of obsidian waned, leaving in its place a sharp black dagger. The blade was small but the handle was sturdy. He held the knife on the tip of his finger, waiting to see which way it toppled.

Perfectly balanced. He gripped the handle, then flung it thirty yards across the stone room. At the other side of the stall was a target with a diameter no larger than a foot. The blade struck perfect center.

Well, of course it did. Alden hadn't missed such an easy shot since he was nine, when his father first introduced him to the craft. At twenty-three, he had more than mastered the assassin's weapon of choice. This was only his warm-up.

"*Reditio.*" The blade pulled itself from the target, zipped back those thirty yards, and landed in his outstretched palm.

He turned his back to the target. The knife twirled between each of his fingers, quick enough that a misstep could cost him a pinky, but smooth enough that there would be no chance. As the blade finished dancing around his thumb, he caught the tip with two fingers. Then, with a flick of the wrist and toss over his shoulder, the blade zipped across again. This time, the dagger spun as it travelled, its final landing point unpredictable.

Well, unpredictable to most.

The knife struck its target. Perfectly horizontal. Perfectly centered. As expected from an assassin who mastered that trick at twelve.

His ears perked at the faint but high-pitched slew of notes, like someone skimming their hand at the top of a piano. It grew louder as its source grew closer, but he kept his focus on the target. He didn't need to look to see who that source was. These days, not many people sounded like that. Only Graye.

"I thought you were supposed to be working on the plans?" the woman said.

She closed the black stone doors behind her. The heels of her black boots clicked against the red and black flooring as she strode toward him, smiling. There was no one in the world he less desired to see than his little sister.

"They're nearly done," he said. "*Reditio.*" He caught the blade.

"Father wants them as soon as possible," she said. The magma river that streaked through the sealed flooring and walls emitted a glow that deepened her ebony skin and illuminated her hair, the latter of which was manipulated to be redder than blood. "He wants to attack in the next week or so."

"I know what Father wants. What is it that *you* want?" Alden flicked the knife behind his back. It stuck perfectly, again.

Graye flashed a toothy grin. The notes moved faster.

"Can't a girl want to check in on her big brother?"

"A girl, sure. But, you're no girl. *Reditio.*"

"Ouch," she said, feigning being stabbed in the chest. "I have feelings, you know."

"Strange. I thought sociopaths were incapable of feeling." Another toss, another bullseye.

She moved to her brother's side. The knife returned as fast as it left, and she pulled it from the air, grasping it between two fingers.

"You think you're so funny," she said.

"No, I think you're unpleasant—" he grabbed the blade "—and a waste of my time. If you came to taunt me, let's get on with it. I'm busy."

His sister folded her arms and leaned against the block of obsidian. "I heard you helped Kiva sneak into Nysa."

"Yeah, and?" He glanced at her sidelong.

"Nikita didn't like that."

"Yes, well, I could overthrow Esmerelda today, and Nikita would shame me for the outfit I was wearing when I did it. I'm not worried about him."

"You don't think Kiva will get caught? Get killed?"

He lifted a brow. Graye Caldwell had never worried about anyone but herself in her life. "Do you have a crush on him or something? He could use a girlfriend."

She laughed, but her faint slew of notes faded to a monotone, steady drumbeat. "I'm asking because I care about you."

"That's bullshit if I've ever heard it."

He threw the knife. Another perfect hit.

"Are you not worried about him, then?" Her drumbeat slowed. "I mean, you left him all alone in enemy territory with a wounded shoulder and the alloy who gave it to him."

"Should I be worried?"

"He's your best friend."

"And a grown man. He can take care of himself."

She tilted her head. "Can he?"

"What are you getting at, Graye?"

She shrugged. "I mean, I would think a shoulder like that would really slow a person down. And what if the alloy turns on him? He has so much working against him. I'm just hoping the next job goes well—that he doesn't get caught in the clash." She tucked her hands into her pockets and waltzed back toward the entrance. "But if you say he can take care of himself..."

"Is that a threat?"

She stopped at the door. The slew of high-pitched notes returned with the satisfaction on her face. "I need to get going, but you should really get back to Father with those plans."

Alden whirled to face her and released the blade.

"*Specta, specta!*" she shouted before the handle left his palm.

A single mirror appeared in front of her, held steady mid-air by her own sheer will. The blade passed through the mirror, leaving a wake of glass behind it.

He spun back around to find another mirror at equal height, also held mid-air, yet this one faced his training target. In the moment he turned, a sharp edge emerged from its surface. Once the dagger was free from the glass, it darted toward the target, steady and true to the bullseye. And stuck.

"Betrayed by my own brother," his sister half-sang along to the melody. "I thought we were a team."

"Go away, Graye, before I do something worse."

"Please. Like you could hit me if you tried." She left the room, the mirrors plunging to the ground and shattering.

CHAPTER 30
EMBER

Book in bag, Ember took the landsailer and made for the south side of the island, spending the next four wearisome hours stopping and starting and sinking and skidding across the town, through the suburbs, and toward the mountains. Her frustrations didn't make concentrating on her manipulation any easier, but she did get to invent some new curses on her journey, decorating her vocabulary with phrases like "Kiva-ass-shit" and "red-eye-motherfucker."

When the sand became rocks, she was forced to stop. She pulled out the map and brushed away the sweat on her brow. The author's residence was at least another half-hour walk further. She glanced at her shoes and groaned.

This side of the island was steep and growing steeper. The rocks loosened beneath her feet, the trail had thinned, and there were fewer plateaus where she could rest. She didn't think she was climbing a mountain, but her body thought otherwise.

The sun beat down her neck, and she cursed herself for not

bringing at least a hat. If she didn't hurry, she'd become a tomato.

At last, there appeared a small house, precariously perched on a cliff. Violet hibiscuses surrounded it on one side, and it overlooked a steep drop and miles of ocean on the other. As far as she could see, this was the only house out this far. And unlike every other building on this island, it didn't appear to be made of sand but rocks—hot pink.

She slowed as she stepped onto the porch, pulse thundering in her ears. She gripped the strap of her bag tightly with one hand and lifted her other fist in the air. Eyes closed, she breathed, and knocked.

The waves crashed against the cliff below, filling the achingly long moment of silence. The palms of her hands moistened, and her spine chilled. The butterflies in her stomach pounded for an escape.

I can't do this. She turned to step off the porch.

"Hola?" a woman said behind her.

Ember stiffened. The woman at the door was long and thin, her coarse black hair tied up in a turquoise headwrap. A sleek green dress painted in splashes of blue with willowy sleeves and a flowy skirt draped over the woman's ebony skin.

This woman knew her parents. Ember's heart beat in her throat.

"Are you Liliana Caldwell?" she stuttered out in Spanish.

"Who's asking?" the woman said in perfect English.

Alright, hint taken. Work on pronunciation.

Ember offered her hand. "My name is Ember Slade. It's nice to meet you." The words tumbled from her mouth.

The woman looked her over from head to toe. Ember supposed she should've expected this from someone who lived so cautiously, but the scrutiny felt violating nonetheless.

"My, my," the woman said at last. "You are her spitting image. Please come in."

A warmth washed over Ember as she entered the author's home. The candlelight filled the room, brighter than any space in the castle. The cozy couches and chairs were large enough for several guests and covered the entirety of the floor. Hundreds of framed pictures of so many different people decorated the walls. Some people looked like family. Others were clearly cherished friends. But every single person held a genuine smile.

"I never thought I'd live to see this day," the woman said. "Please, sit down. Would you like a guarapo? I'm sure the hike was draining."

Ember nodded. As she took a seat in a chair near the mantle, the anxiety rushed out of her. This place was safe. She knew it.

"It's quite the rare occasion that I get visitors out here," the woman called from the kitchen. Soon, she returned with two cups of what looked like punch and took a seat across from her guest.

Ember grabbed the cup and sipped. Cold sweetness teased her taste buds, cut by hints of lime. "Thank you," she said as the sugar dissolved on her tongue.

"My pleasure, dear. I have plenty more for you, so drink up. Now, I'm sure you have a number of questions about your parents."

She set down her glass. "You *knew* they were my parents."

A simper spread across Liliana's lips. "I've known your mother since we were teenagers. We had the same tutor and spent most of our free time together, getting into all sorts of trouble. I met Victor years later when Ana introduced us. They started dating when she was in her early twenties I believe. He wasn't much of a looker, but she insisted he was the best—"

"Thank you," Ember interrupted. She needed to know about the author, no one else. But realizing how rude she must've sounded, she put on a smile. "That's a lot. Thank you."

Liliana seemed unbothered. Her smile grew warm, like the comfort of a blanket on an icy winter day.

"Miss Caldwell, how did you know about me before today?"

"Honey, I was Ana's best friend. I was there throughout her pregnancy."

"Did you know that I was left in the Soulless Realm?" Ember asked as heat formed in her palms.

The corner of Liliana's mouth quirked. "As I said, I was there throughout your mother's entire pregnancy."

Ember refrained from scowling, but the flames still crawled up her forearms. "And you didn't step in to raise me? Or help me? Or even write about me in your damn book?"

The author said nothing; she only sipped her drink. And a moment later, the heat within Ember dissipated. It was like talking to Kiva again, only receiving half-truths. Though, this woman felt more like she wanted her to discover her lies.

She held up her locket. "Have you seen this before?"

Nodding, Liliana said, "Your parents waited years to give it to you."

"Why doesn't it come off?"

The author blinked. "I wouldn't know. Perhaps, it's broken?"

Extremely broken.

"Did you know about my powers?"

"That you're stronger than most magicks? Of course, I did. You're an alloy."

"Not that. I mean the lightning. Do you think my parents knew about it?"

Liliana's brows knit together. "How would they know what

doesn't exist?"

"But they must've known something," Ember argued. Her hands remained surprisingly cool. "They died two days after I was born, Miss Caldwell. One day after leaving me behind. I can't believe that's a coincidence. If it wasn't the lightning, why'd they leave?"

The woman frowned, her eyes flitting between her hands and Ember, as she seemingly tried to remember whatever she had apparently forgotten. "Remind me your birth date, dear?"

"January tenth. They died January twelfth. Over twenty-two years ago."

She nodded and looked away, mumbling beneath her breath. Gradually, her expression grew hard and her stare distant, and she inclined her head as the mumbling intensified.

Ember narrowed her eyes. "Miss Caldwell?"

"A moment, dear," Liliana said without raising her gaze. "I can barely recall it."

Ember waited another minute, watching the woman mouth nonsense. Though her speech was indecipherable, she spoke with a noticeable rhythm, like she was reciting poetry.

"She becomes light," Liliana whispered loud enough for Ember to hear. She looked up. "Oh, I'm such a fool. I never realized, and it was right before my eyes. You were born the day the prophecy was engraved!"

Ember dug through her bag for her notebook, flipped to where Ademure's handwriting began, and handed it to her. "Do you mean this?"

The author studied the page. "Where did you get this?"

"In el Alcázar's Archives."

"And you managed to get it past the Delfinos? Incredible. I've never been able to get any prophecy past the serpions in Agartha." She handed the notebook back. "It's not exactly the same, but it seems to refer to the same event. And, now that you've mentioned the lightning, I presume this will begin fulfilling soon, if it hasn't already."

Liliana then spoke to herself. "To think, Ana. Your daughter, the light."

Ember grimaced. *Ana has nothing to do with this.* And with that thought, her forearms ignited again, heating faster and stronger. The flame burned through her back and her chest, then started toward her—

"Your anger and apprehension are strong, dear," Liliana said. "What plagues your mind?"

The heat vanished. Ember was even-headed once more. She flipped her arms over and rubbed them, but they were completely cool. *What the hell? I haven't thought of the raindrops once.*

She looked up at Liliana who gave her another smile.

"Are you messing with me?" she asked intending to be angry, though she felt unusually calm.

"I'm sorry if it bothers you," Liliana said. "I can pull back if you wish. I just hate to see you so distraught."

"But how? I thought—"

"You have enough to learn as it is. Don't concern yourself with this. Not yet."

Now that Ember noticed it, she couldn't not feel it. It was like a giant weight pressed on her emotions, stopping them from spilling over. With them repressed, she could easily focus on her plans. But what was Liliana doing to keep her anger at bay? How could she exact so much control?

It didn't matter. The woman was right: she had too many other things to worry about.

"Miss Caldwell," Ember said, "I need a way to go home."

Liliana sipped her guarapo and pursed her lips. "I don't know that I can help you with that, honey. I have a ship at the harbor, but that's it."

"You can take us away, then!"

"Us?"

"Princess Ademure and me. She also needs help leaving."

Shaking her head, Liliana said, "I can't fight the estrellas. Not without several other magicks more powerful than myself."

"But if we get enough of a head start—"

"They'll catch up to us, dear. I'm well aware of how strong they are. The princess, especially, wouldn't make it out alive."

"Is there another way? A plane? A bridge?"

"Unfortunately, no. Believe me. I've tried them all."

Ember's excitement waned, though she wasn't sure if it was natural or not. "What about the prophecy thing? Does it tell me how to control the lightning? How do I make it so that I can't hurt anyone I don't want to?"

Liliana shrugged her mouth. "I wish I could help, I really do. But it takes weeks to understand even a couple lines. It would be months before I would be able to tell you what that says about your magic. All I can say now is that it will be vital to the war."

Ember sank into her chair and covered her face in her hands. Hours of reading. The dive into the Archives. Damian's plans. Ademure's safety. So much *emotion*...invested into a dead end. She groaned in exhaustion.

Her exhaustion faded.

"I hope you don't mind," Liliana said, smiling sheepishly. "But you have a long journey ahead of you. I can't have you giving up yet."

Ember thinned her lips, but that little amount of genuine care was more than she had ever before received. She had to admit it felt nice to be looked after.

"Who are you, Miss Caldwell?" she asked after a moment. "Were you an activist too?"

"Soulless rights?" Liliana said, chuckling. "Elysium, no. I was simply a tutor. I loved your mother, but I never understood that drive. Understood her less when she decided to marry one of them."

"Marry one of them?"

"She went to Tokyo, came back with him. A shock to us all, you can imagine. And a bit of a predicament, considering the times we were in. Leon and I eventually warmed up to him, but it was quite a feat, let me tell you."

Ember raised a brow. "Wait. Are you trying to tell me my father was a soulless?"

Liliana tilted her head. "Ember, what do you think an alloy is?"

"I don't know. A powerful magick?"

"Yes, of course, but that's not what defines them. Alloys are mixed-race, born of soulless and magick blood. You're Nysan on your mother's side, of course, and on your father's side, American."

"But they met in Tokyo?"

"He traveled quite a bit for work."

"And what was she doing in Tokyo?"

She shrugged. "She traveled quite a bit for fun."

Staring blankly at the wall of photos, Ember took some time to process this new information. "Why didn't you mention any of this in your book?"

"It wasn't well-known at the time, and the attitude toward soulless was very hostile. Still is today, but it's mostly cloaked by this stupid cold war with the Agarthans." She waved her hand. "Your mother manipulated Victor's eye color and said she met him in South America, in the mountains. But the Crown didn't believe her though they couldn't prove otherwise. So she constantly kept him in her sight. Eventually, no one cared except the queen. And when Ana started her crusade for soulless rights, well, she didn't exactly curry favor with Su Majestad."

"Then they were killed."

The woman smiled sadly as she sipped her drink.

"That's them, right there." She pointed to the mantle which held three picture frames. On the left were Ana and Victor Slade. On the right, an unfamiliar couple. In the center was a picture featuring four faces, all gleaming.

Ember looked closer at the latter frame. The woman pictured, as well as the children, looked very much like Liliana, but the boy and girl had their father's eyes—his *scarlet* eyes. She looked back to Liliana who still smiled, her green irises sparkling. *She's alone.*

"Why do you live out here?" she asked.

"To get away from the nonsense. The estrellas and queen have been increasingly reckless. They stir up whatever drivel they want, deliberately ignoring the consequences, and I want no part of the fallout. I wouldn't mind if el Alcázar de Maldojo came down with a sudden incurable affliction quite frankly."

"So you're not a fan."

"Since the king and my husband left the castle, things have spiraled out of control. Between the nymphs and Agartha, I don't know how much longer our little island can survive the rule of Su Majestad."

"Why don't you leave?"

"This is my home, honey. The only other place in the world I would go would have me killed before I could step foot on the obsidian. I have nowhere else."

And there was silence. Liliana sipped her guarapo, as if she were waiting for Ember to say more, but she sat quietly, her hands folded across her lap, her gaze wandering about the room.

"I'm surprised, dear," she said. "You came all this way. You truly don't want to know anything else about your parents? I've told you so little, and my book wasn't at all comprehensive."

She was right. The book mostly focused on her parents' activism, not their personal lives. And if Ember herself wasn't mentioned, there was no telling what other details Liliana had skipped over.

They could've meant to protect me, Ember began to argue with herself. *They could've left to protect me.*

"You've told me enough."

"You're afraid," Liliana observed.

"I'm not."

"You are. You're afraid to know more about them."

"No," Ember insisted. "I just recognize they're dead. There's no reason to learn more."

"I think that's all the more reason to learn. You never had the chance to talk to them."

And what would I have said if I did?

Or worse, what if she found out their leaving didn't actually matter? What if she still would've...regardless of whether they had stayed? Or what if her parents did try to help her, but she scared them away?

Or what if what they said or did or could've done otherwise meant nothing at all, because no matter what, she was always going to act on her stupid emotions and get herself...here?

What if, just maybe, it wasn't her parents that she should blame?

"What they've done can't affect me any more than it has," she said. "They're gone, always have been. They don't matter."

The anxiety retreated once more, her head clearing. Liliana looked at her with pitied eyes.

"What?" she asked.

"I guess I should tell you about your parents."

"Really, Miss Caldwell, I don't care to know about them."

"They're alive, dear."

Ember looked up, and time stopped.

Then, the world stopped.

Then, her heart...stopped.

"What? But you—"

"I did," Liliana said. "I wrote that they were dead. I lied."

Her tongue grew thick, and her throat constricted. A tear formed at her lash, sweat at her brow. Her head throbbed. The room was closing in.

"Why?"

"For your safety and theirs. It was only a matter of time before an 'accident' befell them. They escaped to the Soulless Realm."

The beating, the pulsing, it wouldn't leave her ears. *But why the Soulless Realm?* she wondered. *How did they know when? Who else knows about them?* Yet, as she spoke, her mouth ran dry, and all she asked was:

"Wh-where?"

Then she forced herself to swallow.

"Where are they now?"

"I believe they've since separated," the author said. "At least, they had when I last spoke with Ana. As far as I know, your father is back in Tokyo continuing his research, and your mother is in the Andes mountains."

So her parents had convinced entire nations that they'd tragically died in a fire and had made themselves out to be martyrs for the cause. Her parents had fooled the king and queen—the *estrellas* for decades. They were incredible! They had to be! Intelligent, cunning, people who really believed in something, they were probably decent fighters, and—

"Why didn't my parents find me once they were safe?"

Liliana's smile faded. "I...don't know."

—they'd never come back for her.

"I'm sorry, Ember."

But that apology hardly removed the dagger that split her in two, at the mind and the heart.

"Don't be," she said. *It's not like I expected anything else.*

"I'm sure that when you find them, they'll have some explanation."

Ember couldn't heat under Liliana's dampening, but she wanted to, even if it meant losing control. She wanted the island to burn, the world to burn. Her parents to burn.

Fortunately, the author's magic was strong, so she instead let out a cold laugh.

"Find them?" she said. "If they've forgotten about me, I've forgotten about them. I'm not finding them."

"Ember, they're your parents."

"No, they're my DNA donors."

Liliana set down her glass. "I understand what this news must feel like, and you have every right to hurt however you see fit. But don't let that hurt stop you. You'll need to grow quite a bit before Fate calls."

"My fate is to return to my apartment in Dallas and sleep so long I wake up thinking this was all a fever dream."

"Your fate is to stop the war."

Ember stood and threw her bag over her shoulder. "Thank you for your hospitality, Miss Caldwell, but it's time for me to go."

But before she could take a step, the author grabbed her shoulder, keeping her firm in place.

"If not for your parents, then why did you come here today?" she asked. "Do you not wonder about who you are?"

"I think I've got the gist."

"You truly think that you are meant to be someone who is on the brink of rage at all hours of the day?"

At that, Ember met her gaze and twisted her lips.

"I think," Liliana said, her eyes brightening, "that when you have the chance, you need to find Ana. Find out who you really are through the person who brought you into this world."

Ember touched her locket with cold palms. "I've learned everything I'll ever need to know about her."

"You haven't."

"I have," she said more sternly. "Miss Caldwell, I know you meant well telling me they're alive, but in all honesty, I liked them better dead."

Liliana took Ember's hands in hers. She met her stare with a warm smile, and though Ember wanted to break away, something kept her feet firm in place.

"I implore you to seek her out," the woman continued. "You must prepare for the war to come, and to do that, you must know yourself. Don't let your parents' mistakes stop you from pursuing your path. You must find Ana."

Ember looked at the mantle once more where Ana and Victor Slade were frozen in an everlasting smile. Parents by blood only.

"I have to go," she said. "Thank you for your time today, Miss Caldwell."

Liliana tugged on Ember's hand, wrapping her into an unexpected hug. Ember was stiff, her eyes widened. But she let herself sink into it, wrapping her arms around the woman in return.

"Honey, you are welcome here anytime."

The door shut, and Ember stepped outside into the angry Nysan sun.

CHAPTER 31

ADEMURE

Light broke through the stained-glass windows. Birds chirped in the courtyard. The smell of breakfast wafted through the air. Without the estrellas, the dining room was substantially warmer and, without her mother's presence, this morning was almost pleasant. She soaked in every moment.

"Ademure?" the alloy said as she entered the dining room. "Where is Cadeña? Won't the twins see you?"

Biting into her delectable toast, Ademure said, "Good morning to you too, Ember. Damian informed me that Nieve and Sombra just left the island, and, when I started my morning prayers, I realized there was no one standing watch in the hall. I wouldn't dare miss the opportunity to leave my room."

"This doesn't feel right."

"I don't care. I'm dead anyway." She swallowed. "Did you see that author yet? The last thing I saw in my notebook was your rewrite of Nieve's diary entry."

Ember grimaced. "I saw her a few days ago."

"And?"

"Nothing. She was a dead end."

Ademure frowned and was surprised to find herself a bit disappointed. "I'm sorry. I told you we shouldn't rely on her."

Ember plopped herself down in the seat next to her. "I know, I know. But the more I think about helping you, the more ridiculous I feel. I'm not a fighter. I'm not an escape artist. I'm barely an adult, honestly. And yeah, I might have some absurd magical powers, but I can't tap into them without going ballistic. I just thought if Liliana Caldwell knew so much about my parents, then maybe she could help. Clearly, I was wrong."

"Don't give up yet," Ademure said, faking her own shaken confidence. "What about your original plan? Before the author, how did you think we were going to get away?"

Ember took an irate bite of pineapple. "I planned on stealing one of the estrellas' boats."

"Okay, what about that? We can still do that."

"Ademure, do you know how to sail?"

She shook her head.

"Then it's also a dead end," Ember said. "I've been practicing for weeks, and I still barely go anywhere, even when I put all my energy into it. Not to mention we'd somehow have to sneak you past the estrellas and onto a landsailer—which I barely know how to use—to even get you to the harbor."

Gulping down her resurfacing anxiety, Ademure reached for the alloy's arm. "That's okay, you'll learn. You'll practice more, and you'll get it, and we will be fine. We have time."

"Do we?"

"You haven't been told when to do it, right? You said so yourself. If you haven't attacked, then it's not yet my time."

"Yeah, I guess."

A stout figure burst into the room before Ember could say

more, and what little remained of Ademure's stoicism shattered.

"Princess Ademure! Alloy Slade!"

Amá.

Oh no.

"How pleasant to see you both!" Esmerelda chimed. "Although Ademure, you look sallow. And Alloy, you look dreadful."

Ember moved her arm in front of Ademure, as she had that night in the library.

"Come now," the queen said. "Don't be like that. I'm only here for a quick talk."

The room grew hot like that night in the library as well. Ademure reached for Ember's forearm, but when she touched it, her finger singed. She ripped it back, waving off the sting.

"Not now," Ademure whispered to Ember. She glanced back toward the door to see both Estrellas Bailón and Cadeña standing at the watch. They weren't the Delfinos, but Bailón in particular wasn't someone she wanted to cross. "We won't win."

She didn't know if Ember had heard her, but the sweat on her own brow started to dry. Ember lowered her arm, and instead gripped the wood of the table—something the twins would've done in case they needed to manipulate a weapon.

Ademure's stomach turned at the sight of her exuberant mother, but like a true royal, she put on a smile anyway.

"To what do we owe this honor, Amá?"

"Daughter," the queen said. "Dear sweet, youthful Ademure. I have only come to announce an exciting event to take place this Friday. Something the entire island will enjoy."

Furrowing her brow, Ademure said, "Friday is el Día de la Independencia."

"It is. And we will be having a parade. I'll want you by my side."

She glanced at the estrellas. Cadeña wore a sinister grin and toyed with his monocle. Bailón simply seemed annoyed. *What is going on here?*

"I must admit that I didn't expect to be included in this year's festivities," Ademure said carefully. "I thought you didn't want me to mislead our people any further than I supposedly already had?"

Her mother's laugh was unnaturally shrill. Ember straightened in her chair as if she was readying for an attack, but when the estrellas stepped forward, she sunk back, still gripping tight to the wood of the table.

"You are mistaken, dear Ademure," Esmerelda said. "Of course, I want you by my side. Actually, I've come to realize that you are key to helping my plans move forward."

"I am?"

"You are. Our last stop will be in the plaza, near the fountain. There, we will have you give a speech to those people who so adore you, encouraging them in these dark times. You will tell them to hold on a little longer, and that the end of this madness is in sight, now that the Agarthans have extended an olive branch."

"An olive branch?" Ademure repeated. "When did this happen?"

Bailón stepped in quickly, saying, "Don't burden yourself with the details. Just be ready on Friday in your best dress." She turned to the queen. "I believe that's more than enough, Majestad. I would advise that we move on with your busy schedule."

"Of course," the queen said, but she was looking at Ademure as she said it, her green eyes glowing.

"Cadeña, stay here with Su Alteza," the captain ordered. "Alloy, you should head to training."

A sweltering heat followed Ember as she dutifully crossed the dining hall. Before leaving, however, the alloy glanced back at Ademure with troubled eyes. With a single nod, they both knew. This was never going to be a celebration.

No. This was the end.

"Sweet Ademure," Esmerelda said. "Is there something wrong?"

"No." Cadeña at her side, Ademure's fake smile fell. "Nothing at all."

"Eat something, then. You look sickly."

"I'm alright, thank you," she said, but her racing pulse and churning abdomen said something else entirely.

"Suit yourself. If we have to carry you to town, we will." Her mother grinned. "But you won't be missing for any reason. The people only really listen to you."

The moment her bedroom door closed, leaving Cadeña in the hall and the princess with her privacy, Ademure tore her notebook open, pen in hand. But a message was already waiting for her.

Tell Damian.

Luckily for her, the half-nymph arrived through her balcony door ten minutes later. At the end of her lengthy, overwrought explanation, she was sitting on her bed with her elbows on her knees, head in hand, running her fingers through her hair, and taking the deepest breaths she could summon.

"I'm not ready," she sputtered.

"You can't think like that, Princesa," Damian said at her side. "We have three days left before this parade. Señorita Slade and I have been preparing for this. It will work out."

She nodded, but heat still flooded her cheeks, and her lashes were soon lined with salty tears.

A warm hand lay on her back.

"You will leave," he said. "We'll find a way. In the meantime, would you like to see the plans?"

"You and Señorita Slade will probably enter at the north entrance to the town," Damian said, making himself comfortable in the chair in her room. "That's where I'll be waiting."

"And how will you get the estrellas' attention?"

"I'm thinking I might sing for them. Slow them down a bit. What do you think?"

"That they'll easily overpower you," Ademure said, shaking her head. "What about your nymph side? Any special abilities there that the twins won't have? Maybe with the rhythms?"

"Listening to them won't do anything but warn me about where they are. And I can't fade in the sand either. I'm out of practice. I might accidentally suffocate myself."

Fade? What else did Ademure not know about the nymphs? Unfortunately, there was no time to learn more.

"What about poisoning?" she said. "That's a nymph specialty, right?"

He looked down. "That's not something we do lightly, Princesa."

"But the other alloys—"

"I haven't been to Nyseion since I was nine. I don't know the nymphs' reasons, only that they thought it was fair.

Anyway, they have trained nymphs to do that job. I'm not nearly as skilled."

"You could practice," she insisted.

"With what time and on what dummy? Princesa, if I could successfully poison someone, there would be far fewer estrellas threatening you. Besides, what you want is a display. Something to catch the Delfinos' attention. Poison is too subtle."

She glanced at her empty vanity. "What about mirrors, then?"

"Mirrors?"

"There's nothing that will catch their attention more than a national security threat, right? If someone manipulated something like, I don't know, sand, into a ton of mirrors, the estrellas would be forced to hunt them down."

"But what if an Agarthan does breach security?"

"I doubt any Agarthan would know to enter at the moment the mirrors are manipulated, and it wouldn't take long for the twins to smash them. But even if someone did get through, isn't that what we want? A big distraction?"

Damian started scribbling in the margins of the map, on the little space that wasn't already drowning in notes. "It might be crazy enough to work. I like it."

Ademure leaned her head back against the headboard and looked up.

"What?" he asked. "It's a good plan."

Not really. She glanced at her notebook. It was shaky at best, and it almost entirely relied on Damian and Ember. But not her.

And how could she expect it to? She wasn't strong. She hadn't trained in years. She didn't have special magic. She hadn't done anything to help Ember but take her to the library and endanger them both. Ademure was dead weight in an escape attempt doomed to fail. There had to be something she could do.

"Our plan would be better if Ember could figure out her lightning power," she said. "We could use a bit more in our arsenal."

"I don't disagree, but she's not going to figure it out in a matter of days."

"Maybe she could, if I could figure out this prophecy. Of course," she sighed, "I've already been working on it for nearly a week without any hint of a breakthrough. And especially without the library, I don't know where I can find more information."

"Valentina's?" he suggested.

She shook her head. "I thought about that, but I'd be recognized before I could get a foot outside the castle. Not possible."

She flipped back several pages to the rewritten text.

Seek Pandora stared at her, written at the bottom of the page.

"Who is Pandora?" she whispered.

"She's the first woman," Damian answered, standing beside her and looking over her shoulder.

She rolled her eyes. "Yes, I know that. I'm asking who she is today. Surely this can't be referencing the same Pandora from several millennia ago. She couldn't have lived that long."

He rubbed his chin. "My mother told me she did. I think most nymphs believe she's still alive today, actually."

Ademure stared at her notebook. *Is that possible?* she wondered. *Pandora isn't dead? How can I confirm that?* Her eyes trailed up to the rag hiding Damian's ears, the sparse green strands buried in his brown hair, the lankiness of his build, the neon-green of his irises.

"Damian, I have another ludicrous idea."

"Yeah?"

"What if I went to the nymphs?"

His eyes widened. "That *is* ludicrous, Princesa. Why would you want to do that?"

"They're the original denizens of this island, right? Long before humans inhabited it. They are the literal manifestations of the magic of Nysa, the protectors of the nature of magic themselves! I bet they know more about this." She raised the notebook. "About all of this."

"But it'll take you hours to walk there, and that's the only way in unless you can fade."

"I'm not going to forego whatever help I can give to Ember because of a little hike."

"I don't know. The nymphs aren't kind toward humans. Even I make them uncomfortable."

She stood. She was much shorter than the teenager, but that didn't stop her from looking him in the eye. "Damian, we need more help. Who else would be willing to decipher this?" she asked, raising her notebook. "Who else could?"

"I should go instead, Princesa. They'll be less hostile toward me."

"No. Ember needs you. If I fail, she still has to succeed. *You* still have to succeed, and make sure my mother doesn't."

"And if you don't come back? What then?"

She pressed her lips. "Then it'll be easier for Ember to drive the landsailer and sail off this island."

"Princesa, this isn't wise."

"I don't know that what is or isn't wise matters. In three days, if our plan doesn't work, I'm dead anyway." She tucked her notebook away. "I don't expect you to understand."

He tugged at his kitchen towel, then looked at the clock. "The twins will be back before dark. Think you'll return before then?"

"Twelve hours?" She bit her lip. "I think so."

No one had visited the forest in years. Not a soul.

With a bag over her shoulder, she marched out to her balcony. Damian held her arm as she lowered herself over the ledge.

No, Ademure thought. She would not let herself overthink this one. The twins would be back tonight, and she would be in their sight once more. She would never get another chance like this. *You can't continue to hide and expect miracles.*

She landed on the courtyard grass.

The staff glanced at her through the windows of the kitchen. Those glances followed her as she calmly walked past the gazebo, some of the cooks even calling after her, shouting questions about her well-being. She ignored them. It was probably strange to see the princess anywhere but the dining room or her bedroom. Never mind that she strolled toward a forest no human had neared in ages or that she did so in an afternoon gown and slippers. It was nice to know that at least the kitchen staff still liked her.

Once she was behind the temple and out of sight, she sprinted.

Pop, pop, pop!

The waist of her skirt tore free from her bodice as she tumbled head over heel. The strap of her bag tangled her arms so that she couldn't reach out, and she hit the ground with a grunt, knocking the breath from her lungs. On her back, she felt her ribs ache, but thankfully nothing worse.

As she lay there, the sun forced her eyes shut, and she decided whether to move again. She hadn't even left the court-yard yet, and she had failed.

"How did I get so weak?" she said aloud, still lying in the grass.

Seven years of hate, abuse, solitude. Seven years of standing by as she watched the estrellas grow crueler, her mother grow sicker. Three days more and it would all end. Perhaps that would be simpler.

You will leave. Damian's words infiltrated her thoughts.

Then Ember's. *I won't leave this island without you.*

And she thought of how Ember had shielded her from the estrellas, twice.

Damian and Ember were so determined to rescue her at such a high cost to themselves. And here Ademure was, not yet having left the castle grounds, contemplating death. Not a hundred feet into her new plan, and she had already fallen. She wasn't worth their efforts. It was time to give up.

I won't convince them of that, though, she knew. *They'll try to save me anyway.*

And that made her angry. Why couldn't Damian have forgotten about his oath? Why had Ember finally grown a spine?

Why had she let herself get so *fucking* weak?

Damn them all.

She groaned as she rose from the ground, pitying the grass stains on her torn skirt. Remembering the leggings she had on beneath, she finished the job, ripping through the last of the skirt's seams, so that only the bodice of the dress remained. Then, she packed away the fabric, and started her jog once more.

Three days left to be alive, and she would make the most of every minute.

CHAPTER 32

KIVA

Kiva sat at the Round Table with his head in his hands, staring at his reflection in Profe Valentina's wall of mirrors. His awful green eyes stared back.

Over five weeks of hiding in this horrible nation. Five weeks of flirting with the most distrusting blah of a person he had ever met. Five weeks of sand in his socks. And what had he gotten in return? A purpled scar that perpetually stung. And when he neared that blah, a purple wound that burned.

"Kiva?" Valentina said as she closed the door to the showroom behind her. "You're looking especially glum today."

"I'm just in my thoughts," he said.

"You've been thinking for four days straight, then? Have you even left the shop since Friday morning?"

"I thought you enjoyed my company."

"Only when you have more personality than a grain of sand. What's going on?"

He put a finger to his temple. "Profe, I'm tired. I don't really want to talk."

"Are you having girl problems?"

He glared.

She laughed, then promptly jumped up to take a seat at the table's edge, letting her legs swing below. "Honestly, Kiva, how can you be so bad at this?"

He ruffled his hair as he dropped his head, letting out a drawn-out groan. "It's not my fault women are irrational creatures."

"Now, now. No need to generalize." She clicked her tongue. "Besides, it's not that women are naturally irrational. Perhaps, we only lose reason to men."

"Tell me, Profe, what is it men do that sap a woman's reason?"

"The novel I could provide wouldn't help you. We only need to know what *you* did to sap Señorita Slade's reason."

Normally, his tutor's quips didn't irk him so easily, but at the moment the stinging in his shoulder occupied most of his tolerance.

"That damn woman is too suspicious for her own good."

His tutor's legs stopped swinging. "What happened?"

"I offered her an escape, and she figured that I was Agarthan and was trying to kidnap her."

Her nose wrinkled. "Was that not what you were trying to do?"

"It was."

"Then why are you upset?"

"Because she was supposed to trust me enough for that not to matter!" He shot to his feet, gripped his hair, and aimlessly paced the room.

"She was supposed to trust you enough that *kidnapping her* didn't matter?"

"No, of course not." He looked at the floor. "She was supposed to trust me enough that being Agarthan didn't matter." *Okay, yes, I hear how ridiculous it sounds.*

She rapped her nails on the table. "I'm not sure that it does matter."

"Tell that to her."

"I think she made her thoughts obvious enough. She knew you were Agarthan, and she still tolerated your presence for at least a little while, right? I see that as a point in your favor."

"She discovered that I was one of the men who attacked the twins."

"Oof. I retract the point."

"And I also accidentally admitted to her that I planted the book on her parents. She thinks I did it to hit on her."

"What exactly was it that you were going for, then? It sounds like you botched the whole thing."

"My gods, I was trying for a little honesty." He dropped back in his chair and set his head in his hands. "Giving her a little bit of the truth so she would trust me. Letting her know that I could offer her an escape from the estrellas."

"Ah, the damsel in distress approach." Valentina clicked her tongue again. "Kiva, I hate to break it to you, but though you may sit at the Round Table, a knight in shining armor you are not. You can't so carelessly toy with the emotions of a magick like her and expect to come out unscathed. She's untrained and an alloy—an extremely delicate bomb. Woo her. Charm her. But don't trick her."

"Yeah, well." *You could've told me that sooner.* He massaged his shoulder, biting back the pain. Striations of blood vessels peeked out from underneath his sleeve, purpling his bicep.

His tutor gasped. She slid off the table, took his arm in her hand, and yanked up the sleeve.

"This looks much worse than before," she said as she traced each straggling line. The glasses she wore magnified the care and worry held within her eyes. "She didn't strike you again, did she?"

"No. I'm honestly not certain *what* happened," he said, but at seeing her worry worsen, he quickly followed with, "but I'm okay, I swear. It's really not that painful."

She frowned, then pressured his wound. Fire seared through his shoulder and into his back. He jerked free of her grip and adjusted his sleeve whilst holding back tears.

"You've always been a terrible liar," she said, folding her arms.

"You're the second woman who's told me that this week."

"And yet, you still seem to wonder why all the women in your world have lost their reason." Her bun bobbed as she huffed away.

He massaged his shoulder in his chair alone, while the sounds of drawers opening, metals clinking, objects toppling echoed from behind her wall of artifacts. Then a few doors slammed shut, and not a minute later, Valentina returned, holding a pointed glass vial in her outstretched hand.

"Here," she said.

With his good arm, Kiva reached for the vial and held it close. The vial itself had three different fishtail-shaped insignias melted into it.

"Mermaids?" he asked.

She nodded. "Healing water."

"How did you get it?"

"How I get all things. Now drink."

Shaking his head, he insisted, "This is part of your collection. I'll heal on my own and be fine."

"Kiva." She bent down to meet his level. "You don't understand. This wound is not natural. I can see it in the veins. Whatever she did to you will only get worse with time, and I refuse to outlive one of my students. So please, drink."

Profe Valentina had never apprenticed for alchemy—she didn't have the attention span for eight years of schooling—

but Kiva trusted her instinct more than anyone in an alchemy ward. Traveling the world in search of the rarest treasures had made her one of the wisest magicks in the fields of injuries, illnesses, and potion-making. So if she thought his condition was serious, it was.

He popped out the cork. The water swirled inside like a whirlpool, creating a steamy substance that emanated from the vial, though it was much colder than steam. He breathed in the air, feeling a rush of ice fill his lungs.

Then, he lifted the vial and tipped it into his mouth. The taste of the liquid was so pure and light, nothing like any water he'd had before, and he tilted the vial further until nothing was left.

It was as if steam expanded to his every toe, every hair, every cell of his body. But the steam was cold. Refreshing. Most of the chill targeted his shoulder, icier closer to where the wound was worst. The ice froze the pain, encapsulating it, and dispersed it to the rest of the steam. His shoulder ached, then dulled, then numbed entirely in a matter of seconds. Then, the steam escaped his pores.

He felt reborn.

He looked at his shoulder. The striations remained.

He held the vial upside down once more, mouth agape, but no water—not even a lagging drop—escaped.

"I was afraid it wasn't enough," Valentina said. "There won't be anything left in that. That's perfect glass made specifically for the healing water. All of the water will have drained already."

He set the vial down onto the table. "That's okay. At least, the pain is gone." He stood up, swinging his arm around. He punched at the air, stretched to the ceiling, lifted the chair.

Absolutely nothing. No soreness, no sting.

Amazing.

"I'll make a trip to Atlantis and beg the mermaids for more once this is all over," he said.

"Unfortunately, I doubt more water will heal you further." She scuttled closer, reaching up to inspect his shoulder.

"What do you mean?" That water had relieved him of so much relentless agony. Surely, it could fix a scar?

"Healing water isn't omnipotent. It's designed to heal the wounds that are both fresh and what mermaids have encountered before. It partially healed you, probably only because you reinjured it so recently. But the wound itself..." She lifted the sleeve once more. The purple had definitely faded, but the skin it had darkened was raised. "This was created with magic they —and I know for sure *I*—have never seen. It's quite terrifying, really."

"It won't ever heal completely, then?"

"I can't know the answer to that." She pulled a chair out and sat down. "The world of modern alchemy is evolving, having to keep pace with natural magic's evolution. It's not entirely uncommon to come across magic never-before discovered."

"So, there could be a cure in the future?"

"Possibly. But it's hard to create a cure when I don't know what happened in the first place. How did she create the lightning the first time? How did it get worse?"

He slumped in his seat, racking his brain for an answer. "I really wish I knew."

That day in the Soulless Realm, he had wondered why the alloy hadn't fought back earlier, why she hadn't electrocuted him sooner. Why had she waited until the last second to strike, when he and Alden had nearly killed the twins? Why would someone with that kind of power even hesitate?

But then, she was nothing but hesitation. She had an idea of what she could do, but nothing more. She knew nothing about magic, and especially nothing about lightning. All she knew was that she had the ability to do some serious damage.

"I think she got lucky," he said, instinctively rubbing his now pain-free shoulder. "She knows less than most ten-year-olds. She just also happens to be three times as powerful."

"Lucky? But she hit you square on."

He remembered that morning at the beach. The shock when he'd told her what had happened to him. The sadness when he'd showed her the wound.

"Yeah, she did," he said, "but it was an accident."

Valentina cocked her head. "Let's go back to the beach on Friday. What happened right before this got worse?"

Kiva thought for a moment. "Nothing at first. She was just mad at me. But after I mentioned planting the book, I think—I think her eyes were brighter than normal? And that's when I felt it, electricity charging through my shoulder. I couldn't think straight."

"And when did it stop?"

"When she did. When she realized I was in pain because of her." He sat with that a moment longer, and his heart ached at the thought. *She was afraid of hurting me.*

"You know," his tutor said. "A similar thing happened when I said she looked like her mother. Do you think she was angry then, too?"

Could this really all be about her parents? "It's possible."

"You really are terrible with women."

"Excuse me?" he said with a tone that lay somewhere between shock and amusement. "How could I possibly have been expected to know that she was angry that first night? I was a bit preoccupied with keeping my shoulder attached."

His tutor pointed an accusing finger. "You made her angry with that white knight bit on Friday, too."

"Not intentionally! She was angry before the sun had even

risen, but it wasn't until I mentioned the book that she became incensed." He blinked, recounting that conversation. "Then she was like another being altogether."

"This will be hard for you, Kiva, but I think my alchemist advice for this wound of yours is to not make your girlfriend angry."

"She's not my girlfriend!" he shot back, ignoring the flutter in his chest. "Besides, I've been hit with tons of spells, and subsequently made a lot of the magicks who produced them angry. Yet they've never carried on past the initial blow. Why does it matter if I make her angry or not? Why did this wound still hurt at all? I've never known any magic to do that."

"All good questions," Valentina said as she hopped off the chair. "I had been wondering the same thing since I first saw your arm and decided to do a little research."

She scuttled toward her never-ending artifact collection. It still amazed him what she had amassed over the years, and how he had gone so long without knowing its full extent. The shelves truly did extend into oblivion, likely with the help of some amber-eyed stretching innate—the outside of the shop was nowhere near large enough on its own. And each industrial shelf extended to the ceiling, stuffed with almost anything one could think of.

There were the magical artifacts, of course: the healing waters and magical boxes of the world. The historical ones: the Round Table and several mummies, for example. She had a shelf for soulless things—she had a strange interest in lawnmowers. And she had more than a few walls in place of shelves for the overwhelming amount of art. As she walked, she passed a wall of paintings, though he recognized only one—and he did a double take. He was certain that hardly smiling woman was in a museum in Paris.

"Ah, here it is." His tutor bobbed her way up a ladder to

reach something cylindrical from her topmost shelf. At the bottom, when she stepped off the last rung, she held it out—a scroll. "I assume you're familiar with old magic?"

"Like the innates?"

She glared at him. "I surely hope you know more than only the innates."

"I can assure you, I don't."

"It hurts to know that I've failed as a tutor," she said, shaking her head.

He rolled his eyes. *You should have been a drama tutor.*

"The innates are forms of old magic, yes," she continued as she unrolled the scroll, "but there is more to old magic than just the basics."

Completely illegible symbols were scribbled next to completely unintelligible pictures. She seemed able to comprehend the code easily, but all Kiva recognized was the leaf-shaped symbol decorating the upper right hand of the parchment.

"You took this from the nymphs?" he asked.

"This was a gift from the minister when I visited him last year."

"You *visited* the nymphs?"

"Yes. And surprisingly, they aren't all terrorists."

"But you never told me."

"You never asked." Shrugging, she added, "The nymphs lived on this island first, you know. We should be grateful they let us bickering fools stay. Anyway, kindness breeds kindness, and I wanted to learn more about their culture, so I offered up my own in exchange."

"But they killed magicks. Mercilessly. How could you want to know more about that?"

She eyed him, a glimmer reflecting off her glasses. "Only

when we stop communicating, does violence becomes the language."

There was no levity when she said it. Behind the bobbing bun, the oversized glasses, and the exorbitant enthusiasm for learning, Kiva sometimes forgot the darkness his former tutor had seen.

"Nonetheless," she continued, reclaiming her bubbly state, "this scroll is a relic of Ancient Nysa. The language scribed here is Old Nymph which *as you'll remember*—" she gave him a stern look; he returned an annoyed one "—fell out of practice over three hundred years ago." She laid the parchment on the Round Table, stretching it across the diameter. "Outside of the innates, there were at least four other forms of old magic as well as a form of antimagic." She pointed to the leftmost illegible text that was scribbled next to an unidentifiable pictogram. "This discusses the first old magic—the magic of the nymphs."

"You mean magic that only nymphs can do?"

"Not exclusively, no, though predominantly nymphs use it. You remember learning about the rhythms, right?"

Oh, that's what Ember was talking about, he thought, recalling the waterfall.

"You know," she continued, "not many modern humans know about empathy magic, though, at the time of this text, it wasn't uncommon for human magicks to use it as well. The learning curve for us seems to be a bit steeper, however. I guess when we developed spells for viciousness, we lost the need to feel."

She skipped to the next scribble and picture.

"This is the second old magic—the one you used earlier."

"Healing magic," he said. "The magic of the mermaids."

"Right. This magic is absolutely exclusive to them as far as we know. Though, thankfully, they can bottle it for us."

Kiva again massaged his shoulder, still awestruck at how quickly the pain had faded. He was thankful for that magic indeed.

"Then there's premonition magic. It's strictly hereditary, and unfortunately, at the moment, it belongs to some fairly dreadful people."

"Yeah, no kidding."

"Fourthly, we have glamour magic."

"What the serpions in Agartha use," he said, looking at the fourth picture and illegible text.

She nodded. "Like the mermaids, we're fairly certain only the serpions may use glamours. Though, unlike healing magic, the boundaries of glamour magic are not well-known. The serpions are much too secretive for that.

"Lastly, we have feeding," she said, moving her hand to the rightmost scribble and picture. The writing was still indistinct, and the image was angular and heavily shaded. "The sole known antimagic belongs to the kiras of Lemuria."

Kiva shivered. The kiras were creatures that fed on someone's magic until the soul was so weakened, the heart stopped. They dressed in all black to match their raven wings, and hunted at night because it was easier to feed when most magicks slept. By the time the prey realized their magic was draining, it was too late. He thanked the gods those creatures stayed to themselves on the other side of the world.

"This is fascinating, really," he said. "And receiving a lecture from you is a trip down memory lane. However, I'm not sure I see the point you're trying to make here. I wasn't aware these magics were considered 'old' or whatever, but I am familiar with them. I just don't know why they're relevant to the alloy's magic."

Valentina huffed, and with a flick of her wrist, smacked her former student on his bicep—which was the full extent of her reach.

"I haven't gotten to my point yet," she said. She gestured to the last several lines of the scroll, all beneath the original five texts and pictographs.

"This is where it gets hazy. My Old Nymph is pretty decent, but I can't make out these last pieces of script. I sent a letter to the nymphs, asking for their guidance, but they were of little help as well. It seems like this portion was actually written much earlier than the rest of the text, and the language is too complicated to decipher.

"What I do understand is that this says something about the number seven and hope. And below that text, there is a large zig-zag pictograph as well as seven little pictures. The pictures are difficult to make out but I do see a spade-shaped object and what I think is meant to represent a ring. After that, I know nothing else."

He looked at the larger zig-zag image and reached for his shoulder, tracing the striations emanating from his wound. There was no doubt.

"That's a lightning bolt," he said.

His tutor nodded. "I wasn't sure at first, but I think I agree with you. I believe your girlfriend has somehow acquired a lost old magic."

He stared at the text, trying to decipher what he knew he couldn't. If what Valentina said was true, then no one in the present day had any memory or knowledge of what this old magic was or what it could do.

Well, except for him.

But, what did those seven smaller pictures mean? Did she have seven other old magics as well? How did she acquire the first, if she didn't even know she had it?

A bell chimed, and the chest in the corner of the room

started to vibrate, its seven strange locks rattling. Valentina, clearly bewildered, scurried to it. She bent down to inspect it, brushing her fingers over the locks and the casing, but it ignored her touch. She even whispered, "*tardo*," a charm that should've at least slowed the vibrations, but it continued to shake as if she hadn't cast a spell at all.

"Have you ever seen it do that before?" Kiva said, walking to her side.

"Never," she said as they stood over it. "I'll have to take a closer look after I take care of the customer out front."

"I'll follow you out. I need to get going anyway." He had to reach out to Ember again soon. No more moping or weird artifact distractions. The longer he stayed on this island, the longer he risked being flayed by the estrellas.

But finding another way to reach her... It wasn't like he could send another message. Perhaps, he could try the beach again...if she didn't walk away when she saw him coming.

He remained lost in thought as he stepped out from behind the reverted plain wooden door into the main store. He focused on his shoulder—damn, did it feel good—not catching any of the bookcases in the tight aisles. Valentina had already scuttled ahead, nowhere to be seen.

But as he rounded the last corner, he spotted his tutor at the front desk looking back at him...and giggling.

In front of her, a tall woman with long blonde curls and fierce green eyes dug through her bag in search of a few diamond chips. And despite his inexplicably quickening pulse, he grinned.

CHAPTER 33

EMBER

"You're kidding me," Ember said, stashing the book she'd just bought and diamond change into her bag. This island wasn't big enough. "What are you still doing here?"

"Hey now, I was here first," Kiva said, hands up in front of him. "You followed me this time, ice queen."

She scowled. "I don't have time for this."

"Ember, wait."

This is what I get for playing hooky from Ozamiz, she grumbled to herself.

The bells chimed as she pushed the front door open. The town had a fervent energy this time of day. The plaza smelled of baked goods and salty ocean air. Children chased one another around the fountain. Landsailers cruised down the streets, around men and women with hands full of cloth shopping bags. Shopkeepers stood at their entrances enticing them to buy more.

He caught up to her side.

"Kiva," she said under her breath as she walked the main

thoroughfare, "I'm telling you to leave me alone. It's time to accept your loss, go home, and stop wasting my time."

"As long as you and I are here, I can't have lost yet. Come now, you didn't think I'd give up that easy?"

"I sincerely hoped for it."

"Your animosity never ceases to sting."

She couldn't stand his smug grin for half a second. So she returned her gaze to the sand pavement, wondering, *How did I ever let myself break my own rules for this ass?*

"What can I say to make you go away?" she asked, refusing to look at him again.

He kept pace with her anyway. "Come with me to Agartha."

"No. If I haven't made myself clear, I'm not taking part in this war. I won't hurt anyone for you."

She entered an empty coffee shop, sat down at the nearest table, pulled out the map book she'd purchased and her own notebook, and her pen went to work. He took a seat across from her.

"Why are you in town?" he whispered, as if he hadn't heard her refusal at all. "Doesn't el Alcázar have a library?"

Just ignore him.

She traced from the north side of the town to the plaza. After her *discussion* with Bailón this morning, Damian had made a quick visit to her room. He'd mentioned that the plaza was where the royals usually stopped for speeches. It would be the most public moment—all eyes would be on the princess. That was when the twins would want Ember to strike.

"The town isn't that big," Kiva said, leaning over her shoulder. "What could you possibly need that for?"

If you don't respond, he'll get bored and leave, she told herself.

She attempted to refocus. They had to escape before making it to the plaza. If Damian could cause a distraction for at least the Delfinos, then she and Ademure could try to sneak by the others. Ember could have Damian set up a landsailer, and they could make a break for the harbor. If only she could figure out how to sail.

"Have you ever manipulated magma before?" Kiva asked. "When we get to Agartha, there's some fire spells I want to teach you and—"

Ember slammed her notebook shut. "You know the world doesn't revolve around you, right?"

The smile that played at his lips fell. "I'm sorry. I didn't realize... Is everything okay?"

"Everything is fine," she lied, her palms hot. "Or it would be, if you would leave me alone."

He tilted his head as if he didn't believe her. As if he was worried for her. And she hated it.

Kiva, you've already embarrassed me once.

"Look," he said. "I know what you must think of me after the other day, but I'm not playing around anymore. I don't know how much longer I can stay here."

"That's your problem, not mine."

"If you don't come with me, it'll soon be our problem."

"Goddammit! How many times do I have to say no?" She shot up from the table and fumed out the door.

He sped after her, saying, "You don't understand. The war—"

Outside the sky blue shop, she whirled back, palms on fire. "Oh, I understand plenty! I understand the queen is a maniac and the estrellas are psycho minions. I understand that no one gives a fuck what I want, just what I can do for them. And I understand that this all probably means nothing in the end. I understand the war is for show and I'm supposed to be a puppet." She exhaled. "I won't be a puppet."

"You wouldn't be a puppet in Agartha."

She squinted at him. "You can't possibly say that with a straight face. Kiva, you dangled that fucking book in front of me like it was a carrot, knowing who I was, who they were. You messed with my head solely to control me. Like a *puppet*."

"And I'm sorry for it. That was only supposed to be a small part of my effort to convince you on Agartha. I had no idea that you cared for your parents so much."

The heat slid to her wrists. "Let's get this straight. I don't give a *fuck* about my parents. My problem is with you using them to manipulate me."

His shoulders dropped. "Sure. Okay."

The heat grew hotter.

"What is that supposed to mean?" she spat.

"That you're as guilty of lying as I am."

"I am not."

"You are. To me, as well as yourself it seems. But did you know that your magic tells the truth?" He pulled up his sleeve. "Lightning and your parents. Quite the baffling link."

Her eyes widened at the wound. *The purpling. It's gone.*

"When we get to Agartha," he continued, "this is the first thing we'll practice. Of course, we'll use a trigger that's less sensitive."

A muscle in her jaw twitched. "They are *not* a trigger. How can they be when they weren't there? When they've *never been* there?" *Raindrops.*

"Seems pretty obvious to me."

"You're unbelievable!" She threw her hands into the air. "After what you've done—after what you've *admitted* to doing —you still have the audacity to taunt me like that? To claim that people who I've never known affect my powers over twenty years later?"

"Do you have any reason to think that they don't?"

No. She knew they did. She had always known they did.

"I'm not going to Agartha with you."

She marched back inside. Heat moved away from her arms and toward her cheeks, a tear forming at the corner of her eye. She folded her arms tight to her cooled body and returned to her table, Kiva dutifully doing the same. Then, she reopened her notebook and started writing out her plans once more.

"It's okay to care about them, Ember. If I didn't know who my parents were, I'd probably care about them, too. Especially if they died so tragically."

But mine didn't die.

"I can't care about them," she said. "Caring is the real trigger."

Expectedly, he met her gaze with a smile and...sympathy?

She cast her eyes away. "Stop that."

"Stop what?"

"Stop giving me that look. I told you I don't need your pity."

Chuckling, he said, "Tell me, whose pity is it that you use? Seems to be a lot of your own."

The heat in her face rose, but the rest of her body remained cool. She continued to scribble, aimlessly now, as it was hard to focus on anything she was reading.

"You know what I'm curious about?" he said after a while. "You didn't have that book I bought you on your evening train. So what had you thinking about your parents then?"

She ignored him, doodling the same locket that weighed heavy around her neck. *I need you to help me escape I need you to help me escape I need you—*

"How have you trained that magic so far with the twins?" he asked.

She gripped her pen harder. The doodles were bleeding ink and the pen tore through the page.

"C'mon, Ember. You're not going to tell the guy you shot with lightning what he said to set you off?"

She closed her eyes and mumbled, "I don't remember."

"What?"

"I don't remember," she repeated a little louder, her cheeks growing pinker. "I don't remember anything that happened that day on the train."

His stare could've bored a hole through her face. "Really?"

"And there's that pity again. Kiva, I really have something urgent to do—"

"That's terrifying."

She glowered. "I'm aware my powers are terrifying."

"No, stupid, I mean not knowing. Has this happened before?"

She looked through the shop's window, at the children laughing along the sidewalk. *Raindrops.*

"For as long as I can remember," she said. "Usually, it's only a few hours here or there. But full twenty-four-hour blackouts... That was the second time."

"Does anyone know about this?"

"You. The twins. Me."

"So, no one."

She shot him a glare, but he didn't abandon his pained expression.

"Doesn't it get lonely?" he asked.

She twisted her locket with one hand, sliding it along her chain and brushing her thumb over the engravings. "I'm used to it."

She took the following moment of silence to focus on the raindrops, even drawing a few in her map book. Though really, she didn't need to. Even her palms were completely cool. But other emotions throttled her breathing, her mind, and raindrops were much better than teardrops.

"You really think you're a monster, huh?" Kiva said at last.

Her pen stalled, trembling above the page. "Don't you?"

"No. Not at all."

She frowned. "I've hurt so many people, though. I hurt you. How can you believe that?"

He laughed as he shook his head. "I've seen the real monsters. You're nothing like them."

At that, her breath hitched.

Kiva lied constantly, about who he was, what he was after. And she hated it—she'd hated it every single time—but not like this. None of those lies were as excruciating as this one. The others might have made her palms warm, but this one stabbed at her chest, stole air from her lungs. It really was just another one of his lies, and yet it bothered her so much. Why?

Because it feels like he's telling the truth.

He seemed to notice her hurt. But when he reached for her forearm, she yanked back and rose so quickly, she nearly toppled her chair.

"I don't understand you," she whispered, gripping her books, warmth returning to her hands. "Why did you come after me now? So I would spill all my secrets to you? So you could puppet me back to Agartha?"

"What?" He stalled, glancing at the empty service counter and clearing his throat. "Of course not."

"Why then? Did you think this would persuade me to join you?"

"I'm not sure making someone upset is a great persuasion technique."

"So you didn't follow me to convince me to go to Agartha?"

"Damn it, Ember!" He rose from the table, too. "Yes, I want you to go—*home*—with me, but no, I'm not trying to exploit your feelings to do that. I was only trying to be a friend."

"I don't *have* friends."

"I wonder fucking why! I've never seen someone so allergic to kindness. You know if you actually opened up once in a while, like trusted someone, you might make a few of them? Do you have even one person in your life who you give a shit about?"

"Yes." She met his eyes without wavering, her fists tight about her books without quivering. "She's why I don't have more."

With a deep, frustrated breath, he ran his hands through his hair and wrung it.

Ember loosened her grip on her books and walked back out onto the street. Not fast, this time; she didn't mean to avoid him. She simply needed air.

But then she realized he wasn't following her at all. She looked through the shop window and found him—his hand still in his hair and eyes locked on his shoes as he paced around the floor, well on his way to digging a trench.

For some reason, that made her sigh. And then something must've possessed her because she went in one last time.

"Why go to such lengths to come after me, anyway?" she asked as she held open the door. "To what end?"

He looked up, brows raised high, and scoffed.

"To stop a war," he said. "That's the end." Then, he lowered his voice. "My people will die if the estrellas have their way."

With lips pressed shut, she considered him, his words... how similar those words were to Damian's.

She gestured for him to follow her.

His brows raised higher, as if asking if she was sure, and she huffed before repeating the gesture. Quickly, he then made his way to the door, and they spoke quietly as they walked side-by-side along the street.

"I won't kill for you," she said. "Either of you."

"We don't have to kill thousands. Only leadership."

"That's still murder if I'm not mistaken. And how can you just casually suggest that we kill some of the strongest magicks in the Realm?"

"It's what needs to be done."

"You don't understand. I can't be a part of that."

He stopped mid-walk and buried his head in his hands. Then he closed his eyes, leaving the air with sounds of only birds and wind and the faint anthem that played in town.

"Fine."

She turned. "What?"

"I said fine. You win. I won't bother you anymore."

"That's it?"

"Well clearly, I should have accepted the loss last Friday. I can't risk fighting you again, especially not in Nysa, and it's not like you'd ever consider going to Agartha willingly."

"I never said that! I'd leave in a heartbeat, but I don't want to hurt anyone to do it."

"I don't see a distinction frankly. You won't be able to avoid bloodshed so long as you stay here, but I'm sure you already knew that."

She knew.

Her palms were hot again. "But why do I have to do that to survive? This isn't my home, my people, or my war. I didn't choose to be here. Why am I the one being forced to kill?"

He took a careful step toward her, the levity in his eyes now gone—so close that, with the gravity laden in his demeanor, in his next words, he could have collapsed the world around them.

"I think you need to stop fantasizing about what life used to be for you and focus on what it is now. Returning to solitude is no longer an option. Your choices are whether you work for us, or you work for them." He nodded toward el Alcázar on the hill in the distance. "And I don't have to tell you, there's a difference."

She returned his hardened stare. "I won't kill for either of you."

"Then I'm done here."

But she wasn't.

As he started to walk off, she shouted at the back of his head. "What happened to the Kiva who would stop at nothing to get what he wanted?"

And he spun, a simper hanging on his lips. "He was twice electrocuted from the inside out, and he's trying to avoid a third round."

She stiffened. "I never—"

"Stop," he said, pulling her wrist away from her locket. "Lightning may have been a bit of an extreme punishment, but I can't say that a punishment wasn't warranted. Besides, I'm fine." He moved his shoulder and arm as if to prove the point. "Don't waste an apology on me."

The breeze caught his unkempt brown locks. His smile no longer played on his lips. And though his eyes were still green, he seemed, for once, honest.

"You're really giving up, then," she said.

"Isn't that what you wanted?"

"Absolutely. I just really didn't expect you to stop."

He smirked. "Who knows, I may change my mind. But as of today, I simply don't have the right words to convince you otherwise."

He turned away then, and she nearly let him go, but something tugged at her. The escape was in three days. Would she see him after that?

Did she care?

"What about tomorrow?" she said.

He stilled. "Tomorrow?"

"Yeah. What if you came up with the right words tomorrow? Would you come back to tell me?"

He put his hand to his chest, widened his eyes, and opened his mouth as much as his jaw would let him, mocking her with every gesture of excitement.

Oh, god, this was a mistake.

"Ember Slade, are you telling me that this is the argument that won you over? That *you* want to see *me*?"

"No," she said quickly, blushing. "Well, yes. But only if you have the right words and that it's this new honest Kiva who brings them. Otherwise, forget coming at all."

He laughed. "You drive a heavy bargain, but I think I can agree to those terms. Tomorrow then. At the plaza. And you should bring honest Ember as well."

CHAPTER 34
ADEMURE

Ademure stumbled over a branch, tearing yet another hole in her leggings. Her hair served as a resting ground for twigs and leaves, her arms for scratches and scrapes. Her legs ached as she hiked up the steep inclines, and the few dips in the terrain served only to hold enough water to soak straight through her slippers. Naturally, that also made her desperate for a drink. She pushed on.

Living in Nysa her entire life, she'd always thought she knew how green something could be, but this forest proved just how mistaken she'd been. Small, waxy leaves and vines dominated the space above her. Longer, glossier leaves and their leaflets fanned the space around her. And dark, pungently flowery shrubs covered the footpath that had long succumbed to overgrowth. What ground she had covered in a matter of minutes in open air took her four times as long to trek underneath the canopy, and the tiny incessantly screeching frogs made that trek feel like hours. Water trickled from her brow, though she wasn't sure if it was her own—the air felt as wet as the ocean itself.

From what she remembered of the many maps she'd studied, Nyseion couldn't be much further. The maps had never really detailed the nymph territory, but she was certain that it was directly north of the castle. Keep going, and she would eventually find it.

Her legs wobbled as her hike grew steeper. Sweat drenched her bodice. Hair fell in pieces around her face. After another few steps, she dropped to the wayside, cursing herself for not packing water.

Kneeling over a puddle of water so deep she could see her muddied image in it, she watched her tired reflection exhale. She must have caught her mother's sickness thinking she could do this on her own. She wouldn't make it. She hadn't trained anywhere nearly as intensely since she was a child, and since the oracles arrived, she'd rarely left her room without an escort. She'd rarely left her room at all. She was too weak.

I should turn around while I still have some wits left, she thought. *Ember will surely figure something out.*

"Fool!" she said out loud, slashing a hand at the puddle. "Ademure, you're a dimwitted fool! That's the sort of thinking that landed you in this damned forest."

Newly clad in mud, she forced herself off the ground, ignoring her begging legs, charged toward the wall of green, and swept the enormous leaves aside.

She screamed.

"This forest is the dwelling of Pan's children," the green man said. "It is where Dionysus himself was born and raised. It is where Dionysus's grapes grow. It is anything but damned."

The figure had at least a foot on her but was just as slim. His ethereal arms draped by his side. His legs stood tall. He wore a pale pink tunic that hardly covered his lean torso, and pinned to his chest was a green rose, remarkably similar to the one her mother wore in her crown. His dark green locks brushed his shoulders, and he held a spear by his side. His face could only be described as beautiful.

A nymph. She had found them.

"I'm deeply sorry for my insult. I meant no offense." She curtsied. "Ademure Maldojo, Princess of Nysa. Pleased to meet your acquaintance."

The beautiful green man stood perfectly still. "Why are you here, Princess Ademure?"

She hadn't thought that far ahead. What should she say? That she'd voluntarily traveled to an, at best, unfriendly land to find information that might or might not have been recorded about a figure who might or might not exist? Better to ease into it.

"I was hoping the nymphfolk could help me find some answers," she said.

"Answers regarding what?"

She dug into her bag and pulled out the small notebook. She flipped to the page with Ember's handwriting and held it out to him.

"What's this?" he asked as he reluctantly took it.

"Mythos of the first woman, Pandora, and what I believe to be a prophecy."

"You would have us engage with those who slaughtered us?" His voice boomed through the forest. "How dare you ask us to help further your villainy!" He threw the notebook at her feet.

Cautiously, she bent down to pick it up as she mulled over his words. The only slaughter that she knew of was of the alloys, seven years ago. But the nymphs?

"I'm afraid I don't understand," she said. "What slaughter? When?"

"You humans are all the same." He lowered his spear, the point glinting a few inches from her neck. "You murder thousands of innocent lives and call it sport. Train your elite forces using our people as target practice. Then come to us, as if nothing ever happened, begging for our help to repeat your atrocity."

"I promise," she said, carefully considering each word before she spoke it, "I'm not trying to do anything of the sort. I truly don't know what you're talking about." The point grazed her throat. "You have to believe me!"

"You'd ask us to believe you, a human? We have shared this island with humans since they first came to be. An honest human is rarer than a kira in white."

Her breathing quickened. What could she possibly say to make him believe her? What had she read about the nymphs that she could use? There was so little information on them in the library to begin with, and what she had read was either Nysan propaganda or quite literally ancient history. All of it... except that romance book, of course.

Wait.

"The rhythms," she said, meeting the nymph's glare. "My rhythms. You can hear them, right?"

She waited for a response, hoping he understood. He stayed quiet, but his eyes were on hers. Then, his ears twitched.

"What rhythms do you hear?" she said.

He shifted his stance but still held tight to his spear. "You are disharmonious. The rhythms of frustration and fear ring loudest."

"Are those the rhythms of a liar?"

"They could be. Most liars have fear."

"Fear alone?"

He narrowed his eyes. "Fear and guilt. Or joy."

"And I have neither."

"You could be an exceptional liar."

"I could be," she said, "but I promise I am not." She took half a step back from his spear. "Tell me, what's rational? That I am an incredibly fantastic liar? Or perhaps, you might consider that I am an incredibly desperate princess?"

He furrowed his dark green brows before slowly drawing back his weapon. When the spear returned to his side, she could finally catch her breath. He was reasonable. She could work with reasonable.

"To ease your mind further about your choice to disarm," she said, eyes still on the spear, "you should know that in three days' time, my life will have ended. Thus, I am not a fantastic liar, but a very desperate woman indeed."

"You come for protection, then."

"I come for guidance." She held out the book again. "I believe decoding whatever this prophecy means is the key to preventing war."

His expression darkened. "Prophecies are evil magic. It was your prophets who led the charge against our civilians."

She tilted her head. "Do you mean the twins?"

"I do not know. It was seven years ago, and I only saw them from a distance. One had hair as white as the clouds, the other black as night. And with them, hundreds of alloys."

Her eyes widened.

Ademure had never really believed that the nymphs' attack on the alloys had been unprovoked, but even experiencing the Delfinos' cruelty first-hand, she had never considered that it had been them who'd *incited* it. They would've been what? Twenty-one? Her own age now, and as far from becoming vice-captains at the time. Such a young age to have caused so much harm.

Thousands, she thought as her heart broke. Nysans, nymphs, alloys, *lives*. Dead. And they labeled *her* the traitor, knowing full well it was actually them who deserved the title. She had to have been the most foolish, daftest princess—

Stop it. She took in two deep breaths. She couldn't be self-critical, now. Ember was enough for the both of them. She needed to help the alloy in any way she could, and this was her way. *I must find out about Pandora.*

"The prophecy belongs to them," she said at last, "but I'm far from on their side. If I can understand what they know, then I can stop them from doing the same to the people of Agartha."

"We don't mess in human affairs," the nymph said. "We cannot help you."

"You understand that if the humans go to war, that it will be fought on our lands? We can't travel like the Agarthans do. They'll bring the fight to us. Do you really think you'll be left out of the battle?"

"What I think is of no importance. We will not help you humans in your death games."

"I'm trying to prevent death. Can't you see that?"

"Are you asking us to simply forget the tragedy your kind brought upon us?"

"Tragedy which you in turn brought upon us," Ademure said defiantly, her chest heaving, "killing thousands of innocents around the world."

"How dare you compare thousands of lives to the genocide of our people."

"I'm not comparing! I'm showing you that it's a cycle. A cycle that your people are not completely innocent in. A cycle I'm trying to break."

He raised his chin.

She went to her knees and put her hands together. "Please. I don't know what else to do. I care for my people and for myself. If I leave here empty-handed, I may as well begin digging my own grave and many of yours as well."

She leaned further, resting her arms on the ground and dropping her head. This had to work. She couldn't return to el Alcázar yet.

"I'm Princess Ademure Maldojo of the magick nation of Nysa, begging the children of the holy god Pan, the guardians of the holy god Dionysus, to hear my plea."

She kept her head on the forest floor. Sweat dribbled down her neck, and her hair mixed with mud. But she didn't care. She would remain there for the night if needed. She wouldn't leave without gaining something. Anything

"Stand, Princess," he said at last.

She obeyed, her legs aching more so than before. She wiped the mud from her forehead.

"It is not in my authority to deny a refugee," he said. "On the merits of your claim, I will take you to see Minister Calix. He will have the final say on your request." The nymph turned toward the foliage and disappeared.

Her brows raised.

Was that a yes?

CHAPTER 35
EMBER

As she entered through the wrought iron gates of the castle, Ember tried to rid herself of the thought that she could, and likely would, hurt someone...again.

Not again. Never again.

But Kiva's wound wouldn't leave her mind. Nor his words. Something had definitely changed in him. But why? For what reason? Nothing had changed about her.

Those questions continued to plague her as she walked through the foyer and the corridor, right up until she passed Ademure's door.

No Cadeña? she thought.

She frowned and knocked. After a moment of silence, she pushed on the princess's door. Empty.

Maybe she's in the temple? Doesn't matter. It's Damian I need anyway.

She sprinted down the stairs to the dining room, where the staff set silverware and place settings. The air smelled of roasted pork.

"Alloy Slade," the butler Mateo said before bowing.

"Dinner won't be ready for another half-hour. Was there something you needed?"

"Is Damian here?" she said. "It's urgent."

"I'm sure young Damian is around here somewhere. I'll fetch him." His coattails flipped behind him as he strode toward the kitchen.

She leaned one hand on a wooden chair, waiting for the gangly sixteen-year-old boy to appear.

"Señorita Slade." Damian came through the kitchen door and bowed. "Did you get what you needed from town?"

She nodded before moving closer to him and dropping her voice. "Will you go to the temple with me?"

"Of course." He turned back to the door and called out, "Mateo, I'll be outside with Alloy Slade if you need me!"

"Understood," Mateo said through the closed door.

The half-nymph turned back to her. "Let's go, then."

A moment later they were atop the temple steps. Ember pushed open the door.

Also empty. *Where is she?*

"So what did you want to talk about, Seño?"

She handed him the map book.

"I've marked it up," she said, flipping to the pages of the plaza. "Bring two landsailers here." She pointed to the north entrance of the town. "You'll probably have to set at least one out the night before."

"I can do that," he said.

"One will be for Ademure and me, and the other for you. She probably told you that we'll be headed for the harbor." Ember waited for his nod. "Good. I think your best chance will be to draw Sombra and Nieve toward the forest on the other side of the desert." Her cheeks grew suddenly hot at the memory of her and Kiva's trip, but she quickly gulped the intrusive recollection away. "There aren't any nymphs nearby and no Nysans ever enter. I think that includes the twins. You should be safe there, at least for a little bit.”

“What about sailing?”

Her shoulders fell. “I’m practicing some more before Friday, and we’ll just have to hope that we can learn to read a nautical chart on the fly. I wish we had more time to make a better plan, but I’d rather try my luck with the ocean than the estrellas.”

“And where are you going?”

“Florida, if I can figure out how to get there. I know it’s where they expect me to go, but I haven’t traveled outside of the U.S. It’s the best shot I have at gaining a home court advantage.”

She could tell Damian didn’t quite understand the idiom but he nodded anyway.

Leaning back against a pillar, she asked, “Did you and Ademure come up with a plan to distract them?”

“Somewhat,” he answered.

“Somewhat? What do you mean somewhat?”

He adjusted his rag. “The princess had other ideas for how we should go about it.”

“And you didn’t agree with them?”

“No.” He inclined his head. “Did she not tell you?”

She frowned. “Tell me what?”

“I thought she’d have written it in that notebook thing. She left this afternoon.”

“*Left*? The castle?”

He nodded.

“I don’t understand,” she said. “How is that possible? Was she planning on coming back?”

“Yes, but,” he looked out the stained glass windows, “she’s supposed to have been back by now.”

This can't be happening, Ember thought. Not now. Not when they finally had a plan. "Where did she go?"

"Curious," said another, familiar voice. "We were wondering the same thing."

Arms ablaze, Ember stepped between Nieve and Damian. The twin's white eyeliner looked exceptionally sharp today, like the dagger she held in her hand. Ember pulled Damian closer.

"Now, now, there's no need for that," Nieve said, hands raised as if in surrender, though one still clutched a knife. "We only want to know where Su Alteza has gone."

"They've just come back from a job," Damian whispered behind Ember.

A job? As she devised several ways on how she was going talk her way out, or fight the twins off, her eyes fixed on Nieve's dagger. Red tainted the tip. *Oh.*

Oh fuck.

"Honestly, Nieve, I'm tired of this." Sombra stepped out from behind her sister. Her liner was blacker than her soul, a shadow to her minacious stare. "Alloy, my sister has given you every opportunity, every benefit of a doubt, and still, you would rather live life as a ticking time bomb than do what needs to be done? You would rather let a traitor escape?"

"Step back, Sombra. We're not certain of what happened," Nieve said, tucking her knife beneath her cloak and putting a hand on her twin's shoulder. She then looked at Ember and asked, "What do you know, Alloy?"

Ember put on her best remorseful expression, though she was much more terrified than penitent. "I don't know anything."

"But he does," Sombra said, staring at Damian.

With determination in his eyes and grit between his teeth, he tried to move forward—but Ember stopped him before he did. He might have been tall and strong. He might have even had a few nymph tricks up his sleeves. But he was just sixteen, and this wasn't his fight.

"Don't come any closer," she said to Sombra, heat flowing up her shoulders.

The oracle laughed derisively. "Is that a threat?"

"Yes."

She didn't see the fist, but she felt it. Knuckles connected to her chin, her teeth smashing together so hard one might have cracked. Her sight went fuzzy, as did her mind, and she hit the tiled floor with a thud.

"Sombra!" she heard Nieve say. Ember had yet to open her eyes.

"What?" Sombra said. "I didn't even use a blade." A pause. "Now, kitchen boy, would you be so kind as to tell us where Su Alteza is?"

Ember heard only silence.

"Nothing?" Sombra mused. "I know! What if we promise to let you join us on the float on Friday? You can stand next to the princess. It will be a once-in-a-lifetime event."

"*Sombra!*"

That forced Ember's eyes open. She sat up, jaw aching and head throbbing. Her arms slipped when she put weight on them. Six figures stood in the room now, each person with a double. Damian—assuming there was still only one—gave her a questioning look.

He doesn't know what to do, she thought, holding her head. *Hell, I don't know what to do.*

She had to live, else the queen lost her superweapon. Ademure had to live until Friday at least, else the Crown lost whatever show they wanted to make out of her. But Damian... Damian was nothing.

Through a groan, she said, "That won't be necessary. He'll tell you."

"Oh, good!" Sombra said.

Damian lifted a brow, asking if Ember was sure. She wasn't, but she nodded anyway.

He closed his eyes slowly before turning his attention to the twins. "The princess went into the forest a few hours ago," he said. "I haven't seen her return."

"Thank you, Damian," Nieve said through gritted teeth, eyes hardened on Sombra. Then she bent down close to Ember and inspected the extent of her sister's damage. Ember turned away.

"Relax," the oracle said calmly. She set a hand on Ember's cheek, brushing a thumb over her now-sensitive chin. "It's bruised, but not broken."

She gently moved her head so that they faced one another; Ember kept her gaze averted.

"I'm sorry for this, Alloy, truly. Sombra is on edge. Su Majestad is on edge. A known traitor has just escaped the castle, off to make a deal with the same monsters that annihilated us before, so we're all a little on edge. I hope you can understand."

Does she really think I'm buying this? Ember thought, though she knew she had to at least act as if she was. They already suspected she was conspiring with Ademure. No reason to amplify those doubts.

So she looked Nieve in the eye and, slightly nauseous, said, "I get it. Things are tense. Emotions are high. But in the end, we're family. And family is there for you no matter what, right?"

The oracle gave a satisfied smile and let go of her chin. "Heal up before Friday, Alloy. Fate is depending on you."

Nieve then left the temple quickly, but Sombra lingered behind, her cold eyes washing over Ember.

"Thank the gods I didn't break your jaw," she said, though she actually sounded sort of disappointed about it. "Next time, do us a favor and remember who's in charge."

The temple door shut behind her.

Ember stayed on the floor and closed her eyes, ashamed. All the lessons, the studying, the training, to be taken down in one blow. Where was her supposed lightning magic? An ability that no magick could fight against, that had cursed her since adolescence. Yet, when she needed it most, she couldn't produce a spark.

"Damn it!" Damian shouted. "I was so distracted, I didn't hear them at all. I could've taken them, Seño."

She opened her eyes to find him staring at the temple door.

"Don't be stupid, Damian. If you could've, you would've a long time ago."

"I could've, though. I could've...I don't know—poisoned them."

"I'm glad you didn't. They would've killed you first, and I need you alive."

He continued glaring. "Señorita Slade?"

"Yes?" she said, squinting, fighting off the painful pulsing in her ears.

"The princess will be alright out there, won't she?"

"Out there, I think she's fine." She pushed herself off the floor, head spinning, and then reached for a nearby pillar. "Friday, I'm not so sure."

"I'm sorry I didn't tell you that she'd left sooner."

"It's not your fault she's gone. I just hope she made the right decision. Did she say why she left? Was it really to start a second massacre?"

He shook his head. "She thinks the nymphs can help you with your lightning magic."

"She thinks *what*?"

"I tried to talk her out of it, but she was set on going."

You've got to be fucking kidding me, Ademure. You sure as hell picked the perfect time to start saving yourself.

"Seño Slade?"

Ember sighed, holding tightly to the column. "What is it, Damian?"

"We have to win."

"I know."

"Will you hurt them for me?"

She lowered her chin. "Hurt who?"

"The twins. Will you hurt them the way they hurt my dad?"

In that moment, she heard his truth, the reason for helping them that he had hidden behind his brilliant green eyes and carefree smile. She saw the years of frustration, pain, and sadness he had buried beneath his youthful, eager bravado. In that moment, she felt his hate.

He was right. Payback wasn't the word.

He wanted revenge, and more.

"No," she said. "I won't."

Damian didn't frown. He didn't react at all, in fact. No, instead, it was like he'd already known her answer before she'd said it. Like her rhythms had given it away.

CHAPTER 36

ALDEN

Alden knocked on the door.

"Come in," said a deep booming voice.

With a considerable push, the heavy door swung open. His father's study was grand—larger than the drawing room, possibly larger than any other study in the castle. Leather-bound books upon books filled the shelves. Carefully crafted maps and schematics decorated the walls. A large wooden desk sat in the center of the room covered in a smattering of papers and a single soulless laptop—his father had an affinity for soulless technology, and this piece had proven useful.

Behind the desk stood a bureau ten feet high and twelve feet long, filled with trophies. The latest additions—a handkerchief and a glove—belonged to the president of Lemuria and pharaoh of Atlantis, respectively, both since deceased.

Next to the cabinet, a glass enclosure held an emaciated kira. Dressed in ill-fitting black linens and poised with his head in his hands, the man-like winged creature sat on his stool so still, that were it not for the small risings of his chest, Alden would've thought him dead. Though, looking closer, death didn't seem far off. At the kira's feet was a tray of salmon, untouched, and black feathers littered the bottom of his cage.

Meanwhile, in a straight black suit and red tie, Leon Caldwell studied his corkboard, rubbing his neatly trimmed beard between his thumb and finger. The magma light that dripped like candle wax behind the semi-transparent cobalt walls and ran in rivers along the perimeter of the cobalt-obsidian ceiling and floor emitted a light that glowed against his dark bare head, shadowing the rest of his already ebony skin. His melody was slow and soothing, the song of someone entrenched in thought.

"Father," Alden said.

Leon shushed him and continued to stare. Alden waited patiently knowing that any further attempt to catch his father's attention would be in vain. Leon Caldwell would decide when he was ready to speak.

"Alden," he finally said, turning to face his son, "what's the status?"

"The plans are finished." Alden straightened his posture. His father's thunderous voice could command an army. It soon might. "Execution will be flawless."

Leon nodded. "Good. Well done. I'd expect nothing less. Tomorrow morning, the three of us will convene to review."

Alden nodded in return and started toward the door, but then... *I hope he doesn't get caught in the crossfire.* Graye's words had troubled him for days. What could she have meant by them?

"Father?"

His father had already returned to his corkboard. "Yes?"

"About Graye..." He trailed off, unsure of how to broach the topic.

"What about your sister?"

Figuring there was no going back now, he cleared his throat. "She said something to me last week. When I try to wrap my mind around it, I can only come to outrageous conclusions. I'm asking for some insight."

"Out with it, Alden. I don't have all day."

His chest tightened. "Do you plan on killing Kiva?"

Leon's chin dipped—not the reaction he had hoped for.

"I should've known better than to trust an eighteen-year-old with such sensitive information," his father said. "An oversight on my part."

"So, she wasn't lying to me?"

"No, she was not."

"But why?" Alden asked, heart sinking. "What does he have to do with anything?"

"I wish I could tell you, son. I assure you, you will learn soon enough. But for now, you are too close to the target. I cannot risk your interference."

"He's on our side, though! He's tracking the alloy as we speak!" It was rare that he raised his voice at his father, but it was much rarer that his father targeted his friends.

"That's enough, Alden. Leave me to my work."

"Father, I don't see the logic in this decision. It would be counterintuitive."

"Enough," Leon warned.

"But Father—"

A palm deftly struck Alden across his cheek. He stumbled backward.

Leon stood, chin high with eyes cast down. Under the magma light, the red in his irises were a severe scarlet. He replaced his hand in his pocket, saying, "I told you that was enough. You have me treating you like you're still an adolescent."

The stinging surged, and Alden put a palm to his face—

which now radiated heat. He should've expected this. He had pushed too far.

"I apologize, Father," he said, straightening. "I only acted out of care for my friend, but I was ignorant. Surely, you have your reasons."

Leon sighed. "It was my mistake in telling Graye. I expected you to react as such when you found out." He strolled to his desk and sat down.

Alden nodded. His father was nothing if not accountable. He grabbed a chair and sat opposite him. "I promise not to press you any further, but can you help me to understand one thing?"

"If it is something I can at this time disclose, then I shall."

"How does killing Kiva help our cause in Nysa?"

The corner of Leon's mouth quirked up.

Indignation lit within Alden. "Did I say something amusing?"

"No. Just assumptive. Your entire question is predicated on the notion that we have a cause in Nysa."

"Do we not?"

"Our mission is much broader than that," his father said. "Nysa is hardly an immediate threat. In fact, I'd much prefer them to be our allies."

"*Allies?*" Alden leaned forward in his chair, wanting to make sure he had heard that correctly.

"I know that it's far-fetched."

"Father, it's more than far-fetched. We tried and outstandingly failed just a decade ago. The wounds are still fresh in both nations."

"Yes, I'm aware. But an alliance of all the magicks would be the most beneficial in the long-term."

"Long-term? What does that mean?"

The red in Leon's eyes seemed to darken, and he put his

folded hands to his lips. "It means that we have been oppressed for too long."

Alden's brows furrowed. His family was wealthy and well-respected: his father was Counselor to the king himself. They could consume what they desired, spend endlessly, and travel the world (excluding Nysa, of course). The Caldwells were many things, but oppressed?

"For centuries our kind have been persecuted," his father continued. "Forced into the corners of the Earth, to its deserts, atop its peaks, beneath its waters, beneath its crust, all in order to survive. I'm tired of hiding from those horrid beings."

"Father, I don't understand. By 'horrid beings' you mean—"

"Soulless, yes." He locked eyes with Alden. "Like Lemuria and Atlantis, Nysa is simply a stepping stone, albeit a larger one than I originally intended. But the goal is not the genocide of the Nysan people. Every magick is precious."

"Except Kiva."

His father thinned his lips. "Kiva is a part of that stepping stone. Though it is unfortunate, it is a necessary sacrifice. His life will be given for the greater good of our people."

"Ultimately, then, you plan on warring with the Soulless Realm."

"I plan on obliterating the Soulless Realm."

The words hung heavy in the air.

"Could we not attack now?" Alden asked after a moment. "With our manpower, magic, and training we should be able to win handily. Why wait for Nysa's defeat?"

"You haven't met soulless," Leon said, grimacing. "You underestimate their technology. We would be overwhelmed if we were to attack with the numbers we have now."

Alden went silent. He still couldn't fathom why Kiva was so important—or, for that matter, why Nysa was. And the disharmonious chords emanating from Leon were as strange as the hatred in his father's voice. Not once in planning a mission had he ever heard him speak with such emotion.

Nor had he ever seen him create plans as odd as these. As per his father's instructions, their previous jobs were much simpler. Complexity increased errors, so a plan as elaborate as this? He didn't understand. But, in all his life, he'd never known his father to act without reason. If he said the soulless were a threat, then they must've been.

And yet he couldn't shake the feeling that there was more to this. Something his father was hiding from him, that went further than the assassination of his best friend.

"Have you told Graye?" he asked.

"Not yet. I had intended to inform the both of you after Friday's job."

He nodded a final time. "Thank you for telling me what you could, Father. I've left the plans on the table over there, and I will see you and Graye tomorrow."

"Understood. Until tomorrow."

Alden left his father's study, the doors swinging shut behind him, and headed for his own room. Once there, he took the two mirrors in his room and set them in the hallway, then locked the door behind him.

He dropped himself in front of his desk and pulled out his pen and paper. Furiously, he scribbled, jotting everything he could remember from what his father had said, then ripped out his notes, folded them, and slipped them into the slim wallet he carried on his person. When it was all done, he found himself shaking.

Did his father really want to war with the world?

CHAPTER 37
ADEMURE

Nyseion connected to everything it touched.

Ademure and the nymph stood at the base of the tree. She held tight to Xander's arm as the color drained from his body. With a translucent hand, the nymph touched the wood, sinking into it. The same magic tingled her own arm before it too was lost to the trunk. With eyes closed and a deep breath, she faded into the tree.

Rush. The only word she could think to describe it. She felt the texture of the bark, the density of the heartwood, but her body simply rushed through it. Like she was a part of it, it was a part of her.

They surged upward. The forest spanned below them, so vast, she couldn't see the castle or the harbor, or any part of human-populated Nysa.

Though Xander had told her the method behind their travel, she couldn't grasp the concept. He had said it had to do with the intensity of the magic in Nyseion, that somehow, they were all one with it, but she couldn't sense that oneness at all. He had also mentioned how loud the rhythms were, that

Nyseion itself emoted. She took him at his word, but again she didn't understand. It was just a tree, wasn't it? Did mountains and rivers emote as well?

They rose into the crown. Each branch they passed hosted a village of a dozen homes, all one-story cabin-like houses made of wood and leaves. Couples swayed to unheard songs in the village centers. Children chased one another, fading into the branches of what Ademure believed were small schools. Elderly rested in the petals of massive flowers, simply reading.

At the top branch, Xander and Ademure slowed to a halt, and she gasped. This branch had hundreds of tendrils, thousands of leaves, all swimming over one another, weaving in and out, dancing and twirling through the top of the crown, ultimately coming together as one magnificent fortress.

It was all so beautiful.

They stepped forward. The tingling beneath her skin subsided, and the weight of her body returned. She was flesh once again.

"Xander," another nymph said, coming from the entryway. He dressed in similar fashion to her guide, wearing a pale pink tunic and a pinned green rose.

"Isidore." Xander half-bowed.

"Is this the human you were sent after?" Isidore asked, nodding in Ademure's direction.

She lowered her head. "I am the Princess Ademure Maldojo. It is an honor to be welcomed here."

"Welcomed?" Isidore scoffed. "Humans are far from welcome here. Xander's ill-judgment does not buy you entry."

"I'll wait for the minister's opinion on that point," Xander said. He looked at Ademure. "Come, Princess."

Inside the fortress, the same tendrilled branch that formed the outer structure also made up the furniture, staircases, and chandeliers that decorated the halls. And hundreds of nymphs filled the corridors. Some were dressed like Isidore and Xander. Many dressed in fuller gowns, even the males. All the clothing was a smattering of pale hues, but several wore brightly colored sashes across their dresses. And all wore a familiar green rose.

She followed Xander up the staircase, careful not to lose him in the rainbow crowd. She already heard their whispers, felt their heads turn. She even saw several of them gesture in her direction.

They entered two arched doorways, just tall enough for Xander and plenty tall for her.

The room wasn't overly large nor ornate, but it was orderly, clean. Like the main hall, all the wares were made of branches woven together. There was one desk, with one chair. And the veins of the bark all radiated from the very center of the room. One window behind the desk lit the entire room, and several nymphs stood in a circle, one on each vein, hovering over some engraving in the bark below them. One nymph stood out from the rest, dressed in a beige gown and green sash, and of course, a green rose.

"Minister," Xander said, standing taller. In the presence of so many large nymphs, Ademure felt pressed to stand taller, too.

The nymph in beige stepped apart from the others. "General Xander. Who is this unusual guest you have with you today?"

With a bow, she said, "Princess Ademure Maldojo. It's an honor."

"Ah." The minister returned the bow. "Calix, Minister of the nymphs of Nysa. To what do we owe your presence, Princess?"

Amongst these ethereal giants, she felt inadequately human, but she raised her chin all the same. "I seek a record of sorts. I have it on good authority that you might know about Pandora?"

The minister frowned. "For what reason would you like to know about her?"

Ademure looked at the other nymphs in the room. They continued to pore over the engraving in the branch, unaware their minister had ambled off. Still, she would rather not raise alarm in more nymphs than she had to.

"Minister Calix, I'm sorry, but is it too much to ask for a private room? The information I'm looking for is sensitive."

"Of course." He walked toward a nearby wall and pushed. An unseen door opened, revealing yet another room to this wonder of architecture, and the three went inside.

Her eyes widened. The room was a complete contrast to the last two—the tendrilled branch almost seemed to stop at the door. In its place, there were plastic floorings and sheetrock walls. The cabinets and desks were all a stark white. And on those desks sat computers, calculators, cameras. Telescopes, telephones, televisions. Technology of the Soulless Realm.

"Ahem," Calix said. "Princess."

Her cheeks burned. "Right." She pulled out her small notebook and flipped to Ember's handwriting. "I have a prophecy."

"Prophecies aren't well-regarded here, Princess."

"I understand, Minister. And I promise that I'm here entirely of my own accord. I have no desire to assist the oracles. But, for my nation's sake and my own, I have to know what this means." She handed it to him. "Any bit of information you can provide would be immensely helpful and appreciated."

His eyes skimmed the page in silence.

"The part about 'daughter of Hope,'" he said at last.

"Yes?" she said, refraining from showing too much excitement.

"We did have a scroll that briefly mentioned the same line.

That and these 'evils' mentioned here on this other one, but we we're unable to decipher the rest. Unfortunately, that scroll is no longer in our possession—not that I'm sure it would've been useful to you anyway. The rest of this prophecy is largely unfamiliar. Pandora predated even our people."

"Oh." She dropped her head.

"Hm..."

Her head shot back up. "Yes?"

"Well, after a second pass, the 'evils' mentioned could also refer to the green rose sickness."

"How so?"

"It says 'Evils dead. Evils reborn.' And green rose sickness was an evil thought long dead. So long, in fact, that it was mostly believed to be myth, until it reappeared a little over two decades ago." He handed her back the notebook.

"This was written over two decades ago. It could be relevant. What is the sickness?"

"Roughly twenty years back, Nyseion birthed rare flowers that only bloom once a millennium." He tapped his chest, pointing at his brooch. "The green rose. The flower of our people. So naturally, we believed these flowers to be lucky and all garnished them. At the time, it was custom to visit your kind's town and exchange gifts with the humans.

"Soon we found out, however, that though nymphs remained unaffected by the rose, humans had intense reactions. Many changed moods, became simple-minded. Often, the wearer became so attached to the flower they were willing to kill for it."

Ademure stiffened. That sounded painfully familiar... "Did the humans ever become jealous?" she asked. "Obsessively so?"

Calix shook his head. "Obsessive yes, but rarely were they envious of one another."

"How many roses are left today?"

"None in the human world. It was a brawl, but we painstakingly removed every last green rose from your part of the island. The humans that survived returned to their initial natures."

"My mother's crown has a green rose."

He paused. "That's not possible. It's likely a fake or another flower."

"It can't be a coincidence. The lack of emotion. Simple-mindedness. Willingness to kill. It's been a much more gradual change than you say, but I've witnessed it."

"But she hasn't acted on these impulses, has she?"

"No," she said, "but that's only because her estrellas have held her back."

He shook his head. "The last humans became barbarians after only a few days. How long has your mother had hers?"

"As long as I've been alive. What does that mean?"

"That it's not the green rose."

"But it is!" Ademure pressed. "It looks just like yours." She gestured to his chest.

Calix looked at her, unconvinced. "Then, she must be exceptionally insusceptible to its effects. Even so, assuming it is the green rose, any human subjected to such prolonged exposure... I'm not sure anything can be done."

"Can't we just remove it like you did the others?"

"The others had theirs for less than a week, and it was a nightmare to remove. I can't imagine the attachment your mother has formed over twenty years. Only in death is she likely to part with it. I'm sorry to say it out loud, but your rose-bearer is a lost cause. If I were you, I'd focus on the other Evils of your prophecy. Apparently, there are multiple, after all."

But Ademure couldn't accept that. Whatever the other Evils were, they would have to wait. She wanted her mother back. She wanted her life back. *There has to be a way*, she thought. *I need more time here to discover what that is.*

"Minister Calix," Xander said, closing the door to the lab. "I've received word that two more humans are at the root of Nyseion. What would you like us to do?"

Ademure looked out the window to see the sun disappearing behind the horizon, and her heart dropped. *Oh no. I've been gone too long.*

"Princess," the minister said slowly, "I thought you came alone."

She swallowed. "I did. But I wasn't supposed to come at all."

"If you've brought us danger," his eyes sharpened on her, "then leave with it."

"No," she said a bit too loudly. "Not yet. If I leave now, Nysa will go to war."

"That is not a problem of Nyseion."

"It will be! The war will be fought on your lands. You think Agartha would leave you unscathed?"

"We have lasted several millennia, Princess. We will last several more."

"Minister Calix, please." She put her hands together and raised them to her bowed head. "I have to stay. I have to understand how to reverse this sickness. What can I do to facilitate that? What do you need?"

Surprisingly, he paused and lifted a brow. "What do you have?"

She furrowed hers. *What do I have? Not a queendom. Not any worthwhile magic.*

"My mind," she said. "And my hands."

For some reason, that seemed to catch his attention. Calix leaned into Xander, and the two whispered between themselves, out of earshot.

"What do you know of the Soulless Realm?" Calix finally asked.

"I know what I've read from el Alcázar's library. And I'm acquainted with a magick who was raised there."

The two nymphs exchanged knowing looks. Calix walked over to a cabinet, grabbed several notebooks stuffed with pages of scribblings, and laid them on the desk in front of her.

"You will record everything you know about this magick from the Soulless Realm, as well as spend your days in this laboratory researching soulless technology. Xander will check on you, and I will have another come acquaint you with the current state of affairs. In exchange, you may access whatever records or otherwise we have to complete your own research in your off time. Fair terms?"

More than fair. Ademure made an effort to not nod so vigorously.

"Good," he said. "Well now, it seems I have more pressing matters on my hands. If you will excuse me."

Calix left, and Xander remained at his post outside the lab, watching her. She didn't look at him. Instead, she looked through him, through everything, at nothing. Because, for the first time in a long time, she could breathe.

She pinched her skin, trying to wake herself from this dream. But it wasn't a dream. It was something viable. Something logical. Something other than relying on an unpredictable magick, feeble at her craft, to overpower the most elite force in the Magick Realm.

I'm out.

CHAPTER 38

ADEMURE

Minister Calix had told the staff of Ademure's situation shortly after her arrival yesterday evening. Still, she received varying looks of disgust when she walked the hallways—which, to be fair, wasn't all that different from life in el Alcázar. And it wasn't unexpected, considering the twins' arrival had been confirmed just an hour later. The oracles hadn't yet moved from the root deep in the forest, but no one expected that to continue much longer. Of course, the nymphs would hate the person who had brought them here.

Being that person, when she could, Ademure opted to resign herself to the room the minister had offered her. But the research lab was clear across the fortress from that room, so at the moment, she couldn't. Instead, she sped through the halls, wishing she had green skin.

She had to admit, though, she was excited to work in the lab today. Yesterday evening, she'd met with one of Calix's top soulless experts in the research lab. He'd spent several hours walking her through all of the progress they had made so far on the technology. He'd explained what each piece did and the basics of how they worked. They had even recreated the connections needed to power objects like the phone and laptop. (They connected to something called an Internet?) When she'd asked how, he'd thoroughly elaborated on the process—how it had taken months to dissect and build. And though the details eluded her, she was absolutely fascinated.

"Oh gods!" she exclaimed. She picked up the phone she'd accidentally dropped onto the laminate tile. Thankfully and surprisingly, it hadn't shattered, though it was clearly made of glass.

Still, she couldn't figure out how to turn it on. The nymph yesterday had said anything she needed to know about the basics of the tech would be in the notebooks, so she set the phone on the table before setting her hands on her hips and looking at the wall of them.

In a matter of minutes, she'd scattered the notebooks across all three tables, holding the one about phones in her hand.

That has to be it, she realized. *The phone lost all of its power.*

She pulled a wire from the pile of technology that looked like the sketch in her book and attached it to the phone and corresponding holes in the table. An image of a rectangle, partially filled in with red, appeared on the phone's previously blank canvas.

"Whoa."

Immediately, she pushed all the buttons, moved her hand along the screen. Anything she could do to make the image disappear, but it didn't. She looked back at her notes.

"An hour? How can the soulless wait all day for their technology to power?" She sighed, then turned to the next interesting piece of technology—the laptop.

She opened it and followed a similar routine. Also blank. She sighed again.

~

"Princess?" Xander said, entering the lab.

Ademure was huddled in a corner, her nose deep into a notebook about a camera. "Yes?"

"Would you like to join us for dinner?"

She looked out the window to see the sun setting. Then, she glanced at her mess. Loose pages were strewn across the room. Messes of wires hung from what the researchers called "outlets." Soulless technology precariously rested on various table edges.

You can come back to this tomorrow, she reminded herself.

And then, she nodded, feeling weirdly calm. Weirdly unpressured for time. Weirdly...free.

Xander waved a hand toward the door. "This way."

She followed the nymph down the vast staircase and into a rustic dining room. All of the stagnant furniture was made of the tree's tendrils. The chairs and other décor were made of the trees leaves. They did use candles for light, which surprised her considering the wooden makeup of the fortress, but they floated in the air—far away from any dry branch.

Calix sat at the head of the table. Isidore, the oh-so welcoming nymph, sat to his left. Next to Isidore sat a nymph with more curves and longer hair. Ademure didn't recognize her, but she too wore a pink tunic. Three chairs were filled with three of the nymphs the minister had met with yesterday, when Ademure had interrupted him. And those three all wore non-pink pastel gowns and vivid sashes. The two chairs to the minister's right were empty.

"Good evening, Minister," Ademure said before bowing,

holding out the skirt of her own gown—another gift from the nymphs.

"Good evening, Princess," Calix said. "I'm glad to see you will be joining us."

Xander gestured for her to sit in the chair immediately adjacent to the minister. She obliged, and the general sat in the final seat.

"I hope you find the food to your liking," Calix said. "It's not what you're used to, I'm sure, but it's a delicacy in Nyseion."

A mixture of leafy greens and colorful grapes and berries filled her plate. Roasted poultry sat on top. An inhale and her mouth watered; her stomach grumbled.

"It looks and smells wonderful," she said. "Thank you."

Digging into his own plate, he smiled. "Our pleasure."

The rest of the room joined him in tearing into their feast. And, delightfully not under anyone's critical eye for the first time in as long as she could remember, Ademure quietly took bites of her food, too, finally allowing herself to give in to her hunger.

"You know," Calix said, "these grapes are grown just outside—"

"Minister," Isidore interjected. "I hate to tear you from your diplomacy, but are we not going to discuss the oracles? They are less than ten miles from the base. They've covered the distance much faster than we anticipated. We must decide what to do."

Calix shot his general a look of displeasure, but his fork stilled as he seemed to consider the substance of the interruption. "Ophelia, what do you think of this? What should we do?"

"The oracles have proven their strength before," said the nymph with longer hair. "There's no need for us to wait until they strike. I believe we should operate on the assumption that they can climb Nyseion, so we shouldn't allow them to try."

"And what say you, Xander?"

"I agree with Ophelia. I believe the oracles are an immediate threat, and we should respond in kind."

"If I may, Minister," said a nymph dressed in a light blue gown and bright orange sash.

"Please, Magus."

"I don't know that striking the oracles first is the best strategy. They can see the future. Won't they be prepared for us? Why not continue to watch them instead?" He took a drink from his goblet. "Let them endure the climb to Nyseion, and once they tire out, strike them in their sleep."

The minister rubbed his chin. "What do you think, Princess?"

Ademure choked on her grape. "Me?"

"You've interacted with the twins much more than any of us. You know their weaknesses."

She stifled her coughs by gulping down water, hoping it would cool her flushed cheeks. She had gone so long without being asked for an opinion, she had nearly forgotten how to give one—and in a strategy meeting, no less! When she felt as if she could breathe again, she spoke before she could make herself out to be any more of a fool.

"But I don't know their weaknesses," she said. "Only their strengths. I know that it's not their future sight that you should worry about, but their present. And I know that they can see everything that happens around them within a sizable range, as if they were a fly on the wall of each room within. They'll see you before you see them."

"And how do we circumvent that?" Ophelia asked.

"You don't," Ademure said. "There is a half-nymph in the castle that claims the twins are blind to him, but I haven't had a chance to discover why—it could be any number of things. Either way, I don't think that it's wise to make the first move in a full attack should they see you coming, nor do I think we should continue watching them from afar and make ourselves willing victims."

Calix nodded. "We'll send a scout crew, then. Have it report back regularly. And if we're fortunate, we'll discover that their blind spot applies to more than young Damian."

Ademure's eyes snapped to the minister. "You know Damian?"

"I know all my people, Princess," he answered casually. "It's settled, then. Isidore, you will take your team and scout the oracles. Report to Xander and Ophelia each morning. Magus, you will prepare the other sages accordingly, and we shall improvise from there. Understood?"

"Yes sir," the nymphs said in unison.

After a brief silence and an exchange of dishes for desserts, light conversations rose at the table. The sages spoke with each other and the generals amongst themselves. Meanwhile, Ademure contented herself with picking at her cold green cream, her ears catching the occasional gossip or strategy or nymph curiosity, her mind swimming with thoughts and questions and hopes and fears.

"You're a quiet one," Calix said.

She felt his eyes on her, but rather than meet them, she continued to scan the room. "Am I?" she said. "I guess I don't often have much to add to the discourse."

"I don't believe that, though you do seem distracted." He leaned into her line of sight. "What are you thinking?"

She swirled her leaf-made spoon in her leaf-made bowl. "I'm wondering why you asked for my opinion. Why heed an enemy's advice?"

"You are not my enemy, Princess."

Her spoon stopped. *I'm not?*

"Each war is new," he continued. "New enemy, new terrain, new magic or technology. Strategy is fine, but most 'experts' don't last from battle to battle. What truly matters is intelligence, information. Knowing another's weakness and how to exploit it. Knowing our own and how to protect it. No, you may not have battle experience, but between the soulless realm and the oracles, you're a wealth of knowledge. A weapon in its own right."

"But what if I'm wrong?" she asked. "What if I'm sending you down the wrong path?"

He laughed. "And I was beginning to think you had little confidence, Princess. How arrogant you must be to think yourself so necessary to our cause."

"But I'm the reason you're facing the twins!"

"No, this was inevitable. You've only given us a reason to act now."

She fell back in her chair, leaving behind her dessert entirely. Her stomach still didn't sit right. She didn't doubt the nymphs' strength, but she knew the twins. And she knew how often she had successfully stood up to them—all zero times. Despite the nymphs' backing, she couldn't help but feel as if she was leading the people of Nyseion into a trap.

But he did say it was a long time coming, she reminded herself.

"What happened, Minister," she asked, "when they attacked?"

He frowned. "Are you aware of the nymph statue in the plaza?"

She nodded.

"That was where General Linus fell," he said. "He escorted my people's trip into Nysa. Once gifts were exchanged, he was expected to guide them back to Nyseion. His statue was a gift from the queen to commemorate him and the others that died."

"Why would we commemorate someone we attacked?"

"As a cover, I suppose. We didn't know that there had been an attack at all. Not initially. Before we even knew they were dead, your mother sent word with one of our survivors that a tragic accident had occurred. The glass gifts your town had given us were somehow tainted—with what the Crown never specified. But the moment they were exchanged, thousands of my people dropped dead."

Ademure frowned. Tainted glass? What would even taint glass?

"Oil," he said, as if hearing her thoughts. "The glass was tainted with crude oil. Death in a liquid."

"How did you know?"

"A defector of yours told me."

She inclined her head but said nothing.

"During my investigation, I met with her," Calix continued. "She dressed remarkably similar to the oracles, so I had my doubts about her, but then she told me that what had happened was no accident. That the alloys were acting on the oracles' orders. That they were attempting to fulfill a prophecy and used my unknowing people for training. And her rhythms sang only verity."

"But to what end? Why kill the nymphs? What does that accomplish?"

He sighed. "I wish I knew. Since humans first inhabited the island, we've refrained from involving ourselves in their politics as much as we possibly can. However, once I'd learned the truth, I couldn't refrain any longer. Civilians, children. All dead because of the Nysan Crown's selfishness. And so, I acted selfishly in return."

"Poisoning the alloys..."

"I know it sounds cruel. Perhaps it was. But if the prophecy required trained alloys, that was what I had to deprive the world of."

The other dinner conversations thundered in their silence. She'd always known that what had happened seven years ago wasn't her fault, that she didn't deserve the ire she'd received. And now she had confirmation, two feet in front of her—the nymph who demanded the deed be done.

And she didn't blame him.

"You know that you missed one," she said. "You left an alloy alive that day."

"Did we? I assure you, it wasn't intentional."

"She was in the Soulless Realm. Almost sixteen at the time."

"She must not have made Cristian's list." Calix shrugged. "Anyway, it's much harder for us to fade where the magical connection is weak."

"I thought fade could only be used in the forest?"

He lifted a green brow and asked, "Where would you get an idea like that?"

"Damian said he couldn't use fade in the sand."

"Damian probably can't."

As she sat with this information, she furrowed her brow. "Is that how you found the alloys, then? Used fade to detect their magical strength? Then again to travel?"

The minister looked at her inquisitively. "Something like that."

"And oceans and the earth don't stop you? That's how you could travel to Atlantis and Agartha?"

"Somewhat."

"But what about the poison? How were you able to poison so many so easily? Many of the alloys hadn't even consumed anything before they died."

"Princess," he said, "I know that your inquiries arise solely out of curiosity, but considering your position amongst your people, pardon me if I don't find it sensible to divulge all of the nymphs' secrets to you."

Ademure only then realized how far over the table she had leaned, how tight her hands had pressed to the wood's surface. She leaned back.

"Of course," she said and bowed her head, hiding her flushed face. She hadn't rambled on a topic like that in so long. Her mother would have slapped her silly before she had gotten out a single question. "My apologies, Minister."

He raised a hand; she winced. He seemed to notice, eyeing her, then set his hand down and shook his head. "No harm done, Princess. Actually, I should be thanking you."

"Thanking me? For what?"

"A quite fascinating conversation."

After dinner, Xander escorted her back to her room in silence. But as she started to shut her room's door, she realized that the general wasn't leaving her behind.

"What are you doing?" she asked. "Go home. Get some rest."

"I apologize, Princess," he said, "but I cannot leave you alone. Minister's orders."

"What? Why?"

"'A royal shall never be without their escort,' the minister said."

"But I shouldn't need a bodyguard in friendly territory. " She glanced at the empty hall—shadows danced not only around corridor corners but through the divots of every ridge of every branch that twisted together to form the hall. Presumably, nymphs could fade through every one of them. "Unless not everyone is as friendly as you," she added.

Xander was silent, but the look in his eyes told her everything.

"Right," she said. "I guess I shouldn't expect every nymph to let go of their need for retribution so easily. Were you here last night as well?"

"I was."

"Are you not exhausted working almost forty-eight hours straight?"

"We nymphs don't require as much sleep as humans."

If I make it past Friday, she thought, *I must start tracking these idiosyncrasies.*

"Even so," she said, "do you not have a spouse? A child?"

He recoiled, appearing almost offended. "We would never allow someone who has a family to fight—families are what we protect. How can we do that if we separate them?"

Track that one too. "So how long will you be staying outside my room?"

"Until I find someone who can take my place. Ideally two others. Then, we will rotate watches."

"And how long will that take?"

He bobbed his head. "As long as it takes to find someone with the right rhythms. I cannot give you a time."

So she pulled a chair from her room and placed it just outside her room's threshold.

"What are you doing, Princess?"

"You've gone to such extraordinary lengths for me. First by allowing me to plead my case to the minister, and now by protecting me day and night." She sat down. "The least I can do is keep you company."

"That's not necessary. You need your sleep."

She waved a hand. "I'll fall asleep at some point, I'm sure. Until then, let's talk—if you don't mind, of course."

He eyed her. His chest remained high, his spear tight in his hand. "Whatever you wish."

"I only wish whatever you wish, Xander. I don't want to burden your job, nor to make you uncomfortable."

"You've done neither."

"Good. Please let me know if I do."

"Yes, Princess."

"Ademure." In seeing his raised brow, she continued with, "I'm a princess in name only. So, if you would please, call me Ademure."

"As you wish, Ademure."

She folded her hands in her lap, looking out at the dark corridor. It was scarcely lit by candlelight, essentially rendering her blind. In the morning, these halls had been flooded with nymphs, bustling to and from meetings, chatter and footsteps echoing off the veiny wood. Now, they were empty and silent.

"Xander?"

"Yes, Ademure?"

"Did you always want to be in the military?"

He nodded once. "For as long as I can remember."

"Why?"

"I wanted to serve my nation."

She chewed the inside of her lip. "Sure. I also want to serve my nation. But aren't there other means of doing such a thing? Running for an office perhaps?"

"Bureaucracy is above me. I can serve better with my body than my mouth."

With a tilted head, she countered, "But you're a general. You command troops."

"I do. But only when I have to."

"And you never wanted a family?"

"The idea has never appealed to me. Ophelia and Isidore and the others are my family. They are enough."

"You don't have parents? Grandparents? Aunts and uncles?"

He shook his head. "My mother was the last. When she died, I was finally eligible to join."

Ademure could never imagine such a desire for herself, especially if it meant voluntarily giving up a family. But then, she hadn't had a family in so long, perhaps it was worth considering.

She glanced up at Xander, whose face was shadowed by the single candle that floated above them. Then she caught the faintest twitch in his ear—so small, that had she blinked she would have missed it. She waited another moment, and again, there was the twitch.

"Do you know why humans can't hear the rhythms?" she asked.

"I don't. I suspect it has to do with training, as I know that there are some humans who can."

"There are? Who?"

"I don't know more than that."

"I assume they're Nysan?"

"Again, I wouldn't know. I only know that there were several who trained with the nymphs well over a decade ago."

"Do the estrellas know about them?"

"I have no answer."

"I bet not," she said to herself. She had never heard Sombra or Nieve talk about the rhythms before, much less humans who knew them. And considering Damian had never divulged such a secret to her, she couldn't imagine many humans knew at all.

How interesting...

"So, you can hear my emotions?" she said. "Any and all of them?"

"Yes."

"And I assume you can hear other nymphs' emotions, considering the lengths you're going to in order to listen to them right now."

He eyed her. "Yes."

"Can you control each other's emotions?"

His face hardened, his hand tensing around his spear. He said nothing.

"Oh," she said, shifting in her chair. "Oh my gods. You can, can't you? Or..." She looked in his narrowing eyes, then looked away. "Perhaps, you can't. Or, at least, you shouldn't."

"You are correct," he said, pressing his lids shut. "We shouldn't."

"But you do. Maybe not you in particular. But someone does."

Xander only returned his gaze to the shadowy halls.

And Ademure's thoughts ran wild. To not only hear someone's emotions but to control them as well. Play on someone's pride, someone's jealousy. One could quell or incite riots, maybe even wars. What incredible power!

But then, that was why Xander was hesitant about it, wasn't it? The nymphs hadn't fought in years, though. Even the slaughter of the alloys seven years ago had been just that: a slaughter. There was no fight. Why be so hesitant when it wasn't ever used?

"Have you ever controlled someone's emotions before?" she asked.

"No," he said firmly. "I lack the ability."

"But you're in the minister's cabinet. If you don't have it, who does?"

"I am uncomfortable with this topic."

She blinked. "Of course. I'll say nothing more of it."

"Thank you, Ademure."

She smoothed her skirt, making a mental note to copy down what she'd learned tonight. Then, reluctantly, she changed subjects.

"Do you know Damian?" she asked.

The tension in Xander's shoulders seemed to loosen. "I only first heard of him tonight when the minister mentioned him. That poor boy."

"What do you mean?"

"He's part human."

"And?"

"Can you imagine living his life? Being ostracized by both sides? It's a terrible fate."

She wrinkled her nose. She knew that Damian hadn't visited the nymphs in so long, but she had never considered there to be a reason for that.

Then again, he'd had a choice to live with his mother in Nyseion or live as the son of a traitor, and he had chosen the latter. That alone should've tipped her off.

"He's a good kid," she said. "Without his help, I would've never made it here. And he never did tell me about the rhythms. I had to learn from a book."

"I had wondered how you knew about those," Xander said. "You surprised me when you begged me to hear yours."

"Is that why you let me pass?"

"Among other things."

"What other things? My charm?" She plastered a toothy grin on her face and met his eyes.

He let out a single chuckle. "Not quite."

She laughed—which felt amazing—and rested her chin in her hand. "What was it then?"

"Your honesty. And your humility. Not many people of your

station would kneel in the mud to an inferior, whether that be human or nymph. I've only known Minister Calix to show such modesty to his subordinates."

Her smile faltered. "Oh."

"Your rhythms don't sound content with my answer. Nor your tone."

"It's not discontent with your answer, I assure you. I'm merely unhappy with myself."

"Why?"

"Because I fear you're confusing weakness for humility. As I've said, I'm a princess in name only. I have no strength or power in which to have pride. What you saw yesterday was desperation. Nothing more, nothing less."

"Hm."

She lifted her head. "You don't agree?"

"Forgive me. I haven't known you long, but you managed your way not only past me but past the minister as well. Not even Sofia stayed longer than a few hours."

Her brows raised. "Sofia? As in Sofia Valentina? Small woman, large personality?"

He nodded, chuckling to himself. "The very same. The only other human who made it to Nyseion—invited, I should say. But you should know, she did not spend the night."

Ademure tilted her head, considering what that meant for herself. "I doubt Sofia had reason to."

"Perhaps not, but that does not change the fact that you have negotiated your stay."

"Yes," she said, setting her chin back in her hand. "By selling my limited knowledge of the Soulless Realm and lacking ability to research it in turn."

"I don't believe that's as much of an affliction as you are trying to make it seem. I also doubt that Minister Calix would have given you a job that you would not enjoy. After all, it can be quite boring sitting around the fortress all day."

"Oh, I can imagine." It was probably much like sitting around a castle all day. "It's not that I'm ungrateful to you or the minister. And you're right, the job isn't the slightest bit tedious. But I fear that my stay is only burdensome. I mean, you're now dedicated to spending your nights outside my room! Wouldn't that time be better spent elsewhere?"

"If you weren't here, yes, my time would be diverted elsewhere. But the task of protecting you is not any less important. Did you not hear how enamored the minister was with you when you arrived yesterday, asking after your knowledge? Or how he latched onto your every word at dinner earlier tonight? He thinks you are valuable, incredibly so. If he didn't, you would not be here. He is a good man, but he puts his people first. Which means, you are the furthest thing from a burden; you are an asset. That seems like a power to me—one that is the most difficult of which to show humility."

She pressed her lips together. Xander had never said so much to her or anyone else in the day she had spent with him. Even on their long trek from the forest to Nyseion, he was quiet. He inquired about nothing, kept his eyes forward and his feet moving, or else his ears listening. She had no idea that he might have had so much to say.

"Thank you, Xander," she said at last. "I don't know how to take that."

"You don't believe me. That is expected. You will come to." He bowed his head. "Princess."

CHAPTER 39

KIVA

K iva sat at the Round Table, again staring at his disgustingly green eyes in the mirror. Today, the alloy—*Ember*—wanted to see him. It'd been a year since Alden's informant had first leaked the Delfinos search for an alloy, that she'd traveled each day into Pegasus City. An entire year Alden and Kiva spent tracking the Delfinos' movements, her movements. A year of plotting, persuasion, dumb luck. And finally, *finally*, he had made some sort of progress.

Why did he feel guilty?

No, this is a good thing, he tried to reassure himself. *Take away Nysa's weapon and use it against them. If I can convince her to leave today, I can save Agartha. I get my life back.*

That felt wrong—so wrong. But it was right.

Right?

He put his head on the table and groaned.

"Kiva, are you there?"

He lifted his head. His best friend was reflected in the mirror.

"Alden!" he said, grinning. "I thought you'd still be on the job. Or did you finish already? Was it a heist? What'd you steal? Actually, I've been meaning to ask you more about—"

"The job hasn't finished yet," Alden interrupted. "Look, I don't have much time to talk. In a few minutes, I'll go completely dark."

"What do you mean?"

"I really wish I could explain everything, but just listen to me."

Kiva pulled his chair closer to the mirror. "Listening."

"In two days, there's going to be an event in the plaza in Nysa. The entire nation is going to show up."

"Yeah, it's Nysan Independence Day."

"You can't be there."

He frowned "Why not?"

"You just can't!" Alden shouted, and Kiva jumped. "I'm sorry," his friend continued. "I can't tell you more than that."

That disturbed him. Alden was always vague, but never scared. Something must be wrong.

"Alden, am I in danger?"

"Not if you don't go." His red eyes flashed from demanding to begging. "Please, I know you have this complex, or whatever it is that makes you want to do stupid things, but this time, listen to me. It's not safe."

That was hardly an answer, but Kiva nodded nonetheless. "Okay. I won't go."

The tension in his friend's face loosened just a bit. "Thank you. I'll talk to you more in a few days."

And then he was gone, leaving behind Kiva's green-eyed reflection.

He sat there for a moment, then looked toward Profe Valentina's collection. At the upper right of the top metal shelf, an hourglass-shaped clock leaned against a giant tooth. It was almost noon.

He would have to ponder more on this later. But for now, he had an appointment he could not miss.

~

The plaza was busy today, people decorating the shops in preparation for the holiday. Even the nymph fountain had green and white ribbons ornamenting its base. Nysa's anthem blared from a variety of instruments, people, birds.

The Nysans were undoubtedly the most isolated of the Magick Realm, but unlike Agartha, this town was *alive*. If it weren't for their monarch, Kiva could almost see himself staying here.

He scanned the plaza. On a bench near the fountain, he spotted a familiar curly-haired blonde woman, entirely oblivious to everything but the notebook she huddled over, frantically scribbling in, and his pulse quickened.

"Hey, ice queen."

Ember sent her book and pen flying. "Damn it!" she shouted. "Don't sneak up on me like that!"

He bent down and grabbed her things, dusting off the sand before handing them back to her with a sly grin. "Don't blame me for your complete lack of peripheral senses."

She reopened her notes with a scowl. Her pages were stained with illegible markings—the thoughts of someone unhinged.

"What is it that you're working on anyway?" he asked.

"It's none of your business."

"I can help, you know." He reached in his pocket for a shell —one he'd clad in a bright Nysan-green. "I've been known to plot a thing or two before."

She stared at his open hand, her mouth just as open. Then

she threw her book in her bag and slung both over her shoulder. "This was a mistake."

"Whoa, whoa, whoa." He held out both hands, letting the shell fall to the sand. "You're leaving already? Because of what I said?"

She started toward the castle without a word.

"Ember, what the hell?" he yelled before running after her. "Weren't you the one who invited me here?"

She looked back at him and glowered. "I asked honest Kiva to come today. Not an insincere flirt."

"I don't know what you want from me. I am being sincere."

"If this is the real you, then you're a waste of my time." She eyed him up and down. "I'm not going to let some immature playboy get in my way."

Her words stung a little more than usual, but in her glare, he saw bloodshot eyes, darkened circles, and pain. A lot of pain. *Something's off.*

She started walking again.

"Wait," he said before joining her once more.

"I'm done, Kiva. I've got things to do, and I can't spend any more energy on you."

"Ember, I'm sorry. I'm really truly sorry. But give me five minutes—that's all I need."

She didn't stop.

"Godsdammit, didn't you hear me?" he shouted. He reached for her shoulder, halting her mid-step. "I told you I'm sorry!"

"Don't touch me!" She shoved his hand off. He backed away. And the air around them grew warm. "Your words are worthless to me," she continued. "I can *never* tell what's a lie, and I'm tired of trying to figure it out."

You can always tell. A bead of sweat formed on his hairline. *I can't be the only reason you're this heated. There's something else.*

But what, he couldn't begin to fathom. He supposed if he were around the Delfinos all the time, he would be angry as hell too.

He took in a deep breath and recovered his calm. "Look, I didn't come here to fight you again. I'm being genuine: I'm sorry. Sorry for touching you. Sorry for lying to you. For using you. All of it. I just want you to listen to me."

She stared at him in silence, as if she were waiting for him to prove his regret.

Without taking his eyes off of her, he moved slowly, lowering himself onto the edge of the nymph fountain, and tapped the space next to him. "Will you sit with me?"

Her voice was barely audible. "Why?"

"Because I have a lot to say." When she didn't budge, he added, "Please?"

As if it pained her to do so, she sat next to him. And the temperature drop—though small—was noticeable.

"What more can there possibly be to say?" she asked before he could start. "You want me to kill for you, right? Just like everyone else."

"Please," he said again, making no effort to conceal his frustration. "You're the one who keeps begging me to tell the truth. I'm trying to do that, so let me. Please."

She gave him yet another dirty look and folded her arms, but neither motion held the same wrath as before, and she stayed quiet as the air completely cooled.

"If there were other alloys," he started, "we wouldn't have cared about you in the slightest—us nor the estrellas, I assume. For some time now, alloys have only been considered weapons of war, and we used to have plenty of them. I doubt that's consoling at all, but I need you to know that none of this was ever personal."

Her arms were still tight across her chest, but the lines in her forehead softened, and she seemed attentive to what he had to say.

"Until seven years ago," he continued with a slight boost in confidence, "Agartha had a host of alloys. Not as many as Lemuria, but they could have held their own against the Nysan alloys, and that's what really mattered. The issue was that our elder alloys were dwindling. We were relying more and more on our up-and-coming ones."

He glanced at her, and now her arms were at her side. She had leaned in. He took in a deep breath.

"Our most senior military officials were tasked with protecting the newest recruits, acting as their guards until the alloys were trained enough to become guards themselves. And they were guarded, sure, but since Agartha is nearly impossible to access without the ability to mirror, Agartha itself was usually all the protection needed. So often, if an official had to take on another duty, or something came up, the military left the recruits to me. The alloys became good friends of mine. One even was like a little brother." He turned his gaze to the sand beneath his dangling feet. "Then, I watched him die."

He heard her breath stop, but he couldn't pull his gaze from the ground. He clenched his fist, fighting back the heat in his face.

"He was twelve, and he'd never harmed a thing. He never even had the opportunity to because he never left the watch of the Black Sky. He never saw it coming. None of them did."

He could feel her eyes on him, wandering about him, digging at him. He refused to meet them. The sounds of running water and Nysan anthems claimed the air until, at last, he felt like he could continue. "Of course, my failure left Agartha exposed as well."

Ember shifted, but she still said nothing.

"Cold wars can't stay cold forever," he said. "Either someone collapses, or someone attacks—and we were vulnerable to both. The lords, ladies, and businesspeople of Agartha had become increasingly dissatisfied with King Nikita's rule. If he couldn't fight off a Nysan strike, Agartha would fall to Nysa. And with how fractured the lords' armies are and no alloys to protect us, the only defense was to force Agarthans underground permanently.

"But it wasn't long before the lords began asking what the difference was between that and imprisonment. They wanted more than protection: they wanted the king to go on the offensive against Nysa. And if he didn't win back their freedom, then they would find a new king who could."

He instinctively grabbed at his scarred shoulder. "My failure left Agartha susceptible to not just the Nysans, but ourselves. By not protecting the alloys—my friends—I fractured the kingdom. So I had to reconcile it. I needed to find someone to unify our armies and lead the charge. Who better to do that than the last alloy?"

Her lack of reaction made his heart race. She studied him for a moment, the corners of her mouth downturned, and then she pulled away, like she was lost in thought or contemplating what to say next or judging him for what he'd let happen to the alloys or maybe what he'd done in response. The resulting silence was unbearable, but there was no way to undo it now.

Finally, she spoke. "Kiva, why tell me this?"

He swallowed down his rising pulse. "You asked me to come back if I found the right words. That's what these are. They aren't pretty, but they're right."

Another silence.

But much shorter than the last.

"Sounds like Agartha is a house of cards. I don't think it's fair to blame you for knocking it over."

"Yes, well, tell the king that. When we get to Agartha, I'll introduce the two of you."

He caught her eyes when he said it, hoping for the faintest of smiles.

She gave him a minute upturn of a single corner of her mouth.

Thank the gods.

"You really don't know when to give up, do you?" she asked.

"You gave me a reason to keep going. Don't forget that." He winked.

One upturned corner became two.

But as her attention settled on the castle in the distance, her smile faded. He glanced at her bag. The notebook she'd spent the last two days scribbling in sat on top.

"It's not just me, is it?" he asked, his gaze returning to hers. "That has you in a frenzy. I'm not the one that put you on edge today, am I?"

She dipped her hand in the fountain, swirling the water with her finger, and shook her head. "I'm trying to help someone," she said. "And things aren't exactly going as planned."

"Who?" he asked.

But she only swirled in response.

He frowned and tried again. "Why do you need to be the one to help them?"

Her hand froze; her eyes hardened on the water. "Because I failed to protect someone else."

"What happened to..." realizing what he was asking, he added only, "the one?"

She looked at his shoulder. "I'm guessing what happened to you."

"You don't know?"

"I know she's alive. I know that Child Protective Services stepped in and separated us. I know that I've tried to contact her a million times and she's rejected me every time, and I know that I deserve the silence. But more than that," she looked away, "no."

He put a hand on her dry hand, trying to catch her attention. But she pulled it away and wouldn't look back.

"Ember, if you don't think I can be blamed for what I did, why are you blaming yourself?"

"Failing to keep someone alive and actually killing someone," she laughed mournfully, "are two different things."

He raised a brow. "But she's alive?"

"My foster parents aren't," she said, splashing the water. "And she was hurt. Badly."

The unbearable silence returned, so much heavier than the last. His chest constricted and his stomach somersaulted. Not knowing what to do, he tried to reach for her.

"Don't," she said before pulling her knees up to her chest and wrapping her arms around them. "I don't need condolences."

Her face tightened with guilt, with sadness, loneliness—a different emotion etched each wrinkle in her forehead, each muscle in her cheek.

He hated seeing her this way.

"You didn't know who you were or what you could do," he said. "You didn't know—"

"I *wanted* to kill them." She spoke quietly, like a weight pressed on her vocal cords. "I wanted them dead. And I knew enough about myself to know that I could make that happen. You keep thinking you know me, Kiva, but you don't. I'm not innocent. I know what it means to murder. What it costs to murder. That time, my sister was the price." Several tears traced her etchings.

He exhaled, finally understanding. "That's why you believe you're a monster."

"It's how I *know* I'm a monster. They knew it, too." She

nodded toward the nymph statue that loomed over them. "If only I had died that day with the other alloys. None of this would have ever happened."

"Don't say that," he said quickly as his neck flushed with heat.

"Why not? It's true."

"You don't know what's true." He gritted his teeth, his mind reeling with how wrong she was. She was powerful and lethal, yes. But she was also caring, compassionate—never mind how much she pretended to be otherwise. He knew no monsters like that. "You couldn't possibly know what's true."

"My sister—"

"Would still be without her sister. You've been gifted what others had stolen, yet you waste it on pitying yourself for things you can't change. How selfish of you to think it doesn't matter that you survived that day."

She glared at him, and he waited for the air to grow warmer—he dared it to—but it stayed as cool as she did. She looked back at the water.

"You're right," she said—and that confused him. Then she swung her legs over the edge, stood, and grabbed her bag— and that confused him more. "I should go."

But when he realized she was heading toward the castle path, he caught her by her bag strap. "Hold on. You're really going back? You're choosing them, knowing full well who they are?"

"For now. I have to make up for my mistakes, too." She started walking.

"Then why make time for me?" The words were out of his mouth before he could stop himself.

Like stone, she stilled where she stood. However, he didn't hesitate to cover the distance between them. Then he waited with his hands in his pockets and his heartbeat drowning out the town's anthem as she fumbled with the clasp of her bag and pulled at the ends of her hair.

"I don't know," she said.

"No," he said, shaking his head. "Not good enough. You could've let me go yesterday. I would never have bothered you again. If you weren't going to Agartha with me, why did you ask me to come back?"

"I..." She closed and opened her mouth several times, then cleared her throat. "In two days, I'm leaving Nysa anyway."

He frowned, again confused. "How?"

"Oh no, I will not have you following me." She jabbed a finger into his chest. "Nysa is way easier to leave than Agartha."

"But you felt the need to tell me you're going?" He grabbed her finger in his hand.

The pink of her cheeks contrasted the sparkling green of her eyes as she said, "It didn't feel right not to say goodbye."

"I don't understand—"

Her lips were on his, soft and sweet. Her hands were on his neck, warm and wanting. And the moment of shock, of surprise, faded into one of bliss, of lust, of happiness as he realized...

He kissed her back.

His right hand went to her hair, tugging her curls, wrapping a finger in her soft locks. His left hand wrapped around her waist, pulling her tighter to him, so he could protect her, so he could keep her to himself, so he could stop her from leaving...

He broke away and put his forehead on hers. "You're leaving."

She looked up at him with a sad smile, rosy skin, and wild, blonde hair. "If things were different, and your country didn't depend on me as a war weapon, perhaps we could have actually been...friends. That's why I'm saying goodbye. I'm leaving this world entirely. Leaving this war entirely."

"No," he said automatically as he tried to comprehend all this. But he couldn't, and so the butterflies in his stomach began speaking for him. "This can't be goodbye. I'm going to see you again. I have to."

Chuckling, she gently pulled herself from his arms, then gripped the strap of her bag. "I never really believed you'd leave me alone."

With that, she turned on heel and headed back toward el Alcázar de Maldojo, her curly blonde hair floating in the breeze.

Fuck!

CHAPTER 40

EMBER

"Fuck!" Ember shouted, slamming the door behind her.

She dropped onto her bed and stared at the ceiling. She had told him so much. Too too much. About Ademure, then Daphne, and then her foster parents.

My foster parents! She groaned. She had told him of how she had *murdered* her foster parents. Why on earth had she felt the need to tell him that?

And then he had asked her that question she had asked herself all morning. Why had she asked to see him again? Why had she wanted to say goodbye? And why, when she could've easily lied to him, had she *kissed him* instead?

God, he was so certain he would see her again, too. Luckily, because of either her escape or her death, he probably wouldn't.

"Señorita?"

She sat up. "Damian? Don't you know how to knock?"

"I did several times, Seño." Folding his arms, he looked her over. "You're back from the harbor late."

"I had to make a stop in town." She dragged the covers over her knees.

He scrunched his nose. He definitely didn't believe her.

"What do you need?" she asked.

"Princess Ademure hasn't returned."

She furrowed her brow. "What about Sombra and Nieve?"

He shook his head. "Them either."

It's been two days... I should reach out to her.

She turned her notebook to the first empty page she could find. But on the page before that, she found a note she didn't recognize.

Ember,

I'm sorry I left without notice, and I'm sorry for getting to you so late. I thought that I would be back in el Alcázar by now. I went in search of the nymphs for guidance, and they were extremely accommodating. I plan on doing more research.

I'm sorry to leave you like this, but I hope you understand.

If you can, you should escape north. I know it's not the Soulless Realm, but the nymphs have been so kind to me. I'm sure they'd be kind to you as well.

Hope you are well,
Ademure.

Ember dropped the notebook.

"What is it, Seño? Is la Princesa okay?"

She got out, she realized. *She escaped. She found protection with the nymphs.*

That was fantastic! Ember should've been relieved. Should've been ecstatic.

She wasn't.

"Ademure is fine."

〜

Thursday morning, Estrella Bailón sat in the dining room alone, no twins in sight. Sitting down in a chair across from the captain, Ember grabbed a plateful of food.

Just one day, she thought, *I'd love to come to breakfast and see no one at all.*

"Good morning, Alloy," the statuesque woman said.

"Morning," Ember said with a mouthful of pineapple.

"Sleep well?"

"Does it matter?"

Bailón laughed. "Well, I hope you'll sleep some tonight. Tomorrow is the big day."

Ember ate another piece of pineapple in silence.

"The parade will be in the evening," the captain continued. "I'll have Capote lay out a set of clothes for you to change into beforehand. You, Princess Ademure, Queen Esmerelda, and the Delfinos will all ride in the finale float. Cadeña and Capote will be in the first. Rodriguez and Maduro at the tail on landsailers."

"What about you?"

"I'll be keeping an eye on the crowd. I won't be in the parade."

Playing with the fruit on her plate, Ember asked as casually as she could, "Did you want me to kill her in a particular manner?"

Not that it mattered, since there would be no princess to kill. But she was curious how this was supposed to work.

The estrella's eyes lit up. "Ah, so you have taken an interest! That's wonderful."

Ember popped another diced pineapple.

"It'll be quite painless actually," Bailón said. "In your dress tomorrow, you'll find a gun."

Ember frowned. Surely, she hadn't heard that right. "You want me to shoot her?"

"Yes."

"Then, all of that training, the combat drills and spells with Profe Ozamiz. What was that for?"

"We're playing to your strengths. When taking a life, there are already so many decisions to be made. We want you to only make one: pull the trigger."

"What if I miss?"

The estrella smiled. "You best not miss."

Ember stabbed another piece of fruit. "I don't get it. Why am I doing this? Why can't you or the Delfinos or someone else do it?"

"Because the public does not know you," Bailón said. "There will be no suspicion when you arrive dressed in red."

Ember's fork clattered against her plate. "I'll be posing as an Agarthan?"

"You're comfortable with changing the color of your eyes, I presume?"

"Why would an Agarthan be in Nysa? Or in the parade at all?"

"You didn't hear the news?" Bailón laid a newspaper out on the table. "The Agarthans have been our friends for a month now."

Ember swiped the paper and read the headline.

AGARTHAN DIPLOMAT NEGOTIATING PEACE TALKS WITH CROWN

"I'm the diplomat," she said distantly.

"Yes. Tomorrow, you'll put a bullet through our beloved princess's tiara, and, well, I don't know that there will be much peace left to negotiate."

Ember set down the paper with a trembling hand. "Bailón, do you really believe the princess is a traitor?"

"Of course, we've told you this."

"I know what you've told me. I want to know if you believe it. If *you* think she knew what she was doing all those years ago."

Bailón looked hard at her, hiding her breath behind steepled hands. "You have not been here long enough, Alloy. In recent years, Nysa and its people have worsened significantly, and the princess is not innocent. I believe things must change."

Ember nodded absently and reminded herself that Ademure wouldn't be back, that the princess was safe. She even managed to say, "I understand," to the estrella.

But she'd been lying when she said it. And she rushed to the nearest bathroom.

Ember stole the kitchen's landsailer for the second time that week. She still jerked the contraption intermittently, but compared to her first drive, she was now a master at the craft, and so she headed for the harbor.

"Alloy Slade," the massive admiral said as she entered the building. His head nearly touched the top of the doorway. "Good to see you."

"Good morning, Admiral," she said, bowing.

"Back already for another practice session? I thought yesterday would've worn you out. You were out there for hours."

"I floated for hours. Today, I have to sail."

Guerrero grinned. "Determination. I love it! Very well. Please take care of yourself today." He sniffed the air. "I believe there's a storm on the horizon."

She glanced out the windows but found only crystal blue skies and calm waves. Not a puff of white tainted the air or ocean.

"Where?"

His booming laugh echoed off the walls. "Just be careful. The storms move quickly out here. Once the sky grays, it'll be on you before you know it." He turned on heel and started toward his office.

She spotted the port where the ships sat unmoving—like she was probably about to be.

"Admiral?"

He stopped at his doorway. "Yes, Alloy?"

"Is there a trick to sailing?"

"A trick?"

"Like an easier way of doing it? I've been practicing for over a month, and I still haven't figured out how to do anything but sink. Is there something specific I should be thinking about when I manipulate the water?"

Scratching his trim beard, the admiral said, "I don't know what sort of answer you're looking for, but sailing is very similar to landsailing. Focus on the air in your sails rather than the push of the water. Does that help?"

"Unfortunately, I can't really landsail either."

"I'm sure you're fine, you just need more time out there. You'd be phenomenal to master sailing after only a month, even for an alloy. After all, it's a massive hunk of metal you're controlling. It takes a lot of energy to move a thing that large."

If only I had time. "Thank you, sir."

He smiled and entered his office, and she headed for the dock.

The three familiar estrella ships sat where she had left them, or rather, where they'd left her. The center one was her favorite on which to sunbathe.

She jumped onto it, untied herself from the dock, and grabbed the helm. The water was so still today that even the swells hardly moved her. Maybe she didn't need to manipulate the water.

"*Maior*," she said into the breeze.

A gust of wind blew by, nearly knocking her into the wheel. She locked her arms and gritted her teeth, waiting for it to pass.

Once it did, she looked back at the dock and saw that she had barely moved five feet.

She groaned.

"*Maior*," she said again, this time bracing herself.

The wind came once more, sending her hair into a flurry. But otherwise, she was still. She looked at the sail, fluttering but not taut. Then, she glimpsed the dock, ten feet away, and cursed into the wind roaring at her backside.

She knew she had the magic. She had to have it, or she wouldn't have been in this mess in the first place. *Damn it, how do I control it?*

She inhaled. What had Kiva told her at the waterfall? When she couldn't control the leaf?

Magic comes from the core. The soul. Let the magic speak.

She listened. A growing warmth swirled in her abdomen— the full extent of her power, within reach. She focused harder, deeper, trying to break whatever barrier shielded it. *You're a damn witch,* she told herself. *A damn powerful witch. C'mon, you can move this thing.*

Finally, like the engine of a car, the magic roared.

The warmth spread to her chest first, then her shoulders. Down her arms and legs. To her fingers and toes. Up her neck and through the top of her head. Her heartbeat resounded in her ears. She looked to the sail that still fluttered.

Then, she willed the wind.

"*Maior*."

It rushed up, trying to take her clothing and hair with it. But she dug in her feet and leaned her weight back. After a moment, the wind passed, letting go of her and instead taking the sail, and the massive cloth suddenly grew taut.

The ship jerked. Ember hit the back railings with an echoing of metal and a grunt. Rolling to her back, she shielded her eyes from the blaring mid-morning sun with one hand, and held the back of her neck with the other.

But the sound of churning water forced her up. The dock receded, shrinking from view faster and faster. Then she peered over the railing and there it was. A white, worthwhile wake.

She was moving.

She was moving!

She pushed herself from the deck and onto her feet. The shoreline passed by. Then, the forest. Nysa became a speck on the horizon. And then, she was in open water.

For over an hour, she played at the helm, turning the wheel to the left, cutting sharp to the right. She created wakes, then skipped right over them, and then back again. She wanted to see how fast she could really go, push her magic to its limit. And *damn*, could she go fast! The salty sea spattered her face and tongue, wind whipped by her ears, and she was...happy.

When her arms finally tired and her skin reddened, she moved to the covered seating, the wind still in the sail. She leaned back against the cushion and—for the first time in a long time—relaxed. Maybe tomorrow's plan would work after all.

But I don't have to wait for tomorrow, she realized.

She didn't have to wait for the princess any longer, and the twins were still gone. She was already on a boat set straight north, which should have taken her to somewhere in the United States, and she was moving at top speed. In fact, today might have been her best shot at leaving this hell for good.

She looked at the calm waters and clear sky. Could she really do it?

She lacked food and water, but she might not have needed any. Nieve had sailed from Houston to Nysa in one night, and Ember had had a large breakfast this morning. She could surely go half a day without.

And if she got lost? Then, she would wait for nightfall. Find the North Star like they did in fairytales.

She grinned. She could do this. She would do this.

She would make this the beginning of her happy ever after.

The sun painted the sky orange.

Ember sat on deck, tracing each cloud as it appeared on the dusky horizon. It was tedious, but it kept her mind occupied on something other than the sea and her stomach. Thankfully, actual sailing wasn't as nauseating as landsailing. She was sure she wouldn't have made it this far with her arms around a bucket.

Thunder bellowed in the distance, and the non-manipulated wind picked up. The water grew choppy, colliding with the side of the boat. Above her, the orange disappeared behind a deeper gray sky. And behind her...

It was black.

Electricity enervated the air, and the sky went bright white. Then a sound—like the crack of a whip.

Then black again.

"Shit."

Ember pushed more wind into the sails, but the surrounding winds grew just as fast, countering her fuel. She focused more energy, more willpower, more soul. Her abdomen grew hot, and her winds overwhelmed the others.

But then, the ship rocked. Full waves crashed against it, some large enough to wet the deck. With tumultuous waters, the winds she produced were no longer enough to keep her going.

Another clap of thunder. Louder. Closer.

She rushed to the helm. The wheel spun, catching every shift in the current. She took it, used all her strength to hold it in place, but the gusts fought her, prying the steering wheel from her hands until, at last, she dropped to the deck, exhausted and overheated.

A drop of water splashed on her forehead, and she looked up. The charcoal skies had caught up to her, leaving only a sliver of orange on the horizon. Another drop hit. Then another. Then the drizzle turned to rain. Then a downpour.

"You're fucking kidding me."

Lightning flashed across the sky. Winds that started as whispers grew so strong she couldn't tell whether she was being soaked by the rain or the sea.

Still, if it weren't for the unrelenting ocean, she could've made it out of this mess. But each time she steadied herself, readying a manipulation of the rain or the wind or the wheel, another wave bashed the side, knocking her to her knees. If only the waters could smooth, she would be long gone.

She thought for a moment about manipulating the waters anyway, but for now she could still weather this storm below deck, then reassess after it passed. If she manipulated the water, and messed it up, she might not have a ship—or a life—to reassess.

She hurried below deck and entered one of the four bedrooms. Here, the roars of wind and claps of thunder dulled, crashing became almost silent, and finally, she could hear herself think and breathe.

Except she wasn't breathing.

Breathe, she told herself. *Breathe! BREATHE!*

But her breath wouldn't slow. She panted like she was running a marathon, her face flushed and sweat streaming from her head, yet she was completely still.

She dropped onto the mattress, but nothing changed. A scalding heat radiated from her core, like when she was angry, but at this moment, she was mostly scared.

And then she remembered. *The winds.*

She had been manipulating them for hours. A perpetuating spell—of course, she would tire out. She had to stop them before they drained her completely.

Her arms and legs already aching, she rushed up the steps to the deck above her, but when she tried to open the hatch, she found it to be immovable. Confused, she shoved it harder, but the wind above pushed back with equal strength. She eased up, then threw all of herself into the hatch again. Still, it didn't move.

It's so hot, she thought, and her fear skyrocketed—heat *never* bothered her. *I've got to get out.*

But how? If she manipulated the hatch, she didn't know if she'd be able to manipulate it back—not with how tired and unsteady she was. And if this storm was going to continue like this, she was going to need all the shelter she could get.

She scanned the four rooms below deck for something she could push into the hatch to jam it open, something wide enough and strong enough that wouldn't absolutely destroy it. She took a deep, slow breath. Then another. Then—

My breath. I can use the air in here.

Being in a sealed space, she'd probably constrict her own supply for the moment, but with enough force, she could crack the hatch and the storm would take over from there.

She stepped away from the stairs to the hatch and moved behind any freestanding chairs, appliances, knobs, and other knickknacks that could thwack her, then took one more deep breath. She held her hands in front of her. "*Maior!*"

The wind below deck matched the wind above— stronger, even. Ember forced her eyes open, dug her heels further, held her aim steadier as the blankets and pillows and lamps and candles and dressers and a million other things crashed into the walls of the cabin. Her breath fled her, her hair pulled her, but she kept focus until finally, a crack.

The hatch snapped open, and rain pelted her face, gales blowing her hair in the other direction. She dropped her arms —and with that, the cabin air—and trudged forward, fighting off gusts of water and wind. She was demolished, but she had to keep going. She had to get above deck.

It was a mere few feet up the stairs, but against the elements, it could have been a mountain. Still, she climbed. When her eyes peeked out above deck, she connected with the winds that fought futilely against Mother Nature. Shielding her face from the goddess herself, Ember yelled, "*Minor!*"

Her core cooled. But nature's winds, without her magic to impede them, strengthened. She pushed herself to grab the chain that attached to the hatch, and, using all of her body weight and another quick "*maior,*" ripped it from the deck. The hatch raised halfway, and gravity took over the rest— although, she wasn't ready for the impact of such a move, and when the hatch snapped shut, she hit the lower deck with a thud.

Fuck. With heavy effort, she crawled back to her now disheveled mattress and took a deeper, cooler breath.

Her body swayed with the ship. If she closed her eyes, it was almost relaxing, like being rocked to sleep. But the longer she stayed there, the louder the thunder grew, fueling her anxiety, and she couldn't lay there anymore.

She stared at the metal beams above her. *This is my ticket to freedom*, she reminded herself. The storm was a bump in the road, but enduring it would pay off. Once it passed, it wouldn't be long before she would make it back to the States, get back to Dallas, beg for her job back, and live a boring life once again.

Because being boring was better than being a weapon.

Not that she had to worry about hurting Ademure anymore, of course; the princess had found refuge—all on her own. And Ember sincerely hoped the nymphs would protect her far better than she ever could.

She laughed to herself. That ridiculous plan to seek help had actually worked in Ademure's favor. Maybe this ridiculous plan could work in hers.

There was a crash of water. A crack of glass.

She lifted her head. A thin line formed in the center of the window. More crashing, more crackling and the line branched into more lines, like the limbs of a tree. Then, like raindrops, ocean water raced down the pane.

She sprung to her feet.

"Oh shit, oh shit, oh shit." What spell would hold the window together? Could she even manipulate the glass without letting all the water in? But the water decided before she did.

A wave bombarded the bedroom with a splash, shattering the window, soaking the mattresses in one hit. She sputtered before another wave spilled through, drenching her further. With a second of air to breathe, she pulled away the hair glued to her face and looked down. The water was at her ankles.

She was going to drown.

What had Profe Ozamiz taught her? What had Sombra and Nieve? What had Kiva? She raced through her training routines, but could only recall how to create weapons and camouflage and ice, none of which would have any effect on an ocean. The twins taught her nearly nothing but how to avoid them. Kiva had taught her how to change colors and—

The forest. The waterfall.

She started singing.

The water continued to pour in, forcing her to cough, interrupting her melody. She started again, but the water still refused her tune. Then, her arm wrapped around a bedpost, hands aimed at the water rushing by her feet, she shouted, "*Maior!*" before succumbing to another wave. The water sped toward the hatch like it was coming from a hose, and again, the hatch broke free.

The winds alone could've knocked her overboard, never mind the swells that threatened to capsize the ship. Yet, Ember managed to climb on deck.

She ran and slipped to the nearest thing she could hold onto—the mast at the center of the ship—and gripped with her life, chest heaving, as another wave knocked the ship so hard that the sails nearly touched the water.

The lightning was blinding, the thunder deafening. And *goddammit* could those winds let her go?

But even in the chaos, the uncertainty, the fear, she still felt the familiar prickle on the nape of her neck.

Raindrops, she thought. Not because she was angry, but because she needed to focus.

Another swell crashed against the ship, but without the

waves to choke her, this time, she could sing. She shouted above the winds, the waves, the thunder. She was going to make the world hear her song if it was the last thing she did—and it might well have been.

I will stop this storm, she told herself. And like that day in the forest, the song surged within her.

And then time slowed...to match her tune, to match her fire. To match the power inside her. Never before had she been so alive. So awake.

She was the magic. The magic was her.

The ship leaned on its side as the swell grew, her feet leaving the ground as she hugged the mast. The sail almost touched the water, but she paid it no mind. She simply sang.

And time slowed further. The swell no longer swelled. The rain floated down at the speed of falling bubbles. The lightning, thunder, and wind carried on as normal, but her song was only getting started.

The ship tipped so slowly now that without close inspection, one would've assumed it stopped. She hung from the mast, seemingly fixed in the air, singing at the top of her lungs. Then, she swung herself to the top like a trapeze artist to a tightrope, and edged her way to the vertical deck, not daring to cease her melody.

Still standing on the mast, still singing her song, she scanned her surroundings for something that she could use as a raft. Carefully, her footing shifted, and she glanced at her feet, where the mast now angled down. The sail had dipped in the water.

The ship was going to flip.

Her breath quickened, as did her clocking, and the swell moved faster. The hull left the water. The sails were upside down.

Slow down, she told herself. *It's all me. I've got this. I can—*

Her foot slipped completely, and she fell into the water. And, without her song, the ship did too.

Forward, sideways, end over end. The current juggled her mercilessly, stealing more of her breath every second. She forced her eyes open in the stinging sea just as it threw her into the submerged railing, knocking out the last of her air.

She floated, frozen in the waves, with screaming lungs and overwhelming silence.

Her locket drifted in front of her.

Her heart. Her noose.

I could just die. Her head throbbed. Her arms and legs ached. The spark at her neck burned. The scars on her wrist pulsated. *It's not like there's anyone to live for.*

Because Rachel wouldn't know. Ademure would probably never know. And if Daphne knew, she'd be delighted. Kiva or Damian might care, but in the end, they would still get what they wanted—Ember wouldn't become an estrella, and the queen wouldn't have her superweapon for war.

She touched the locket. *Slade. January 10th.* The only information her parents had left behind. Funny, how they'd gotten to live in secret this entire time, the life she had craved, that she'd craved *because* of them. Even funnier that she'd thought they were dead, when instead it was her that death was coming for. All those years wondering where they were. All those train rides imagining who they were. Then finally learning! And she would never meet them anyway.

She smirked. *There was never anyone to live for.*

But then her heart-shaped locket flipped.

And she stared at the engraving. *Ember* stared back at her. For a second. Maybe two.

And she began to swim.

I need air. I need a spell.

Chest on fire, she grabbed the railing of the capsized deck, fighting the current as she held tight. With her last bit of adrenaline, she yanked herself around the outside of the ship and swam to the hull, water pounding her ears, heart begging her to stop. But the surface was close. Fresh air, so close.

She breached it. But a quick gasp and another wave pushed her back under, tossing and turning her in the current.

Damn it. I need a spell now!

In the half-second the water gave her, she broke herself from its grasp, forcing her head above water for another breath, but the waves and winds wouldn't let her speak. Her spark threatened to burst.

I need... I need...

Her lungs begged for air, her body begged for rest. Still she pressed on, her hand finding the metal she sought. If only she could rip it from the ship. She needed to float. She needed her magic.

And it answered her call.

Her soul was as electric as...

...that morning on the train.

...that evening in the kitchen.

Her body remembered what happened next—familiar as the feeling of the locket around her neck: hopeful.

I need. To live.

The spark burst.

The crack deafening. The water steaming. Metal melting. Her makeshift raft free. Unfazed by the blinding light or boiling temperature, Ember peeled back the sheet of metal from the rest of the ship's hull, sensing the electricity that still sizzled at its edges, and pulled herself onto it. And, finally uninhibited by the desperation of the sea, she breathed.

Her legs still hung below the water, and her arms were spent, but she clung to that jagged piece of hull for life as she watched the rest of the ship sink below the surface.

Then as fast as the storm came, it went. When the waves calmed, she rolled herself to her back, watching the rain slow to a drizzle, listening to the thunder quiet. The lightning continued to flash, but lightning had never been anything to worry about anyway.

She looked at her hand and wiggled her fingers. A current still hummed at the tips. *I did it.*

Riding the swells on her raft, she then stared at the dark skies, the vast open ocean.

And I'm alone again.

Good.

If her foster parents had left her alone maybe they would've lived. Daphne had lived long enough to learn to leave. Though, the wisest of all were her birth parents, who'd left the day after she was born.

Ademure had been the most foolish. The princess had known what she was capable of and had stuck around anyway. Long enough to convince her that they were in this together. That they could solve what was wrong with her. Together.

Daphne had convinced her of that, too, once.

Ember pulled her legs completely out of the water, wrapped her arms around them. And cried.

She knew they were all right to go.

She'd just overinvested again.

Then, a latent clap of thunder interrupted her tears, sending a torrent of heat to her palms, and she looked to the sky.

"You think you're funny, do you? Is my life some sort of joke to you?"

A small rumble came from behind the clouds. Then a flash. Then silence.

Heat grew, and she scowled. "Is that a yes?"

Another low rumble.

"What's your name anyway?" she asked. "Pan? Jesus?"

Full silence this time.

"Neither?"

Another silence.

"Both?"

Nothing.

She clenched her fists, arms shaking with exhaustion. "Well, fuck you too, Panjesus. You have a twisted sense of humor. What happens next? My death? I can see it now: the girl who conducts lightning, killed by it! Almost has a nice ring to it, don't you think?"

The clouds rumbled.

"No, you're right. It's too poetic—not your style. You wouldn't be so merciful."

The rumbling was louder this time. Heat rushed to her shoulders.

"Strike me down, damn it!"

Lightning streaked across the sky, followed by a roaring thunder.

Then, the clouds parted. The few rays left of the setting sun stained orange on the gray backdrop, and the thunder completely stilled. Ember frowned.

"You missed."

She lay back down on her raft.

The waters calmed. The rain stopped. The wind was now a breeze. Aside from the lingering lightning, it was perfect weather for sailing.

As she floated, waiting to die a slow and—as the sun left the sky—increasingly cold death, something appeared on the horizon. She had been tossed so heavily in the water, she had no idea which way was which, so, she looked to the sky. The first and brightest star indicated the object was coming from the south—and it was growing closer.

She sat up and rubbed her eyes. It was a ship. A massive ship. With three massive sails. The rose insignia on the center sail was colored the shade of a very familiar green.

"This isn't funny anymore, Panjesus."

Some thirty minutes later, Ember could discern the massive man behind the helm of the massive ship, and, another fifteen minutes after that, the ship slowed to a stop.

A line of rope dropped into the water. Mechanically, she wrapped the rope tightly with her legs. And then, she left the sea.

Before she could say a word, a blanket fell across her shoulders and a steaming bowl of rice and beans and a glass of water were dropped into her hands. A sailor even managed to rub aloe on her face as she ate.

"Alloy Slade," a voice boomed. Guerrero descended the stairs. "Are you alright?"

She nodded robotically, unsure of what was happening. Was she really on another ship? Had the admiral really found her?

"Estrella Bailón noticed you were missing at dinner and sent out a search. When I realized your ship had never made it back, I feared the worst. We sailed straight for the storm, but it was as black as the Agarthan sky—we couldn't see anything. Luckily, there was this incredibly bright bolt of lightning that illuminated the ship—otherwise, we would never have found you at all."

She gulped the last of her food so quickly, another sailor was sent to the kitchens for more.

"I'm sorry about your ship," was all she could say. Maybe the sea was getting to her. Was any of this real?

Guerrero shook his head. "Ships are expendable. You are not." He put a hand on her shoulder and guided her to the cabins. "Let's get you a change of clothes and back to Nysa. The queen would be beside herself if her prized alloy missed the celebration tomorrow."

Nodding, Ember gripped her locket, following the man in stride, finally registering the miracle. Then, she paused, and she looked up with a glower.

Oh, Panjesus, you are hysterical.

CHAPTER 41

ADEMURE

Ademure lowered her shoulders, opened her chest, and unclenched her fists. It took effort for her to remember to relax, especially when today was the day.

This morning, she started with the laptop, opening the Internet. A small image of a magnifying glass appeared.

"Search," the screen read. *Search what?*

The strange arrangement of the letters in front of her was dumbfounding. She tapped the letter *n*. When it reflected on the screen, she straightened, a thrill running through her. It took a moment of hovering to find *y*, then another for *m*, and so on until she saw "nymphs" displayed next to the magnifying glass. Then, as the notebook instructed, she hit enter.

The blank screen filled with paragraphs upon paragraphs of information. It read like any book she would find in the library, but with so much less effort to find it.

So interesting...

Her eyes latched onto a word at the top of the screen: "Images." She dragged her finger along the rectangular pad below the keyboard and moved the arrow above the word. Then she tapped the rectangle, and the screen changed again, inundated with sketches, drawings, and paintings of the ethereal creatures.

Is this what the soulless believe nymphs to be? she wondered. The art was stunning, but their depictions were much more fantastic than the real thing. Still, the laptop was fascinating. What else could she research?

"Green rose sickness." Enter.

The search was less promising. It still flooded the page with paragraphs of information—but about gardening and fungal diseases. The images were less than pleasing.

Unsettled, she decided to try something else. "Pandora evils. Reborn. War." Enter.

Now it was soulless fiction and a summary of Pandora's box. Nothing specifically helpful, though it was impressive that Pandora's history wasn't entirely misrepresented.

But it doesn't know everything. Where can I find more?

"Libraries." Enter.

Her eyes snapped to a paragraph in the center of the screen. "Library of Congress." She had read about that in el Alcázar. It was the largest library in the world, home to hundreds of thousands of papers, artifacts, and history. Books in hundreds of languages, decades of periodicals and magazines, maps and music...everything. There had to be documents on magicks as well.

If she could get off Nysa, she would go.

She closed the laptop and moved to the cell phone. The design was similar to the laptop and yet, so different. The notebooks told her the phone was more powerful, but she didn't see how it could be, given its size—

Crack!

Ademure crashed to the floor. The ground shook like an

earthquake, and she scrambled for shelter under the nearest rooted table. Frames fell off the walls, books tumbled from the shelves. The camera and phone both vibrated off the desk to a shattering demise.

At last, the shaking ceased. She crawled out slowly.

What was *that?*

She carefully made her way to the door and pushed it open.

The nymphs scrambled. Several shouted frantically for help and several still were pinned under various pieces of furniture, screaming. And though Ademure's loyal general stayed at his post, his expression was grim.

"Xander, what happened?" she asked.

"One of the lower limbs of Nyseion fell. No one has yet reached the ground to search for survivors, but we're expecting none."

Her eyes widened. "Where are the oracles?"

He blinked. "Isidore hasn't yet reported this morning."

"We've got to get to the minister."

Xander and Ademure rushed down the stairs. Minister Calix was in the foyer assisting several other nymphs in lifting the limbed chandelier off a staffer. Together, the nymphs heaved one side, allowing the staffer to escape, then let the piece down.

"Minister," Xander said as he and Ademure caught up, "have you heard word from Isidore?"

"No," the minister said, starting in another direction. They followed closely behind. "He is supposed to report to you."

"He hasn't today."

Calix remained stoic, steps steady. "Have you contacted Ophelia?"

"Not yet."

"Minister," Ademure said. "Do you know what caused the branch to fall?"

"No," he said as the three turned a corner. "In over three thousand years, Nyseion has never lost even a leaf. This is devastating."

"I fear the oracles are behind this."

"Impossible. We've kept eyes on them in the forest. They would not have made it this far undetected."

"Whose eyes, Minister? Isidore's?"

Calix stopped. "Xander, send Ophelia and her men to the ground for reconnaissance. Your team will act as backup to theirs."

"And Magus?" Xander asked.

"Magus says the sages are prepared. If the oracles make it to the canopy, we will be able to fight them off. But let's not let it get that far."

"What do you want me to do, Minister?" Ademure asked.

He looked at her with hard eyes. "Hope you're wrong." He resumed his strut down the hall.

Xander cut in front of Ademure before she could follow him. "Princess, you should stay in your room for the foreseeable future."

"No," she said, shaking her head, "this is my fault. I'll see through to the consequences of my actions." She tried to push past him, but he stopped her again. "Please, let me go to the base of the tree."

"And what if you need to fight? Are you trained in combat?"

That made her hesitate. Of course, she had no training. It was why she came here in the first place; she needed others to fight for her. She was weak.

"I'm what they're after," she said. "They won't stop until either they're dead or I am."

"With due respect, Princess, this is our job. Let us do it."

"It's my life, Xander. I'm going to fight for it."

"Princess—"

"I will stay out of the way until I am needed. *Lacrim.*" The piece of fabric she touched tore apart from the rest of her sleeve. "But when I am needed, I want no one to stop me again." She pulled back her hair with the improvised ribbon.

He lowered his chin. "I cannot guarantee your safety on the ground."

"You can't guarantee my safety here either."

The nymph grumbled. "I must contact Ophelia and her crew. In ten minutes, we will fade down." And he left.

Ademure headed for the trunk of the tree at the center of the fortress, where they had entered three days prior. The entire way, civilian nymphs continued to scream, to cry, to panic. Many faded—she assumed they left for their own branches. Most stood frozen, unsure of what was to come.

I brought this chaos. She hadn't known what the twins would do, but she knew what they could do all too well, and she had ignored that. She should never have voiced her opinion to the minister. She should never have asked for their protection. She should never have sought help. Her chest tightened with her thoughts.

But there is no time to dwell, she reminded herself. *A branch has already fallen. Lives have already been lost. I can't lose more.*

Outside the fortress, soldiers stood in formation, all dressed in tunics not unlike Xander's, though these were much darker shades of pink. Xander was nowhere to be seen, but his orders had clearly been heard. Ophelia stood alone, facing the rest of the crew.

As Ademure approached her, she drew her lips into a thin line. "Princess Ademure of the human tribe. You have brought enemies to our lands."

Ademure's stomach flipped. "I did. Thank you for fighting."

"We fight for Nyseion and our minister. Not you."

The other soldiers carried the same look of disgust as

Ophelia. Ademure pulled at her elbow-length sleeves, wishing they were long enough to cover her hands, to wrap around her body, to hide her face from the world.

At last, Xander returned and took his place between Ophelia and Ademure.

"Soldiers," he yelled. "Our sacred home is crumbling. The unknown we face is daunting, but you are the bravest nymphs I know. We will overcome." His soldiers stood tall and uniform as he spoke. He commanded so much more respect than Ademure's mother could ever hope for.

"Our intelligence suggests that we face an old enemy," he continued, "and if true, they are few. But fair warning. Approach with caution. They do not respect codes of honor or rules of battle. They seek to kill for killing's sake. Blood spilt until they attain what they desire. We shall give them the satisfaction of neither.

"We have not yet heard from General Isidore and his crew. Act as if they are alive, but expect them dead. Similarly, if you find victims of the fallen branch, help those that can be helped, but leave behind the others. As a first priority, the enemy must be stopped from further destruction.

"Ophelia's crew will go first. Span the base of the tree, and move forward from there. My crew will follow closely behind. If you come upon them, do not engage. Return to base, and report to Ophelia and me. Now, ready your weapons."

Xander held out his spear, tip pointed up.

The nymphs nodded once, mimicked his stance, and awaited their final direction.

He scanned the unit, and he nodded in turn. "Good. Ophelia's first faction, go."

Ademure stood behind Xander, awed at the tempo with which the nymphs marched. When her mother had regained Nysa, she disbanded their army in fear of a coup. She'd claimed her estrella force was stronger, more loyal. But seeing these nymphs, Ademure doubted those claims. These soldiers were strong in unison. Loyal without bounds. From her own experiences, the estrellas' allegiance seemed much more fickle.

Perhaps they had a shot.

"Princess, you will stay by my side," Xander said.

"I thought you wouldn't protect me."

"I cannot guarantee that I will protect you, but that does not mean I will not try."

She splayed her palms over her skirt. "You should focus on protecting your troops, your people. Not me. Not a human."

"No," he said simply. "You have good in you. Human or not, that is something I cannot ignore."

She looked up at him. He kept his focus on his troops, jaw tense.

"Thank you, Xander. For everything."

He looked at her, then at her gown. "You won't be very agile in that. Shall I grab a tunic?"

She massaged the dress slower and weighed the soft but sturdy fabric between her hands. "No need. This is a simple enough design." She then inhaled and closed her eyes. "*Vesti braca.*"

The cloth shrunk from her hands, laying flush with her legs. The bottom of the skirt split in the center, the tear traveling to her waist. At her hip, the material turned inward, wrapping around her thighs, and finally, the wraps sealed with stitching that lined her inseam.

The jumpsuit was simple, but considering she hadn't used that spell in years, it was more than satisfactory.

She took Xander's arm as the last of the nymphs faded. Ophelia, Xander, and Ademure stepped up to the bark, the tingle returned, and they became the tree.

The rush was disorienting this time, and Ademure realized

Xander must have moved slowly for her before. When they solidified at the base, the trunk ripped from her body, and her own weight hit her like she had been smacked into the bark. When her color flooded back to her skin and what had been greenery became flesh, her vision cleared. She endured it all without complaint.

The soldiers disappeared into the foliage, leaving the three alone. Ademure skimmed the forest and the tree. From this side, the fallen branch was invisible—the trunk was the size of a small mountain.

"Let's walk the perimeter," Ophelia said. "The last thing I want is to be blind to an attack."

"Agreed," Xander said.

Ademure was thankful for the change in garments. She could only imagine being caught in the tendrils of the roots with the bodice, ripped leggings, and slippers she had worn two nights ago. The hike was difficult enough in proper attire: her jumpsuit still snagged on the bark when they slid down the other side of the first root.

And then, as her feet touched the ground, an unsettling thought hit her. *When I stepped on the roots two days ago, I had been detected immediately.* The twins had as well. Today, however, no one mentioned sensing anyone—twins or otherwise.

When they reached the top of the next root, a nymph faded out of the trunk.

"Soldier," Xander said, "What's the report?"

"We found the enemy, general. Two women, two roots over. Their rhythms are loud. No sign of General Isidore or his crew."

Xander nodded. "Ophelia, send word to retreat. We've found our targets. Soldier, return to your squadron and await orders."

The nymph saluted and faded back into the tree.

Ophelia knelt, placed her hands on the root, and pushed down. Only her right hand faded. Her eyes and skin glowed, her hair floated, and green lines diverged from her wrist, shooting radially along the ridges of the bark. When she released her breath, the glowing ceased.

"I've sent word to those I could reach, but I can't feel three of the roots north of the tree," she said. "The connection is lost."

Xander put a thumb to his chin. "That's where Isidore started his watch."

"What would cause a connection loss?" Ademure asked.

"I don't know. And that we didn't notice until now concerns me. From here on, we should fade rather than walk."

A chill went up her spine. She didn't know much about battles, but she knew communication was what won them.

"Tell the other nymphs to fade and gather at the northeast root," Xander said to the other general.

When Ophelia's glow faded, so did they. Xander grabbed Ademure's wrist and pulled her into the bark.

The odor was revolting.

"This is it," Ophelia said before her eyes glowed again. But the ridges surrounding the three of them didn't light.

Ademure's nostrils burned. Her eyes welled.

"What is it?" Xander asked. "Why are you not connecting?"

Ophelia shook her head with disbelief. "I feel nothing."

"What do you mean nothing?"

"Nothing, Xander," she said. "No enemy, no plant life, not even the root itself. The root is dead."

His eyes darkened. "We lost so much more than a village today. Those roots provide entire ecosystems. What have those humans done?"

"Destruction magic," Ademure said. Since her mother had

used it to destroy her vanity mirror, the stench of it had plagued her life. Outside the tree, it was undetectable, but inside, it reeked. "Only ever used rarely, and never on living organisms. They committed taboo by destroying the inside of the roots."

She was going to be sick.

"We won't be able to use fade further than here," Ophelia said. "I can't even feel my crew."

"They will have gathered there already, if they received our message at all," Xander said. "We will have to risk climbing again."

The three stepped out of the trunk and onto the dead root. Xander released Ademure's wrist and grabbed his spear, holding it out. Ophelia mimicked his stance.

Ademure took the moment to inhale the fresh air, when something dangling from atop the next root caught her eye.

"What is that?" she asked, pointing.

Xander squinted. "I'll go ahead and see. The two of you stay down here until I give you a signal."

Ophelia saluted and Ademure nodded. Xander found a loose vine and scaled the root with agility that was thrice that of her own—proof that she was the reason they were slow-moving. In a matter of seconds, he reached the top, keeping his body close to the tree. Then, he was out of sight.

Ademure's arms were forced behind her back.

"What are you doing?" she exclaimed. She tried to move her hands, but Ophelia bound her wrists with something foreign. She couldn't manipulate herself free.

"Xander may have fallen for your sorcery, but I have not," Ophelia said, murder in her eyes. "Is this a trick? Are you leading us to our deaths?"

"No!" Ademure said. "I swear it!"

"I cannot fade? I cannot feel my comrades? I am no fool,

Princess. These things did not happen before your arrival, and you know the magic that caused them."

"I know! I know! But I *didn't* cause them."

"Your rhythms do you no favors. They are so dissonant." Ophelia pulled her spear forward. "Tell me the truth. Has Xander met his end?"

Ademure trembled at the oak tip staring her down. Its point looked sharp enough to pierce her like a needle through cloth.

"Ophelia," she begged. "I am no foe. I want to protect Nyseion as much as you."

The nymph's neon eyes were so bright, so unnaturally green, and so unblinking. Unshifting. They fixated on her with such an intensity, such a ferocity, Ademure felt as if she'd become stone.

The nymph's ear twitched.

"Then you will not mind the precautionary tactic until he returns." She drew her spear back and turned her attention to the root.

With an amplified pulse and hands still tied, Ademure too, looked up.

Please, Xander, she begged. *Come back already.*

In the wait, Ophelia remained quiet and still. Meanwhile, Ademure fidgeted with the back of her jumpsuit, repeatedly bunching and dropping the fabric, contemplating whether she should try to manipulate something to release her bonds. Eventually, she decided against it, recognizing she was no match against the nymph either way, and staying bound was more likely to keep her alive.

But when an entire hour had passed—or at least, it felt like one had—her hopes of living dimmed altogether. She was sure she would burst, from her heartbeat, from her headache. The absolute silence was tearing her apart.

Finally, Xander leaned over the edge, waving, and she immediately collapsed.

She looked at Ophelia, pleadingly—but understandingly, knowing very well had the roles been reversed, Ademure would have done the same. Ophelia narrowed her eyes and untied the bonds. Then she scaled the root like an acrobat, leaving Ademure on the ground.

With a shaky hand, she grabbed the same vine Xander and Ophelia had and pulled herself up.

She nearly heaved. Bodies littered the ground, intestines spewed, green blood sluicing in the crevices of the bark. The odor of decay, of destruction magic tainted the air. The object she had seen dangling was the hand of the nymph who'd reported to them earlier, now lifeless. A crew of soldiers had been slain where they'd stood.

She covered her mouth before she could scream. There was so much death. *And I've drawn it.*

"I can hear the enemy's rhythms—prideful and joyous," Ophelia whispered. "But not the rest of our crews'."

"If they so casually took out this unit," Xander said, "I have little hope that the others survived."

"How do we defeat such a powerful enemy without our nymphs?"

"We use their rhythms to track them and surprise them."

"But how do we do so without fade?"

"Clocking," Ademure choked out, steadying herself on Xander's shoulder. "I can slow down their time."

Xander frowned. "Could they not diminish the effects of your clocking with their own?"

He was right, of course. And though the nymphs might have been hidden from the twins' sight, she absolutely wasn't. Not to mention, the oracles could manipulate faster and better than Ademure, and the nymphs could perform no spells at all. Still, what else could they do?

"I can delay them, at least," she said. "Even if they see us or hear me, I can slow down their hesitation and give you two an opening."

"I still think we should find backup," Ophelia said. "I doubt all of our soldiers made it to the dead roots yet."

"I wish we could wait for backup as well," Xander said. "But the longer we wait, the more nymphs I fear will die."

"What about the sages?" Ophelia asked.

"They are a last resort. Minister Calix would rather save their energy for a future threat."

"And what future threat could be direr than now?"

He gave her a warning look. "I put my faith in his leadership. Do you?"

She stared back just as hard. "How do we proceed?"

Though the nymphs remained locked in a battle of gazes, Ademure knew the question was for her. "I'll need to at least be able to see the oracles," she said. "That means they'll be able to see me. You need to get out of range so that you can't hear their rhythms but you can still hear my voice. I don't know if you appear in their sights at all, but I don't want to risk anything. Then, I'll start singing, and the time around them should slow down."

"How long will we have until they react?" Xander said.

"If I'm by myself, they'll be suspicious. I'm guessing they'll hesitate for just under a second. I can extend that to ten full seconds for two people, before they fight back. Is that enough time for you to cross two roots?"

"Without having to protect you, that's more than enough time," Ophelia said. "We'll have five entire seconds to gut the brutes."

Ademure bit her lip and looked at the sky. The sun peeked

through the canopy, meaning it was almost noon. If this failed, she had less than five hours before the parade started—*less than five hours to live.*

"Another branch could fall," Xander said. "We must go now."

The three went their separate ways. Ademure slid down the root, heading north, as Xander and Ophelia jumped from the other side toward the south. When Ademure reached the ground, alone, she gulped.

I'm so glad I can't hear the rhythms of my dread, she thought. *My heartbeat is more than enough.*

After a struggle, and more than enough time for Ophelia and Xander to get in position, Ademure heaved herself over the top of the next root where she stumbled upon another dozen mangled nymphs, all with substantial decay. The smells of necrosis and destruction mixed, creating a nauseating stench much worse than the previous graveyard. These deaths weren't fresh.

Covering her mouth, she moved closer to one in particular. He had a familiar strong chin and prominent brow, his green hair slicked with green blood. His pink tunic was ripped apart, and between his chest and pelvis, a pool of rotting organs spilt. It had been at least several hours since Isidore and his crew had been killed.

This time, Ademure couldn't help but vomit.

A minute later, she wiped her tears and her mouth and backed away from the bodies, doing what she could to put the horror out of her mind.

A twig cracked.

She whirled, sweating, squinting, praying to see nothing through the trees. It was quiet. Densely green. She searched for a leaf out of place. The twig that had broken. And finally, when she decided nothing was there, she breathed a sigh of relief.

Promptly, a breeze passed through, drawing back the leaves. Two women stood no more than a hundred yards away—one with charcoal hair, one with snow, both dressed in white.

And they saw her.

Nieve sang.

Ademure stilled, feeling the edges of the song's reach tug at her muscles. *Where are the soldiers?* she thought. *Where are Xander and Ophelia? Where is Ember? I can't do this. I can't fight! I'm going to die! I'm going to—*

Sing!

She opened her mouth, but nothing came out. The twins, raced toward her with breakneck speed, Nieve moving to the second note, tugging harder.

Ademure reminded herself that it took time to clock, even for the twins. She still had time to gain time back. The sooner she started, the harder it was for Nieve to have full control over the minute.

But when she tried again, she still couldn't produce a note. The generals' plan was failing because of her. More innocent nymphs would die because of her.

The twins were on her root, scaling the vine with skill almost comparable to Xander's. In a matter of seconds, Nieve had pulled herself and her sister to the top, both estrellas unfazed by the climb.

Ademure couldn't take them, couldn't fight them. They were going to—

Stop thinking. Just sing!

She forced herself to cough. And then she hummed. It wasn't anywhere near the correct note—her mind couldn't recall the words or melody—but her vocal cords started, and that was enough.

Nieve hesitated.

Exactly what I needed.

Ademure took in a full breath before fleshing out the tone in the melody. Soft at first, but when she recognized what her voice had done, the volume intensified. From muscle memory the song left her lungs, freed to the air. Her voice grew louder, her lyrics crisper, and the magic about her so much stronger. The slight hesitation became a nearly full stop. They had ten seconds.

She continued to sing, but as expected, the twin's melody rediscovered its footing. As if wading through syrup, Nieve drew in breath and Sombra drew a blade. Ten seconds became eight.

Knife held out in front, Sombra took one step, her weight shifting for another. Nieve started her exhale, her eyes lasered in on Ademure. Ademure didn't relent. Six seconds.

Another step closer for both oracles. Nieve produced note after note, each one weightier than the last, each one threatening to fully topple Ademure's song. She heard rustling behind her. Five seconds.

Nieve made it to the third note. Sombra took three more steps, now noticeably faster. Ophelia and Xander flew over the side and charged the twins. Three seconds.

Sombra fought at a walking pace, fending off Xander's first thrust, and Ophelia pierced Nieve's shoulder. But the estrella only winced, and her song still strengthened while Ademure's still waned. One second.

Zero.

As Nieve's song took hold, Ademure broke off, the oracle's innate overwhelming her. Xander threw another, now exceedingly slow jab at Sombra who attacked at full speed.

Then Ophelia ripped the spear out of the singing twin's bicep, drawing from Nieve an animalistic scream and interrupting the innate so that everyone fought at present pace.

Ophelia drove at the oracle with the bloody tip again and again, and despite missing her again and again, she prevented her from resuming the tune. Nieve's white suit was drenched in red.

Ademure stood paralyzed on the side, as if the clocking still affected her. In a way it did. She wanted to sing again, to slow them down again, but there was no way she could clock only the oracles and not the nymphs, and there was no other way to force them to slow.

So all she could do was watch and pray.

Please, Pan, Dionysus. Please.

Sombra went lunge for lunge, kick for kick with Xander. She pulled out a second dagger, twirled both, and sliced at the general. She fought with haste, with precision, but also with worry, intermittently glancing at her wounded sister. Her forehead lined with vexation; her eyes filled with distress.

Xander had no mercy. He cut off each blow, returning it in kind, forcing the raven-haired twin to parry, to dodge, to fight him. And fight him she did.

Nieve grasped at her wound. She was slower than her sister, but she still managed to sidestep and spin around Ophelia's spear with relative ease. She wouldn't last long with the amount of blood she was losing, but Ademure knew Nieve didn't fight long anyway. As if on cue, despite her right shoulder, the oracle threw a left-handed punch, connecting with Ophelia's chin. But Ophelia simply rolled out of the punch, and swept the spear beneath the oracle's feet.

And Nieve fell. Her shoulder stained the wood red.

"Nieve!" Sombra shouted, but she was still trapped in her ruthless spar with Xander.

And then Ademure heard humming. It was so soft it was difficult to make out over the clash. But it was there, the familiar tune, and it wasn't her own.

Her eyes widened.

Ophelia moved on top of the snow-haired woman, oblivious to the hum, spear held firm over the oracle's neck.

There was time. Clocking took time. Ademure could sing. Even if it wasn't precise, she could counter. *Sing!*

"You are a barbarian, oracle," Ophelia said. "It's unfortunate that such a holy gift must end with you."

Ademure fought to draw breath as time dragged her voice back. *Come on, come on, come on.*

Ophelia raised her spear.

Her vocal cords vibrated, low in her throat. *You can do this. Steal it back. Steal back time.*

Ophelia plunged the spear.

Sing, damn it, sing!

Nieve opened her mouth.

The spear slowed to a near halt, an inch from Nieve's flesh. Sombra ripped away Xander's spear—his reaction slow too— and pointed it at Ophelia. Her sister rolled out from under Ophelia's attack.

Then Sombra drove the stolen spear into the nymph's neck, piercing through completely. Green spewed down Ophelia's collar. She clawed at her throat.

Then the clawing stopped, and the nymph collapsed on the root as if she were a doll: lifeless, eyes open. Nieve's song drowned Ademure's scream.

The twins made their way to Xander who was mid-step, reaching out for his fellow general. Sombra forced his arms behind his back, then knocked him to his knees. Nieve put her hand on his throat and released her grip on time, allowing Xander to struggle at a normal pace in vain.

Her speaking voice carried through the air, strident and chilling.

"Good afternoon, Alteza."

"Stop it, Nieve! Please!" Ademure cried, hot tears cascading down her cheeks. Her knees scraped the bark. Her hands shook in prayer. "Please! I'll go back with you! Leave him alone! I'll do anything! Please!"

"And risk you not learning your lesson?" Nieve turned back to Xander. "*Evorto.*"

Viridescent flesh ripped from the muscles with a pop, and the following stench was poisonous. Nieve wiped her hand on her pants, staining it the same jade that now painted the root, and when she and Sombra let go, Xander's body dropped forward with a thud.

Ademure fell to her elbows to heave, but her stomach was empty—all she could do was cry. The village of the fallen branch. Dozens of soldiers. Isidore, Ophelia, and Xander—her advocate and protector. Gone.

Nieve sang for a final time, and the next moments flew by in an instant. Together, the twins tied Ademure's hands, bound her legs, and levitated her, leaving her hair to fall over her face.

And then Sombra spoke. Her words were distant, fast, and barely audible over her sister's melody.

"Why on Gaea's green earth did you think of fighting us, Alteza? You were always going to lose."

CHAPTER 42

KIVA

"Thinking about your girlfriend?" Valentina asked as she walked into the back room.

Kiva sat with his chin on his fist, rapping the knuckles of his free hand on the Round Table as he stared down his reflection in the wall of mirrors.

"She's not my girlfriend."

She waved her hand. "Semantics."

He stared deeper in the mirror, hardly hearing his tutor say, "So, she's not the only thought on your mind today? That's a nice change of pace."

He didn't respond, his thoughts lost in what Alden had said two days ago. Why was he in danger? Should he leave now? What about Ember? If she was to be believed, today was his last chance at getting her to come with him.

Valentina hopped up on the table and waved in front of his face. "I don't like it when you ignore my teasing. Makes me uneasy."

He glanced at her concerned bespectacled gaze. "I'm sorry,

Profe. I don't mean to make you worry. It's just that Alden told me to not go to the parade today."

She lifted a brow. "Why?"

"He didn't give me a reason. But I don't understand what makes this any more dangerous than before. It's not like it would be pleasant to be caught by the estrellas, and I risk that outcome every day. And I've worked so hard to find the alloy, to gain her trust. I can't lose her now!"

Valentina chortled. "So, it is the girl. I should've known."

"Of course, it is. She's the entire reason I'm in Nysa. And now I'm about to return from this dreadful place with nothing to show for it."

"Kiva, what are the chances she actually makes it off the island?"

He thought about that a moment, then sighed.

"Minimal," he said. Though Ember's confidence the other day had him questioning otherwise.

"Then wait her out. Go to the edge of town, away from whatever danger supposedly awaits you here and wait. If she fails, you're still here. If she succeeds, you live to find her another day."

"If she succeeds, I'll have to find her all over again. Do you know how long it took me to find her the first time?"

"The price you pay for love."

He rolled his eyes before returning them to the mirror. "I could just go back to Agartha right now. Face whatever scorn awaits me."

Holding her hands to her face, Valentina gasped obnoxiously loud. "Kiva, are you giving up on love?"

"Oh, shut up. I'm exploring my options. And that one happens to be the easiest and most sensible."

"Sure, but you are Kiva. You do not do easy, and you certainly do not do sensible. That's why you have Alden."

His eyes narrowed.

"Also," she continued, "you'll be back to square one if you go back now. Brink of war, no alloy, and a prick of a father who's embarrassed by you. At least if you wait, you have the potential to turn one of those things around. What's the harm in postponing your return for another few hours?"

He again considered her words a moment. *Gods, I hate it when she's right.*

"Fine," he said. "I'll wait her out."

"Good." She hopped off the table. "Now, give me a hug before you go." She stretched her arms wide.

"Ugh, Profesora…"

"I won't hear it! There's a chance you're leaving me today, and I refuse to let you go without a proper goodbye."

"Did we not just establish that that chance was minimal?"

"Kiva!" she shouted. "If you don't give me a hug this minute, I will rat you out to the Delfinos myself!"

He rolled his eyes again, then leaned down, wrapping his arms around the small woman. She returned the hug, her own arms barely meeting behind his back, then snuggled her head into his chest.

"You've grown up so much," she said. "I can't believe you're the same Kiva who asked me to manipulate you a toy sword all those years ago."

"I believe I asked for a real sword."

"Well yes, that's just what I needed. A six-year-old to chop his hand off while playing pirates." She pulled him in tighter. "You can't leave me so soon."

He rested his head on hers. "I'll be back, Profe. I promise."

～

Before he left for the tracks, Valentina's hourglass clock in the back room had indicated he still had ninety minutes until the parade.

He parked his landsailer just outside the stadium, then climbed to the top of the bleachers where he could see anyone who might attack him, all the festivities, and, hopefully, Ember.

In a way, he was glad to not be able to partake in any of the frills below. There were always too many floats this holiday, too much green. Also that nauseating anthem, and who could forget the crowds?

No, it was significantly better here where he was far, far away from all that *patriotism*.

Though, he did wonder if his sister would be down there today.

The sky colored orange, and the breeze picked up. He looked over his shoulder, toward the south side of the island, where a dark mass loomed on the horizon.

Another benefit of Agartha, he mused. *It never rains.*

He held a pair of Valentina's binoculars to his eyes. He could see the plaza clearly. The entire royal court usually rode in the final float, so, unless she somehow escaped before then, Ember would likely be there. But if it started to rain, he would lose sight of her—maybe lose her completely. He could always move closer, but...

Damn it, Alden. Couldn't have told me what I was up against?

He manipulated the sand bleachers to form a shelter. Gods, he hated waiting out storms.

CHAPTER 43
EMBER

Ember pulled the map out from under Damian's nose and rolled it up. They sat where they had all morning, on the asphalt of the basketball court, arguing. She had hardly been able to apologize to Ozamiz for missing training when the half-nymph had tracked her down, his heavily annotated plan in hand.

"Don't give up, Señorita," he whispered urgently. "You can try again. You have to escape."

"And I will. But not right now." She handed the map back to him. "Ademure made it out safely. The estrellas can't hurt her."

"Do you truly want to fight for them? After what you've come to know? After what they planned for her?"

"I was never going to fight for them, Damian. I've only ever been fighting for me." She touched her locket. "I'll leave before they want me to, I promise, but I first need to learn more about what I can do."

"You can go somewhere else to train!" he shouted, and she shushed him. He lowered his voice, but his intensity was still audible. "Anywhere else."

She shook her head vigorously—she had pondered Kiva's offer from two days ago, but:

"They all want me for the same reasons—to be their weapon. If I'm going to be that, then I should at least train with others who have the same powers."

"And who else wields lightning, Seño?"

But when she started to answer, Damian whipped his attention to the forest. He pulled his rag up slightly, revealing his pointed, twitching ears.

"What is it?" she asked.

"I hear the estrellas."

"Well, their return was inevitable."

"There's a third rhythm." He squinted. "I think it's the princess."

Ember shot to her feet. "Ademure? They've got her?"

"Shh! Her rhythm is faint. Almost like she's sleeping, but she's not."

Soon enough, Sombra and Nieve emerged from the forest and strolled across the courtyard, Sombra's hand outstretched over her head. A mix of red and green tainted their usually pristine white outfits, and Nieve favored her arm.

And then there was the diminutive figure that floated above them. She wore an unrecognizable outfit stained in dark green, and disturbingly, her eyes weren't closed. Ember didn't know if she could move, but she could see that Ademure was very much awake and helpless.

"Hello, Alloy," Nieve said. "Damian."

Sombra lowered the princess to the ground, then dropped her. Ademure grunted when she hit the grass.

"Damian," Sombra started, "could you please find Cadeña and Rodriguez so we can get Su Alteza bathed and dressed?"

The boy stood still, defiant, a jutted chin locked in place. Sombra and Nieve were quiet, too.

Now is not the time, Damian, Ember thought, hoping the sentiment was evident in her rhythms. *We will figure this out. Do what they say.*

And perhaps the thought was evident, because, reluctantly, he did. Or at least, he left, and she hoped he did.

"You should probably ready yourself as well, Alloy," Nieve said. "We'll meet in the foyer in an hour."

Ember nodded, but her feet wouldn't move. She looked down at Ademure who still lay on the ground, staring blankly, her skin pale. She fought the urge to kneel next to her.

Fuck, Ademure. What happened to you?

"It looks worse than it is," Sombra said, a familiar disgust in her voice. "She was not hurt."

"Okay," Ember said, because that was all she could think to say. But her palms were hot. And her stomach was sick. And her locket was strangling. And her scars were burning. And there was screaming in her ears.

And there might have even been a small spark on the back of her neck.

However, she said, "I'll see you in an hour."

Ember stood in leggings and a wrap that she had fashioned tight like a sports bra, and she stared at the crimson gown that draped on her bed. She slid it over her head, laced up the side, smoothed the bodice, and fitted it at her waist. Once in place, she looked at the vanity. The frame was still empty.

Right.

And so she looked down instead. The dress was beautifully scary, she gave it that much. Rather than a nasty tulle puff, it draped smoothly over her legs, preferable for running. It also had a train long enough to cover her boots—actually ideal for her purposes.

She tugged at the skirt once more, and her hand brushed against something firm. She dug through the fabric to find a small pocket located at her back, beneath her thigh, and through the material, she grabbed the object, its shape unmistakable.

She pulled out the gun. It was a small pistol, roughly the size of her hand. The weight of it was outmatched by the heaviness of the skirt in which it sat. It was loaded.

You only have to carry it, she reminded herself. *We'll be long gone before you have to shoot.*

She packed it back into the pocket, along with her green shell for good luck. Then, she tied her hair back, out of her face, and hoped Ademure had the common sense to prepare similarly.

Damian met her just outside her door.

"Is she okay?" Ember whispered.

"Um," he said, twiddling his thumbs. "When she sobers up, she will be."

"'*Sobers up?*'"

"What about the plan?" he said quickly. "Are you still intent on staying here?"

She shut her mouth and lifted the hem of her skirt, revealing the toe of her boot. "Of course, not. We're getting out of this once and for all."

He grinned. "I set the landsailer outside the plaza this morning. I was hoping that effort wouldn't go to waste." Then he turned and ambled down the hall.

But before he passed the corner at the end, he stopped and spun back around.

"I'm glad I was right about you, Seño."

A quarter-hour later, Ember, Cadeña, and Ademure were in the foyer, the latter of whom swayed where she stood. She reeked of wine, but at least Cadeña had pried the bottle out of her hands.

At the same time, Ember had to admit she was impressed. Ademure had consumed at least two and a half bottles in less than an hour. If only she hadn't done so right before a jailbreak.

Queen Esmerelda stepped into the entrance hall, wearing a gaudy green gown that floated as she walked. Sombra and Nieve followed closely behind, each in a fresh white jumpsuit, cloak, and heeled boots. Curiously, Nieve no longer favored her arm.

Following the twins were Estrellas Capote, Maduro, and Rodriguez, each also fashioned in white. Estrella Bailón was nowhere to be seen.

"Eyes, Alloy," Sombra said. "Bailón told you, didn't she?"

"Yes," Ember answered curtly. She covered her eyes and said, "*Colora rubrum*," and when she opened them again, Sombra gave her a smug look of satisfaction.

Outside, the party was met with two different floats. The first float was entirely white and shined against the setting sun. It held two seats decorated in green and gold trim, shaped to look like chariots that "pulled" an ocean, white shifting to a blue wave.

The second float was as exceedingly green as the queen's dress, with faux roots and grass trilling around the edge. Bits of brown twisted together in the center to form the silhouette of a nymph, and there were stairs on the back that led to three seats at the top of the nymph's head. Both floats rested on skis reminiscent of a landsailer.

Estrellas Cadeña and Capote took their seats in the chariot of the white float while Sombra and Nieve stood by the feet of the nymph one. Estrellas Maduro and Rodriguez each grabbed a landsailer.

Esmerelda took the lead in climbing the nymph float's stairs.

"Come now, Ademure," she said. "Don't dawdle."

Ember stood behind as the princess dragged up the steps. If possible, Ademure's skin paled further.

"It'll be okay," Ember said, resting a hand on her back, partially to comfort her, partially to make sure she didn't fall.

"Yes, Ademure," the queen said from the head. "Listen to the alloy. Public speaking is nothing to get sick over."

Esmerelda took her seat in the front, while Ember helped Ademure find hers.

"I know you're nervous," she whispered, "but please, trust me. This will work."

"I'm not nervous." Ademure looked toward the north, toward the forest. Her voice was distant. "I'm done."

Ember lifted a brow. "What do you mean, 'done'?"

"Do not save me."

She frowned, but Ademure's avoidant disposition told her not to press for more. However, she curled her fingers, feeling the magic about them, the heat behind them. And she remembered the concealer Daphne had wiped away all those years ago.

Sorry, Ademure, I can't do that.

The parade started moving, and for a moment, Ember lost herself in the sporadic jolts of the float. She breathed in the damp, salty air. The sky grayed above. One. Two. Three drops of rain splashed on her forehead. And electricity prickled the back of her neck.

Out of the corner of her eye, she watched Ademure shift in

place, except rather than anxious, the woman looked stoic, her eyes fixed on a single point in front of her. Ember followed the princess's gaze to the queen—specifically, to what was sitting on her head.

What is she thinking?

Thunder rumbled.

Ademure lunged.

"*My crown!*" Esmerelda screamed.

Ademure pulled the diadem into her chest before scrambling to stand. But when she reached the stairs, she tripped over her dress. Still, she fought forward anyway, crawling like a lunatic on the ground, one hand holding tight to the crown, hyperventilating. She made it to the second step.

"*Erigo.*"

Ademure hit the railing, tossed across the deck of the float like a ball, the cling of metal reverberating. Nieve bent down to pick up the crown, Sombra on the step behind her.

"*Give it to me now!*" the queen yelled.

The white-haired twin knelt before her with outstretched arms. Esmerelda swiped the diadem from her palms and replaced it on her head, then spun toward her daughter, who remained on the ground, holding her neck.

"Insolent child!" the queen said, before kicking her. Ademure grunted. "You've finally revealed your true colors, have you?"

Ember's palms went hot, and the electricity in the air was palpable.

"Amá, please," Ademure said meekly, holding her stomach. "It's cursed. Please, you have to believe me."

"I have to do nothing of the sort. *I* am the queen. *I* make the demands."

Sombra pulled the princess off the ground and dragged her back to her chair.

"Did your father put you up to this?" Esmerelda spat. Sombra and Nieve tied the princess to her seat. "What did he expect to happen? That just because you'd have my crown, you'd take my place? A crown does not make the queen, Ademure."

"Listen to yourself!" Ademure said louder as she thrashed in her chair. "Apá is a million miles away! How could I be doing this for him? You are sick! You have the green rose sickness!"

Ember's focus snagged on that, but no one else seemed to pay it any mind.

"Your lies and treachery have gone far enough," the queen said as she strutted back to her seat. "And I won't hear another word of it."

"Amá, please," Ademure cried, no longer fighting her restraints. The twins descended the stairs. "Please, I did this because I love you."

The queen sat silently.

"Amá? Amá, you have to believe me. I need you to believe me. I only wanted you back! Amá, please!"

Without turning around, Esmerelda said, "I told you, Ademure. I'm done listening to your lies."

The princess silenced what she could—but she couldn't mute her weeping.

Green rose sickness, Ember thought as the heat and electricity thankfully left her spine. *What is she thinking? What is green rose sickness?*

Ademure whispered under her breath, and her restraints snapped. She rubbed her wrists and dried her lashes. But she provided no answers.

It didn't matter now, anyway. They had already reached town. There were other, more pressing, tasks at hand.

At least, the town was lively: lights hung against the orange and gray sky, the national anthem filled the air, rumbling alongside the thunder. Men, women, and children packed shoulder-to-shoulder along the streets and in the square, buzzing with conversation and excitement. Everyone was so wonderfully unaware.

And why should they be otherwise? These people expected a celebration. Not an execution.

Any moment now, Damian would make his move.

As their float glided closer to the northern entrance, Ember moved toward the railing, looking for a sign, a mirror, a familiar teenage boy. Something that would tell her when to move. But she saw nothing.

That was okay, though. They still had time. They weren't quite there yet. And it would be stupid of Damian to leave himself out in the open. This only meant she would have less time to find the landsailer, so it would be best to locate it now, before the chaos.

Now, she wondered, *where would he have left it?*

"I'm disappointed in you, Alloy."

Ember turned.

Nieve stood so close behind her, her back was forced into the railing. "I thought we had an understanding."

"What are you talking about?"

"Damian is not down there." She gestured toward the approaching plaza. "The landsailer he left has been returned to el Alcázar."

Ember's eyes widened.

"The boy thinks that because we cannot see him, we cannot hear him either." Nieve clicked her tongue in reproach. "We overheard your discussion at the temple the other day, before we walked in. And we heard him again, when he relayed your plan to our princess. And after those two instances, we've been much warier of locations that disappear from our sight."

Oh no.

Oh no oh no oh no.

This can't be.

He's just a teenager.

"What did you do to him?" Ember said. "It was all my idea, I swear. He had nothing to do with it."

Nieve smiled softly, almost approvingly, and that set Ember's palms ablaze.

"I admire your loyalty, Alloy. Loyalty is what makes a great estrella. It's why I endorsed your staying here, even after you lost your temper." Her eyes flitted to Ember's hands. "Even when you openly colluded with a traitor in the library."

Ember struggled to keep her face stern.

"I thought you would eventually see reason," Nieve continued. "I thought I could win over your undying faith. And I thought, what better way to prove your competence than to have you kill the thorn in our side."

Heat crawled up Ember's arms as the realization washed over her. "So Fate didn't ask me to kill her. You did."

"Perhaps."

"Fate isn't real."

Nieve lifted her chin, eyes cast down and a shadow across her face. "Fate is all too real."

The gray sky darkened. A few sparse raindrops became several. The wind picked up, and the estrella's long white hair floated with it.

Ember felt the wind pull her own. "So what's next, Nieve? What am I doing here? You've known for three days that I'm not going to kill her."

"I'm not so certain of that. I don't like being made a fool, Ember." Nieve, too, leaned on the railing, looking out over the town. "Daphne Rui Liang. Located in Washington, D.C., the United States. Attends Georgetown University where she's pursuing a degree in political science, correct?"

Ember stilled.

The corner of Nieve's mouth quirked up. "You know, I was serious when I offered to take you to see her. Unfortunately, considering the circumstances, I can't continue our original deal. But I will attempt a new one." She put a hand into her pocket. "So, it's your choice. Either you take the princess's life, here and now, in front of all of Nysa, or..."

She pulled out a small square paper—a photo. Cropped black hair. Deep brown eyes. Wide, warm smile.

Daphne.

"...I make a visit."

Nieve handed the picture to Ember, who took it with unsteady hands.

"You can keep that. I have her committed to memory." She then put a hand on Ember's shoulder. "Oh, and we've arrived. You should take your seat."

Their float stopped in front of the nymph statue, and Ember stumbled back to her chair.

Whistling, cheering, clapping. Anthems and drums and singing and laughing.

It was all too loud.

"*Welcome, Nysans,*" Esmerelda announced in Spanish, her voice reverberating across the plaza. The gathered crowd clapped.

Ademure leaned toward Ember. "No Damian, I take it."

She shook her head mechanically, still staring at the photo in her hands, then placed a finger to her ear in an attempt to drown out the noise.

"I hope he's okay," Ademure said.

He's not.

Ember shut her green eyes. Brighter ones haunted her mind. Then brown ones.

"*We are so grateful that you join us in celebrating Nysan Independence Day!*"

Another round of roaring applause.

"Thank you," Ademure continued. "For trying."

"*Today is a commemoration of battle, of grit. A remembrance of loved ones we lost.*"

"No, you can't die," Ember whispered, her eyes still closed. Heat flooded her back. "You *can't* die."

"Why not? I told you. I'm done. Let it be."

"*But as you know, independence came at the cost of losing an old friend.*"

The princess put her hand on hers and gripped tightly, her eyes glistening with new tears. She gripped back.

A distraction, she pleaded. *All I need is a distraction.*

"*She comes to us from the underworld itself, on a mission to make amends. Finally, Nysa and Agartha can begin to heal.*"

"I won't," Ember said, looking at the now blurry Ademure. "I can't lose both of you." She shook her head. "I can't lose all three of you."

"*But first, I present my daughter, Ademure, the Princess of Nysa!*"

Ademure gave Ember a sad smile, then pulled away, wobbling as she stood, and Ember was sure it wasn't the alcohol. The princess then moved to the front of the upper deck.

The cheers were so *fucking* loud.

I need you to help me escape.

"It's time, Alloy," Nieve said behind her, Sombra at her side and blocking the stairs. "Who will it be?"

Ember gripped the photo tighter, and either due to rain or her own sweat, the ink began to run.

I'm sorry.

She rose to her feet, then reached into the pocket of her dress, dropping the photo and grabbing hold of the gun.

Both twins grinned.

Ember took in a deep breath, but it wasn't enough to calm the electricity in her fingers. It wasn't enough to calm the nerves.

Raindrops, she thought.

Raindrops. Raindrops. Raindrops.

Ademure and her mother stood at the railing of the float, side by side, facing the town, giving their speeches.

Ember stood behind them. Her crimson dress flapped at her knees. Her scarlet eyes pierced the rain. Even under this dark sky, she knew, all eyes were on her.

Finally, the crowd went silent.

She aimed.

And pulled—

Ademure screamed.

CHAPTER 44
EMBER

I *hurt her I hurt her I hurt her I hurt her I hurt her.*

The echo froze Ember where she stood, eyes shut, hearing only the crowd's horrific shrieks, torn between the instinct to protect the princess and the desire to stay in the dark about what she had done, if she had done anything. She didn't know.

"*Erigo!*" Sombra shouted.

Ember felt weightless, then heavy in half a second. The floor knocked the wind from her lungs. Her back stung and head throbbed, and she rolled to one side.

Ademure screamed again.

Ember's eyes shot open, adrenaline replacing pain. She pushed herself off the deck and to her feet, then raced to the railing. The people below scattered, stampeded. Charms cast and anthems sung. Children cried for their parents. Parents cried for their children.

And Queen Esmerelda lay on the ground, unmoving, red staining her green gown. But what had caused the red—

An arrow?

Thin in length and so sharp that it had punctured her collar. The queen appeared lifeless, blood spilling from her chest. Sombra and Nieve both knelt by her side, compressing the wound whilst hunting for the shooter. Ademure hid beneath the railing, cowering.

Ember looked around, ensuring there wasn't another arrow headed her way. But without seeing where the first one had originated, she was careful to move.

She grabbed the pistol that lay next to her just in case. Then, to be sure, she checked its chamber.

It's fully loaded, she realized, relieved. *I...I didn't do it.*

But then, who did?

The twins shoved aside the queen's maid who knelt at her side. Two other men clad in gray and green trailed behind them. The four propped up the queen so they could better dress her wound. Sombra raised her arm to apply more pressure, revealing something beneath Her Majesty—what looked to be a shattered mirror.

"You," Sombra barked to one of the men. "Get the alchemists up here, now."

"And you," Nieve barked to the other. "Lock down the streets. No one gets in or out without our knowledge."

The two men saluted, then rushed down the stairs.

Nieve turned to her sister. "We have to take her down, or else she'll lose too much blood."

Sombra nodded. "*Erigo*," she said, her arm outstretched to the queen. Esmerelda rose into the air.

Lightning struck, illuminating something in the corner of Ember's eye.

Another mirror. Floating this time.

"Drop her!" Nieve yelled. An identical arrow shot from the mirror and shot inches above the lowered queen. Ademure ducked and screamed. The estrella shouted, "Where are those cowards?"

Ember glanced at Ademure who had her head buried in her knees. If she could—

"Delfinos!" a voice shouted from below.

Ember looked over the rails.

"It's the Caldwells!" Estrella Bailón continued.

As if on cue, two mirrors appeared in the sand on opposite sides of the two floats. An ebony-skinned man, dressed in all black, pulled himself through the mirror behind the green float. A similar looking woman, though with flaming red hair, pulled herself through the mirror in front of the white one. Both had scarlet eyes.

The red-headed woman smirked. "It's been too long, Delfinos."

"*Evorto!*" the man said with a hand on the green float.

The papier-mâché nymph disintegrated beneath Ember's feet. For a moment, she held in the air, long enough to see the panic on Ademure's face when they came to the same realization. As they plunged toward the earth, they screamed.

"*Erigo!*" the man said, and Ember felt weightless once more.

He slowly lowered them. When they landed, gently, and on their feet, Ademure looked as stunned as Ember felt.

He caught us? Ember thought, then covered her mouth. The air was putrid.

"Not protecting your own, I see," he said. Ember looked up to see the twins and the queen floating down on their own terms.

"We have other priorities, Alden," Sombra said.

"Then give us the queen," the redheaded woman said, "and we'll let you return to them."

Nieve shook her head like she was annoyed to be dealing

with this. "Maduro, Capote, Graye is yours. Bailón, Rodriguez, take care of Alden. Cadeña, keep an eye on the princess and alloy."

The rain poured harder, further obstructing Ember's vision. But she saw bodies sprinting. She heard them pounding on shop doors, begging to be let in. She needed to grab Ademure now.

"Nieve, you insult me," the redheaded woman called Graye said. She knelt to touch the ground. "*Specta quinqua.*"

Dozens of mirrors appeared in the sand, all scattered across the plaza. Each one was the size of the fountain, glass rippling like water. The sight of them did nothing to calm the crowd.

Maduro and Capote shouted at Graye, Bailón and Rodriguez at the man named Alden. But before the spells struck, both red-eyes vanished. The estrellas turned.

Graye took Capote down in a second. Maduro rushed the redhead but with a quick few words, he too was on his knees. Bailón and Rodriguez joined the fight.

"You're all useless," Nieve growled, giving her sister the queen's arm. "Have you forgotten you're Nysans?" She opened her mouth.

A blade plunged for her neck.

Sombra caught Alden's wrist, and followed with a blade of her own. But then Alden disappeared, and her blade hit air.

Nieve tried to sing again, but another mirror formed below her, and she was interrupted by the man once more. Again, Sombra countered.

Again, he disappeared.

On the third time, it was Nieve who struck, and Alden jumped back. Ten mirrors levitated, and through them shot daggers. Each oracle abruptly shifted—left, right, jump, duck —dodging so nimbly that not one blade cut.

As the last blade passed Nieve, she dug in her heel and

charged. Her knife met his, and they locked in a battle of strength as hundreds of bits of shattered mirror floated about them, each one pointed at only him. Sombra rushed the shards.

The shards pierced sand. Alden disappeared again.

"We just want the queen," he said behind Ember. "Though, you are making this more fun."

He was gone again, leaving another round of shards in the sand.

Ember had her head on a swivel. The four estrellas were still fighting the red-haired woman—at some point Maduro and Capote had gotten back on their feet—and now the twins were sufficiently distracted with the man in black.

"Ademure," Ember said. The vague figure of the princess hovered over her mother.

Ember raced to her side and grabbed her wrist.

Ademure fought back. "No! We can't leave her here!"

"We have to."

"She'll die!"

Ember turned her eyes from the blood and swallowed. "She won't."

"We can take her now!"

"We can't, Ademure!" she screamed, and Ademure was quiet—worried. Ember swallowed again. "We can come back to rescue her. But if we don't leave now, I don't know that we ever will."

"*Vincu!*"

"Move!"

Ember shoved Ademure out of the way, falling on top of her as two metal chains whipped behind them. Then she shot to her feet and yanked on the princess's hand, dragging her behind the nymph fountain, where they crouched down. They peeked over the edge. Estrella Cadeña dropped his landsailer in the sand and walked toward them. He held the end of a chain in each hand. "*Vincu!*" he repeated.

Ember pulled Ademure down as the chains whipped at the statue. A piece of the nymph's spear cracked, and she threw an arm out at the princess, keeping her pinned beneath the fountain's edge as the piece fell into the water, splashing them.

She took one quick glance to gather her surroundings. The estrellas and Agarthans were on the other side of the plaza. The queen still lay near the destroyed float, rain splashing on her paling face. Cadeña stood in front of her, whipping his chains like a madman. And the townspeople that had come for the parade had been forced to take shelter under the roofs of the nearby stores. She looked at them for a moment, wondering how she could avoid hurting them, and they looked at her as if they were scared of what she was going to do.

This fucking dress, she thought, then she turned to Ademure who, too, looked at her with wide, questioning eyes.

"Stay here," Ember said.

"What?" Ademure said. "You're not fighting him alone!"

"I have to."

"No, you don't!"

"And what other idea do you have, Ademure? We have to get to the harbor, and I don't plan on running there!"

"But he'll kill you!"

Ember shook her head. "He won't. Lucky for me, I'm still too valuable." She stood up. "Don't get caught."

She leaped onto the fountain ledge, leaving the princess cowering behind it, and walked the perimeter, slowly, deliberately, never taking her eyes off of Cadeña. She bounced on her toes and shook her arms, reminding herself that this is what she and Ozamiz had been preparing for these last six weeks.

"*Vincu!*"

The chains whipped at her like snakes slithering through

the air, reaching for her wrists, her ankles. Clinking and crashing against each other, they threatened to grasp her.

She sang.

The chains slowed, then stopped, fixed mid-air mere feet away. She stepped down from the ledge to side-step their attack and reached for each hovering end. The metal was cold.

Cadeña adjusted his monocle. Then he started singing too.

Her eyes widened. The chains sped up, like the wave had at sea. And just like yesterday's wave, she couldn't regain control. Before she could get away, metal wrapped around her outstretched wrists. She pulled and pulled, but the metal constricted tighter, tighter, so tight her hands purpled and she couldn't risk struggling with it anymore.

Cadeña reeled in the chains like they were a fishing line, forcing her to step forward, toward the other estrellas, and chuckled.

"Powerful, but much too wide, dear," he said. "I'll make a note to Ozamiz for your lesson plan next week. Now, Su Alteza."

"No!" Ember shouted. She yanked on the chains again, harder, throwing her entire weight into it, cutting her wrists, and ripping them from his grip. Then she yelled, "*Reditio!*" and the chains became the sand they were molded from.

She stood tall, her palms on fire. "I'm who you really want. It's just you and me."

He tucked his monocle into his pocket. "Sure. *Vincu quinqua!*"

She jumped back, narrowly missing the chain that shot out from where she stood. She hopped to her left, and another one sprang from the ground. She hopped to her right. Another. One slapped at her shin, another at her elbow. She hissed in pain, but she kept moving back and back and back.

Finally, she jumped back to the ledge of the fountain,

where Ademure still huddled, and looked out at the plaza. Dozens of chains whipping, thrashing, lashing at her. Metal on metal resounded. Most of the crowd hadn't been able to move inside yet, so they had backed up to walls, similarly fearful of the snake-like chains.

What do I do? She looked at the sky. It was blacker than she'd ever seen it, until lightning streaked across it. Instinctively, she grabbed at her neck. Maybe, with just Cadeña, she could...

She looked back to the right, at the Nysans in front of the bookstore. *Out of the question*, she decided. *But then what? The gun? I can't get a clear shot.*

She looked down. The princess had formed a shield of sorts, made of sand, sturdy enough to protect herself from stray chains. "Ademure, what do you know about Cadeña?"

A chain struck the fountain, and the young woman flinched. "I've rarely seen him fight," she said. "He doesn't train as much as the other estrellas."

"But you've seen him fight, right? How can I beat him?"

Ademure thought for a moment longer as Ember continued to dodge the metal snakes. "You'll need a weapon," she finally said. "Then get around the chains, and get close so that his chains no longer work for him—chains are his method and he's not nearly as strong hand-to-hand. But if you continue to fight from so far away, you're going to be the only one who tires."

Ember's eyes lasered in on Cadeña on the other side of the plaza, closer to the parade route, probably a hundred feet away.

"Thanks," she said. She dropped into the fountain and dipped in her hands. "*Telum. Telum.*"

She pulled a set of daggers from the water and tucked them into her hidden pocket. Then, she returned her hands to the water. The chains lashed again, chipping at the statue as they slapped at her like tentacles of an unseen octopus.

"*Inundu!*" she shouted as she threw her hands forward, and the water followed.

A wave. A surge. Water from the fountain, from the air, collected and streamed toward the sea of chains. So much water, like it came from the ocean itself.

"*Glacio!*" she screamed. The temperature dropped. The rattling fell silent. The chains slowed and stopped again, frozen in place by the ice that surrounded them. The pieces that poked through were the only bits still clinking.

Panjesus, I hope this works.

Ember stepped back onto the ledge, grabbed the two daggers from her pocket, and sprinted. Where the ledge met the ice, she leaped.

Cold. So cold. She skated on the perfectly smooth ice, skirt flying back, like she was sliding into defense, arms wide. She held the daggers in one hand, returning the excess chains to sand with the other. In two seconds, she was on the other side.

"*Lique,*" she said before jumping off mere feet from Cadeña. She tossed a knife to her free hand, holding both to either side.

"Bravo. Now, that was creative." His eyes flickered to the bookstore. "But you still cast much too wide."

Some of the people who had taken shelter underneath the store roofs scattered. Those trapped in the crowd were coughing, teeth chattering. Others hugged tight to one another, completely soaked.

She rolled her prickling neck. *A little cold shower, that's all. I controlled my magic just fine.*

She looked back at Cadeña, the rain pouring harder, water dripping off her brow. The chains in the ground had stopped moving, but he still had one in each hand.

"More?" she asked.

He sighed. "You are making me work much harder than I had intended to." Then he lashed out.

She ducked, sliding to the right and stepping within striking range. Her left arm drove up, aiming for his abdomen.

But he spun back, his chains whipping in front of him. Like skipping rope, she jumped over the first one, but the second one struck her in the back, and she yelped. She barely managed to remain on two feet.

The first chain came after her again, this time for her ankle. As she had practiced with Ozamiz a thousand times, she stepped back, then lunged forward, so close that the chains couldn't reach her without reaching Cadeña himself. Her dagger extended, she went for his shoulder.

Cadeña pulled his arm up, sending her wrist to the sky. Without hesitation, she moved her weight into the block, turning about his arm. She flipped the knife in her other hand, and repeated the attack on his shoulder. This time, it stuck.

He howled as she pulled the knife free, tearing flesh, the blade slicked with blood. He kicked her in the gut, and she stumbled back.

Back into the range of the chains.

Fuck. She held her stomach.

"You little bitch," Cadeña said as red spewed down his shoulder. He tried whipping the chains again, but only his right chain responded, his left arm limp at his side. The color of his face matched his bloodied suit. "To think I admired you." He dropped the left chain.

Ember took the opening and lunged, both daggers outstretched. But before she could get close, his right chain whipped *faster*, forcing her to jump to the side and out of the way. She rolled to stand upright, unharmed, but was still no closer to beating him.

She stepped again, moving faster herself. She ducked the

lone chain and pressed forward, coming in high but planning to go low.

Then the chain changed directions.

As she jumped, the chain slapped her ankle mid-air. The snap of bone reverberated over the pattering of rain. She dropped to the ground and shrieked.

Cadeña moved on top of her. "This could have been easy, Alloy." He raised his arm; the chain followed.

She tried to stand. She did everything she could to stand. But no matter how much she begged, her ankle wouldn't give her an inch. *Fuck! Fuck! Fuck!*

The chain was above her like a serpent staring down its next meal. Lightning struck, and it glinted.

It came down.

I can't move. I can't move. I can't...

She thought of her time in the ocean yesterday. That time she'd been underwater, drowning. That brief moment she'd considered letting go. She considered it again, now.

However, unlike yesterday, the outcome of today wasn't death. If she let go, she wouldn't die. Rather, she would be beaten into submission—beaten into the weapon Nysa so desperately wanted.

But how bad is that really? she asked herself. *How different is that from the last six years? It's still just not dying.*

Except, strangely, "not dying" no longer appealed to her.

No, she wanted to live. For Damian, for Ademure, for Daphne...

And for her.

Which meant she had to move, *now*. So she twisted, she squirmed, and she tried again to stand. But her ankle refused all of her commands.

And the chain came slowly. So slowly.

Too slowly.

She heard the song.

She glanced back at the fountain, where despite the storm, the rain, the estrellas, the Agarthans, the princess was singing with all her heart.

"What are you doing?" Ember shouted over the storm.

Ademure didn't answer but kept singing, stepping forward from the fountain.

Cadeña barely moved, every inching step carrying him so gradually he might have been still. In the rain, it was almost majestic, drops floating down around him. His chain less whipped and more dragged. He looked like he wanted to say something with his mouth stuck open and his face beet-red.

"You won't last!" Ember shouted. "Get out of here!"

Ademure ignored her again. Cadeña accelerated, heading straight toward the princess, but she raced by him and joined Ember's side.

Agony pulsated in Ember's ankle. Sharp, throbbing, stabbing agony. She knew she should help, but she also knew she couldn't sing at this moment even if she wanted to.

Cadeña moved at full speed.

"*Clypeus!*" Ademure shouted before his song fully caught on. A wave of sand emerged between them and the estrella like a five-foot-tall wall, a shield. She turned to Ember. "This gives us maybe twenty seconds if I sing again," she said quickly. "Think of something."

She stood so that only her head was above the shield and started clocking once more. The estrella's tune faltered, then Ademure's, fighting one another for who would reign.

They locked in a standstill for twenty seconds.

Nineteen.

Eighteen.

Ember grabbed the pistol from her dress pocket and peeked out from behind the wall of sand. Cadeña wasn't anywhere near as far as before, and only one chain stood in her way. She aimed for his shoulder and pulled.

The bullet slowed. Cadeña sidestepped it.

Shit.

She shifted where she sat and looked behind her. His land-sailer was only ten feet away. Could she reach that in time instead?

Not with this ankle.

She needed something else. Something that could strike at Cadeña from an angle he wasn't expecting. A magic he couldn't anticipate. There was the store, the fountain, the dunes, all out of her reach. Then lightning struck, followed by thunder—*not happening*—and she blinked, water falling off her lashes.

Raindrops. I can reach the raindrops.

"Ademure, when I count to three, duck behind the wall."

The princess's song crescendoed, and it wasn't clear whether she could even hear her. But without breaking a beat, she nodded.

"One. Two." Ember shifted to her knee. "Three."

The princess dropped. Ember barrel-rolled to her side, careful not to put weight on her ankle as she moved outside the protection of the wall, and returned to one knee.

"*Inundo!*" she shouted, her hands above her head. The rain halted, waiting for its next command. She was slow, she could feel it, but Cadeña's clocking hadn't yet fully turned on her. She rushed her hands down as fast as possible. Then forward.

The rain swept down and out, like a million tiny needles—still water, but sharp as a blade. Ember closed her eyes. *I just need a few to land. Give me a couple in the other shoulder.*

She opened her eyes.

The needles never made it; Cadeña moved around each one

of them just like the bullets—no, even more effortlessly. His song had caught.

The world sped up around her. She tried to sing, but it was too late. When the estrella's song finally let go, her hands were behind her, held by chains and buried in the sand. The shield had fallen, and at her side, the princess suffered the same demise.

The estrella lowered his hands. Ember pulled at the restraints to no avail.

"Fucking alloy," Cadeña said, holding his shoulder. "Stupid fucking alloy. I told you your cast was too wide." He gestured toward the storefront.

The screams. How had she not heard the blood-curdling screams? She lifted her shoulders to her ears, not wanting to listen, but they were louder than thunder, louder than the winds.

No, I can't have, she thought.

He replaced his monocle. "So many good Nysan lives, ruined."

"You're lying—" Ember cried.

"Are you deaf? Do you not hear them? Stupid fucking alloy. This could have been easy."

Even through the pouring rain, she could see them. Dozens of people, all bystanders, innocent, had fallen to the ground. They writhed. They rolled. They stilled. A red river flowed from them toward her. She couldn't see their injuries, but she could imagine. A million daggers. A million stab wounds. Torn flesh, thrashed ligaments, punctured hearts and lungs and stomachs.

No, they're okay, she pleaded. *They have to be okay.*

A child screeched. She swallowed down bile.

"And you, Alteza," Cadeña said. He piled Ademure's hair into his fist and yanked. "Filthy, disloyal, nymph-loving traitor." He spat in her face and yanked again. Ademure screamed.

"Let her go!" Ember shouted, throwing her body forward, flailing in her restraints.

Cadeña threw Ademure out of his grip. "*Vincu.*"

A new metal snake slithered out of the sand. It crawled around the princess's waist, around her chest, around her neck, and squeezed. She wheezed.

"*I said let her go!*" Ember ripped harder at her restraints, stray locks fell in her face, but her hands remained firmly buried. Lightning sheared the sky. A prickle sheared her neck. "*Get away from her!*"

"Or what?" Cadeña's fingers curled and the chain pressed harder into Ademure's skin. Her breaths were shallow.

The prickle grew to a spark.

"Cadeña, stop it now! Stop it! *Stop it!*"

He curled his hand further, forming a fist. Ademure looked at Ember with bulging eyes.

I need you to help me escape.

"Cadeña, *please.*" Ember cried hot tears. "*Please.* Stop this. You don't have to do this." Her vision blurred. Her locket was heavy and scalding.

The estrella bent down in front of Ademure. "How does it feel, Alteza? I wonder if it's like being poisoned. You get to see your life slip away. You'll die fast, and yet, not that fast at all."

He twisted his fist. Her face was white. Then purple. Then blue.

Her face blued.

Her face blued.

"*Please!*"

"Viva la princesa—"

The spark burst. The sand melted. Ember saw every grain beneath her knees. Heard every raindrop fall on her hair.

And time slowed.

One crack. Her chains snapped.

"*Clypeus.*" She drew up a sand barrier between the estrella and Ademure.

"*Maior.*" She willed the wind to push the estrella back.

"*Reditio.*" She reverted the chain around Ademure to sand.

And finally, she pointed.

The lightning was brighter than the sun. The thunder louder than gunfire. The air hotter than an open flame. This time, it didn't bother her. This time, she was still standing.

This time, she watched.

She hit him square in the chest, cracking ribs to get to his heart. She was connected to him. She *controlled* him.

Her locket blistered hot against her neck, and vibrated with such an intensity, such a ferocity, as if it were full of wrath. Angry at Cadeña for what he had done to Ademure. Furious that he'd taken joy in her pain. Livid that he'd spared no mercy for her, that given the chance, he would not hesitate to take her life.

The locket demanded that Ember kill him. She listened to it.

Her current traveled through his veins and along his nerves. It fractured into branches like water down a window pane. It popped blood vessels like they were bubbles. He convulsed until he collapsed, purple himself.

Then the electricity left her, and time returned to normal pace. She returned to normal strength. And the all-too-late realization of what she'd done weighed on her lungs.

She crumpled forward onto her elbows, quivering and heaving.

"Ember!"

But she couldn't look up. She couldn't look at all. Her eyes were glued shut by the screaming. The ringing. Her scars burning. His flesh burning.

"Ember, we have to go."

She tried to tell herself he'd deserved it. She tried to tell herself it had been in self-defense. After all, Ademure had been suffocating. Had she not stepped in, she would've died!

Still, I enjoyed it.

"Ember! *Ember!*"

Someone was shaking her, pulling at her. Someone was underneath her, trying to push her up.

She traced the red sand. Her eyes lingered on the people that lay in it. The innocent people.

"Profe Valentina! Thank Pan, you're here. She can't stand!"

"*Pressi.*"

Sand wrapped around Ember's foot, solidified about her ankle. Someone else was pushing and pulling her now.

I enjoyed it again.

"Come on, Alloy. You can't be done yet. Stand."

It was like the command came from across the island. She did as she was told, and the brace did help...

But there's so much blood. So much death.

Someone snapped in her face.

Ember looked at her. It was the small woman from the bookstore.

"Don't worry about them," she said, gesturing toward the storefronts. "A couple of pinpricks, nothing more. Oscar's clocking slowed your charm down quite a bit."

Ember's attention drifted back to the people. *So many people.*

The woman grabbed her chin, forcing her to look into her eyes. "They're fine, Alloy. I promise you've done nothing permanent. The alchemists are on their way."

But electricity still prickled on Ember's fingers. And over the woman's shoulder, Cadeña still lay on the ground.

"And him?" she croaked.

The woman's expression grew grim. "What's done is done. You cannot change the past. Train up, and change the future."

The future...

Daphne. Ember looked to her right. The princess's dress was in tatters. She had bruises on her arms and neck. And her eyes were wide with worry. *Ademure.*

She's right, she thought. *We have to get out of here.*

"Where do we go?" she said, turning her head to the sky. The storm soaked the island. These winds could push mountains. She could only imagine what it would be like on the sea. "Even if I can manage to landsail to the harbor, there's no way the two of us will be able to steer a ship in this weather."

"I could be wrong," Valentina said, "but I think there's someone with a solution just outside of the town."

Ember's attention snapped to the woman. "Which way?"

"To the west, near the stadium would be my guess."

"And you're sure they're out there, in this storm?"

The woman smiled at her. "They've waited in worse conditions. Now, go. I've got a former student to help."

With that, she disappeared into the rain.

Ember didn't waste another second. With an arm around Ademure, she limped onto Cadeña's landsailer. Then, as Ademure wrapped around her waist, she leaned into the handle and connected with the sand.

CHAPTER 45
ALDEN

Alden blocked another blow from Nieve and readied for Sombra's attack. One of them charged. He countered, evading her and throwing weight into her sister's follow-up. They moved as a blur of black and white. One got behind him. The other distracted him in front. He twisted and dodged, leaped out from between the two. Nieve struck and Sombra followed, as quickly as he had left them.

Anyone else would've fallen to him by now, but the oracles presented an unusual challenge: he could slip away as many times as he wanted, but they always saw him, no matter where he went. Surprising them was nearly out of the question.

As he ducked Nieve's strike, he stepped into a mirror, rising out of another one, far away from the twins, to where Graye fought four magicks at once. He watched.

Three of the estrellas wielded a spear, an arrow, and a dagger respectively. The arrow flew first—likely meant to be a distraction—followed by the dagger and spear from either side. The fourth estrella, Bailón, opened her mouth.

Graye stepped into a conjured mirror, leaving the three

attackers to cut through air. Then, she reappeared with a knife to Bailón's throat.

The captain smirked. Graye jumped away as a spear drove up from the ground. Had she moved a second later, she would've been skewered.

Alden raised his brows. *You've improved, Bailón.*

He looked back over his shoulder. The twins levitated the queen as if they were trying to leave. *Now that they've lowered their guard...* He stepped through a mirror again.

Rising, he released his daggers. Sombra easily deflected them, but this time, rather than attack, the twins ran off with the queen in tow. He chased after them.

The oracles led him far enough away from the plaza that there were no more mirrors ahead of him, and unlike at the open-air plaza, the buildings in this part of town blocked his view. Conjuring mirrors now would throw him into a random alleyway.

The twins turned a corner, and so did he. He released a dagger; they deflected it. He increased the wind; Sombra shielded it. He liquified the sand; Nieve solidified it. Attack after attack sent and defended, tiring him. Yet, they never sent an attack in return.

Do they think a jog is going to stop me?

Another corner turned, and the twins stepped into a dead end. He hesitated.

A trap, he figured. *It has to be.* He scanned the higher buildings, the lack of back alley doors, and the smooth, rain-packed sand. *What do they want me to step into?*

He moved forward with caution, but the moment he stepped into the alley, a sand wall rose behind him, trapping them and the queen on all four sides. Nieve lowered her hands and panted—her first sign of exhaustion.

"You're locking us in?" he asked.

"I'm tired of you throwing things at me," she said. "Now, you don't have the range for that mirror and knife trick."

"And you think that gives you the upper hand?"

"It's two-on-one."

"And you have a severe hindrance." He nodded toward the queen whose blood dripped with the rain above them. Sombra lifted her queen onto the roof of the building opposite him, her back facing him. Nieve was the only obstacle between him and his target, now.

The estrella thrust a manipulated spear at him. He moved to the side and forward, ripping it from her grip, then spun it around, point to her chest.

"Don't you know not to use weapons you haven't practiced with?" he said.

She growled before manipulating a long blade, and swung. He ducked, then lunged, and she sidestepped—just as he expected—out of his way.

He left Nieve behind and continued forward with his attack, toward the back wall, toward the other twin.

By the time she'd realized his plan, he was already beyond her reach. And when Sombra must've seen him charge her, she turned to fight him off, but not before his spear skewered her thigh.

She screamed, and the queen fell onto the roof with a crunch. Nieve shot him a seething glare, but didn't dare move. *That's the twins' greatest weakness,* his father had reminded his sister and him before they'd left for Nysa. *They don't know how to fight without one another.* With Sombra hurt, Nieve would second-guess everything.

"What?" Alden said. "Didn't see that coming?" He tore the spear out of Sombra's leg. Blood gushed onto the sand, mixing with the rain and staining the area red. She screamed again, holding onto the wall as she slid to the ground, and he drove down the scarlet tip again.

He heard singing.

"*Specta!*" he said, creating a mirror below him and a mirror back where he had entered. He needed space between himself and the twins. The last thing he wanted was to be trapped in Nieve's clocking.

When he surfaced, Nieve was at her sister's side. She held a sword out in front of them while Sombra chugged a potion. The blood on her leg receded back into its wound as the wound began to close.

"You had healing water this entire time and didn't give it to your queen?" Alden called across the alleyway.

"Someone was throwing daggers at us," Nieve called back. "Anyway, her death has been long fated. My sister's has not."

That's what makes us different. I'd give up my sister for our king in a heartbeat, fated or otherwise.

He looked up to the roof above the twins, where the queen was bleeding profusely. Time was running out.

But creating a mirror so far away, on a substance he couldn't touch—that would be difficult. He had to get closer.

Of course, Sombra was now nearly back on her feet and fashioning herself her own sword. He would need a sparring partner to bypass them both.

Where is Graye? She should've already gotten away.

His ears perked.

That music...

Not singing this time, but a much more welcome tune. It was like a brass section blared in his ears. The sound of determination—strong, loud chords that echoed over the storm. It didn't belong to either twin, and it didn't belong to Graye.

"Don't come closer," Nieve said, looking to the top of the

brick wall. Alden followed her gaze. A small figure stood above them.

The figure landed on the red sand, and despite the rain, he could make out the bun and female frame.

"I'm sorry, dear, I couldn't hear you from up there," Valentina said. "Could you say that again?"

"Test me, Sofia," Nieve said, pointing her sword at the tiny woman.

Alden took the opening. "*Specta.*"

He rose behind the estrella and thrust his spear.

As if she'd known exactly what he would do, Sombra sliced off the spear's head, and in tandem with her sister, Nieve swung her sword to his neck.

Both moments of impressive retaliation cut short, though, when a throwing star came for each of their own necks. Then another at Nieve's back. And another at Sombra's shoulder. They dodged those and each star thereafter nimbly, letting them stick in the wall, but the distraction gave Alden the time he needed to think.

He threw his broken spear to the side—in combat with a sword at this range, it would hardly be helpful—and opted for his own hands. If he could incapacitate one of them, Valentina could take the other, and he could get what he needed without fear of interruption. Between snow and charcoal, he chose snow.

Nieve dodged another star when he charged in and grabbed her wrist. He wrenched her hand, forcing her to drop the sword, and Valentina grabbed the weapon, immediately dissolving it before turning her attention onto Sombra.

Alden wrapped an arm around Nieve's neck, while staying wary of her palms—being the object of her destruction magic didn't quite appeal to him today—and he squeezed, leveraging his strength in such a way that he could easily snap it.

Something stabbed his side, and his hold slackened.

He looked down at the blood gushing from his hip, the dagger stuck in his skin. He heard the melody of victory, the departure of fear. The twins' music was deafening.

Thankfully, his tutor stepped in before either twin could do more.

But she can't fight them both by herself for long, he knew.

Slowly, he pulled, exposing his bone as the flesh peeled off the edge. His blood was hot. His skin was hot. He hissed, biting so hard on his tongue, he almost bit it off.

The twins had cornered Valentina. He needed to help her now.

"*Fringo*," he said, and the handle of the dagger broke off. He would have to leave the rest where it was for now.

"*Specta, specta*," and two mirrors appeared. One next to him, one next to them. He stepped through his and rose in the other one.

And met Nieve's blade.

His quick reaction allowed him to step back, keeping the cut shallow, but Nieve still sliced him from shoulder to waist. The new wound was searing. He held back a scream.

Another counter, another lunge. She wasn't as clever as her sister when she was one-on-one, but her technique was swifter. She scratched his cheek, then his thigh. It was only pure adrenaline that allowed him to continue, but his moves were slowing. Blood was seeping.

Over her shoulders, Valentina still fought, danced, countered like she had done so all her life. Seeing her at the bookstore, it had been easy for Alden to forget her abilities. But seeing her now, battling Sombra, the estrella she once had been had reawakened.

"Sombra," Nieve said. "Do you see her?"

"Yes."

"End it, then."

Alden's footing stumbled and he fell to one knee, feebly holding his dagger. Nieve slashed, creating a gash in his arm.

Great. Another wound to bleed from, he thought. *Where is my damned sister?* The faint high-pitched slew of notes was growing louder, meaning she was close—but not close enough.

Nieve thrust forward. Water and blood slicked off the blade that came for him, that would slit his throat. He knew he should block it, or try to block it, or form a shield, but his mind was hazing, his muscles weren't reacting, and the music was screaming.

Clashing metal.

Nick of his neck.

Flaming red hair and a barrage of arrows.

"About fucking time," Alden said, slinking away from the fight.

Graye laughed. "I got carried away. Now, out of my way. I'm tagging in."

Nieve threw down a conjured shield and charged Alden again. But his sister entered the arena before the oracle could draw her blade.

Alden focused on his breath as he staggered to the side of the building. Then, he looked up to the roof, where the twins had left the queen.

"*Specta. Specta.*"

CHAPTER 46
EMBER

Ember let the rain beat against her face. Manipulating the sand and wind was difficult enough as it was; she didn't also have the energy to redirect the weather. Thankfully, her sand-made boot seemed undisturbed by the water. And despite the downpour, she could make out the stadium's massive shape. She headed straight for it.

"My mother is dead, isn't she?"

Ember couldn't turn to face Ademure, but she heard the heartbreak in her voice. It sounded like the screams in her own head.

I killed him, she thought. *I hurt others. And Damian...*

She tried to shake her mind of the neon-green eyes. "You don't know that," she said. "We can't know that."

"I know it. But it wasn't the arrow that killed her. She died long before then."

Ember didn't know how to respond, and Ademure didn't say another word. If possible, the rain poured harder, and lightning became their sole source of light. With each flash,

Ember scanned the vast desert, searching for someone—anyone who might be waiting for them. Each time, she was disappointed.

She pulled into the lot of the stadium, skimming the grounds.

"They're here," Ademure said. "Look." She pointed toward a garbage can. Behind it sat a landsailer that had fallen to its side. "Maybe they're inside?"

But there was still no sign of life. Ember shielded her eyes with her hand and pointed to the top of the stadium. "Let's go there. We'll be able to see better."

With great assistance from Ademure, they stepped onto a drenched platform.

"Hello?" Ember yelled, gripping on the railing. She couldn't see anything that wasn't directly in front of her, and the rain was so loud, she wasn't sure anyone would hear her. But she had to try. "Is anyone there?"

Ademure joined her. "Anybody? Please, help us!"

They rose higher and higher. Ember squinted in the dark, looking for any resemblance of a human figure—or any figure at all, quite frankly.

"Ember, I see something." Ademure pointed to the center of the bleachers, a few feet higher than themselves. There the sand had been manipulated to look like a dune—which was completely out of place with the rest of the flat bleachers.

The princess raced ahead. "Sofia Valentina sent us here!" she shouted as she leaped off the platform and climbed the stands. "Please, can you help us?"

"Ademure! Wait!" Ember shouted. Once she reached the same level, she resorted to crawling off the platform and hobbling along the seats, the weight of her sand-booted foot making it difficult to suck in breath for another yell.

Then the faux dune liquified. The sand returned to the bleachers, and there stood the tall, chestnut-haired man that she'd thought she would never see again.

"Kiva?"

Jaw dropping, Ember whipped to the young woman next her. *She knows him?*

"Ademure?"

She whipped to Kiva, jaw dropping further. *He knows her.*

The princess rushed him, tears mixed with rain, nearly knocking him down with her embrace. He wrapped his arms around her in return, and Ember's palms heated.

"Ademure," she said, forcing her voice calm, "please explain."

Kiva's head shot up, his fake green eyes wide. "Ember! I swear, I wasn't trying—Are your eyes red?"

The heat shot to her forearms "Kiva, you better tell me what's going on or I swear to god—"

"Ademure," he said like he was deep in thought. He looked down at the princess, then back to Ember. "Ademure. You were trying to save Ademure."

"Wait, you know each other?" Ademure asked, still holding onto him.

He nodded sheepishly.

The fire shot to Ember's shoulders. "Ademure, how do *you* know each other?"

The princess looked up at him. He averted his gaze.

"Well, I haven't seen him since our parents' divorce so he's definitely matured," she said. "But I could never not recognize my older brother."

Brother?

Divorce?

Prince.

"Kiva," Ademure said before Ember could scream, "can you get us out of here? Profe Valentina told us you could."

He rubbed his hand behind his neck. "Yeah, obviously I can. But you won't like it."

"I'm well past the point of being selective. I'm in."

"Great. But you weren't really the one I thought I'd have trouble convincing."

The siblings both looked at Ember, Kiva at her ankle.

Agartha. After all that effort spent avoiding him and his desperate plan to take her away, here she was, begging him to leave. *If you would've told me this is where I'd be, Panjesus, we could've saved a lot of time.*

She gritted her teeth. "Fine."

In response, he smiled, and her heat became scalding.

"You didn't win," she added. "The circumstances changed. That's all."

"Remind me, who's the one who can't tell when they've lost, ice queen?"

Ember balled her fist, and, with every ounce of energy she had left, punched the prince in his shoulder. He grunted, and she shook her hand, flexing out the sting.

"At least it wasn't lightning," he said, grabbing at his arm.

"Would you like to make it lightning?"

His mischievous grin widened, and he knelt to the bleacher. "*Specta.*"

The sand he touched sank away, replaced by a mirror the size of a small pool. Though it rippled like water, when the rain fell, it stiffened like glass. Like this wasn't an enormous portal to the underworld but instead just a mirror, meant solely for reflecting Ember and Ademure's exhaustion.

"Each of you, take an arm," Kiva said. Ademure easily grabbed his left arm. Ember begrudgingly grabbed his right. "This will feel odd for you. But hold on and trust me."

"Yeah, right," Ember said, but she held his arm tighter, ignoring the look he gave her.

"On three, we jump. One. Two. Three."

And she leaped from her good foot, hoping Kiva was there to catch her.

CHAPTER 47

ALDEN

Alden's hand was soaked in blood. He needed an alchemist and soon.

A barely conscious woman, hidden in a pile of green fabric, lay at his feet. Queen Esmerelda groaned as she opened her eyes.

"Alden? You've grown since I saw you last. Has your king sent you to execute me?"

"My king doesn't know I'm here," he said and pulled out a vial. In his other hand, he grabbed the arrow and yanked it from her collar. The familiar smell of iron, feel of slicing flesh. A deluge of blood poured from the wound.

She cursed but was too weak to fight him. He lifted her arm.

"What are you doing?" she asked.

"My father requests the blood of each leader we kill," he placed the vial underneath to collect the droplets, "before we kill them."

"Your father is messing with ancient taboos. It will get *him* killed."

"'Taboo'?" Alden grabbed the green rose diadem from her head. "Care to elaborate?"

She screamed and kicked more violently than she had with the arrow. "Give me back my crown!"

"You've lost your husband, your son, your people, your daughter, and you will soon lose your life," he said, twirling the diadem. "But all you cry for is the piece of metal you wear on your head." He put the trophy out of reach. "I will never understand rulers."

"That is *mine*."

"I don't know how you've lived so long with such a poison affixed to your skull. Most Nysans died within months of the nymphs' gifts, right?"

"The nymphs didn't gift that to me," she said, attempting to reach for it. "Your father did, and I'd like it back!"

Alden frowned. *Why on earth would Father have a green rose?*

He dropped her arm and corked his vial. Over the ledge, his sister and former tutor still fought the oracles. Each woman's technique varied from the other, but they were all extraordinary magicks. It wasn't often that he and Graye took on such skilled foes. They made missions exceptionally more exciting.

His side stabbed.

Time to end this.

"I'm sorry, Esmerelda," he said. "I do wish you and Kiva could have resolved your differences."

"That traitorous boy?" she said, then spat. "He chose his father over me. I'll die before letting him back into my life."

Alden sighed. "Yes, you will. Amazing how you can truly still envy Nikita so. Even now."

"*Give me back my crown!*"

"*Erigo*." Alden wouldn't normally levitate a target before killing them, but he didn't want to test his wound.

Esmerelda floated upright, feet dangling over the edge. He grabbed his dagger from his waistband and held it at her throat.

"Graye!" he shouted. His sister glanced at him and grinned, then returned to her fight. Thirty more seconds was all he needed.

He plunged the knife into the left of the queen's windpipe. His muscles tensed as he ripped it to the right. Then he gripped harder, twisting his blade, the handle smeared in his sweat and her blood. Her eyes remained open as she died.

He released the levitation, dropping her corpse into the red sand.

Done.

He stumbled. It wouldn't be long before he was as weak as the queen. He grabbed the crown and staggered back to the edge.

"It's finished, Graye," he shouted to his sister, before turning his attention to his tutor. *But what will happen to Profe?*

His thoughts slowed with every drop he lost. He couldn't help fight, but if he or Graye could get to Valentina, they could conjure a mirror. Somehow, he could distract a twin. Perhaps Sombra. She was easier. Then he could have Graye take on Nieve while his tutor ran to him. And after, he could fight Nieve, and his sister could leave. Of course, this assumed that he had the energy to both distract and...

Wait, what was he supposed to be doing?

"Leave, Alden!" Valentina said as if she read his clouded mind. "You've done enough! You and Graye need to go!"

He held his head, and the world blurred beneath him. "What about you?" he managed to shout, then winced. *She can't mirror like us.*

"I'll be fine," she said. "Just get out of here!"

He reluctantly nodded. He was in no condition to argue.

"Graye, let's go."

In a second, she was gone, and both twins turned their attention to Valentina. The tutor raised her hands in surrender.

Go, she mouthed as she knelt on the ground.

He grimaced at the sight, but still conjured a mirror and collapsed into it.

CHAPTER 48

EMBER

Mirroring was like being split in two but weighing twice as much. It was worse than sailing, not quite as bad as landsailing. More than anything, it was the sudden change in altitude that made Ember woozy. Her ankle didn't help.

"Welcome to Agartha," Kiva said.

The castle was black. Flooring, stairs, walls. All black. The only color at all belonged to the red and orange banners that hung from the ceiling. Even through the few windows in the foyer, all she could see was glowing magma and black. No clouds, suns, moons, or stars to light up the skies.

It wasn't her first choice, but if it kept her alive, black would be her new favorite color.

"Ademure," Kiva said, "do you remember where your room was?"

"Yes."

"It's currently empty. You should be able to take it back."

She nodded absently. "Are you sure Apá is okay with me coming here?"

Apá, Ember thought. *Father. The Agarthan king. Kiva… royalty.* The heat spread through her shoulders, but she kept her vision clear. *Raindrops.*

"He'll be thrilled, trust me," Kiva said. "I believe Graye has some extra clothes that you can borrow. She should be around here somewhere. I'm going to show Ember to the guest room. I'll come get you in an hour."

He hugged his sister before she left, and Ember's neck was hot to the touch when he turned to her.

"I can't thank you enough," he said.

She glared at him.

"Seriously." There was no humor in his eyes. "I haven't seen Ademure in a decade. After finding you, I'd considered retrieving her myself. I can only imagine what life was like for her being trapped with that tyrant of a queen."

"Your mother," Ember said curtly.

His jaw tensed. "That woman might have given birth to me, but she hasn't been my mother in some time."

Smirking, she shook her head. And though she had no idea where she was going, she limped silently toward the stairs in the middle of the black foyer. Anything to get away from this guy.

"I know you're angry with me," he said.

"Oh no, not at all. What's there to be angry about? I'm sure it was just an accident that you lied about being an agent of the Agarthan government. I'm sure you just forgot to mention that you were the one and only Agarthan *prince*."

"Is a prince not an agent of his government?" he asked with an effort at a smile.

He had no idea how lucky he was that she literally couldn't stand upright.

Though, the look she gave him must have given him some

inkling because he put a hand behind his neck. "I planned on telling you."

"But you didn't."

He looked at her, eyes still green and filled with guilt. "Let me walk you to your room. I'll tell you there." He held out a hand.

She didn't take it. "I'll follow you."

"On that ankle?" He chuckled. But when she didn't return the laugh, he dropped his arm. "This way."

She limped up the steps with him, turned the corner with him, and hobbled down the hall with him without a word. He didn't speak either, only gesturing the directions and, once they'd arrived, opening her door.

Her room was black like the rest of the castle but with gilded moldings on the ceiling and magma flowing where the walls met the floor, lighting the room from below—*as if I needed more heat.* In the center of the room sat a black bed on a golden frame. To her left was a large closet, and to her right, a vanity— one with a mirror. Her reflection, with scarlet eyes, startled her.

"*Colora reditio,*" she said. Her eyes were emerald once more.

"Your eyes are better suited for green," Kiva said, coming up behind her.

She glowered at him.

He looked in the mirror himself. "*Colora reditio.*"

When his eyes returned to their natural red hue, he faced her.

"Go ahead," she said, sitting on the bed, arms still folded. "Explain."

He stayed standing. "The first thing I'll say is that every-thing I told you two days ago was the truth."

"Sure it was." She rolled her eyes. "Listen, you've proven I can't trust anything about you, so if—"

"You trusted me enough to let me take you here."

His words hung in the air, his eyes on hers, both wondering the same question he had asked two days ago. *Why make time for me?*

"I came here for Ademure's sake," she said through gritted teeth.

"Sure you did," he mocked, rolling his eyes in turn. "Look, you're in my country, in my home. You will be witness to everything I say and do under this roof. I have nothing left to hide from you."

"Why did you hide this? I already knew you were Agarthan. Why hide that you were royalty?"

"You knew the queen..."

"I also knew the princess!" She threw her hands up. "Plus, I, of all people, don't judge others for the sins of their family."

"My parents killed your parents, don't you see that?" Forehead creasing, he put a palm to his chest. "My parents are the reason that you grew up in the Soulless Realm alone. I was once the heir to the throne responsible for orphaning you."

She frowned. "'Once'?"

He cast his eyes down and spoke quickly. "My father stripped me of my inheritance and gave it to Ademure." Chin low, he looked back at her. "But the point stands. Would you have ever believed me if you had known any of this?"

"I never believed you anyway, Kiva! But I believed Ademure. And she's just as responsible as you are."

He put his hands in his pockets and closed his mouth, lips pressed tight.

She let out a sigh. "Which is to say, not at all." She shut her eyes and touched her locket. "My parents orphaned me all on their own. Or, I guess, abandoned me. However you want to spin it."

He raised a brow. "What does that mean?"

"Apparently, they're alive."

His jaw dropped. "How—?"

"I don't want to find them," she interrupted, meeting his gaze. "They left. I'm not chasing them down. I don't want anything to do with them."

Which perhaps wasn't the most honest statement she'd ever made, but she knew that if she was going to move forward, it was what she had to tell herself for now. There were so many other things that needed her attention first.

"Okay," he said, somehow seemingly understanding. "So. I'm the Agarthan prince. What does that change?"

"I don't know, *Your Highness*."

"Oof, it doesn't change that." He plopped down beside her. "No, from you, I will only answer to 'Kiva', 'Prince Kiva' but in a sarcastic tone, or 'overconfident dipshit'."

She suppressed a smile. "Don't make me laugh. I'm not done being mad at you."

"Ah, I apologize. I've forgotten the queen must maintain her icy exterior."

He has some nerve, she thought still fighting the smile.

"So, I ask again," he said. "What does me being a prince change?"

She gripped the black velvety comforter they sat on. She had fought so hard to escape the estrellas, to stay out of a war that she had no stake in. Yet now she was here, on the other side of the battlefield.

"I'm your weapon now."

"You're not. You're our guest."

"Does your dad think of me as a guest?"

"I'll talk it over with him. Don't worry about that."

She eyed him. "Are you sure you want me here? You won't be safe around me. The estrellas were able to stop me when I lost control, but you can't clock."

"I'm offended you think that I'm weaker than a damn estrella. I nearly had the Delfinos in Texas."

"You had another with you then. And neither of you stopped me from hurting you. I'm getting better, but if I can't stop myself, you'll need some way to restrain me."

Frowning, he said, "How many times do I need to remind you, I lived? I'm fine."

"You're lucky. I'm just telling you that normally," her eyes flitted to his shoulder, and she gulped down the thought of Cadeña flat on his back, purple, "it's not safe to be around me."

"That's not true. Look at Ademure."

"Ademure is safe because two Agarthan assassins, the weird bookstore lady, and you saved our asses. I drove the fucking landsailer."

Kiva was quiet then, either because he didn't know what to say, or because he knew there was no point in the fight—no matter who was right, she was in Agartha all the same.

She also fell silent, palms hot.

"Well, I'll tell you that nothing's changed for me," he said after a moment. "I'll fight with Agartha to stop the Nysans, I'll train you as much as I can in all of your magic, including your ever-so-deadly-but-I'm-impervious-to-it-lightning powers, and," he smiled, "I won't stop pestering you until you agree."

The one time in her life that she didn't want the heat to recede, and her hands cooled completely. She wanted so desperately to prove to him why he shouldn't cross her, and yet he had already crossed her and paid for it—twice. And here he was, wanting to go a third round. The man clearly did not know when to back down.

To be fair, he'd warned her of that.

"I'll be here for you, Ember. Always." He took her hand, and his lip curled wryly. "Lightning and all."

Instinctively, she started to pull away, but when she saw

his eyes, she stilled. It was as if she was seeing them for the first time—which, in a sense, she was. They were silly but honest, and simmering with heat. Passion. His emerald ones could never compare, especially in the warm magma light.

Then she was distracted by his hair and him brushing it back, pointlessly, because it soon fell over his face once again.

And then by him brushing back hers. Tucking it behind her ear.

But despite all these distractions causing her heart to flutter wildly, she forced herself to turn away.

"I want to go to D.C," she said.

He leaned back, his own cheeks reddening slightly. "Why?"

"Nieve will be after my sister."

He shook his head. "You're too hurt to fight her right now. Even if you were healthy, it'd be much too dangerous."

"She's my sister, Kiva."

"I know that, but so do the twins. They'll be waiting for you there. And I'm not so certain they'll be so hospitable this time."

"Then what do you suggest I do? Just wait? For what? Until when?"

"Lie low in Agartha until we can figure out something else."

"And how long will that take?"

"As long as it takes," he said sternly, his beautiful scarlet eyes searching for reason in her own gaze. He took a breath. "And I'll send a sentry to ensure your sister is safe in the meantime. Does that sound reasonable?"

No.

She nodded.

"Good. I believe the closet has a change of clothes, and the bathroom is through that door. I'll be outside your room with a pair of crutches when you're done and let the alchemists know to expect you in an hour or so. Unfortunately, we do need to meet with my father first."

As the door shut behind him, she fell back onto her bed, wanting to cry. Instead, she stared at the ceiling. The emptiness in her stomach wouldn't leave her.

Today had been a fucking miracle, not at all thanks to her.

CHAPTER 49

ADEMURE

I'm alive. Ademure stared in the mirror. *And I'm free.*

But so many died.

She touched her cheek. Ten years had passed since she had seen her reflection. The circles under her eyes were dark. Her cheekbones were prominent. She was much older. Thinner. Paler. And so much weaker.

She pulled at her hair, picking apart the frayed ends. It wasn't soft. Barely more than a tug, and it would break. She combed it back, out of her face, and into a bun.

So, this was her.

She changed into a loose black gown that brushed the ground as she walked. In the black, magma-lit hallway, Kiva was dressed in a black shirt and slacks. Ember stood beside him in a dress like her own, though she had accessorized her outfit with crutches.

"Are you ready to see Father?" Kiva asked.

"Are you sure this is okay?" Ademure said. "When was the last time a Nysan was down here?"

"Don't worry. I've already alerted his guards and he's

excited to see you and Ember. Besides, you're his heir, remember?"

"If you say so." Her eyes flicked to the alloy. "Um, can I have a moment alone with you before we go?"

Ember raised a brow.

"A quick one," Kiva said. "Father is waiting in the meeting room. I'll let him know you're on the way."

Ademure nodded, and he left for the staircase.

"Let's talk in here," she said, pulling Ember's hand. "The servants here are trained to always be watching. Lord Caldwell's orders. Those were his son and daughter that..."

Her chest stung. Heat rushed to her face. Had she not yet run out of tears?

"That shot your mother," Ember finished as the door shut behind them. They both took a seat on the bed. "I'm sorry, Ademure. But you know the estrellas. She'll pull through."

She nodded, wiping her cheeks. "Yes, of course. They always have their way."

Ember gave her a worried look. "Ademure, before your mom was...hurt, you had an episode on the float. Do you remember that?"

"Yes." She wished she could forget; the welts on her stomach still stung. "When I grabbed her crown."

"You called it the 'green flower' something?"

"The green rose sickness. Something I learned about from the nymphs. I figured if I could remove the crown, I could return her to normal. I think I still can."

Ember shifted on the bed.

Ademure watched the magma flow about the edges of her room. It was so warm in here, and yet, she couldn't help but feel cold. "I didn't thank you for saving me."

"No need. I didn't really save you."

"I think you did. I wouldn't have made it off the float had you not been by my side."

Ember visibly swallowed. "All of those people..."

"Made it," Ademure finished. "I promise. Profe Valentina would never lie to you about that. *I* would never lie to you about that."

The alloy didn't look convinced, but she continued. "Still, I got us chained to the ground."

"And freed us from those chains."

"Yeah." She looked away. "Why did that woman from the bookstore help us?"

"Valentina tutored me, Kiva, and Alden and Graye Caldwell when we were younger." Ademure smiled at the distant but warm memory. "She's a dear friend to our families. And, she was a top estrella before she retired. The estrellas on the force today, she was their captain. Sombra and Nieve were her proteges, and they took her place when she left."

Nodding, Ember then asked, "And why did you want to talk to me?"

Ademure frowned. "Whether you believe it or not, you saved me today, and I thank you, but I shouldn't be alive."

"What are you talking about?"

"Others gave their last breaths, so I could take another." She inhaled deeply, wishing her lashes would dry. "You didn't see them in Nyseion, the nymphs, but they protected me. They offered me food and shelter, and had me serve as counsel. They respected me. They listened to me. And they died for me. And all I could do was let myself be captured. I don't deserve to be here."

"But you are here. Maybe it's for a reason."

At the alloy's newfound optimism, she blinked. "That's what I wanted to discuss with you. I want to go to the Soulless Realm."

Ember cocked her head. "Why?"

"The gods have given me another chance at life. This must be the reason." She went to her vanity and pulled out a sheet of paper, words she'd scribbled on the page. "I copied the prophecy from memory. I'm meant to learn more about Pandora."

But Ember ignored the paper, asking, "Why do you need to go to the Soulless Realm for that?"

"The Library of Congress. It's the largest library in the world. They're bound to have something regarding her."

"Yeah, maybe some myths or statues or something. Nothing magical."

Ademure shook her head. "No, I think you're wrong. I believe there's more there than even we can imagine. And if I can find out what these Evils are—"

"Evils? What are you talking about?"

"The Evils of Pandora's box." She pointed to the top of the page. "They've been reborn. We need to find them and capture them."

The alloy studied the paper for a moment. "Even if you're right about all that, what's the point? There's been evil in the world for a long time. I don't think this will stop it."

"The point is to prevent war. And maybe we can get my mother back. The nymphs told me the green rose could be an Evil." She looked down. "But there are others."

"Ademure, you can't go."

"Why not?"

"You won't be safe from the estrellas! The twins!"

"Their vision does not extend past the castle, Ember, much less to the northern United States. I doubt they even know we've come here."

"Yes, but if they find you—"

"Then I'll die a free woman."

Ember hoisted herself up on one crutch. "Then I'm going with you."

"No," Ademure said. "The estrellas will be especially looking for you, and you're hurt. Anyway, I'd rather have you train than dig through shelves. You'll be better off here."

"I can't let you go alone. Wait six weeks for my ankle to heal, and we can go together."

"I can't wait that long, Ember! So many people risked their lives for me today. *You* risked your life for me. It's high time that I pay my dues."

The alloy jutted her chin, staring Ademure down, but she stood proud and unwavering. She had to do this. Xander couldn't have died in vain. Her mother needed a cure.

Apparently deciding the conversation was over, Ember limped toward the door and said, "I'm going with you. And you can't stop me."

CHAPTER 50

KIVA

"I'll go with you," Kiva said. He stood from the table.

"No," King Nikita said forcefully. The light of the magma running down the walls highlighted the ferocity in his father's crimson eyes. "You must train the alloy. Perhaps Alden or Graye can accompany her?"

Leon Caldwell shook his head. "My children have their own tasks to attend to."

"I'll go with her," Ember said.

"No," Kiva and his father said in chorus.

Somewhat aggravated at how similarly they sounded, Kiva continued, "You need to heal, and you need to train."

"It's settled then," Ademure said. "I'm going to the Soulless Realm on my own."

"Father, talk some sense into her."

"Daughter," Nikita said, stroking his lengthy orange beard, "Are you sure about this? You can't mirror back like we can."

"I'm aware, Apá. But this isn't your decision to make. I'm going."

The king closed his eyes and grabbed the bridge of his nose.

"You are not the little girl I once knew. I trust you'll make the right choice."

"Thank you."

What in the world is she thinking?

Now aggravated by his father's leniency, Kiva glanced across the table at Ember for an answer, but she was only simmering.

"Are there any other items of import that we must discuss?" King Nikita said.

The room responded with silence.

"Then, you are all dismissed."

After exiting the meeting, Kiva pulled Ember aside while Ademure continued down the hall.

"Does she know what she's doing?" he whispered, gesturing at his sister. "Did you talk her into this?"

"Hell no," Ember said. "She thought up this plan all on her own."

"Can you stop her?"

"I tried already. But she's made up her mind. She's not going to budge."

He chewed the inside of his lip. "Alright then. The alchemy ward is just past the stairs and to the left. They're expecting you. Heal up quickly and get some rest. I can't imagine the day you've had."

She tilted her head, eyeing him, or perhaps wondering how to respond.

At last, she said, "No, you can't."

And suddenly, her arm was around him, and he was reminded of their time at the fountain. How had that only been yesterday?

Struggling to catch his balance, he asked, "What's this for?"

"A thank you," she said into his chest as she pulled him

tighter. "For saving us. I'm beyond irritated with you, and this isn't at all how I wanted to leave, but Ademure and I *are* safe. For that, I think you are hug-worthy."

"Okay, then." He returned the hug, enjoying the moment for what it was and swallowing down that ever-fluttering heartbeat of his. "You're welcome, ice queen."

She pulled back with narrowed eyes. "And I'm gone."

He chuckled as she left, then headed for the Caldwells' chambers. Just outside their obsidian doors, a familiar woman with scarlet hair stopped him.

"Graye," he said, "I heard you were in Nysa."

"Prince Kiva," she said with a cool smile. "We were. I was a bit disappointed to not see you there."

"Where's Alden?"

"In his room with the alchemists."

He furrowed his brows. "Alchemists in his room? Is he okay?"

"He's fine. Dramatic. Sombra Delfino nicked him in the side."

She then eyed him for a moment, still wearing her smile, and he didn't quite know what to think of that.

"Well, thanks, Graye," he said finally, pushing past her.

And though it wasn't clear to him just what had amused her, she laughed. "Anytime, Prince Kiva!"

He shook off his chills and rushed toward Alden's room. His friend lay on his bed as two men in black frocks hovered about with forceps, flasks, cleaning potions, and a sewing kit.

"Alden, what the hell happened?"

"Kiva!" Alden said, sitting up—with much trouble it seemed. "I'm glad to see you've come back safely."

His eyes dropped to his friend's bloodied side and chest. "Graye told me you fought the Delfinos again."

Alden grunted as he pulled a black blanket over the

wounds. His bedside was stocked with dozens of bandage rolls, his dresser topped with a variety of pain potions. "Yeah, on my own for a bit," he said. "Profe and Graye did help, but not before Sombra got her shot in."

"Alchemists," Kiva said, "please excuse us."

The two men nodded and left the room. He grabbed a chair and sat at Alden's bedside.

"Ironic," Alden said. "Six weeks ago, you were in bed, and I was at your side."

"What happened?" Kiva asked sternly. "What were you doing in the plaza, and why did you ask me to stay away?"

"You know I can't tell you."

"Ademure saw you, Alden. There is no secret anymore. I need to know what happened, from you."

His friend looked at him with hard eyes and thin lips. "My father sent us to assassinate your mother."

Kiva frowned. "Assassinate? As in...?"

He pulled his blanket higher, grimacing. "Yeah."

"But I thought you were a spy? All those times gone, all the information you gathered..." Kiva slumped back into his seat. "How many people have you killed to get it?"

"You can't let my father know you know."

"Why can't I?" he demanded, but at seeing Alden's severe look, he tried again, calmer. "Is this related to why I couldn't go to the parade?"

His friend gave a single nod.

He was quiet for a moment. "Did my father order this?"

"I don't know. I'm as in the dark as you are. Just keep an eye out—on Graye, especially. I don't know that your target has been lifted."

At the sound of her name, Kiva ran his hands through his hair. He didn't particularly like the woman, but he had known her her entire life. In a strange way, she was like a second sister to him. And she was an assassin, too.

After the last few months in Nysa, he didn't have the mental strength to handle such information at the moment.

"Were you successful?" he asked, clearing his throat. "Today, I mean."

"Yes. I'm sorry."

"Don't be. You did her a favor, I'm sure."

Alden nodded but wouldn't look at him. "What about you? What happened with the alloy?"

"The alloy is here. I start training her tomorrow."

"So, you were successful, too."

"Is this what success feels like?" Kiva said. "Father has yet to say anything of my inheritance. Though, truthfully, I'm not even certain I deserve it. It was all luck, really. Profe just happened to send the alloy and Ademure my way."

Alden's expression grew grim.

"What?" Kiva asked.

"Profe held off the oracles while Graye and I mirrored out."

His eyes widened. "You left her alone? With the Delfinos? How could you?"

"We didn't have a choice." Alden grabbed his side and winced. "I was losing too much blood."

His friend's wound was admittedly not small.

"What will happen to her?" Kiva asked.

"Nothing good."

"We have to go back."

"I won't be ready for combat for a few weeks, Kiva. Plus, even with the element of surprise, Graye and I had trouble fighting all seven, and they had a dying queen to protect. Now they're on edge and it's us who have the most to lose. We can't just go in."

"But we can't leave her!"

"I'm not suggesting we do. Profe is strong. She'll survive long enough for us to create a plan."

With a tense jaw, Kiva shot to his feet and started toward the door.

"Where are you going?" Alden asked from behind him.

He looked over his shoulder. "To prepare a plan."

CHAPTER 51
ALDEN

Alden lay alone in his room, staring at the ceiling, thanking the universe for alchemists and their potions. After Kiva had left, they'd finished patching his side and prescribed him a concoction to alleviate the worst of his pain.

Someone knocked at his door.

"Come in," he said. He tried to move but still lacked the strength. Today was the closest call he'd had yet.

A man wearing a trimmed beard and a black suit appeared.

"Father."

"Alden, I'm glad to see you in good health."

"I don't know that I'd say it's good health, but I am alive," he said. "And the queen is not."

Leon nodded. "Your sister told me you fought well against the oracles, and that your plan went off without a hitch."

"Nearly without a hitch." Alden grabbed at his side. "The Delfinos have gotten stronger. More precise."

"But you performed the execution."

"I did."

"Do you have the vial?"

Alden reached for his bag. He handed his father the flask of red.

"Excellent, son. You have done well today."

"What do you do with those vials?" he asked. "Before she died, the queen mentioned a taboo of sorts."

"It is nothing to concern yourself with. Keep doing as I say and the future will pan out." His father's melody was so hopeful, almost lustful. He didn't like it.

"What happens to Nysa?"

His father held the vial to the magma light, rotating it to inspect its purity. "Given her seniority and position among the estrellas, Marisa Bailón will take the throne. Also nothing to worry about. We're in good hands."

Passionate melodies again. Lusting after Bailón? Or the vial? He'd never known his father to care so much for either.

Alden thought of the trophy case. "I also have this, Father." He pulled out the green rose crown.

Leon slid the vial into his front pocket and smiled. "Keep it. It's time you started a trophy case of your own."

CHAPTER 52
EMBER

Ember rubbed her thumb over the barrel. She checked the magazine. *One bullet gone. Sixteen left.* If only she had stuck to the gun.

I'm glad I was right about you, Seño, he had said.

She shook her head. He didn't hear their screams. He didn't see the red sand. He didn't see him convulse, collapse.

You didn't know that I enjoyed it, Damian.

She stashed the gun in her vanity, next to her questionably lucky shell, and looked in the mirror, staring at her emerald irises. His were greener.

She wanted to know that he was okay. She wanted to know that he was alive. She wanted him to know that she was sorry for leaving him behind and that she would come back for him when she could.

But she also knew she had to make a visit first...before someone else did.

The red dress hung from a doorframe. She reached into its pocket, pulling out the crumpled, smudged photo.

Then, she tied her hair up, grabbed her crutches, and left her room.

~

"Alloy Slade," Alden said.

"Just call me Ember."

"Are you angry with me?"

Reaching for her locket, she said, "No. Why would you say that?"

He shook his head. "Never mind. Please. Sit."

She grabbed the chair at his bedside.

"What are you doing in my room?" he asked. "Not that you're not welcome, but I am a bit surprised."

"Were you the other one who tried to kidnap me a while ago?"

"Yes."

"And yet you saved Ademure and me from falling two stories up earlier this evening."

"Yes."

"I can't figure you Agarthans out. Are you the good guys or the bad guys?"

He tilted his head, taking a moment before answering. "I don't know about the others, but I can tell you I'm not good."

"Yeah, but you're not bad either." She looked around at his black, magma-lit room, filled with nothing but drugs and medical supplies. "Anyway, I thought I'd come and say thank you."

"For saving you from the fall?"

"For distracting the twins so that Ademure and I could run."

"You shouldn't be thanking me. We were after your queen. Distracting the oracles was a part of that plan."

"She wasn't my queen. I'm still grateful."

She then brushed a finger over her scars. There should have been a fourth there now, but after so long without reopening the others, she couldn't bring herself to create a new one. And, physically there or not, all four still burned with the heat in her palms.

"I have to go to D.C," she said.

He eyed her. "I thought Ademure was going alone—"

"I'm not going for Ademure." She looked up, meeting his questioning crimson eyes. "Can you help me?"

CHAPTER 53
DAPHNE

Daphne held a coffee in each hand, her jet-black bob brushing her neck as her heels clicked against the tile of the Capitol Building. Winter break at Georgetown meant she could spend more time in the House of Representatives, learning the ins and outs of democracy. Maybe one day she would be a congresswoman or a senator or perhaps the president herself. But today, she was an intern.

"Here's your coffee, Speaker Jacoby," she said.

"Thank you, Daphne." Speaker Jacoby grabbed the cup and left the office in a rush.

She returned to her cubicle, her desk overlooking the courtyard. Snow painted the trees and pavement white, and she shivered at its chill, marveling at the sight while soothing her aching feet.

Washington, D.C. had been home for two and a half years, now. She had grown up in the city, but never in one with such a harsh winter. She'd never needed snow boots or more than a light coat in Dallas. Though, cold weather was little price to pay for attending her dream school.

Other prices were much steeper.

"Daphne," Cannon said. Her closest friend wheeled toward her. Two other interns stood behind his chair. "Come to lunch with us."

"In a minute," she said. "I need to finish this." She gestured toward her computer.

"See you in a bit." The group left, and Daphne grabbed her purse before heading toward the bathroom.

No one stood at the sink and she didn't hear anyone, but she ducked under every stall just in case. When she was sure she was alone, she opened her bag and dug through its contents. Her finger brushed the familiar tube. She looked in the mirror and pulled down her turtleneck.

Pale pink and shiny, but dry. She traced where the doctors had sewn it back. Like a rag doll. Pieced together. It was her skin, but it didn't belong.

She ran her fingers over the rest of her clothes. Over her shoulder, down her back. Streaks across her chest and along her arm.

Daphne opened the concealer and touched up the patch on the nape of her neck. She readjusted her turtleneck to cover as much as she could. Then, she packed her concealer and headed for the cafeteria.

Speaker Jacoby passed her on her way back from lunch. She nodded at him, and he nodded in return. He couldn't possibly know how thankful she was for him. How grateful she was that he had been a guest speaker for her class her freshman year at undergrad. He had been in politics for some twenty years, a veteran of the game. But what had attracted her the most was one niche society he claimed to be a member of on his campaign site.

"Speaker Jacoby, what is a Newtonian?" she had asked him after the class.

He'd seemed surprised at the question. "Someone who believes in the laws of physics," he enthusiastically told her. "As they were named by Sir Isaac Newton himself."

"Wouldn't that be everyone?"

"Like everything else, there are humans who engage in the unnatural."

It had been then that she'd realized she wasn't the only one who knew. After telling him her story, he'd offered her an internship in his office, saying she was just the perspective he'd been looking for. Of course, she'd accepted.

When Daphne returned to her cubicle, she found an envelope, unmarked but sealed, sitting on her desk. She tore it open and pulled out the paper inside.

Newtonian meeting
Monday, 7 pm
Washington's Tomb

Don't forget your scars.

She read through the note again, then grinned. How could she forget?

These scars ran deep.

THE END

ΤΟ ΤΡΑΓΟΎΔΙ ΤΟΥ ΡΟΛΟΓΙΟΎ
THE CLOCKING SONG

Η ομορφιά της μαγείας είναι οτι υπόρχουν εφτά
Η τελική ομορφιά δεν είναι μια από τα ουράνια
Τέσσερεις απο τις ομορφιες είναι του χρόνου και του χώρου
Τρεις απο τις ομορφιές είναι απο άλλφ φυλή

Ομορφιά ένα τεντώνεται λεπτή ή φαρφυά όσο χρειάζεται
Ομορφιά δύο κοστίζει χρόνου και μαγνητίζει απληστία
Τι ομορφιά τρία αντικατοπτρίζει δεν είναι όλα εδώ
Ομορφιά τέσσερα είναι αυτό το τραγούδι, τραγούδα δυνατά καί καθαρα

Ομορφιά πέντε είναι ένα ψέμα, προοριζόταν να ξεγελάσει γυαλί
Ομορφιά έξι αντιστρέφει τι έφθασε να περάσει
Ομορφιά εφτά είναι η πιο μεγάλη, ένας ρυθμός δίαθεσης
Ομορφιά οκτώ δεν είναι ομορφιά αλλά παρεξηγημένη

Υάρχούν και άλλες αν και άσχημες
Αλλά εκείνες οι οκτώ έχουν χαθεί, παγιδευμένες μέσα σε ένα δοχείο

Υάρχούν και άλλες αν και άσχημες
Αλλά εκείνες οι οκτώ έχουν χαθεί, παγιδευμένες μέσα σε ένα δοχείο

THE CLOCKING SONG
(TRANSLATED)

The beauty of magic is that there are seven

The final beauty is not one of heaven

Four of the beauties are of time and space

Three of the beauties are of another race

Beauty one stretches thin or wide as it needs

Beauty two costs time and magnetizes greed

What beauty three reflects isn't all here

Beauty four is this song, sing loud and clear

Beauty five is a lie, meant to trick glass

Beauty six reverses what came to pass

Beauty seven is eldest, a rhythm of mood

Beauty eight is no beauty but misunderstood

And there are others though ugly they are

But those eight are lost, stuck in a jar

ACKNOWLEDGMENTS

Into Infernal Paradise has been well over a decade in the making —a dream story I devised at twelve and then subsequently had to revise (and revise and revise) when I returned to it at eighteen, twenty-two, and then wholeheartedly at twenty-five. And even at twenty-five, the draft was a mess not much better than the one my twelve-year-old self concocted. So, thank you to Rebecca Raymond, Kelsey Craker, and Bria Garcia, who all suffered through that mess and believed I had a gem. Thank you to my writing friends, Britt, Tae, Viraj, Ellie, William, and J.M. for diving into the next iterations on the quest to unearth the gem. Thank you to my developmental and line editor, Mandi Andrejka, whose sharp eye caught things I'd never before seen. Thank you to my cover designer and marketing genius, Rena Violet, who in many ways brought my novel to life. Thank you to Pete Staviski for his excellent Greek translation. Thank you, of course, to my partner Adam, who both read Ember's journey and encouraged me to publish it. And finally, thank you to you, dear reader, for taking a chance on this debut indie novel from a nobody author. Without you, this reality would remain a dream. I hope you stick around to see what Ember and the gang are up to next.

About the Author

Michelle Toro is a recent law school graduate and avid volleyball player (indoor *and* beach!). A native Texan, she currently lives in Houston with her tabby cats, Arya and Momo. *Into Infernal Paradise* is her first novel.

Follow her!
Instagram: @writermichelletoro
TikTok: @michellentoro
Website: michelletoro.com

If you enjoyed *Into Infernal Paradise*, please leave a review on Amazon and Goodreads—it goes a long way!

www.ingramcontent.com/pod-product-compliance
Lightning Source LLC
Chambersburg PA
CBHW030905300726
48970CB00001B/25